M000194762

SHADOW OF THE COALITION

THE OMNI TOWERS SERIES BOOK 2

JAMIE A. WATERS

Shadow of the Coalition © 2018 by Jamie A. Waters

Cover Art © 2018 by Deranged Doctor Designs
Editor: Beyond DEF Lit

ISBN: 978-0-9996647-1-1 (Paperback Edition)
ISBN: 978-0-9996647-5-9 (eBook Edition)

Library of Congress Control Number: 2018907711
Second Edition *September 2018

THE OMNI TOWERS SERIES

Shadow of the Coalition

CHAPTER ONE

KAYLA GOT down on her hands and knees, eyeing the space between the floor and a collapsed ancient wall in Sector Twelve. It would be a tight fit, but she'd navigated worse in the past. Taking a deep breath, she sucked in her stomach and squeezed through the narrow space.

She stood, brushed the dirt off her helmet visor, and shined the flashlight around what appeared to have once been a common room. *Living room,* she corrected herself, although there definitely wasn't anything living in the room now. Only the remnants of an old fireplace stood in the corner while pieces of broken furniture remained scattered on the floor, a thick shroud of dust and debris coating everything within the room.

Closing her eyes, Kayla took a deep breath to help focus her thoughts. Using what she now knew as energy threads, she opened up her senses to explore the hidden world beneath the surface. The darkness fell away, and Kayla embraced the energy that now swirled in the ruins. The surrounding energy vibrated, its wordless demand inviting her to tap into it. She shivered, her blood humming with a rush of power. Her fingers unfurled as the energy became a tangible thing.

She basked in the warmth and excitement of the intoxicating power. As the energy flowing through her increased, it was a little easier to ignore the strange ache and sense of longing she suspected came from being separated from Alec.

It had only been a month since she'd left OmniLab's towers. After she helped restore control of the towers to those who would look after the best interests of its residents, Kayla had found herself irrevocably bonded to Alec, the new co-leader of the High Council. Even though he was enigmatic and alluring, the shared energy bond scared her more than she wanted to admit.

It might have been easier to remain in the towers and allow Alec to train her, but history had taught her to be cautious. She wasn't willing to blindly trust someone she barely knew and risk being exploited again, especially when it came to these supernatural talents she didn't understand. So she'd spent the past month secretly exploring her ability to manipulate energy within the confines and solitude of the ruins. Once she got a better handle on this aspect of herself, she'd eventually need to face him again and figure out the rest.

Alec was likeable enough, but Kayla had only spent a handful of days with him. They'd exchanged a few messages since she left, but she wanted to proceed cautiously. Trust took time. Kayla had never wanted to rely on anyone before, and the thought she'd need to return to the towers because of this bond was more than a little unsettling, so she was determined to push the limits, train on her own, and figure things out in her own time. Besides, even though they shared a metaphysical bond, she wasn't in love with Alec. It was an OmniLab trader named Carl who had truly touched her heart.

Her face warmed at the thought of Carl, and it wasn't just from the stifling heat in the ruins. Even though they'd known each other for a year when her ruin rat camp had moved to his district, it wasn't until she recently joined his camp that she began to see him differently. Through his altruistic actions, he'd challenged her beliefs about traders and even OmniLab, forcing her to look beyond the surface. Sure, she was still cautious, but a darker side of human nature could be found anywhere, whether it was in the towers or on the surface.

It was a constant challenge to live as a ruin rat on the surface when survival was sometimes dependent upon outsmarting the OmniLab traders and their crews. Kayla enjoyed the challenges Carl provided, pitting her will against his. He was willing to let her go her own way for the most part, but he wasn't beyond resorting to some unethical tactics to prevent her from going too far. The man had a quick mind and was incredibly devious, two traits she greatly admired. More than anything, he understood her. Of course, it didn't hurt that he was sexy as hell too.

With a sigh, Kayla pushed away the errant thoughts in order to focus again on the dilapidated room. Her former camp was depending upon her to continue providing them with tradable credits they could use to purchase vital supplies. Since she'd left them a month ago, they'd taken a hit to their productivity and had been struggling to make up the difference. If she managed to find enough tradable materials on this scavenging expedition, it might be enough to put them back in the clear for another few days, or even a week if she were lucky. She couldn't afford to spend time daydreaming when there was work that needed to be done. Hopefully, tapping into her new energy abilities might help expedite things a little bit.

The energy continued to flow around her, and she channeled it until the mental image of the room shifted and transformed the dingy walls into brightly painted surfaces covered with family photographs. A child played on the floor while her parents sat on the couch and watched an antique vidviewer on the wall.

Kayla opened her eyes and stared at the verisimilitude of the ruined room. A wave of vertigo swept over her as the mental image overlapped with reality. Shaking her head, she pushed aside the image, but the memory of the past refused to leave completely.

An old photograph caught her attention, and she crossed the room toward the cockeyed frame. The glass was cracked and the picture faded, but she gasped at the sight of the image. The family looked exactly like the one she'd imagined. The energy flow around her shifted dangerously, and she swallowed nervously as she tried to regain control.

"Kayla?" Veridian's voice interrupted over her headset. "You okay? Your vitals just spiked."

"Uh, yeah. Sorry about that," she said in a rush, not wanting to alarm her scavenging partner on the surface. He'd been monitoring her progress for the past hour. "I just found an old photograph that surprised me. That's all."

Okay, Kayla, keep it together. You know this energy shit is freaky and you haven't figured exactly how it works yet. Just relax.

A slight vibration under her feet caused her to freeze. The floor felt secure, but vibrations didn't usually happen without reason. More curious than alarmed, she bent down and pressed her gloved hand against the ground. The vibration grew stronger.

"Kayla, get out now!" Veridian shouted over the headset. "We've got seismic activity on the monitors."

The walls began shaking violently. A rumbling noise grew in intensity as the dust and debris fell around her. The picture frame on the wall clattered to the floor. Kayla crouched low against the wall, powerless to do anything else. A loud crash resounded though the room, and she threw her arms up over her head as part of the ceiling collapsed.

Almost as soon as it had begun, the shaking stopped. Dust filled the area, obscuring her vision through the helmet.

"Kayla? Are you all right?" Carl's panicked voice came through her headset. He must have been monitoring the channel from the trader camp.

"Yeah, I'm okay." She tried to brush off some of the dust covering her visor with limited success. The filtration device embedded within her new helmet worked overtime as a cloud of gray powder surrounded her. Apparently, OmniLab had some uses after all—they made terrific toys. "That was scary as hell. I didn't think there was any seismic activity in this area."

Carl sighed. "Thank God. There normally isn't. I don't know what happened. The building you're in is mostly underground, and it's possible some of our equipment may have affected the stability of the chasm. I'm going to have Xantham look into it now. In the meantime, get the hell out of there until we know it's safe."

Fantastic plan. She wasn't a big fan of shaking ruins. "Is everything okay above ground, Veridian?"

"Yeah, I'm fine up here. A few pieces of equipment got knocked over, but that's it. Can you make it back to your harness so I can pull you out?"

Relief rushed through her. In every way except for blood, Veridian was like a brother to her. It was Veridian's mother who'd saved her from nearly dying in a ruin collapse when she was a child. After adopting Kayla as her own, she and Veridian grew up together and had created an unbreakable bond. She couldn't imagine losing him.

"Shit!" Kayla looked around, investigating the now collapsed entrance to the room. "The tunnel's blocked. I can try digging my way through, but I don't know if the area above is stable. Can you run a stability scan? While you're checking that, I'm going to see if I can find another way out."

"On it," Veridian replied.

Carl's voice came over her headset again. "Kayla, don't move. Other areas may have weakened if that tunnel collapsed. Veridian, send me the data as soon as you finish running it. I'm heading out with Cruncher right now to bring some stability supports."

Kayla snorted. Don't move? Who the hell was he kidding? There was no way she was going to sit with her thumb up her ass and wait. She'd been rescuing herself for twenty-one years. No need to stop now.

Visibility was crap, but she could see a few inches in front of her. It would have to do. Moving along the wall, Kayla climbed over rocks and rubble, searching for another way out. Other than the tunnel and part of the ceiling collapsing, the rest of the room appeared to be stable.

A small opening by the fireplace caught her attention. She didn't recall seeing it before the tremor, but then again, they'd only managed to excavate down to this level a few days before. With grim determination, Kayla began clearing away the debris blocking the area. If she could clear enough of a path, there might be another room on the other side. After about ten minutes, Veridian's voice once again came over her headset.

"Kayla, we're going to have to wait until Carl gets here with the supports. It looks like the structural integrity of the tunnel wall is compromised. Everything else appears stable as far as I can tell from here."

"Sounds good," she replied absently and continued to focus on the task at hand. They could do what they wanted, but waiting wasn't an option. When she finished clearing away the rest of the debris, a sizeable hole had been made between the floor and the wall. It appeared to be some sort of natural tunnel sloping downward, and with no debris inside that she could see, she believed it might be relatively safe.

She knelt closer to the opening, and a tingle of energy swept through her. Her heart thudded in excitement. *I knew it. There's something else in this sector.*

Kayla bit her lip, debating whether to explore the tunnel. Carl wouldn't be happy if he knew what she was considering. He'd argue that the strange energy pull was even more of a reason *not* to explore alone. It might be possible to take a quick look and get back before they knew she'd disappeared.

"V, can you send Carl and Cruncher down with a hydrating pack? I'm parched."

Veridian's voice responded in her headset. "Sure thing."

She pressed the button on her wristband to change comm frequencies to an unmonitored channel. Fortunately, neither she nor Veridian had volunteered their little code to Carl's crew. "V, I found some sort of natural tunnel. I think there's something down here."

"Tell me you're not going to do what I think you're going to do." Veridian's voice was strained.

"I'm going to do it," she informed him, pressing her gloved hand against the wall of the tunnel. Even through her gloves, she could tell the temperature was several degrees cooler than the room.

Veridian groaned. "Not a good idea, Kayla. Carl's got to be monitoring your vitals and comms. You may be sleeping with him, but he's still my boss."

She grinned. "Loosen the connector for the control monitoring panel. Pretend the earthquake did it."

"Fine," he agreed. "You better cover for me when he loses his shit."

"Done." Dropping to the floor, Kayla used her elbows to crawl through the narrow opening. It was a tight fit, but once inside, the earthen passage widened. "I'm inside now. There's no debris in here. It's probably safer than the last room. I'll let you know what I find. I'm going back to the other channel now."

"Be careful," he warned.

Kayla pressed her wrist unit again to switch back to the main channel. Sometimes the old saying was true: it really was better to ask for forgiveness than permission. Adjusting the light on her helmet, she crawled through the tunnel where the swirling energy seemed to beckon her further. Rocks bit into her knees and palms, but she continued. After a reasonable distance, the tunnel suddenly ended. It appeared to open up into some sort of chamber, but it was impossible to tell much from her location though.

Twisting her body, she gripped the edge of the dirt wall and lowered herself to the rocky floor below. Kayla pulled out a secondary light and flipped it on to get a better look. She nearly dropped the light, her breath hitching in excitement at the sight in front of her. A huge natural cavern extended back into darkness. There was a distinct noise and she paused, trying to determine what it was. The sound was vaguely reminiscent of the waterfall in the towers.

The light cut through some of the oppressive shadows and illuminated large stalactites and stalagmites filling the cave. Kayla tugged off one of her gloves, unable to resist touching one of the rock formations. A cloud of moisture hung in the air and clung to the rocky surface. Trailing her fingers upward, she felt the dips and jags of the natural stone. She tore her eyes away from the rock and took a step away from the tunnel. The ground was slippery, forcing her to tread carefully as she approached the center of the cavern.

A large underground river flowed through the cavern at a steady pace. In all of her experience, she'd never seen anything like it.

"No freaking way."

Carl's voice came over the headset, breaking through her daze. "What's wrong? Are you all right?"

Kayla swallowed, trying to form a coherent thought. "Yeah. Um, you guys close?"

"We're in the ruins, and we've got the supports in place. Cruncher and I are clearing the debris now. It won't take long until the tunnel is clear."

"Uh, you'll need to excavate a bit farther. I went through another tunnel."

"Dammit, Kayla! We don't know how stable that area is yet. We need to run a full scan of the ruins before you start crawling around."

She laughed into the headset, unable to suppress the giddiness at her discovery. "Yeah, yeah, bitch at me later. You're not going to believe what I found down here. You might need to widen the tunnel entrance a bit, but it gets bigger once you're inside."

Veridian's voice came over the headset. "Huh. Found the problem. The earthquake must have loosened the connection. You should be able to track Kayla's location and vitals now."

There was a deafening silence over the channel. Carl's voice, when he spoke, was strangely calm—a little *too* calm. "You're telling me you just figured this out?"

"Come on, Carl," she interjected before Veridian could say anything, "you know how sensitive some of our equipment can be."

"Fine. Don't move until we run further tests. By the way, we brought you your *hydrating pack*." Carl's voice cut off abruptly, and she could only imagine the swearing that must be going on at the other end. Guess they'd need a new code phrase.

He'd get over his irritation quick enough once he saw the

cavern though. Kayla pulled off her helmet and took a deep breath.

The air was clear from dust but still felt thick and heavy on her skin. The different sounds, smells, and even the taste of the moist air in the darkened cavern gave the impression she'd stepped through to another world. The energy threads felt stronger here, too, but she ignored them. Her focus right now needed to be on scanning the dimensions of the cavern. Reaching down, she dug around in her bag to locate an image mapper.

Activating the device, Kayla moved closer to the river. The ground was even more slippery closer to the water. It was too deep to see the bottom, but the distance across the river was fairly wide. She glanced down the length of the tunnel where the rushing water disappeared into darkness. They'd have to bring down some equipment to cross the river and follow it to its source.

Her excitement was bubbling over, but she managed to keep the image mapper steady and focused on scanning the dimensions of the river and cavern. At least thirty minutes passed before she heard movement from the direction of the tunnel. Dropping the image mapper back into her bag, Kayla moved over to where Carl was climbing down into the room.

Kayla still felt that familiar flutter in her stomach whenever she looked at him. Even in his UV-protective gear, the OmniLab trader was a gorgeous hunk of man.

At the sight of Kayla, he pulled off his helmet. Long, dark hair was tied back away from his face displaying a strong jaw with just a bit of stubble, giving him a more rugged appearance. Although his brown eyes were full of frustration and concern, his expression quickly changed to one of shocked amazement at the sight of the cavern.

Another figure climbed through the tunnel and dropped onto the rocky ground. Kayla recognized Cruncher, Carl's short and stocky right-hand man. A former ruin rat like herself, they'd both developed a deep respect for each other's skills and abilities. He pulled off his helmet and let out a low whistle.

"Damn, girl. What the hell did you find now?"

"It gets better," she promised and motioned for them to follow her toward the river. Stopping just a few feet from the moving water, Kayla turned to gauge their reactions. Both men stopped short and stared slack-jawed at the river.

Their stunned reactions mirrored hers. Underground rivers were extremely rare and critical to their survival. Most water sources were heavily contaminated and unusable. Using special water treatment techniques, they were able to purify and treat a scarce few to create safe drinking water.

"You guys wouldn't happen to have a water testing kit with you, would you?"

"No, but we can quickly change that," Carl replied before speaking into his headset. "Veridian, I need you to send down the water testing kit that's in the compartment of my bike. We've got an underground river down here."

"No way!" Veridian's eagerness and disbelief were apparent, even through the headset. "I'll send it down right now. Grab some images of the river. I want to see it."

"I'll grab the kit from the drop point," Cruncher offered.

At Carl's nod, the older man headed back to the tunnel. Carl turned away from the river and focused on Kayla. She smiled up at him, but it faded quickly at the intensity in his expression.

He took a step closer and abruptly pulled her close, wrapping his arms around her. She stiffened, surprised by the sudden movement. Burying his face in her hair, he inhaled deeply. "I think my heart stopped beating when I heard about the earthquake."

She felt a twinge of guilt at the realization he'd been more than worried. Uncomfortable with the thought, her initial response was to shrug it off, but she hesitated. Although he would never demand it, she could sense his need for reassurance.

The moment she acquiesced and relaxed against him, he let out a sigh and threaded his fingers through her hair. They remained that way for a long moment, and then he tilted her head back to look into her eyes. The depth of emotion in his expression floored her.

Without saying another word, he crushed his lips against hers. Sensations exploded as the heat between them ignited. She wound her arms around his neck, demanding more, and his kiss deepened in response. His hands traveled down her length until they reached the edge of her shirt, brushing at the skin beneath it.

How did this man get her worked up so quickly? The slightest caress seemed to set her off like a blazing inferno. The desire to touch his bare skin became consuming. As though sensing the direction of her thoughts, Carl reluctantly eased away. *Damn him.*

His eyes were clouded with passion, but his hands were gentle. He cupped her face and pressed a tender kiss against her forehead. "How long does it take to retrieve a water testing kit?"

"Not long enough, you two crazy kids," Cruncher's voice sounded over the commlink. Kayla bit back a groan and dropped her head onto Carl's chest. They'd forgotten to disable the audio. *Again.*

"I'd take my time getting your kit, but seeing as we just had seismic activity down here, you two are going to have to wait to get your freak on back at camp."

Carl chuckled and shook his head. Kayla squeezed her eyes shut, imagining the comments Xantham was making. Any day now, they'd probably see copies of Carl and Kayla's greatest hits distributed throughout camp. She'd have to kill all of them if that ever happened. It wasn't so much modesty she was concerned over, but rather Xantham's tendency to assign a point system for performance.

"It's safe to come back. I think we can manage to keep our hands to ourselves," Carl said before focusing again on her. His eyes darkened in concern as they scanned over her. "Are you sure you're not hurt?"

Trailing her fingers lightly over the rough stubble along his jaw, Kayla offered a reassuring smile. "I'm okay. I promise. I did some preliminary scans of the area while I was waiting for you guys."

Carl took a deep breath and pressed his forehead against hers for a long moment. Pulling away, he let his gaze sweep the dim cave again. "All things considered, this is really incredible. We had no idea this river even existed. How did you find it?"

She debated whether to say anything about the trail of energy that led to the tunnel. It was hard enough for her to understand this energy stuff, but it was even worse for Carl. Even though he had some limited knowledge from living in the towers, Kayla suspected his reservations stemmed more from the fact she was permanently bonded to Alec than anything else.

OmniLab claimed she was a descendant of the Drac'Kin, those legendary creatures also referred to as dragons. Supposedly, they'd lost their shapeshifting abilities centuries ago, but they still retained some of their other supernatural powers. At least that was their basis for explanation when it came to her strange talents. In all honesty, the idea freaked her out. Up until a few weeks ago, she hadn't known it was even possible to manipulate energy. If she hadn't experienced it firsthand, she never would have believed it possible.

Deciding it would be better not to remind him of the

shared connection with Alec, she shrugged. "The quake must have opened up the tunnel."

Carl looked skeptical, and she turned away, hoping he would drop it. When she didn't offer more of an explanation, he sighed. "I see. This is an amazing find, but you shouldn't have taken the risk. You could have been hurt."

She glanced back and offered a teasing smile. "I don't die that easily. Besides, I like keeping you on your toes."

His forehead creased, and he rubbed the back of his neck. "Don't think I haven't noticed."

Although touching, Carl's concern left her disconcerted. Would she ever grow accustomed to people worrying about her? Maybe she did take some risks, but they were hers to take. Kayla had been on her own for too long to just sit back and let someone else run the show.

Deciding a change of topic was necessary, she said, "Thanks for coming out here. Do you have any idea what caused the shaking?"

Carl shook his head. "Not yet. Our initial stability scans didn't show any potential for seismic activity, but the readings we just received say different. I notified OmniLab on my way over. I believe they're going to launch an investigation."

Kayla frowned. The scanners should have picked something up. Luckily, there hadn't been any more tremors since the initial incident, but it was always a possibility.

Before she could ponder the issue further, Cruncher returned with the water testing kit. "It's all yours, girl. You found it, you get to take the sample."

She flashed him a huge smile and eagerly took the kit. It was a metallic box with a cushioned lining, which contained several empty vials where samples could be stored and tested. Careful to remove one of the vials without breaking it, she knelt beside the river. Once a small amount of river water had been collected, she slid the detector wand into the vial. A moment later, the unit beeped and displayed the reading on the screen.

Carl took a step toward her. "What does it say?"

Kayla shook her head, studying the display. It couldn't be right. "I must have gotten an error. I'll try it again."

Carl knelt next to her, watching while she collected another sample and ran the test again. When the reading displayed the same result, Kayla bit her lip. She looked down at the river and back at the display, contemplating its accuracy. Was it possible this was the first nontoxic water source they'd seen in generations?

She glanced up at Carl, who was frowning and rubbing his chin. It looked like he was wondering the same thing, but neither one wanted to give voice to their hope. A discovery of a relatively clean water source could revolutionize their efforts in locating new resources.

"There might be a problem with that machine," he said cautiously. "We can take a couple of samples back with us and test it at camp."

Kayla nodded and bent down to retrieve a few more samples. After locking them into the water testing box, she slid the unit into her bag and stood to find Cruncher touching one of the stalagmites with an expression of awe on his face. He shook his head and said, "This place is incredible. I've seen images of caves on pre-war data cubes, but seeing it in person is unreal."

Carl nodded in agreement and motioned for them to start heading out. "We'll need to run more stability tests and get some additional equipment down here. Once we get the water test results, we can plan our next move."

Kayla stared into the darkness and bit her lip, hesitant to leave. Caution was warranted, but she was really curious how deep the cavern went. It wouldn't take long to explore just a little further.

Before she could take a step toward the darkness, Carl wrapped his hand around hers. "Don't, sweetheart, the river will still be here tomorrow. Until we figure out what caused the earthquake, it's not worth risking your safety." She opened her mouth to argue, but he pressed a finger against her lips. "Veridian's above ground. Your little stunt with switching channels aside, he's been worried about you since it happened. Let him see you're okay before you get into a worse situation."

Kayla wrinkled her nose. *That was a low blow.* As much as she wanted to explore, Carl was right. The man had the insufferable tendency to consistently be the voice of reason. Veridian usually went along with her schemes, but he still worried. She blew out a breath and slumped her shoulders. "Fine, but no one else gets to come down here without me."

The corner of his mouth twitched in a small smile, and he nodded. With one last longing glance at the river, she added, "I want to see if OmniLab has some flotation devices and underwater cameras we can use to explore this tunnel. I might be able to rig up an underwater speeder using compressed air so we can find out how far and how deep it goes."

He chuckled, slipping his hand behind the small of her back and nudging her in the direction of the tunnel. "That can be arranged. Figure out what you'll need so we can put in a requisition."

Kayla pulled on her helmet and considered the necessary equipment. Caught up in mentally designing an underwater speeder, she barely noticed Carl lifting her back into the narrow tunnel. Details and possibilities raced through her thoughts while she climbed after Cruncher. The sooner they got back to camp, the faster she could start working.

Excitement lightened their feet, and it took less time than expected to make their way back through the ruins. Once they reached their equipment, Kayla climbed into her harness and pressed the button to pull herself up to the surface.

Veridian's face lit up in relief when he saw her. Taking his offered hand, she let him pull her the rest of the way out of the ruins. Before she could even remove her harness, he enveloped her in a tight hug. She returned the gesture and then ducked out of the way so he could help Carl and Cruncher.

Kayla removed her helmet and grabbed a couple of hydrating packs. She tossed one to both Carl and Cruncher before opening hers. Exhausted, she sat and drank it down while Veridian packed up the equipment.

Now that they were above ground, all three men seemed more relaxed. Carl and Cruncher took turns describing the cavern to Veridian, using gestures to show him the size of the rock formations. Using the back of her hand, Kayla wiped her mouth and tossed the now empty drink container into a disposal bag. "Maybe we can talk you into going down there and checking it out, V. It's incredible."

Veridian's eyes widened, looking horrified at the suggestion. His aversion to going into the ruins was well known, but she held out hope that he'd get over his fear one day. "No, thanks. I'll leave that sort of thing to you guys. I'd love to see the images you took though."

Unsurprised by his refusal, Kayla nodded in agreement. It had been worth a try. Standing up, she grabbed a bag of equipment and began to help load it onto their speeders. Once they were ready, Veridian pressed the button to deactivate the UV guard over the area. The machine emitted a loud beep as it signaled the sixty-second warning before it disengaged. Kayla and the rest of the guys climbed onto the back of their speeders and fired up their engines.

She crouched low on her bike and took off toward Carl's camp with the other three bikes trailing behind her. The hot, dry air whipped around them, and Kayla was thankful for the upgraded OmniLab UV-protective gear and equipment. This time of year was always especially brutal. It made the contrast between the arid landscape even sharper against the memory of the cool underground cavern.

They drove through areas that had once been teeming with life. Now, only collapsed and ruined buildings remained, breaking up the otherwise barren terrain. As they approached the trading camp, Kayla slowed down and pulled up outside the entrance. Carl pulled up alongside her just as she dismounted.

She reached over, grabbing the bag from her bike, and then headed toward the entrance. A large roar from some sort of engine sounded overhead and a dark shadow appeared on the ground. Shielding her visor from the harsh light of the sun, she could make out a sleek aircraft flying over their camp.

Apprehension filled her at the sight of the foreign aircraft. She didn't recognize it as belonging to OmniLab, but she wasn't an expert. Kayla turned back to Carl, but he was already in motion and running in her direction. He grabbed her around the waist, hauling her backward, and she almost lost her grip on the bag. She caught a glimpse of Cruncher and Veridian rushing toward them.

The moment they reached the covered entrance, Carl released her. Kayla swallowed, searching the sky to track the aircraft's progress, but it was almost out of sight. She frowned and headed inside with Carl and the others.

Pulling off her helmet, she tossed it on a nearby rack and looked around at the equally alarmed and confused faces. "What the hell was that thing?"

Carl shook his head. "No idea, but that wasn't one of OmniLab's drones. They would have notified us if they were sending out some sort of new aircraft in our area."

Cruncher rubbed the back of his neck. "Could it have been from another facility?"

"That's the most likely possibility," Carl admitted with a frown and pulled out his commlink.

Xantham strode into the hallway, and Kayla nodded a greeting while pulling off her jacket. The communications expert for Carl's camp was dark-skinned with short, dark hair and eyes. He was an outrageous flirt and a bit of a goofball, but there was no denying his skill as a tech.

He winked at her before turning to Carl. "Boss, I'm glad you're back. Master Tal'Vayr has been calling for the past hour. He needs to speak with you right away."

"Maybe he already knows about the aircraft or something about the earthquake?" Kayla suggested when Carl frowned.

"Possibly," Carl replied, slipping his commlink back into his pocket. "No details, just several urgent messages from him. Xantham, I want you to pull up the camp surveillance and tracking system. See if you can get an image of the aircraft. I want it sent to OmniLab right away."

At Xantham's confused expression, Cruncher filled him in. After hearing what had transpired, Xantham's hands swatted the air in frustration. "Well, shit! This wasn't my fault. I would have seen it if I hadn't been too busy playing messenger boy for the High Council. I'll get on the radar now." He turned and raced down the hall in the direction of the communications room.

Kayla opened her bag, checking to make sure the water samples hadn't been damaged. Thankfully, the case was still intact.

Carl motioned for Cruncher to take them from her. "Cruncher, start scanning the samples for contaminants. I'll call OmniLab and be in there in a few minutes to check your progress. Veridian, check with Xantham to make sure it's clear and then bring in the rest of the equipment. Kayla, do you want to start on the imaging?"

She shook her head. "Not just yet. If you don't mind, I'd like to listen in and see what Alec has to say about the earthquake and aircraft."

Surprise and concern flickered in Carl's eyes. "You sure?"

She hesitated briefly and then nodded. It was no secret she'd been trying to avoid Alec since she'd left the towers. Thankfully, Alec hadn't pushed the issue, at least not overtly. He still believed she would eventually return to the towers on her own. So far, she'd managed to prove him wrong.

"Yeah, he'll be more forthcoming with information if I'm with you." Kayla followed Carl into his office, waiting until he closed the door and engaged the privacy settings.

His office was spotless as usual. A large desk stood in the center of the room with several cabinets displaying unusual artifacts on two of the walls. The third wall held a video screen he frequently used while working. Kayla walked over to the desk and sat on the edge of it.

Carl pressed a button to call Alec on the wall display. A moment later, the High Council leader appeared on the screen. Her heart thudded at the sight of him for the first time in weeks. She bit her lip, convinced this couldn't be normal. It went beyond regular attraction and straight into that weird paranormal bullshit. Suggesting she join Carl to talk to him might have been a bad decision.

Alec's brilliant blue eyes regarded Carl coolly. "Where's Kayla?"

"I'm here." Her voice came out almost as a squeak. Carl gave her a sharp look, and she tried to cover with a slight cough. If she couldn't even manage to speak without issue, this could be a problem.

"The ruins were a little dusty," she offered by way of an explanation. Carl wasn't buying it. Yeah, it sounded lame even to her. Determined to do this, she straightened her shoulders. "I'm good."

With a frown, he stepped aside so Alec could see her.

She offered a little finger wave. "Hi."

Alec was quiet for a long moment, his eyes softening as he drank in the sight of her. The seconds crept by, and when he still didn't say anything, Kayla felt her cheeks start to flush. Finally, he broke the silence. "Are you all right? I heard about the earthquake."

Kayla swallowed and rubbed the back of her neck. How could a stupid video call render her so awkward? In some ways, seeing Alec on screen was even worse than responding to the few messages he'd sent her. It made the sense of loss from their shared connection more noticeable. Thankful that at least he wasn't standing there in person and dumping energy over her, she nodded.

"Yeah, I'm fine." Kayla struggled to regain some semblance of composure. *Ugh, the man makes me feel like a complete idiot.* "Just a little shaking and some dust. We found something you're going to be interested in though."

Alec listened quietly while she described the cavern and the underground river. By the time she finished, he had already shifted back into High Council mode. "Carl, I want you to send over the contamination report of this water source as soon as it's complete."

Carl had been silent up until then, simply observing their conversation. She'd almost forgotten his presence and now, glancing over at him, she realized her mistake. There was no love lost between Carl and Alec. Cruncher let it slip that things had grown increasingly tense between the two men ever since she'd left the towers, but Carl hadn't mentioned anything. In fact, he made it a point to avoid the topic of Alec as much as possible.

Carl stood immobile and leaned against the desk, arms

crossed over his chest. His expression was grim, but his voice remained impassive as he agreed to Alec's request and proceeded to describe the strange aircraft. Kayla couldn't help but admire his cool at handling the council leader.

Alec nodded at the end of the report. "That coincides with our preliminary reports. We received notification that an unauthorized air vehicle entered OmniLab territory a short time ago. We're conducting an investigation now. Send over whatever images you were able to collect. It could help us determine its origin. The towers and surrounding areas are being put on high alert. You should see some exploratory drones in the vicinity while we attempt to make contact."

Kayla bit her lip. "Could the earthquake be related to this aircraft?"

Alec hesitated. "The seismic activity was not natural in design. That's actually the reason I was trying to contact you. Kayla, I need to ask you to return to the towers."

Her eyes widened in shock. "Yeah, right. That'll happen about the same time I manage to pull a photon generator out of my ass. I had my fill of those towers a few weeks ago. Thanks, but I'll stay here with Carl and stick to the ruins for now."

Alec frowned. "I had no intention of asking you to return until you were ready. However, I have some concerns and it would be in your best interest to return. It would be better to discuss those reasons in person."

Kayla crossed her arms, her temper rising. Alec might run OmniLab, but she'd be damned if she was going to let anyone boss her around. "You need to do better than that. I'm not going to just pick up and run back to the towers on your say so." Her eyes narrowed slightly. "I don't belong to you."

A combination of irritation and something akin to regret flickered in his eyes but was quickly gone. "I'm concerned about your safety. In addition to this unknown aircraft and possible threat, I believe the seismic activity was a result of energy manipulation. I don't know if you were the cause or ... someone else. If you were the one responsible, you need to be trained to prevent further incidents."

Uh oh. That doesn't sound good. A feeling of unease crept over her. "What the hell are you talking about, Alec?"

"When you were in the ruins, did you channel energy?"

She glanced at Carl, whose eyes had widened with alarm. *Oops. Busted.* Resisting the urge to squirm, she admitted, "Um, yeah. I didn't do anything that would make the earth shake though. I didn't think that was even possible. You said my talent was finding missing or lost objects." The last part was said almost accusingly. Although, technically, it could be argued that she had managed to find a missing or lost water source. Shit. If the earthquake led her to find the river, maybe the two really were linked.

Alec nodded as though that explained something. "That's only part of your talent. That particular ability emerged when you were a child. Other talents can develop as you go through puberty and become an adult. We didn't have an opportunity to explore your range of abilities before you left the towers."

Other talents? Kayla jerked her head up, locking eyes with his startling blue ones. She could almost feel the pull toward him through their shared connection. On some level, she desperately wanted to return and feel the exquisite sensations of sharing energy again, but there was no way in hell she was going to let herself be controlled through this bond.

Until she managed to figure out more about this aspect of herself, Kayla couldn't risk putting herself in another situation like she had the last time she went to the towers. Alec's father had managed to subdue her a little too easily, not to mention her uncharacteristic reactions every time Alec shared energy with her. Maybe she could try to access Omni-Lab's databases to see if they had any information that might help. Obviously, her attempts at exploring this energy phenomenon on her own were proving rather disastrous.

As though he could tell what she was thinking from there, his calm façade dropped briefly. "Kayla, you can't keep avoiding this. You're not just channeling your own energy anymore. Through the bond we established, your abilities have been amplified. Whether or not the earthquake was your intention, it's likely you were the one who inadvertently triggered it. If not ..." His voice trailed off, and he took a deep breath before continuing. "Regardless, you need to learn how to harness your skills and abilities. If you come back, I can teach you. It's not safe for you to remain there without any training."

Kayla shook her head, crossing her arms over her chest. "Forget it. I'm not ready to come back yet. I won't use my energy anymore. I managed just fine for years without it. If I go back, you'll get all up in my head again. That's not going to happen. I don't belong to you, and I sure as hell don't belong to OmniLab."

Alec looked at her in exasperation. "You're the most hard-headed, willful, and frustrating woman I've ever met."

She rolled her eyes. She'd been called far worse, and that was on a good day. "You need to get out more then. If that's all, I've got a sample to go check."

Without waiting for a reply, Kayla hopped off the desk and strode out of the room. There was no point in arguing with him. It might be foolish to ignore the warning, but considering her unwanted imprisonment during her last visit to the towers, she wasn't willing to risk it. If she knew for sure she could trust him, things might be different. Annoyed that the excitement of finding the underground river was now shadowed by Alec's words, Kayla scowled and headed toward the tech room.

CHAPTER TWO

KAYLA STRODE into the tech room to find Veridian and Cruncher hunched over one of the computer terminals. Veridian glanced up when she entered and raised an eyebrow at her expression. "You look like you want to hit something or someone. What's wrong?"

She glowered at him and slumped down in an empty chair. "Alec wants me to go back to the towers."

Cruncher snorted. "You think? The guy's been pissing Carl off more than usual lately. He's had to start giving him our daily scavenging schedules and coordinates. Not to mention he's been tied into our communication systems. It's making Xantham twitchy."

"He *what*?" Kayla jerked upright in the chair. This was news to her. "He's been monitoring us?"

"Yup," Cruncher said with an amused expression. "I guess since you won't talk to him, he has no way of keeping tabs on you. He just about flipped out when the earthquake happened. Never thought I'd see the High Council leader lose his cool like that. Carl thought he was going to run straight out of those towers and head here himself."

She slammed her hand down on the desk. Veridian jumped at the sound and shot Cruncher a warning look. "That bastard! I should have known. I'm tempted to go to those towers and kick his ass personally. Why didn't anyone tell me?"

Cruncher shrugged. "Probably to keep you from heading back to the towers and kicking some High Council ass."

Veridian sighed, running his hand worriedly over his frizzy brown hair. "Well, it's not like we didn't see this coming. Alec wasn't exactly thrilled when you left. You have a tendency to attract the wrong sort of attention. Leo always said you sucked at keeping a low profile."

When she glared at him, Veridian held up his hands in surrender and grinned. "So ... are you going to go back there? Or are you going to keep hiding out here?"

"I'm *not* hiding," Kayla retorted and folded her arms over her chest. Okay, maybe she was hiding. A little. *Dammit.* She was more transparent than she thought. "I'll just tell Alec to mind his own business and quit checking up on me."

"Uh huh. Right. I'm sure that'll work," Veridian said, turning back to his terminal. Cruncher snorted in agreement. Neither one of them even bothered to pretend that Alec would listen to her.

Kayla huffed, suspecting they were right. The idea that Alec watched her every move was more than a little creepy. It only reinforced her decision not to return to the towers yet. If he was this controlling when she was miles away, it didn't bode well for when she eventually returned.

Drumming her fingers on the desk, Kayla tried to figure out the logistics of disabling the two-way communications with OmniLab. It would serve Alec right if their contact were temporarily cut off. The lesson would do him some good and give her a little breathing room. Too bad this whole aircraft thing was happening. Cutting off communication with the towers right now probably wasn't the best idea.

A loud beep emanated from Cruncher's machine and drew her attention. He studied it for a moment and leaped from his chair, knocking it to the floor with a loud crash. Grinning widely, he gestured to the screen. "Un-fucking-believable. You've got some crazy luck, girl. Check it out."

Thankful for the distraction, Kayla leaned over to take a peek. "You already finished testing the water samples?"

"Yup. They're clean." Cruncher pulled her out of the chair and twirled her around. A laugh bubbled out of her at his exuberance. "We ran three separate tests, and the water's safe. We've got ourselves a clean water source here."

She turned to look at the display more closely. The test results showed the water was completely potable with only minor contaminants. Ever since the war had rendered most of the planet uninhabitable, clean water sources were like mythical unicorns—they just didn't exist. Even with OmniLab's technology, traces of contaminants still remained behind. They had to use specially developed hydrating packs for regular drinking use.

However, Kayla was a realist at heart and eyed the screen with skepticism. Things that seemed too good to be true usually were. "I don't trust it. We can't afford to make any mistakes on this. Aren't there some other tests we can run to check for microbial contaminants?"

Cruncher narrowed his eyes. "You're too young to be so cynical. Besides, we don't have a spectrophotometer here in camp for that sort of analysis. Although, you could always go flutter your eyes at Alec and get him to send one our way." With a smirk, he added, "On second thought, maybe not. If you so much as crooked a finger at him, he'd probably send over a dozen, along with the techs to run them. We don't have that kind of room with all the other crap he's been sending us."

Kayla groaned and half-heartedly punched Cruncher in the arm. The former ruin rat chuckled and turned back to the display. Alec's generosity had been over the top since she returned to Carl's camp. Over the past several weeks, they'd received several shipments of new prototypes and state-of-the-art equipment from OmniLab. It bothered her that everyone knew OmniLab's "generosity" was a direct result of her uncomfortable relationship with Alec.

Before she could say anything else, someone cleared their throat behind her. Kayla spun around, surprised to find Carl had slipped into the room. His expression was troubled, and she wondered what Alec had said after she left. At her questioning look, he simply shook his head. "Find out anything?"

Apparently, he didn't want to discuss it. She could respect that. Kayla sat back down and pointed to the contamination report on the screen. "Cruncher's gotten three test results back. All of them are negative for toxicity."

"I would have thought that was impossible," Carl mused, stepping behind her and leaning over to look at the data. He rested his hands on her shoulders, rubbing small circles as he read through the data. "If this is accurate, do you have any idea what this could mean?"

Kayla nodded, resisting the urge to groan at the way his hands worked her sore muscles. His attentions made it difficult to focus on the conversation. "Mmhmm. OmniLab's going to freak out when they get this news. We need to do further testing before we get their panties wet. I also want to find out where this river goes."

Carl considered her words for a moment. Her head lowered seemingly of its own volition as he hit a particularly tense spot on her neck. The man had magical fingers.

"I heard you tell Cruncher you wanted to do some additional testing. As it happens, I need to return to the towers for a few days. I'll take a sample directly to OmniLab and have them test it using their equipment. That would be the fastest way to get answers. I'll also see about making arrangements for some underwater imaging devices while I'm there."

Kayla tensed, negating the past several minutes of work he'd done on her muscles. "You're going back to the towers? What the hell did Alec say to you? And why didn't you tell me he was spying on us?"

Carl dropped his hands and glowered at Cruncher. "You told her?"

The older man shrugged. "She needs to know, Boss."

Carl sighed in resignation. "It's not what you think, Kayla. Can you come with me to my office? I need to show you something."

Her curiosity mounting, she followed Carl back to his office and took a seat on the edge of the desk. He sat, entered in a few commands on a small tablet terminal, and then nudged it toward her. It was an official notice from OmniLab requesting access to all of Carl's information, including communication logs, trade agreements, and financial records. The record request went all the way back to three years ago when Carl first accepted the trader position. It was long before she'd even met Carl, much less begun working at the camp or scavenging in his district.

Confused, Kayla looked up at Carl. "What's this? What's going on?"

He sighed, leaning back in his chair, and eyed the tablet with distaste. "I probably should have told you weeks ago about Alec monitoring our camp, but I knew it would bother you. As you know, OmniLab owns the trader camps and we're all under contract with them. It's unusual but not unheard of for them to demand access to our daily records and communication logs. Requests for that type of information have been rolling in since we left the towers. Granted, this level of surveillance is a bit unusual. I figured Alec wanted to make sure you were safe, and this was his way of going about it."

Carl gestured to the tablet and his jaw tightened. "But this new demand is something completely different. After you walked out, Alec sent this over to me. Director Borshin wants to audit all my records. They're looking into my finances and interactions between the ruin rat camps now. They've asked me to return to the towers immediately so I can go through my records with them."

Kayla glanced down at the tablet again. "I don't understand. Why would they want those records?"

His expression was grim, and he didn't respond immediately. Finally, Carl sighed and rubbed his fingers over his face as though tired from the entire ordeal. "I don't know, Kayla. Your guess is as good as mine. Alec isn't particularly fond of me, and my first thought was that he might be trying to replace me as a trader."

She stared at him in stunned shock, her grip tightening on the edge of the desk. Before she could say anything, he held up a hand. "Don't worry. I dismissed the idea almost as soon as I had it. That tactic seems a little heavy-handed for him, regardless of our differences. In all honesty, I don't know what he's looking for in these records. I contacted Rand as soon as I ended the transmission with Alec. They've requested his camp's records, too, but they're not focusing on him to the same extent they're focusing on me."

Kayla frowned. "But Rand's only been a trader for a month."

Carl nodded. "Yes, and that might explain why they haven't ordered him to report to the towers. Rand mentioned he spoke with Warig and Henkel earlier today, and neither one of them mentioned anything about an audit. Something about this doesn't feel right to me. But whatever it is, I'll handle it. I have nothing to hide."

Kayla picked up the tablet and scrolled through the long list of requested information trying to find some clue to Alec's motivation. Carl was right though. There was no love lost between the two men, but this didn't make sense. Both Carl and Rand had supported her decision to leave the towers against Alec's wishes. It troubled her that they were both being targeted. Why not the other traders?

Kayla jumped off the desk and paced, too agitated to sit still. "I don't like that you're being singled out. You're the best trader OmniLab's got. Some of the High Council even pointed that out when they were interviewing Rand for the trader position. Alec better not be doing this because he's still pissed that I left with you."

"We don't know anything for sure. The High Council has every right to request the information, especially since the towers are under new leadership. Maybe that's all this is. Either way, Alec has asked me to return to the towers tomorrow to go over my records with Director Borshin. I was asked to extend the invitation for you to accompany me."

She froze at his words and slowly turned to face him. Their eyes locked and understanding filled her. "He's using you to try and get me to go back, isn't he?"

Carl nodded and stood, crossing the room toward her. "That much I agree with. It's possible he's just using this request as an excuse, especially after you refused his invitation. If that's the case, it's just more of a headache than anything else. You don't have to do anything you don't want to do."

Kayla frowned and considered Carl's words. Part of her wanted to stay in the camp and just continue to ignore Alec, but a larger part wanted to go back to the towers and tell him exactly what she thought of his attempts to use Carl to manipulate her. If Alec's actions were just affecting her, it might be different. But Alec's interference was also impacting everyone in Carl's camp, and she couldn't let him continue to do that.

Unaware she was considering accompanying him, he continued, "Your idea about sending the samples to OmniLab for additional testing is a good one though. I'll take them with me. I won't be gone longer than a few days. When I get back, we can head back to the cavern. It'll take a few days to run more stability scans anyway. In the meantime, would you mind helping Cruncher render those three-dimensional images?"

Aware he was waiting for a response, Kayla brought herself back to the conversation. "Sorry, what?"

Carl groaned. "It figures. You're thinking about going because of what I said, aren't you?"

"Maybe." She looked away, not willing to meet his gaze. "So what if I am? Someone needs to tell Alec to back off, and I can do that a lot better face-to-face. He has no right to use you to get to me."

Carl ran his hands over his face in frustration. "You're going to send the message loud and clear that his plan worked. All he needs to do is call me back to the towers and you'll go back too."

She shook her head. "No. I'm going to send the message that he'll never see me again if he tries to manipulate the people I care about. I made my choice already: I left with you."

Carl was quiet for a long time and just looked at her. "Kayla, are you sure you aren't going because you want to see him again?"

Shit. Panic flooded through her at the loaded question. She glared at him and held up her hands, gesturing in frustration. "I can't believe you're asking me that. I've spent the last several weeks trying my damnedest to avoid him and you think I *want* to see that pompous, arrogant jerkoff?"

Carl reached for her hand as she started to pull away. He gripped tightly, not letting her go. "Yes, I do. In the entire time I've known you, I've never seen you back away from anything. You've always met every obstacle and challenge head-on. Something about this situation with Alec is different though. You've avoided him for weeks, but you've changed your mind all of a sudden? It doesn't make sense. I think you do want to see him again, but for whatever reason, you've been trying to avoid it until now."

"That's not true." Kayla's protest sounded weak, even to her. Carl might be right, but she wasn't ready to have this conversation. Not now. Maybe not ever.

Part of her hated how easily Carl could read her. As though sensing her conflicted emotions, he took another step toward her. "I know you're not still angry over what he said in the towers. Your temper is like a flash fire. It burns, and it's excruciating to witness, but it's over almost immediately. You've pretended to be angry with him for weeks. Why?"

"He said I belonged to him!" Kayla yanked her hand back. "I don't belong to him! I won't *ever* belong to him. I don't care about the stupid connection thing. I won't let him control—"

"I'll be damned," Carl whispered. "You're terrified of that 'connection thing,' aren't you?"

Kayla's eyes widened, and her hand flew to her mouth. She'd said too much.

"Sweetheart, why didn't you tell me?"

She shook her head, refusing to answer. With a sigh, he slipped his arms around her. Kayla started to pull away, but the comfort and reassurance Carl offered was irresistible. She leaned against him and squeezed her eyes shut.

His voice was soft as he said, "You can't change who or

what you are. But you can make a choice about how you want to live your life."

"I already did," she whispered, curling her fingers into his shirt. She needed this closeness, needed him. "I chose you. It doesn't make the ache go away though. It hurts all the time."

Carl tipped her head back and searched her expression. "I want to understand. Please tell me."

Kayla swallowed nervously and looked away, not wanting to hurt him. How could she admit that part of her wanted to see Alec again? Her feelings for Carl weren't any less, but the energy ... she desperately wanted to feel it again. It was that incessant need that freaked her out and made her avoid Alec.

"I can't get him out of my mind." She hung her head, ashamed of her admission and weakness. "It's this pull that won't go away. Every day, I think of another reason to go to the towers, and then I have to talk myself out of it. It's hard enough to deal with it on my own, but when I saw him earlier on screen, it brought everything to the surface. I remember the energy and want to experience it again. I hate feeling that way though. I don't want to live like that."

Carl's arms tightened around her. He was quiet for a long moment as though battling an internal war. Squeezing her eyes shut, a sick feeling grew in the pit of her stomach at his continued silence. Finally, he sighed and threaded his fingers through her hair. "Maybe you *should* go back to the towers for a visit. It's possible you've been going about this the wrong way."

Kayla peeked up at him, not sure she'd heard right. "What? What do you mean?"

"Alec told you this would happen," he reminded her. "He knows far more about it than we do. Maybe there's a way to turn it off or make it easier to deal with. We won't know until we ask him."

Her brow furrowed. "You want me to see Alec even after I

told you that? The two of you were throwing off enough testosterone and angry guy vibes to make me think we were headed for another nuclear fallout."

Carl smiled and tucked a strand of hair behind her ear in an affectionate gesture she'd begun to treasure. "You said yourself that you chose me. You also said you want *it*, not him. You're drawn to the energy. I still don't like him much, but I can deal with that."

She frowned, still not completely convinced. "You really think I should go?"

"I do. You've been distracted lately, and I know you're not sleeping well. I can't help but wonder if this is the reason. If there's a way we can either get rid of this bond or figure out how to keep it from hurting you, we should do it. Besides, we need to run the water tests and get some extra equipment to finish exploring the cavern."

Kayla bit her lip, considering his words. Avoiding Alec hadn't made things any better up to this point. She still wasn't sure she trusted him or this energy stuff, but she did trust Carl. He'd bailed her out of more than one tight spot before, and she just hoped he'd be willing to do it again if things went bad. "I guess you're right. If I go, I want you to promise me something though."

He looked at her in surprise. "What is it?"

"No matter what happens, I want you to get me out of there. Even if I tell you something different, make me leave with you. Knock me unconscious if you have to, but when you leave, I want to be with you."

His eyes warmed at her words. "I'm not going anywhere without you. I don't think that's going to be an issue though. You're not going to want anyone else to touch your river."

She relaxed a bit and returned his smile. "Yeah, that's a good point. That river is mine."

Carl bent down to brush his lips against hers. His kiss was

gentle and offered her promises of a future if she'd only open herself up enough to embrace them. One of his hands wound its way through her hair as the other pressed against the small of her back, drawing her closer.

This was what she feared losing if she went back to the towers. The understanding, patience, tenderness, and passion he offered were more consuming than anything she'd ever experienced. Carl might not have Alec's ability to entice her with energy, but he had a way of touching her that transcended the physical and caressed her soul. Carl was her balancing point in so many ways.

Kayla needed him like a breath of air. Fear gripped her at the thought that the strange metaphysical connection she shared with Alec might threaten the precious bond she'd chosen to forge with Carl. In the face of returning to the towers, she needed his touch and reassurance that she wouldn't lose him.

Desperate to touch bare skin, she slipped her hands under his shirt and slid them across his stomach and then upward across his muscular chest. She shivered at the feel of his heated skin under her fingertips. The need for more was overwhelming.

Kayla parted her lips in invitation, saying without words that she accepted everything he offered. With bold strokes, Carl swept in eagerly, possessing her mouth in the same way he'd claimed her heart. The passion between them flared as his kiss became even more demanding, consuming her with its heat.

Carl broke the kiss suddenly, capturing her wrists in his hands. Leaning his forehead against hers, he took a deep breath and struggled to regain his composure. "You have no idea what you do to me, Kayla."

She had a pretty good idea if it was anything like what he did to her. And so help her, if he stopped touching her now, she'd have to hurt him. He always talked too damn much. Kayla nipped at his lower lip. "I'm willing to find out."

"You're a wicked woman." Carl released her wrists and rubbed his nose along her jawline. His hot breath fanned against her neck as he murmured, "If you're going to go with me tomorrow, we should go pack before you distract me completely."

She shivered at the sensations coursing through her. To hell with packing. She'd go naked if it meant she could stay in his arms. "Why bother? Seara dresses me when I'm there anyway."

"You won't hear me complaining." Carl chuckled, and his fingertips brushed against the bare skin under her shirt, sending delicious tingles through her. If he didn't shut up soon, she was going to tie him to the bed and gag him. "Your mother has phenomenal taste. Although, I think you look incredible no matter what you're wearing."

He trailed his lips downward, and Kayla tilted her head to give him better access. It was getting more difficult to form coherent thoughts. "And what—" Her breathing hitched as he reached a particularly sensitive spot on her neck. "What about when I'm not wearing anything?"

He pulled back slightly and raked his gaze over her figure. "It's hard to say. I think I'll need to see that in order to give you a fair assessment."

That was a suggestion she could work with. She took a step back, immediately missing the warmth of his touch. With a playful smile, Kayla reached down and slowly pulled off her shirt. She dropped it on the desk and watched as his eyes flared with heat.

He swallowed. "That's definitely an improvement. But you might want to remove all your clothing so I can make a more accurate evaluation."

Kayla gave him a sultry smile and took another step back.

His eyes followed every movement as she reached down and slipped off her pants. Kicking them aside, she looked up at him. "Is that better?"

Apparently, it was. Instead of responding, Carl yanked off his shirt and threw it on the floor. Kayla squealed in delight as she was quickly airborne and carried into his private quarters. She laughed as he tossed her onto the bed.

He stalked toward her like a powerful predator. She arched an eyebrow and propped herself up on her elbows. "I'm guessing you see something you like."

Carl ran his hands lightly along her thighs, trailing upward to her hips. Pulling her down so she was pinned underneath him, he said in a husky voice, "That's putting it mildly. Kayla, you're the most incredible woman I've ever met."

Her heart fluttered as Carl bent down and kissed her. Unable to resist him or the promise of everything he offered, Kayla wrapped her arms around him and gave herself to him completely.

CHAPTER THREE

THE BUZZING of a commlink alarm woke Carl the next morning. With a grunt, he reached over and grabbed the device. He rubbed his eyes, trying to focus on the screen to determine if there were any messages requiring his immediate attention.

The first was an urgent message from OmniLab. They'd issued an edict declaring the towers and surrounding areas on high alert due to the surveillance aircraft sighting. There was a secondary message from Alec with another strongly worded request to bring Kayla to the towers for her protection, especially in light of this newest development. The third message was from Xantham. He'd managed to extract a few images of the aircraft from the surveillance feed yesterday. They'd already been sent to OmniLab for analysis.

With a sigh, Carl tossed the commlink back onto the nightstand before rolling over and propping himself up on one arm to look down at Kayla curled up against him. It was so contrary to her normally independent and free-spirited nature. He'd never seen anyone look as peaceful and angelic when they slept. It made him hesitant to disturb her. It also brought out every single one of his protective instincts. She'd become an important part of his life in such a short amount of time.

Carl bent down and lightly kissed her nose. The blanket had shifted around her hips sometime during the night, leaving a teasing expanse of soft skin exposed. His eyes roamed over the curves of her lush body, and he cursed his luck. Any other time, he'd consider pushing back their trip for a few hours.

Kayla was indifferent to her natural beauty. In Carl's opinion, it only added to her appeal. She was petite in stature, but the same couldn't be said about her personality. Surprisingly strong-willed and fiery in nature, she had a tendency toward being stubborn and obstinate. Underneath, though, she was far more complex and sensitive than he'd ever imagined.

Her shoulder-length dark hair fanned across the pillow, and he carefully brushed it away from her face. Trailing his fingers across the softness of her cheek, they brushed against dark lashes. Her eyes remained closed, but he knew once they opened, he'd be looking into the most striking green eyes he'd ever seen. From the moment he'd first seen her, she'd captivated and intrigued him.

"Good morning, sweetheart."

At the sound of his voice, Kayla opened her eyes and gave him a sleepy smile. She stretched, causing the blankets to shift even more. His eyes followed their movement, appreciating the rather tantalizing glimpses of what lay beneath.

She raised an eyebrow at his expression. "Mmm. I know that look."

Of course she did. Any man with a pulse would have that look if they had her sleepy, naked form in their bed. He'd bet the rest of his OmniLab contract that most of them daydreamed about it. At least he had the privilege of knowing the reality was even better than the fantasy.

The thought of his OmniLab contract brought him back to the present. As much as he'd like spending the rest of the day in bed with his beautiful siren, pissing off the higher powers in the towers wasn't the best idea. He was already on Alec's shit list.

With a pang of regret, Carl bent down and brushed his lips softly against hers. "I'm sure you do. But sadly, we're going to have to get going this morning. We've got a long drive ahead of us to get to the towers."

Kayla shifted and lightly kissed his neck. Trailing kisses upward toward his ear, she flicked her tongue against his earlobe. "You don't really want to rush out of here, do you?"

His willpower went out the window. They could spare an hour. Maybe two. This woman owned him, body and soul. Burying his face in her hair, he groaned and pulled her closer. "You're an evil temptress."

She laughed and wound her arms around him. He dipped his head to kiss her when his commlink began beeping from the nightstand. With a curse, he rolled away and switched it to audio before answering.

A familiar voice came over the communication device. "Good morning, Carl. Sorry for disturbing you so early, but we had an unidentified aircraft flying through our district about an hour ago. Director Borshin mentioned you reported a similar incident yesterday."

"Good to hear from you, Rand." Carl sat up, his attention now completely focused on the call from the other trader. Another sighting in the neighboring district didn't bode well. "It happened late yesterday afternoon. Were you able to capture an image?"

"Yes," Rand replied. "We sent it to OmniLab already. I'll forward a copy of the image to you too. They were flying low, and it's possible they were conducting some sort of surveillance of the area. You should hear from the towers shortly if you haven't already. They're talking about possibly recalling us. Have you had any other sightings?"

"Not to my knowledge. I have an appointment at the towers later today so I'm getting ready to head there now. Have you spoken with the other traders?"

"Not yet. Director Borshin indicated you were the only one to file a report."

Carl frowned and considered the possibilities. He shared the area to the east of the towers with Rand. It was possible that whoever was piloting the aircraft just hadn't moved into the other districts yet. "I'll have Cruncher send you a copy of our surveillance video from yesterday. Let me know if you find out anything else."

"Will do. Take care and give my best to Kayla."

Carl said his goodbyes and terminated the transmission. Kayla placed her hand on his arm, drawing his attention. "You're worried, aren't you?"

"A bit. I have a bad feeling about this. As far as I know, there aren't many other facilities with surveillance aircraft. If someone else is mapping OmniLab territory, this could be a problem."

"Maybe we should put off returning to OmniLab until we learn more," she suggested. "I could ask Alec to hold off on the audit thing for a while."

Carl didn't answer right away. Part of him was tempted to stay and keep an eye on the situation, but if there was a potential danger, he wanted Kayla in the towers where she'd be safe. After her confession last night, he knew there was no way she'd willingly go to the towers without him. He also needed to get to the bottom of this audit request.

Leaning forward, Carl brushed a kiss across her forehead. Kayla had enough on her plate without needing to concern herself with everything else. "It'll be fine. If there are any more sightings, we can come back. Cruncher will contact us if anything comes up."

"I guess you're right." Kayla frowned. It was clear she still wasn't thrilled with returning to the towers. Her reluctance filled him with a small measure of satisfaction. Aside from OmniLab's frequent nosing in their affairs, the past several weeks with her had been wonderful. He didn't care much for the thought of sharing her again with Alec—even temporarily.

Alec could be conniving when it suited him, and he'd obviously set his sights on Kayla as the prize. With the way they'd left things in the towers, Carl had no illusions that Alec would do whatever was necessary to work his way into her life. He'd been making Carl's work life a living hell for the past month, piling on additional work in the form of tweaking their existing safety procedures, monitoring their comms, insisting upon daily schedule logs, and now this audit had landed on his desk. It didn't matter that his camp was the smallest of the trading camps and they were short-staffed. Alec kept reminding him he could easily be replaced and recalled to the towers if he didn't toe the line.

So far, he'd managed to handle things, but it didn't look like they'd let up anytime soon. He'd played off some of his concerns to Kayla about the audit, but he was worried. There wasn't anything for OmniLab to find, but he wasn't sure how far Alec would go in his pursuit. The sooner they resolved the situation with that damned bond, the better. If the only way to do that was to have Kayla return to the towers, Carl was determined to be right there with her. He just hoped this decision wouldn't backfire on him.

Forcing a smile he didn't quite feel, he tried to bury his concerns. "Why don't you get ready to go? I'll let Cruncher know what's going on and ask him to send the images to Rand."

Kayla hesitated for a moment, searching his expression. He kept his face blank and remained silent, hoping she wouldn't press the issue. After a long moment, she shrugged and climbed out of bed. Tossing a sultry look over her shoulder, she blew him a kiss before stepping inside the bathroom.

Carl watched her go, resisting the temptation to join her. With a sigh, he shook his head and began to dress. Unlike most other relationships, this one continued to confound him. Of course Kayla wouldn't pry. It seemed to be an unspoken rule with most ruin rats. Sometimes it was amazing he'd made as much progress with her as he had. Kayla had no problem with the physical aspects of their relationship, but any hint of discussing emotions had her looking for the nearest exit.

Ruin rats were transient in nature. Even though she might have strong feelings for him, she shied away from putting them into words. One of these days, he'd manage to bridge all of her walls. In the meantime, Carl reminded himself to be patient. So far, she hadn't run. As long as he let her set the pace, she continued to let him deeper into her world.

With one last longing glance toward the shower area, he headed out of the room.

Cruncher, Jinx, Zane, and Lisia were in the common room having breakfast and greeted him when he entered. Jinx was a tall, willowy, redheaded woman who had been working as a scavenger for him for the past three years. He'd come to depend on her quick mind, cool temper, and knack for helping to diffuse tense situations in the camp.

Zane was a blond man with fair skin and an average build. Carl had recruited him from the same ruin rat camp where he'd met Jinx three years earlier. Zane was an excellent scavenger with an almost uncanny knack for working locks and getting into tight spaces. He'd immediately impressed Carl. Zane and Kayla frequently challenged one another. Their playful competitiveness only helped to enhance their already remarkable skills.

Lisia, on the other hand, was a problem that needed to be remedied soon. Carl had been briefly involved with her before meeting Kayla. Unfortunately, Lisia harbored some rather intense resentment toward Kayla and Carl's blossoming relationship. Because of the tension, he'd been giving serious weight to Jinx's suggestion about transferring both Lisia and her brother, Elyot, to Rand's camp. The loss of Elyot would be a hardship, but it might be worth it to have less discord within the compound. Once the audit was complete, he'd speak to Rand about the possibility and begin looking for crew replacements. Either that, or they might be able to work out a personnel trade.

Carl walked over to the table. "Sorry to interrupt your breakfast, but I just heard from Rand."

Cruncher swallowed a bite of his food. "Something up, Boss?"

"Possibly," Carl said and told them about the call.

Zane shook his head. "I was with Xantham last night when he was monitoring the comms and radar. There weren't any other sightings in our district."

Carl didn't bother to hide his relief at the news. "Good. I was debating whether I should cancel my trip to OmniLab. Kayla agreed to go with me. Hopefully, we'll get some answers when we get there."

Cruncher snorted. "I bet she's thrilled about that."

"Not even close," Carl replied.

"Veridian told me about the earthquake yesterday," Jinx said with a frown. "We still don't know what caused it, do we?"

Carl hesitated, wondering if Alec was right and Kayla had been responsible for it. There was no need to worry his crew about it though. "It's on the list of things to find out. At the moment, I'm more concerned about this aircraft. Cruncher, Xantham managed to capture some images from the surveillance feed yesterday. I need you to send them to Rand when you're done eating. If there's any change or any other sightings, let me know and we'll come back immediately."

Lisia had been quiet up until this point. She stood and swept her curly blond hair back. "That's all right, Carl. I need to do some work in the communications room anyway. I can take care of it for you."

Carl raised an eyebrow, surprised at the unsolicited offer. Lisia wasn't known for being particularly helpful, especially not lately. Cruncher seemed somewhat caught off guard, too, but shrugged.

"Makes no difference to me," Cruncher replied and took another bite of his food. When Carl nodded in agreement, Lisia pasted on a polite smile. She dumped her tray into the recycler and headed out of the room.

"That was weird," Zane muttered and looked around the table. "Anyone else think that was weird?"

"Leave it alone, Zane," Jinx admonished with a wave of her fork. "I think it's great she's offering to help out. Maybe she's turning over a new leaf. Besides, getting to know some other trader crews would be good for her."

Carl pinched the bridge of his nose and didn't comment. This new and improved version of Lisia wasn't exactly trustworthy. Unless something dramatic had shifted in the past day, something was going on with her. He'd reminded Lisia a month ago that her and Elyot's contracts were up for renewal, hoping the threat of not renewing with them would change her behavior. Unfortunately, it seemed to have made things worse. Lisia's productivity, while never stellar, had diminished considerably until most of the camp was feeling the strain from picking up her deadweight.

Her changing behavior might be unexpected, but Carl

wasn't about to get into this discussion now. He'd deal with Lisia and her mood swings after returning from the towers.

———

AFTER KAYLA FINISHED in Carl's room, she returned to her private quarters to pack. She might spend most nights in his bed, but there was something to be said about enjoying her own private space too. Such a thing had been outside of her experience until she moved to the trader camp. It was still a novelty.

Carl had offered to move her belongings into his room, but she'd managed to dodge the issue so far, unsure she was ready for something so ... permanent. As a general rule, ruin rats didn't do permanent. Losing someone you cared about was hard enough, but when you dropped your defenses and had that expectation they would be there, your entire world could be upended once they were gone. She squeezed her eyes shut, remembering when Pretz had died. She'd been careless afterward, making so many mistakes. In their line of work, mistakes were frequently deadly.

If she'd had that much difficulty coping with Pretz's death, losing Carl would be a thousand times worse. It was hard enough keeping a modicum of distance between her and Carl while living here in his camp, but she had the feeling it would evaporate entirely once she took that next step and moved into his room.

With a sigh, Kayla finished packing her bag and left it on the bed before heading toward the common room. Jinx and Zane were still finishing up breakfast when she entered.

"Morning, Kayla," Zane greeted her. "We heard you and Carl are headed back to the towers."

"Looks that way," she admitted. Reaching over his shoulder, she grabbed a fruit stick off his tray and winked. He narrowed his eyes but allowed the theft and then chuckled.

Jinx pushed her tray aside and stood. "Could I talk to you, Kayla? I know you guys are trying to hurry and get out of here, but it'll just take a minute."

Kayla cocked her head and took a bite of the pilfered food. Jinx shifted from foot to foot, not meeting her gaze. The tall redhead was normally confident and self-assured, but something had Jinx nervous. Curious about the cause, Kayla nodded in agreement and followed Jinx to the workroom in the back of the camp.

The large room was originally designed as a practice room, but with all the new equipment Alec kept sending, it was now quickly becoming more of a secondary storage room. Kayla grumbled under her breath about the excess waste and carefully stepped around some boxes piled by the door. Maybe they could donate some of these things to her former ruin rat camp. They could use the extra supplies. Hell, Leo would probably dance around camp for a week when he got a look at some of these gizmos.

Jinx closed the door behind them and anxiously twirled a red curl around her finger. "Sorry, I just didn't want anyone else overhearing yet."

Kayla looked at the young woman in concern. "What's wrong?"

"I didn't mean to alarm you," Jinx said quickly, almost stumbling over her words. She clasped her hands together as though trying to keep from fidgeting. "It's nothing bad. At least, I hope it's not bad. I just wanted to talk to you about Veridian."

"V?" Kayla asked in surprise, growing more concerned. "What about him? What's going on?"

"This is sort of awkward. I know you're protective of him. I mean, you guys are really close. I just thought you should know that we ... um ..." Her voice trailed off as her face flushed to match the red in her hair.

Kayla's eyes widened in astonishment as realization dawned. "Holy shit! You and V?"

Jinx nodded sheepishly. "Yeah. I'm really into him. He's an amazing guy. We've been spending a lot of time together lately. He was going to tell you himself, but he's on shift later so he's still sleeping. I know you and Carl are heading to the towers in a little while. I didn't want you to find out from someone else. Besides, I figured if you were going to kill me, it would be better to tell you now in case I needed time to run."

Kayla stared at her blankly for a moment and burst into laughter. Jinx still looked unsure. Both amused at Jinx's reaction and thrilled Veridian had finally made a move, Kayla couldn't stop the huge grin from spreading across her face.

Jinx bit her lip. "Okay, laughing and smiling is good. Right? You're okay with it?" She looked hopeful at the thought. "I wasn't sure how you'd react. I know you two are close, and I didn't want things to be weird."

Kayla shook her head, still amused over Jinx's apprehension. "No, it's not weird. I'm glad for both of you. You guys deserve to be happy. Just don't break his heart or I'll have to hurt you. That would really suck since I like you."

Jinx let out a long breath and slumped against the wall. "I don't plan on it. Man, I feel like I just dodged a minefield. I didn't want to cause more problems in the camp. I know things are still tense with Lisia."

The reference to that particular Pandora's box caused Kayla's smile to slip. "Right. Well, I think it's great about you and V. I'm still kinda shocked though. He's had a thing for you since he first met you, I just didn't know he acted on it yet."

Jinx's eyes lit up and she smiled, making the normally

pretty girl positively radiant. "Yeah. I had to drop some pretty big hints to get him to take that step. He was worried about making me uncomfortable or moving too quickly. It sounds silly saying it, but he's a complete gentleman. It's a big change from most of the other guys I've known."

"Yeah, he's definitely one of a kind," Kayla agreed. Veridian was usually reserved around women and tended to be extremely protective of them. As far as she knew, he'd never had any sort of romantic relationship. He was the stereotypical nice guy, and most women ended up thinking of him as a brother or good friend. Kayla had known about his infatuation with Jinx and was thrilled his feelings were reciprocated.

"Well, I just wanted to give you a heads-up. I know you've got stuff to do before you head out, so I'll let you go take care of it."

Kayla smiled at Jinx. "When I get back, I want to hear all the details. Knowing V, he won't say a word, so you're going to have to spill your guts. Take care of him while I'm gone."

Jinx laughed. "It's a deal."

With a grin, Kayla turned and headed down the hall wondering how she'd completely missed that development. She was still shaking her head when she entered the tech room. Cruncher was hunched over one of the terminals working on the images from the cavern.

Kayla leaned across the desk to get his attention. "Heya, Cruncher. Think I can snag a copy of those images? Carl's dragging me to the towers for a couple days and I want to take the files with me."

"Sure thing," Cruncher replied and pulled up another screen. "Maybe with you two lovebirds gone, some of us can get some actual work done." She made a move to swat him, but he held up his hands in surrender. "Okay, okay. I'm sending it to your commlink unit now."

He entered a few commands, and Kayla's commlink beeped a moment later, acknowledging receipt of the files. She thanked him, and he added, "I'm going to start rendering the images in three-dimensions. I'll send them to you at OmniLab when they're ready. When Veridian drags his ass outta bed after playing with Jinx all night, I'm going to have him work on aligning the images with our topographic maps. We might be able to determine the path of the river based on that."

Kayla's eyes widened. "Shit, you knew about Jinx and V too?"

Cruncher laughed. "They've been making eyes at each other for the past couple of weeks. When they disappeared together last night, we all had a general idea what was going on. It's a genuine lovefest in here. I'm going to have to go find myself a woman."

Kayla blew out a long, drawn-out breath. "I can't believe I've been so out of the loop."

He grinned and patted her shoulder. "Judging by the amount of time you've been spending with the boss and dodging Alec's calls, I'd say you've got more than enough loops of your own."

He might have a point, but she wasn't going to admit it. "I was doing pretty well with dodging Alec until yesterday."

"It was only a matter of time. We all knew this would happen, so enjoy the sights and the food and then get your ruin rat ass back here to work. We're going to need you for that cavern."

Kayla smiled at Cruncher's words. Even with all the teasing about her birthright and ties to the tower, he hadn't treated her any differently. Although regarded as a derogatory slur by some, she was proud of her ruin rat ways and still considered herself to be one. She felt a pang of longing and realized she missed Leo and her former camp. In some ways, life was much simpler there when it was all about survival.

Making a mental note to try to visit her old camp with Veridian, Kayla put the thought aside to focus on more urgent matters. "Did Carl forward you a copy of the aircraft image Rand sent over this morning?"

Cruncher raised his eyebrows at the question. "You didn't see it?"

She pulled up a chair in front of another terminal and sat. "Not yet. I want to look at Rand's images and the ones Xantham extracted. I'd like to see if they're the same design."

"No problem." Cruncher gestured to her terminal. "You can view them both on Lisia's machine. She was looking at them a few minutes ago."

Kayla entered the commands to bring up the two aircraft images. The request was rejected. She frowned and glanced up at Cruncher to ask him about it, but he was fully engrossed in his project. Unwilling to disturb him, she circumvented the system and extracted the files from the archive server. She'd have to ask him and Lisia later if they'd changed some of the system settings. Carl would be wanting to leave soon, and she didn't have time to investigate the issue.

Based on what she could see, the design of the aircraft was identical. She enlarged the images to take a closer look and caught a glimpse of something on one of the wings. There was a partial image on the one Xantham had extracted as well.

Kayla manipulated the picture to overlay Rand's image with the one from Carl's camp. It appeared as though some sort of emblem had been painted on the wing of the sleek aircraft. She enhanced and sharpened the image even more.

Once it was complete, she sat back and eyed the finished product. It was an unusual design that looked like a circular shape with a line extending through it. She saved the new image and sent it to her commlink along with the unmodified images of the aircraft.

Cruncher glanced at her screen. "What's that?"

"Some sort of design on one of the wings." She shifted the screen so he could view the image. "Have you ever seen anything like this before?"

He frowned and shook his head. "No. I can send it over to OmniLab and have them run a search through their database though. I didn't catch that when I saw the images."

"Catch what?" Carl's voice interrupted as he entered the room.

Kayla turned in her chair. He was wearing his UV-protective gear and looked like he was ready to leave. She pointed to the monitor. "This image was on the aircraft. Have you seen it before?"

He walked up behind her to get a better look at the screen. Carl studied the image and shook his head. "I can't say I have, but I haven't made a study of other facilities. You just found this?"

She nodded. "Yeah. I overlapped the images to get a clearer look at it. I'm going to send it to Alec."

Carl waited while she sent the image directly to Alec along with a short message explaining how she found it. She turned back to Carl when she finished and said, "Maybe he'll know something by the time we get there. You're ready to go?"

"Yes. The bikes are already packed. I grabbed your bag off your bed."

Kayla picked up the water samples and put them into a secure carrying case. Unable to think of any other reason for delaying, she sighed. "Okay. I guess it's time to get this over with."

Cruncher chuckled and waved them off. "Have fun, you

two. I wouldn't mind if you brought me back a couple of those sandwiches."

She grinned, recalling the last time they had been in the towers. Cruncher had become obsessed with the food Seara, Kayla's mother, had served them. Her mother had been delighted with Cruncher's appreciation and had sent them home with a full box of sandwiches. It wasn't much of a surprise when they'd been devoured within a day of arriving back at the camp. The pre-packaged foods the camp normally kept on hand were tasteless compared to the food in the towers.

After promising she'd mention his request to Seara, Kayla and Carl headed to the entrance so she could gear up. She pulled on her protective equipment, and they both headed outside into the bright sunlight. Kayla scanned the horizon, half expecting to see the aircraft again, but there was no sign of it or anything else.

Although the towers could be seen from where they'd been scavenging in Sector Twelve, they were too far away to see from the trader camp. Even without a physical presence, Kayla felt a strange pull coming from their direction. It might be her imagination or because of Alec, but either way, it made her uneasy. The thought of this bond thing having that sort of control worried her. She refused to be dependent on anyone or anything, real or imaginary.

Taking a deep breath and pushing aside her reservations, Kayla climbed on the back of her bike and followed Carl away from the trader camp.

———

THE DRIVE to the towers through the ruined landscape was long and uneventful, but Kayla began to feel a stronger mixture of apprehension and anticipation once the two buildings came into sight. The main tower primarily catered to the human residents, while the other tower housed their more unusual residents: The Drac'Kin. The towers stood out boldly against the barren horizon like an imposing beacon, offering both a potential haven and a warning.

Steeling her resolve, she followed Carl's lead and parked behind him outside the main entrance. She climbed off and stretched once she'd shut off and secured the speeder, her legs feeling leaden, partially from the long drive but also because of nerves. Carl reached over and grabbed the bags from the backs of the bikes and hefted them over his shoulder before leading her inside.

Kayla pulled off her helmet as soon as she stepped through the large doors into the immaculate entrance area. The blaring whiteness of the interior contrasted sharply with the dust, dirt, and grime from the outside world.

One of the OmniLab attendants she recognized from her previous visit rushed up to them, intent on relieving them of their belongings. Determined to stop any signs of obeisance before they started, she sidestepped the attendant and hung up her helmet. "Heya, Melvin. How's it going?"

The man stopped short, his eyes widening at the unaccustomed familiarity. "Uh, it's going well, Mistress Rath'Varein."

"Kayla," she reminded him, grimacing at the formal title. She'd cure the whole blasted tower of their annoying deferential attitude if it killed her.

He hesitated before nodding. "Of course, Mis—Kayla. Are—Are you doing well?"

Kayla flashed him a smile. *One Omni down, a few thousand more to go.* "I'm great, thanks for asking. Although, I think my ass went numb from sitting on the speeder for so many hours."

Melvin continued to stare at her, completely bemused.

Carl leaned close and whispered, "You're going to torture all of them, aren't you?"

She whispered back, "Only until they start treating me like a regular human being."

An elderly woman with graying hair approached them and waved the young man away. As he scampered back to his station, the woman addressed Kayla and Carl in a clipped but polite no-nonsense voice. "Welcome back to the towers. Master Tal'Vayr informed us of your arrival. Trader Carl Grayson, please sign into the terminal so we can modify your access for this visit."

Carl hung up his helmet and went over to the console on the far wall. After completing a retinal scan, he placed his palm on the machine until it emitted a loud beep. He spoke his name clearly and then turned back to them.

The woman glanced down at her handheld tablet and nodded. "Thank you. Master Tal'Vayr has given you clearance to visit the Inner Sanctum during your visit. Your biometric signature has been authorized for use within the priority elevators."

The side door swung open and an unfamiliar man with short, brown hair stepped into the room. He was slightly shorter than Carl with a trim waist and heavily muscled arms and chest. Kayla hadn't seen many other Omnis with such an athletic physique.

His gaze swept across the room and seemed to absorb every minute detail. Kayla guessed the newcomer was somewhere in his mid-twenties, but the intensity in his hazel eyes made him seem older. She recognized the same look many ruin rats possessed, and it instantly put her on alert. This was a man who'd seen the darker side of human nature.

The gold OmniLab Ouroboros symbol was a stark contrast against his dark jacket. It was a miniature depiction of a dragon circling around and grasping its tail in its mouth.

Veridian, who had a love for history, had explained once that it represented the concept of cyclicality. As an example, he told her the story of a bird called the phoenix that had the ability to rise from its own ashes to begin anew.

Kayla pushed these thoughts aside to focus on the man wearing the symbol. Her gaze traveled down his length, and she stiffened at the sight of the weapon holstered at his waist. Given her previous experience in the towers, this wasn't good news. Kayla glanced at the exit and tried to calculate how long it would take to grab their helmets and make a run for it.

The man noticed her reaction and froze. They stared at each other for several heartbeats, both assessing and considering one another. He slowly raised his hands in a passive gesture, indicating he intended no harm. His voice, when he finally spoke, was low and soothing and reminiscent of someone trying to coax a feral animal into approaching. She nearly snorted at the realization she was the feral animal in this scenario.

"I apologize for startling you. My name is Brant Mason. Master Tal'Vayr and Director Borshin were unable to meet you personally. They both send their apologies. Master Tal'-Vayr has asked me to escort you to your family's quarters. He'll be joining you there shortly."

Kayla wouldn't have lived long as a ruin rat if she trusted everyone at their word. She shook her head, gesturing to the weapon at his side. Alec's father had used the same type of weapon when he knocked her unconscious weeks earlier. "Why do we get an armed escort?"

Brant's expression remained neutral. He continued to hold himself still as though aware that any sudden movement would have her running for the door. *Smart guy*.

"It's a standard issue security device configured to stun and subdue. All security escorts carry them," Brant said carefully, trying to assuage her obvious apprehension. "I understand your last visit to the towers wasn't altogether pleasant. I assure you, I have no intention of harming you or forcing you to do anything against your will."

"I'm sure it's fine, Kayla."

She glanced at Carl, who gave her a reassuring nod. His vote of confidence made her feel marginally better, but she wasn't completely convinced.

"I'll go with you on one condition," she proposed, determined not to fall into the same trap as last time. "I want my own weapon if you're going to keep yours. Either level the playing field or I'm out of the game."

Brant's head jerked in surprise, and his calm façade dropped for a moment. His obvious shock at her request pleased her. It was about time these Omnis were shaken up a bit. Kayla put a hand on her hip and gave him a cocky grin. When Brant's eyes narrowed, Carl smothered a laugh and looked away.

Brant hesitated for several long minutes as though deciding. Kayla tapped her foot impatiently, giving a pointed look at the exit door. With a scowl, he bent down. Keeping his movements slow, he lifted his pant leg. Kayla hid her surprise when he withdrew a second weapon from an ankle holster. He turned the device around, aiming it away from them, and then slid it along the floor toward her. Her eyebrows arched in surprise. She didn't think he'd actually give her a weapon.

Kayla picked up the device and studied it for a moment, itching to take it apart and find out how to replicate it. As a general rule, most ruin rats only had weapons they were able to create or scavenge. OmniLab wasn't exactly eager to arm the masses on the surface. Experience, however, had taught her never to be without a weapon and she now carried a knife embedded within her belt.

The new device Brant had given her was a slender, cylindrical weapon with a small touchpad. At the bottom of the touchpad was a grooved trigger.

"It's an electrolaser gun. It stuns your target for several minutes."

She nodded at Brant's words and admired the way the device fit in her hand. She was definitely keeping it. The ankle holster wasn't a bad idea either. She'd have to see about getting one of those too.

"All right," Kayla agreed and pocketed the weapon. If Brant was willing to take a leap of faith, she could do the same. However, there were going to be some rules. "But you have to call me Kayla. I don't like the whole Mistress and Master thing. And if you even *look* like you're going to pull out that weapon, I'll have you crying on the floor like a little girl before you know what hit you."

Brant blinked and studied her as though she were a puzzle he couldn't quite figure out. Finally, he took a step back and gestured toward the open elevator doors. "I won't harm you, Kayla."

She flashed him a smile and walked over to the priority elevator. With a slight chuckle, Carl adjusted the bags over his shoulder and followed them. Once they were inside, Brant leaned forward and programmed their floor into the control panel.

Kayla fingered the weapon in her pocket and looked out the glass window into the huge courtyard area as the elevator shot upward. Flowering plants and vines were scattered throughout the enclosure creating a rich gardenscape. The view in the towers was extraordinary, and she wondered if this was the way the world used to look before the last war.

Carl moved to stand behind her, wrapping his arm around her. When she leaned back against him, he brushed his thumb against the bare skin at the edge of her shirt. His warm breath whispered against her ear, "It's beautiful, isn't it?"

She nodded, catching a glimpse of Brant out of the corner of her eye. The security escort was watching them with a disapproving frown. She caught his eye and his expression quickly blanked. With a polite nod, he turned back to watch the elevator console. Kayla glanced up to see if Carl had caught the exchange, but he was focused on looking out the window.

The elevator signaled their arrival, and the doors opened to a large corridor. Recalling her last visit, she recognized the simulated miniature stream flowing through the hall surrounded by trees and foliage. A cobblestone path twisted through the landscape toward her family's quarters.

The door was decorated with a large tree carved into its surface. Strange creatures she now recognized as dragons, or Drac'Kin as they were referred to in the towers, were flying above the tree and cradled within its branches. She lightly traced over their image with her eyes before pressing her palm against the plate on the side of the entrance.

The door slid open, but before she could enter, Brant said, "Your mother has been informed of your arrival. Master Tal'-Vayr will be here shortly. I'll wait outside until he arrives."

Kayla glanced at the man, still unsure what to make of him. Unable to do much except nod, she left him at the entrance and headed inside with Carl. The large circular-shaped common room was decorated in soft cream colors. Ornate pillars added an opulence to the room while the plush seating and decorative flowering plants invited guests to linger. The room might appear welcoming, but it just served as a reminder she was out of her element.

Seara Rath'Varein, Kayla's mother and current co-leader of the High Council, rose from her chair. The petite, dark-haired, older woman moved forward to embrace her daughter.

Slowly becoming accustomed to her mother's displays of affection, Kayla returned the hug and brushed a kiss against her cheek.

Seara beamed in response and took Kayla's hand. "I'm so glad you're here. I was ecstatic when Alec told me you were coming back. Please, come in and put your things down. Your old room is still ready for you. I can show Carl where to put everything." She motioned for them to follow her down the hall, still nervously chattering. "I hope you don't mind, but I picked up some extra things for you to wear. I just couldn't help myself. I was going to send them to your camp, but Alec suggested I wait because you wouldn't wear them on the surface. I've left them all in your room for you."

Kayla smiled at the woman's enthusiasm. Their relationship was still too new to feel comfortable, and Kayla suspected Seara's purchases were a way of trying to make up for all the years they'd missed together. At Carl's nudge, she said, "You didn't have to do that, but thanks."

"Oh, I couldn't resist. One of these days, I'm hoping you'll join me. I'd love to take you shopping." Seara laughed, her green eyes twinkling as she beamed at Kayla. "Sorry. I keep going on and on. Of course you'll want to get settled in and unpack." She turned to flash a smile at Carl and added, "I'm sure Kayla wants you to stay with us here. I went ahead and put some extra toiletries in the room for you too."

Before Carl could reply, a loud chime sounded at the door.

"That's probably Alec," Seara mused. "Kayla, why don't you let him in while I show Carl where he can put everything?"

"Uh, sure," she managed, and her gaze traveled back down the hall. The thought of opening the front door had the same appeal as touching a live electrical circuit just waiting to zap her.

"Kayla?"

She blinked at the sound of Carl's voice. He and Seara were both watching her stare down the hallway like a dumb-ass. At Carl's questioning look, Kayla swallowed her reservations and gave him a tentative smile. She needed to get her shit together and quick.

"Yeah. I'm fine. Go."

He hesitated briefly, but then nodded and headed into the bedroom with Seara.

Kayla took a deep breath, trying to push aside the nervousness about seeing Alec. *Pull it together, Kayla. Just forget about the energy and the stupid connection. You can do this. You're not going to let him use Carl to get to you.* Steeling her resolve, she took a deep breath and marched to the front door.

It slid open, and she found herself face to face with Alec. Any residual anger she'd been experiencing fizzled at the sight of him. He was about the same height as Carl but that was where the similarity ended. Alec's golden hair fell neatly to his shoulders, and Kayla flushed at the memory of running her fingers through its silky softness. Brilliant blue eyes studied her intently as she admired his strong jaw and elegant bone structure.

The man looked like some sort of ethereal figure standing in a long, white tunic embroidered with golden thread over a pair of white pants. A gold chain lay around his neck, and there were several rings on his fingers. His appearance was so far removed from everything on the surface that it felt a little surreal. *How the hell does he always manage to look sexy, exotic, and mysterious at the same time?*

"Hello, my love."

His voice struck a chord, almost hypnotizing her with the sound. A slight smile played on his lips as she looked up into captivating blue eyes. Longing, desire, and a flood of other emotions rushed through her. Desperately wanting to touch and channel energy toward him, Kayla struggled against the urge to throw herself into his arms and succumb to her desires.

Alec lifted her hand and pressed a small kiss against it. Just the slightest touch from him had her senses reeling, and she gasped as a small amount of energy trickled over her. Kayla trembled, and her resolve further weakened as his warm energy enveloped her.

He took a step closer so they were standing barely inches apart. The intoxicating scent of his skin along with the faint aroma of incense filled her nose. Completely aware of her conflicted emotions and desires, Alec offered a slow, triumphant smile. "I admit, I wasn't sure what sort of reaction I would get when I saw you again. I'm glad it was this one. Are you going to invite me inside?"

Time seemed to stop, and Kayla blinked in confusion. Her eyes widened as she recalled they were still standing in the doorway.

Yeah, real classy. Way to go, Kayla. Just stare at the gorgeous man like a complete idiot and fantasize about jumping him right there in the hall. Shit, I'm in big trouble here.

CHAPTER FOUR

"I've missed your wit," Alec said with a chuckle.

Suddenly snapping back to herself, Kayla's eyes narrowed. The intrusive bastard didn't know when to stop. She found the energy thread linking their thoughts together and severed it abruptly. The first sign of wariness crossed Alec's face.

"Kayla?"

She clenched her fist and swung at him, connecting squarely with his jaw. He flinched from the blow and took a step back, astonished by the attack. *Damn, that felt good,* she thought even though her hand was throbbing.

"You arrogant, manipulative prick," she hissed.

Alec stared at her, clearly shocked that her emotions had shifted so quickly. She took another step forward and shoved him. Hard. He took another half-step back and tried to capture her wrists, but she jerked away from him. "How dare you use Carl to get me to come back here. The whole audit thing was nothing but an elaborate ruse, wasn't it? And the surveillance to track my every move? Now you're dumping energy on me like you're hoping I fall at your feet?"

"Kayla," he began, holding up a hand and gingerly rubbing his jaw. "Let me explain."

"What's there to explain?" she demanded, pleased his smug and cocky expression was gone. At least now they were both feeling unbalanced. "The only reason I'm here right now is to tell you to back off. If you keep harassing Carl or anyone else I care about, I swear I'll walk out of these towers and you'll never see me again. But I'll kick your ass so completely before I leave that you won't be able to walk for a week."

"Excuse me, Mistress Rath'Varein," a voice interrupted. Kayla spun in surprise to see Brant standing by the door. *Oops.* She'd been so focused on Alec that she'd completely forgotten about him. Judging by the look on the security escort's face, he'd seen and heard the entire thing.

"My name is Kayla," she reminded him, annoyed all over again. "What the hell is it with all of you and these stupid titles?"

Genuine amusement filled his expression at her words. "Excuse me, *Kayla*, but perhaps it would be better to have this conversation inside? It might be difficult to explain why one of the High Council leaders was beaten up right outside your door."

Kayla crossed her arms over her chest. Brant had a point, but she still hadn't finished making hers. She turned back to Alec. "Fine. Come inside and risk getting your ass handed to you. Otherwise, walk away. Your choice."

Turning around, she strode back into the common area to find Seara and Carl had both returned. Seara was seated, and although the older woman appeared elegant and refined, her forehead was creased with worry. Carl stood next to the couch with a knowing expression on his face as though he'd guessed what had occurred outside in the hall. Keeping his voice polite, Carl offered a shallow bow to the High Council leader. "Hello, Master Tal'Vayr."

Alec rubbed his injured jaw and acknowledged the greeting with a brief nod. Seara's gaze flitted back and forth between Alec and Kayla. "I heard shouting. Carl assured me everything was fine though. Alec, are you well?"

Alec's gaze didn't leave Kayla. "Your daughter is displeased with me again, Seara."

Kayla gave an unladylike snort and waved her hand in the air. "He's fine. For the moment anyway. He's got a hard head so there's no permanent damage."

Seara gasped in shock. "What did you do?"

"Nothing that wasn't warranted," Kayla replied, shrugging and then pointing her finger at Alec. "I want your word right now that you're going to stop all the nonsense and leave me the hell alone. No more games with the surveillance. No more messages. No more elaborate equipment. No more checking up on me."

Alec's jaw clenched, but she had to give him some credit. The High Council leader kept his cool for the most part. He flicked the barest glance at Carl before turning back to her.

"Contrary to what you may believe, the audit and surveillance aren't my way of punishing this *trader* for his indiscretion. As part of my duties, my goal is to protect the towers. That's what I'm doing. Even if you were living in the towers, I would still be doing exactly what I'm doing."

Kayla paused and cocked her head curiously. Alec seemed to be telling the truth, but it was hard to tell without their telepathic connection. She hesitated for a moment and then reached toward him to reestablish their mental connection. Her energy meshed seamlessly with his, and she realized he'd been waiting for her. The familiar sense of him filled her, but it was annoying that his nearness was a comfort.

Alec's voice filled her head as he spoke telepathically, *"You can always reach for me, Kayla. I'll always be here for you."*

"Stop it. You're confusing me. I just wanted to know if you were telling the truth."

"Then feel my thoughts and my sincerity."

Knowing he could sense her unease, Kayla bit her lip and asked aloud, "So you're saying this whole audit thing has nothing to do with getting me to come back here?"

"Not in the way you think. We asked all the traders to supply us with their records. This is part of an OmniLab investigation. We aren't accusing them of anything. In fact, Carl was asked to come here to help us go through their files. I believe he may be able to help expedite our analysis."

She didn't sense any deception from him and frowned, wondering if she had misread the situation. Carl looked as perplexed as she did.

"What are you hoping to find?"

Alec hesitated and then said, "It's a long story. We can discuss it later once you've settled in."

"I don't want to upset your mother by discussing this now. It's an emotional subject for her," he added silently.

Knowing Alec was protective of Seara, Kayla immediately nodded in agreement. She might be curious to learn the truth, but not at Seara's expense.

Alec gestured to Brant. "Seara, you remember Brant Mason, don't you?"

Seara gave the man a charming smile. "Of course. It's always a pleasure, Mr. Mason. I'm sorry you had to witness all of this. You're working with Director Borshin now, aren't you?"

"I'm honored to see you again, Mistress Rath'Varein," Brant said with a bow. "I've been temporarily reassigned from tower security to handle some affairs for Director Borshin and Master Tal'Vayr."

When Seara nodded, Alec turned back to Kayla. "Regardless of what happened outside, I'm glad you decided to return. Unfortunately, things in the towers have been somewhat unsettled since my father's death. Until they're back to normal, we're taking a few slight precautions. It's nothing for you to be concerned about, but I've asked Brant to act as your security escort in the event you decide to explore the towers on your own. He has the clearance to take you anywhere you need to go and can answer any questions you have."

Kayla glanced at the man and shrugged. The thought of having a babysitter was annoying, but at least she got a weapon out of it. Losing him was always a possibility if he became a pest. Maybe he could even point her in the right direction of trying to find out more information about these abilities. She glanced at Seara, debating whether she could ask her for some guidance. Although, Kayla had the sneaking suspicion Seara would probably encourage her to ask Alec for training.

Alec sat on one of the couches and leaned back, draping an arm over the back of the couch. The man seemed to exude power without even trying, and Kayla felt the pull along the connection they shared. Taking the opportunity to explore their bond, she realized being this close to him made the connection feel even stronger. Everything inside her was screaming to channel energy toward him. She wondered if he felt the same way and was just better at hiding it. As though Alec sensed her careful exploration of their bond, his eyes warmed and he offered her a slow smile.

Frustrated and unwilling to give in to her desires, Kayla sat on the couch opposite from him. *"I love Carl, dammit."* Alec's eyes flashed with emotion, but his expression remained neutral. He continued to watch her, almost waiting and daring her to channel energy toward him.

Annoyed both at herself and him, Kayla decided to focus on the issues at hand. "Okay, so you're doing some sort of investigation which has nothing to do with getting me to come to the towers. Fine. I believe you. I'm not apologizing for hitting you though. You deserved it for the other two times I wanted to hit you and you stopped me."

Carl coughed as though trying not to laugh. Seara merely sighed and folded her hands in her lap.

Alec inclined his head. "I believe that was the first time in my life someone actually hit me."

"Definitely not the first time someone wanted to though," Kayla retorted.

He gave her another slow smile. "You're probably right."

"Stop being charming. It's pissing me off," she told him silently. Alec's smile grew even wider, and Kayla mentally kicked herself. Time to focus on why they were here. "Did you ever find out anything about that aircraft?"

Alec nodded, and his expression grew serious. "Yes, thank you for sending over that image. It helped speed up our analysis quite a bit. It turns out the emblem you pieced together is from another facility. They call themselves the 'Coalition'. They were originally established back when the tower construction was in its infancy. It was a collaborative effort of several pre-war governments to create a secure facility that could withstand natural and man-made disasters. After the war, communications with different areas mostly shut down. Since we never advertised OmniLab as being anything other than a private medical and research center, it's doubtful they knew about our existence until recently."

Carl had been silent up until then and casually moved to sit next to Kayla. "Do you know why they're in our flight zone area?"

"Not yet." Alec replied, eyeing Carl's proximity to Kayla. "We suspect they are conducting surveillance and mapping the areas. Our communication experts have been trying to contact them since this morning. They haven't yet responded to our inquiries. We're currently on high alert. The size of their surveillance aircraft leads us to believe they have at least one base camp nearby. Drones were dispatched this morning to try to determine their location and intent."

Kayla frowned. She didn't have any experience with other groups, so she was at a loss. Up until then, OmniLab was the only "big bad" she'd had to endure. "Are they a threat?"

"It's too soon to say, but we're being cautious. They're one of the larger remaining facilities with satellite camps spread throughout the world. We've never had any sort of dealings or conflicts with them in the past. It's my understanding they've absorbed several smaller facilities over the years. If they're looking to add OmniLab to their ranks, they'll be disappointed. We have no interest in being under their rule. We'll hold our own, if that's what's necessary. Until they engage us in a dialogue, however, most of this is speculation. In the meantime, our defense systems have been activated and we're monitoring the situation."

Kayla rubbed her arms to ward off the cold chill that went through her. It sounded like Alec was taking the situation seriously. She wanted to know more about the defense system they had in place, but the worried expression on Seara's face made her switch gears. Remembering the samples in her bag, she leaned forward. "Oh, I brought those water samples with me. Is there any chance we can get them analyzed?"

"Of course. If you want to take care of it tonight, I'll contact the lab and let them know to expect us. I'll also make arrangements for dinner afterward." Alec paused and considered her for a long moment. *"Provided, of course, you can keep your hands to yourself."*

She rolled her eyes at his double meaning. *"Don't piss me off and we have a deal."*

Alec smiled and pulled out his commlink. At the mention of going out, Seara stood and clasped her hands together excitedly. "Well, since you've gotten your little spat out of the way, I found the most gorgeous dress the other day for you, Kayla. You can wear it to dinner."

Panicked at the thought of wearing another evening dress and heeled shoes, Kayla swore under her breath. Carl laughed outright at her horrified expression. She glared at him and muttered, "I'd like to see you wear one of those getups. Then we'll see who's laughing."

At Kayla's dour expression, Seara gave her an indulgent smile. "It's not bad. It's nothing like last time. This is a much more casual affair."

She eyed her mother warily, not believing the woman understood the concept of casual. "Please tell me there are no crazy shoes."

"No crazy shoes," Seara promised.

"All right," Kayla agreed reluctantly and stood. Seara took her hand and practically dragged her down the hallway.

———

CARL WAS STILL CHUCKLING when Kayla and Seara disappeared around the corner. After they were gone, he turned his attention back to Alec.

The High Council leader pressed a button on his commlink and a woman's voice answered. "Sheila, let Dr. Bathrin know I'm going to need access to his lab. Also, contact the maître d' at Bliss. I'd like a private reservation for four. We'll be there sometime after six."

"Of course, Master Tal'Vayr. Is there anything else you need?"

"That will be all," he said and terminated the connection.

Alec stood and slipped the commlink back into his pocket. Appearing completely at ease in Seara's quarters, he walked over to the bar against the wall and poured himself a drink. Alec turned to Carl and gestured to the bar. "Care to join me? Brant's working, or I'd offer him a glass."

Carl glanced at the security officer and nodded. If Alec wanted to play nice, he should probably take advantage of it. If Carl's suspicions were correct, it wouldn't last long.

Alec poured another glass of the dark, amber liquid and handed it to him. Carl took a drink and watched as Alec absently rubbed his injured jaw.

He could relate. It wasn't that long ago he'd been the recipient of one of Kayla's enthusiastic greetings. "For being so petite, she packs a hell of a punch, doesn't she?"

"Yes, she does," Alec admitted, took a sip, and then glanced down the empty hallway. "But she's absolutely breath-taking when she's furious."

Carl's expression darkened, and he lowered his glass. That took less time than he expected. Alec might be baiting him, but Carl wasn't going to let the comment go without reminding him of Kayla's intentions. "She doesn't plan on staying here. We're leaving as soon as I'm finished in the towers."

"I'm aware of your plans," Alec acknowledged, seemingly unperturbed by Carl's comment. The council leader's uncon-cerned response only served to heighten Carl's suspicions. His next question set Carl even more on edge. "You've known her far longer than I have. Tell me, does she frequently do that?"

"Hit people?" Carl guessed.

"Mmhmm," Alec replied. "Or get angry enough that her eyes look like green fire."

Carl swirled the drink in his glass, wondering what sort of game the High Council leader was playing. "Only when you piss her off. Kayla grew up in a different world, *Master Tal'-Vayr*." He didn't bother to hide the disdain from his voice at the title. Kayla and the other ruin rats were rubbing off on him more than he thought.

Brant stiffened slightly at his insolent tone, but Alec held up his hand to stop him from responding. Carl's jaw tightened as he studied the security officer. At the very least, Brant's presence was a neat little reminder of the power play at work within the tower. *Dammit.* He needed to be more careful. If he wasn't so worried about Kayla struggling to deal with this energy bond, he wouldn't have encouraged her to come here.

Turning back to Alec, Carl continued, "Titles, cold looks, and carefully worded jabs aren't part of Kayla's make up. She'll tell anyone exactly what she thinks of them and worry about the consequences later. She took a swing at me back when she thought she was still a ruin rat."

Alec's eyes glinted at the news as he leaned forward. "Out of curiosity, what did you do to provoke her?"

Carl hesitated. This new role reversal was opening his eyes. It was easier to understand the ruin rats' reluctance to discuss their personal business with traders if this was how it felt. Carl eyed Alec with suspicion, unwilling to discuss his private history with Kayla but unable to outright refuse without creating more problems. He decided to settle on just revealing the basic facts. "It was when I was still trying to recruit her. She fell through a floor in the ruins and injured herself. I paid off her camp leader to keep her above ground until she healed up. She was pissed off enough to hunt me down and let me know exactly what she thought of my interference."

"I see," Alec mused thoughtfully. "Her temper is quick to ignite but seems to fade just as fast. I thought she'd been avoiding me because she was still angry with me. That's not the case, is it?"

Carl frowned, wondering what sort of information the High Council leader was trying to get out of him. Feeling as though the drink was nothing more than an attempt to lower his guard, he put the half-empty glass down on the bar. Alec might run OmniLab, but there were some lines Carl wouldn't cross. "No, she's not still angry about that. You'll need to ask Kayla about her reasons for avoiding you though. I won't betray her trust."

"Very well," Alec agreed. "I need to begin training with her tomorrow. I'll speak with her then. Director Borshin will be meeting you at his office around noon to go over some of your records."

"I received the request," Carl said with the slightest hint of irritation. "I'm curious to know what you're hoping to learn from me. Two of the other traders have more field experience than I do."

Alec nodded. "Very well. I didn't want to discuss this in front of Seara, but we have some time now. They'll most likely be a few more minutes." Alec gestured to Carl's abandoned drink. "Would you care for something different?"

"No."

Carl crossed his arms and waited for the council leader to continue. Alec finished his drink and put the empty glass back on the bar. He adjusted one of the rings on his finger and said, "There has been some instability within the towers since I accepted the position of High Council leader. Of course, this is to be expected with any regime change. My father's death left a lot of people angry, both for what he did to obtain his position and while he held it."

"That's hardly unexpected."

"You're right, it's not," Alec agreed, but his hands curled into fists, belying his feigned nonchalance. "Some individuals are wondering how far the proverbial apple has fallen from the tree. A few of these people believe it may be beneficial to have me permanently removed from the High Council."

Carl resisted the urge to comment. He wasn't surprised

the High Council leader was already making enemies. Deciding to take a neutral approach, he said, "I don't see what this has to do with auditing my records."

"My security advisers have brought it to my attention that threats have been made against me. Unfortunately, they're having trouble determining the origin." Alec paused, looking toward the hallway again where Kayla had disappeared. "Kayla's name has been brought up several times in connection with these threats. As such, we're investigating all possible leads. Some references have mentioned the trader camps, specifically your district and Rand's district. Since Kayla has such strong ties to the surface, we're concerned."

Carl stared at Alec, shocked by what he was hearing. "Are you trying to tell me you believe Kayla has something to do with the threats against you?"

"Absolutely not," Alec said sharply. "My security advisers are concerned someone may try to use her to get to me."

Carl stiffened at the insinuation. "You obviously don't know her at all. Kayla would never allow someone to use her like that. She'd chew up and spit out anyone who tried."

Alec turned away and strolled toward one of the shuttered windows. "While your defense of her character is admirable, it's sorely misplaced. You forget I can feel the purity of her thoughts and feelings with our connection."

He pressed a button, and a panel slid aside to expose the outside world. Through the sealed and filtered glass pane, darkness was beginning to fall. The fading sunlight painted an eerie canvas of shadows over the dismal landscape. Alec stared out across the large expanse of land. "I wanted her here to protect her and prevent anyone from trying to harm her. Even with the instability in the towers, I believe she's safer here than outside. I can't control what happens outside these walls, but here, I can protect her."

Alec motioned toward the security officer. "Unfortunately,

my duties won't permit me to remain by her side at all times. Brant is the best ICS agent in the towers, and he'll make sure she's safe when I'm not around. If I can't convince her to remain here, he'll return with you to your camp. I refuse to allow anything to happen to her."

Carl turned back to the security officer, eyeing him with grudging respect. "Shit. You're an Inner Circle Shadow?"

Brant inclined his head. "I am."

Carl frowned, growing increasingly concerned about the severity of the situation. General security within the towers was handled by OmniLab security officers. Their duties were to investigate, deter crime, and keep the residents of the tower safe. A more elite sect of this group was referred to as the Inner Circle Shadows. These individuals were skilled bodyguards assigned to protect Inner Circle members from adverse threats. Carl had heard rumors that although they weren't Inner Circle members themselves, they'd developed tactics to manipulate energy to a lesser extent.

Even so, they weren't common. It was worrying that Alec felt the bodyguard's presence was necessary. It also implied the threat was coming directly from another Inner Circle member. He wished they were more forthcoming with information about this energy usage so he could be in a better position to understand the situation. Even though he'd been born in the towers, Carl wasn't part of the Inner Circle, and he was very much an outsider to all of them, as Alec so frequently reminded him.

"How much danger do you think she's in?"

Alec hesitated briefly, and Carl saw the truth in his eyes. Kayla was more than just a link to Alec; she was a specific target. "If she's in danger from the Inner Circle, she's safer back in my camp. Are you so desperate to get your hands on her that you're willing to let something happen to her?"

Alec's expression went cold, but it was Brant who intervened. "You're out of line, Trader. Until Mistress Rath'Varein receives sufficient training, she's a security liability regardless of whether she's in the towers or on the surface. Right now, their bond is vulnerable and could easily be manipulated by a skilled energy user. Her weakness leaves Master Tal'Vayr vulnerable. She leaves the *towers* vulnerable."

Carl rubbed his forehead. It all came back to that damned bond again. If there were some way they could just eliminate the entire thing, everyone would be better off. He blew out a breath, thankful that at least Kayla wasn't the primary target in all of this. Even so, more information was needed so he could help protect her. With a brief nod, Carl said, "All right. I'll help anyway I can. What do you know about this threat?"

Brant glanced at Alec and the High Council leader nodded, indicating his permission to discuss the situation openly. The security officer turned back to Carl. "As Master Tal'Vayr mentioned, there has been some dissent since he took over control of the towers. The public announcement of the engagement and claim between Master Tal'Vayr and Mistress Rath'Varein a month ago has both helped and hindered the tower's stability. Most are pleased with the proposed union. However, a few others are expressing their concern that too much control is being filtered to one family."

Carl felt as though the floor opened up beneath him. Blood pounded in his ears and he clenched his fists tightly. He barely managed to control his anger at hearing Brant's words. Resisting the urge to pummel the High Council leader, Carl instead pierced him with a fierce glare. "You left the announcement standing? You know Kayla has no intention of marrying you and living here. What the hell are you trying to accomplish by allowing the public to keep believing that lie? She probably wouldn't be in any danger if you had withdrawn the announcement and cut ties with her."

Alec stiffened, and his eyes turned cold as ice. "If it were that simple, I would have done it immediately. I've been trying to protect her not just from the towers but from herself. How do you think people would react if they knew Kayla had no interest in the towers and couldn't care less about governing her family's legacy? The fact that she's bonded to me has stayed more hands than not. Like it or not, she's vulnerable, Trader. After the display at the High Council meeting, there's no doubt to anyone within the Inner Circle about her remarkable potential. Not many people can wield the sort of power Kayla can. I know many people would jump at the chance to exploit her, if given the opportunity. And trust me, it wouldn't take much to do exactly that."

Carl didn't reply, trying to squash the burning sensation in the pit of his stomach. He wanted to lash out and demand Alec recant the announcement, but he forced himself to hold back. As much as he hated to admit it, Carl suspected the High Council leader might be right. The thought pissed him off even more, almost as much as the idea of Kayla publicly agreeing to be another man's wife.

Carl pinched the bridge of his nose and cursed inwardly. He'd been so distracted by the additional work in his camp lately that he hadn't been paying enough attention to the current political climate in the towers. If people believed Kayla didn't have any loyalty to the towers, there was no reason for them to have any loyalty to her either. It would have been better if she could have retained some anonymity after her identity had been discovered. Unfortunately, her unique parentage and the circumstances behind her disappearance put her directly within the public spotlight. He'd heard some of the rumors but dismissed them as idle gossip. Kayla's return to OmniLab was something of a fairy tale and celebrated by the masses.

Alec must have taken his silence for acceptance because

he continued, "As far as our engagement is concerned, I have intentionally decided not to withdraw my formal statement to protect both her and the towers. I know Kayla will be less than pleased when she realizes we're still engaged, but I'm hoping to convince her it's in the best interest of the towers to leave things as they are for now. The thought of our families merging, even in marriage, sends a powerful message of unity to the towers at a time when it's needed the most. If I publicly cancel our engagement, the unrest and political tension in the towers will just escalate. Right now, it's just a small group that's unhappy. That's manageable. Widespread dissent and fear could topple the towers."

Carl rubbed his temples, trying to ward off the impending headache. After Kayla's father had been murdered, the towers had been in turmoil without a leader. Protests, riots, and crime had escalated dramatically. It was only when Alec's father, Edwin Tal'Vayr, had stepped in with an iron fist that the towers had stabilized. But even then, it had taken several years before things settled back into a regular routine. Now it appeared to be happening all over again.

"I see your point," Carl admitted grudgingly, forcing the words. "But you don't fool me either. I know part of you has kept that rumor alive because you're hoping to change her mind."

"I'm not denying it," Alec said plainly. "I fully intend on marrying her when she's ready, but my personal desires come second to the needs of the tower. It just happens that they both align in this particular situation."

Carl's eyes narrowed, and he took a threatening step toward Alec. Brant's hand slapped to the butt of his weapon, warning him away. "I swore an oath to protect Kayla Rath'-Varein and Alec Tal'Vayr. If you lay a hand on either of them, I'll be forced to subdue you. She may take a swing at him without my interference, but you, Trader, will not."

Carl glared at Alec and tried to rein in his temper. There was no doubt Brant would step in if he laid a hand on the council leader. In a low voice, Carl said to Alec, "You're going to be waiting a long time. I have no intention of giving her up."

"That's your choice, as are the consequences. For now, I expect you'll keep this conversation between us until I've had a chance to speak with Kayla in private. I don't want to have this discussion in front of Seara. It would only serve to upset her."

Carl closed his eyes and nodded. The thought of keeping anything from Kayla didn't sit well, but he understood Alec's reasons for not discussing the matter in front of her mother. There was a certain frailty to the woman as though one strong blow would topple her. Unfortunately, Alec wasn't finished.

"If you decide to remain near Kayla while she's in the towers, you'll also need to stay vigilant. If you see or hear anything suspicious, let Brant or myself know immediately." Alec paused for a moment and then added, "As far as you and your 'relationship' with Kayla is concerned, it no longer exists outside her family's quarters. For her safety, you will need to maintain your distance and treat her in a manner befitting any other Inner Circle member."

"Fuck that," Carl snapped. If Alec thought he'd just lie down and let him move in on Kayla, the council leader was sorely mistaken. "If you want to try to play these games, that's your call, but I won't sit by and keep my mouth shut while you act the loving fiancé. Kayla made her choice. I'll take her out of these towers and back to my camp before I let you interfere in our relationship."

"You're making a mistake."

Carl scoffed. The only mistake he'd made was bringing Kayla back here. He should have known Alec would try something like this. "It's just killing you that Kayla walked away from you, isn't it? I wouldn't put it past you to have orchestrated this entire conspiracy."

Alec's eyes flared with anger, but it was Brant who stepped between them. "I assure you the threat is real. You were asked to come to the towers specifically because of your close relationship with Kayla. You have knowledge of her past, including names and dates that may match up with our compiled evidence. Director Borshin will go over all of this with you tomorrow. In the meantime, however, you need to get hold of yourself, Trader. Put your personal issues aside and look at this from a different viewpoint. How do you think the public would react to seeing Kayla with you when she's supposed to be marrying Master Tal'Vayr? Right now, she's beloved, and that same adoration helps protect her. If the masses turn on her, what's to stop the Inner Circle from going after her?"

Carl paused, and his gaze flickered to the security officer. If the entire towers were under the impression Kayla and Alec were a happily engaged couple, any untoward contact would be looked upon with disfavor. He didn't care much for this political game or Alec's personal intentions, but Carl wouldn't do anything to put Kayla in jeopardy. The political arena within the towers could be volatile, and Kayla didn't have enough experience to navigate it on her own. Carl's jaw tightened, but he didn't argue. There was no point. Taking a deep breath, he let it out on a slow exhale. "I won't let anything happen to her."

Brant nodded and took a step back. A noise from behind had all three of them turning around to see Kayla and Seara walking back into the room.

Kayla's dark hair fell loose around her shoulders. She wore a simple, emerald-green dress that matched the color of her eyes. Low-cut and held in place with two slender spaghetti straps, it accentuated the gentle curves of her body as it cinched slightly at her waist, the material floating downward and stopping mid-thigh. As Seara promised, Kayla wore a pair of matching shoes without any noticeable heel.

Carl's heart thudded at the sight of her. After hearing Alec's speech, he wanted nothing more than to tear her away from these towers, throw her on the back of a speeder, and return to his camp.

Kayla frowned, eyeing all of them warily. "What's going on?"

"Nothing," Carl said quickly and tried to bury his concerns. Knowing Kayla, she was far too perceptive and would quickly discern the truth. In an attempt to distract her, he strode toward her and gestured to the dress. "You look amazing."

Kayla's eyes warmed at the compliment. Resting her hand against his chest, she stood on her toes to kiss him. When she pulled back, her mouth tilted upward in a teasing smile as she spoke in a low whisper so only he could hear, "Wait until you see what I have on underneath it."

Carl chuckled and covered her hand with his. Turning to Seara, he said, "I was just telling Kayla the other day how much I admired your taste."

Seara beamed and gazed at Kayla with obvious affection. "Thank you. I've missed having her here, even if she is an unwilling victim in my dressing room."

He glanced down at Kayla to find her still smiling up at him. He trailed his fingers across her cheek before tucking a loose lock of hair behind her ear. Brant cleared his throat, interrupting the moment. Carl looked up to meet the security officer's gaze.

The meaning behind Brant's expression was clear. It was a reminder that intimate gestures such as the one he'd just displayed were no longer acceptable outside these rooms.

Carl's jaw clenched as he lowered his hand. He took a step away from Kayla, and it felt more like a wide chasm forced between them rather than a small step.

His anger at the entire situation was about to boil over. The longer he remained in the room, the more likely he'd say or do something he'd regret. Nodding to the rest of the room, Carl said, "If you'll excuse me for a moment, I need to check in with my camp and get changed. I'll be back in a few minutes."

CHAPTER FIVE

KAYLA FROWNED and watched Carl disappear down the hallway. The turmoil she'd seen in his eyes was worrying, and she hadn't missed the look he'd exchanged with the security officer either. Something was going on and she was determined to get to the bottom of it.

Before she could go after him, Alec's hand brushed against her arm and a trickle of energy washed over her. Kayla's eyes shot up to meet his alluring blue ones. Desire and something else she couldn't quite distinguish through their shared connection flared to the surface.

"Carl's right," he said quietly. "You're absolutely breathtaking."

"Thanks," she managed, unable to tear away from his gaze. Alec took a step closer, blocking her view of the hallway. He lifted her hand, his eyes holding a thousand promises as he brushed a soft kiss against the back of her hand.

Kayla swallowed, feeling both uncomfortable and enthralled by his attention. She closed her eyes and took a deep breath. Alec's nearness was overwhelming, and she needed to get her thoughts together. This was bad. Very bad.

Steeling her resolve, she opened her eyes and lifted her chin. *"Back off, Alec."*

The corner of his lips curved up into a hint of a smile, but he released her hand. He didn't move away though. Instead, he held her gaze. "Would either of you lovely ladies like something to drink while we wait?"

Seara declined, but Kayla nodded in agreement. She'd need whatever liquid courage he was offering to keep a handle on the situation. With a cocky smirk, Alec moved away from her and toward the bar area.

Kayla barely managed not to sigh in relief. This whole bond thing was worse than she thought. Was it this potent the last time she was in the towers? It was imperative she learn how to control it. Although, she was beginning to have her doubts about asking Alec. He seemed to be enjoying her muddled reactions.

He finished pouring two glasses of the amber liquid. As he handed one to her, his hand lingered over hers for a long moment. Just that slight touch brought more shockwaves to her system. She jerked away and cursed, nearly spilling her drink. The bastard was definitely doing it on purpose. If he touched her again, her drink was going over his head.

Silently hoping Carl would come back soon, Kayla took a sip and scowled at Alec. She wasn't sure which was worse, feeling these conflicting emotions or knowing Alec could sense her feelings.

"You can sever the mental connection again if it bothers you. I'll still be able to sense some of your emotions, just not your thoughts."

She didn't answer, content to sip her drink and glare at him over the rim of her glass. Alec's gaze was scorching, and she felt her breath hitch. A trace of a smile still played on his lips.

He turned to glance at the other two occupants in the

room. "Seara, would you and Brant mind giving us a minute? I'd like to talk to Kayla privately."

Kayla's eyes widened, and her mouth dropped open. "What? No. Why? I don't ... that's ... not necessary." *Shit. Shit. Shit.*

"Why? Are you afraid to be alone with me?"

"No," she lied.

Alec raised an eyebrow, making it clear he didn't believe her. She continued to glower at him. Being alone with him was a very, very bad idea. In fact, this whole trip was a bad idea. Kayla glanced back down the hallway toward her bag. She could be changed and back on her speeder in ten minutes. Maybe less.

Unfortunately, that wouldn't solve anything. Her shoulders slumped as she discarded the idea. It was time to get her head together and show Alec he didn't intimidate her. Tossing her hair back, she decided to go on the offensive. If she pissed him off, so much the better. She needed him to back off enough to give her some breathing room and nothing else had worked so far.

Kayla put down her glass, took a step forward, and poked her finger against his chest. "Of course not. I just don't like you."

"Kayla!" Seara gasped, her eyes darting back and forth between them with dismay.

Alec chuckled and dismissed Seara's concern with a wave of his hand. "Oh, she likes me well enough. In fact, I'd dare say Kayla likes me enough that she's afraid of being alone with me." He took a step closer to her. The challenge in his hypnotizing eyes was unmistakable. "It's a shame, Seara. I thought your daughter was braver than this, but I suppose I was wrong."

Kayla's entire body stiffened, and her eyes narrowed at his words. It seemed like the annoying man almost enjoyed when she was obnoxious to him. "I'm not afraid of you. You want to risk talking to me alone, fine. Bring it on."

His eyes lit up in victory. Kayla's fists clenched, and she resisted the urge to smack him upside the head for being so damn cocky. What was wrong with her that she found that trait attractive?

"I suppose," Seara relented with a frown, clearly questioning the wisdom of leaving them alone together. "Brant, would you mind helping me? I have a suspicion I'm going to need to get the medical kit in a moment. It's on one of my top shelves."

Brant inclined his head and dutifully followed Seara out of the room. Once they were gone, Kayla crossed her arms. It was the safest way to keep from touching or strangling him. She wasn't sure which option was more appealing at the moment. "Okay, you got rid of them. What do you want?"

"Such hostility," Alec admonished, but the light dancing in his eyes conveyed his amusement. "And here I was trying to be nice and give you a gift."

She frowned and shook her head, recalling all the gifts he'd been sending to Carl's camp. "No more gifts. Not here. Not to the camp. It's got to stop, Alec. I don't need anything. I don't want anything."

"I haven't been giving you equipment as a gift," he corrected and reached into his jacket pocket. "I've been giving it to the camp so they can keep you *safe*. You, my love, have a tendency to get into trouble. I figured they needed all the help they can get."

She harrumphed. He'd do well to remember most of her so-called troubles were tied to OmniLab. Before she could remind him of that fact, though, he distracted her by placing a small box in her hands.

The material on the outside of the black box was soft and fuzzy. It was unlike anything she'd ever felt. Despite her earlier objections, she ran her fingers over it and wondered about the contents. It definitely wasn't another generator.

"Go ahead and open it," he encouraged.

Kayla carefully lifted the lid, and her mouth dropped open. All her usual snarkiness dissolved at the sight of the gorgeous, square-cut emerald pendant resting within the box. Shocked by the extravagance of the necklace and the enormity of the gift, her eyes flew up to meet his. "Holy shit, Alec! Where did you get this? Do you have any idea how much something like this is worth?"

He reached down to remove the gold necklace from its resting place. Lifting it up, the gem caught the light making it sparkle even more brilliantly.

"I hope you don't plan on selling it, love. It's been in my family for centuries. I believe my mother would be pleased to know it belongs to you now."

Kayla shook her head in protest. The dragon statue he'd given her was one thing. Heck, even the glass globe had been elaborate. But this gift was beyond compare. In all the years she'd been ruin diving, she'd never come across anything even remotely close to the magnificence of this necklace. Her fingers itched to take it, but her moral compass insisted she refuse. "I ... I can't accept something like this. It belonged to your mother."

"Kayla," Alec said softly, squeezing her hand, "if she had lived, I know my mother would have given it to you personally. You were like the daughter she never had. It would mean a lot to me if you'd allow me to honor my mother's memory and accept it."

She looked up into Alec's eyes. The sincerity of his emotions coursed through their bond, and her objections faded away. Although words escaped her, she managed to nod.

"Thank you," he whispered and slipped the necklace over her head. Kayla moved her hair out of the way so Alec could fasten the clasp behind her neck. A small shiver rushed through her as his hands brushed against the bare skin on the back of her neck. When he finished, she turned back around to face him. Emotion swirled in his eyes as he admired the necklace on her. "It becomes you."

Kayla looked down and touched the emerald resting between her breasts. "I've never had anything like this. I've always wondered about the jewelry in the ruins and why people wanted something like that. I think I might understand. It's beautiful. Thank you."

Alec reached up to gently caress her cheek. A slow wave of energy washed over her, and she closed her eyes at the exquisite sensation.

This is what she had desperately wanted to feel again, she realized. Leaning into his hand, Kayla trembled with longing for more and instinctively sent a small pulse of energy back to him. She felt his exhilaration at the contact, and then his lips lightly brushed against hers. She parted them in surprise and he swept in, drawing her closer and consuming her. The world around them faded away as she rode on the crescendo of energy flowing through them. Kayla's fingers curled into his shirt as she pressed against him, returning his kiss. Through their shared connection, she felt both of their desires heighten as they each experienced one another's sensations simultaneously.

Alec slowed the kiss and gradually withdrew his energy from her. When he finally pulled away, his hands cupped her face and his hot breath mingled with hers. She blinked open her eyes and tried to focus on him. The headiness of his touch left her a little unsteady, and she tried to understand what had just happened. Alec gazed at her as though memorizing every detail. Through their bond, she could feel his desire as intense as a flame in front of her.

"I've never met anyone so responsive and passionate. Your

energy is like a brilliant white light holding all the memories of our ancestors and all the promise of the future. I've never felt anything like it."

Kayla's heart thudded as part of her desperately longed to continue exploring what had just occurred between them. But as alluring as the power was, she couldn't bring herself to do it. Regardless of what just happened, her heart belonged to Carl. She shook her head and started to take a step back, bumping into the bar area behind her. "Alec, I ... I can't. That shouldn't have happened."

He searched her face for a long moment and nodded in understanding. "You don't have to explain."

A tumult of emotions coursed through her. She wasn't sure which were hers and which ones were his. She might not need to explain, but words held power on their own and she needed to say them aloud for her own benefit. "I don't want to hurt you, but I can't give you what you want. I'm in love with Carl."

Alec shushed her and took her hand. He threaded their fingers together and placed another kiss on the back of her palm. "You have nothing to worry about, my love. Even if you won't say anything, I know how you feel about me. If I have to wait a few months or even years until you're ready, I'm prepared to do that. You're worth it."

Kayla frowned. Someone cleared their throat, and she turned to find Carl watching them. He had changed and was wearing his more formal OmniLab clothing. Fury lit his eyes, and Kayla hastily pulled her hand out of Alec's grasp, wondering how long he'd been standing there. Judging by the hard look on his face as he glared at Alec and the whiteness of his knuckles as he clutched the water samples, he'd seen and heard enough.

Kayla bit her lip. Her gaze darted back and forth between

the two men. Yep. It was official. This trip was a *really* bad idea.

She straightened her shoulders, ignoring the churning feeling in her stomach, and gestured to the necklace around her neck. It pained her that she'd put that look into the eyes of the man she loved. "Alec just gave this to me. It belonged to his mother."

Carl stalked toward them. He glanced down at the necklace before turning his hardened gaze back on Alec. "That's a very generous *gift*. I'm surprised you wouldn't want such a valuable family heirloom to stay in your family."

Alec didn't reply, but she could sense his building irritation and subtly disguised anger. The two men continued to glare at one another, and Kayla wondered how long it would take before they came to blows. She was supposed to be the hot-headed one. The sudden role-reversal didn't suit her.

Given the circumstances and Carl's protective nature, distraction seemed like the best approach. Since she was already metaphorically in the middle, she might as well get up close and personal. Sometimes actions said more than words. Stepping between the two men, Kayla turned and rested her palms against Carl's chest. She ran her hands upward until they cupped his face.

Carl hesitated for a moment before tearing his gaze away from Alec. When his eyes fixed on hers, his shoulders relaxed a fraction. Kayla tilted her head and gave a nod toward the water samples in his hand. If he clutched them any tighter, he'd break them. "What do you say to dropping those off and getting some dinner? Other than a fruit stick I managed to swipe from Zane, I forgot to eat before we left camp."

Carl frowned. "You're hungry?"

"Starving."

"I'll collect Seara," Alec said from behind her. Kayla ignored his retreating footsteps and leaned closer to Carl. She stood on her toes and brushed a kiss against his cheek. When she sank back to the floor, she gave him a small smile.

"You looked like you were about to hit him."

Carl managed a half-hearted chuckle. "As satisfying as that might be, you already took care of that. Besides, if I'm arrested for assaulting the High Council leader, you'd end up turning everyone in the towers on their heads staging another elaborate escape." His expression darkened slightly, and she knew his anger was still simmering under the surface. "Although, I won't make any promises if he touches you like that again. I'd hoped we could at least manage to make it through this evening before he tried something."

Kayla fingered the pendant. "I don't know what I'm going to do with this necklace once we get back to camp. It's not like I can sell it or wear it in the ruins. It seemed important to him that I take it though. I just ... I wasn't expecting what happened afterward." She looked away, thinking once more about her reaction to their shared bond. Losing control like that was unacceptable. "I need to get a handle on how to control this energy."

Carl's fingers took hold of her chin and he tilted her head back. There was an uncharacteristic hardness in his eyes. "What happened afterward, Kayla?"

She winced. "He kissed me."

A thousand emotions rushed over his face. His closed his eyes and took a deep breath as though trying to calm himself. Kayla bit her lip. It was a probably a mistake to say anything, but if she were in his shoes, she'd want to know the truth. It was fine to deceive people in some situations but not about something like this. She respected and cared about Carl too much to do that to him.

Carl was quiet for a moment before he opened his eyes and spoke again. "I don't care much for Alec or for what happened, but I heard what you said to him." He let out a long sigh and, with his free hand, reached up to tuck her hair behind her ear. The small gesture reassured her slightly. "We'll figure it out, sweetheart. Alec gave me a brief update on what's going on while you were getting dressed. It's not good. We need to talk about it, but it'll have to be once we're alone."

She raised an eyebrow, but he didn't elaborate. Instead, he focused on something over her shoulder. Kayla turned to see Alec and Seara appear with Brant trailing behind them. As Alec approached, a wordless conversation passed between the two men.

Carl bent down to kiss Kayla's cheek and then whispered into her ear, "I'm going to escort your mother to dinner. I'll explain everything later."

He gave her a slight squeeze before turning to address Seara who looked delighted as he held out his arm for her. Kayla couldn't help but smile at the way Carl charmed her mother. A hand grazed her lower back, and she looked up to see Alec standing beside her.

"Shall we go?"

She hesitated, glancing back at Carl but he was focused on Seara. The older woman was laughing at something he'd said. Something was definitely going on. With a frown, she accepted Alec's arm and let him lead her toward the door. Kayla just hoped he kept his energy to himself. They didn't need another repeat of what happened earlier.

He gave her a small squeeze, letting her know he'd heard her thoughts. It wasn't a promise, but she'd take what she could get.

"I think you'll enjoy seeing the lab. We won't be able to do much more than drop off the samples tonight, but I'd be happy to take you on a tour some other time."

"Sure," she agreed absently as they approached the elevator. Even without the energy, Alec's touch was distracting. It felt as though every single nerve ending was alight with awareness.

They filed inside, and Brant programmed the elevator to take them to one of the lower levels. To distract herself from Alec's nearness, Kayla focused on the view out the glass windows. There was no denying the beauty the towers offered, but she wondered if the occupants even really saw it anymore. Maybe you had to see a darker side of the world before you were able to appreciate what was in front of you.

The elevator beeped, and Kayla turned back around to exit a level that appeared to be more clinical with its stark-white floors and walls. Bright overhead lights beamed down upon them as Alec led them down the tiled hallway toward two double doors. He pressed his palm against the outside plate and it beeped loudly before opening.

A tall, thin, balding man wearing a long, white lab coat greeted them as they entered. The security clip on his jacket identified him as a Dr. Bathrin.

"Master Tal'Vayr, your assistant told me you would be stopping by. I understand you have some samples that need to be tested?"

"Yes," Alec replied and introduced them while Carl placed the water samples on the counter.

Carl gestured to the collection. "My trading camp collected these water samples. All of our preliminary tests came back negative, so we need a more in-depth analysis. We'd like to have them run through a complete analysis and testing cycle."

The doctor collected the samples and studied them closely. "Of course, Trader Grayson. I'll oversee all the tests personally."

"This is a priority," Alec reminded him.

"Absolutely. I'll let the staff know and have this expedited.

As soon as the results are ready, I'll send them directly to you."

Kayla leaned against the counter. "Do you know how long it will take?"

He frowned, looking apologetic. "I'm sorry, but there's no way to know until we begin running the tests. It depends on what we find."

Kayla bit back a groan. She'd guessed as much but had hoped for a different answer. She was anxious to get back to Carl's camp where things were relatively normal.

Alec must have picked up on her tension because he sent soothing vibes along their bond. Kayla shot him a dark look. The sensation immediately faded.

"My apologies. Would you like to head to the restaurant now?"

She nodded, feeling guilty for her knee-jerk reaction. It was difficult to stay angry with Alec when his use of energy seemed to be instinctual. In all fairness, it was rather sweet of him to try to make her feel better. She just didn't like the idea that her emotions were being manipulated.

In an effort to smooth things over, Kayla took Alec's arm again. "Sure. Are we going back to the big dining hall from my last visit?"

Seara shook her head. "No. We'll be taking you into one of the commercial districts. Unfortunately, you didn't have an opportunity to visit this area last time you were here. Your last visit ..." Seara paused and then frowned in remembrance. Kayla's imprisonment in the towers was still fresh in everyone's mind. "Let's just say it wasn't what anyone wanted for your first experience here. I hope you'll give the towers another chance. There's a restaurant called Bliss that Alec thought you'd enjoy. It's much more casual than those silly political affairs in the Great Hall."

Alec rested his hand over hers and gave it a small squeeze

before directing them back toward the elevators. Brant kept a slight distance behind the group. When they stepped inside the lift, he pressed a button on a communication device attached to his wrist. Unfamiliar with the type of device and intrigued by any new technology, Kayla leaned over to get a better look. Brant lowered his wrist immediately and took a step backward, careful to maintain his distance. She frowned and narrowed her eyes, wondering about his strange behavior. Now that she thought about it, he seemed to avoid getting close to both her and Alec. It was tempting to reach out and wiggle her fingers in his direction just to see if he'd jump, but the elevator arrived at their destination before she could test her theory.

Nothing in Kayla's experience could have prepared her their exit into the large commercial area. Countless shops and restaurants lined a busy thoroughfare with possibly more than a hundred people in this one area alone who were either looking inside shop windows or heading toward unknown destinations.

Several people stopped at the sight of them and openly stared. The unfamiliar people, lights, and noise were almost overwhelming, and Alec pulled Kayla closer in order to wrap his arm around her waist when her fingers unconsciously tightened on his arm. Kayla was too busy trying to see everything at once to object to the possessive gesture. Carl moved up to stand on the other side of her and spoke softly in her ear.

"These are some higher end stores. This area is open to the general public, but it caters more to members of the Inner Circle. A lot of people come here to window shop rather than buy."

"Window shop?" she questioned, unfamiliar with the phrase.

"They come to look at the items for sale," Carl tried to

explain. "They rarely purchase anything. They just daydream about owning them one day."

Kayla strained her neck to peer into one of the windows and saw a wide assortment of merchandise. She'd grown up living on the move. All her worldly possessions could easily fit into one or two bags. If she couldn't fit it on the back of her speeder, there wasn't much use for it. "I don't understand. Why do they daydream over this stuff?"

He grinned. "Pretend there are a bunch of OmniLab prototypes in the windows instead. Imagine these stores filled with the latest sensors, frequency detectors, and stability monitors."

Kayla's eyes widened in understanding as she nodded. "Hell yeah. I totally get it now. Except I wouldn't just sit back and window shop. I'd find a way to take them with me. I doubt their security is all that great. Look at that. All that stuff is just lying around begging for someone to lift it."

Alec had been listening to the conversation, and he chuckled at her words. "You're an interesting woman, Kayla. It's rare to find a woman who prefers technology over the usual baubles and trinkets. I assure you, though, you'll never want for anything ever again. Just say the word and it's yours."

Kayla wrinkled her nose, still trying to scope out their security system. Promises didn't mean much—not in her world. "I've never had much use for trinkets. If it doesn't help you survive, why bother with it?" But even as she said it, she fingered Alec's necklace thoughtfully. He noticed the gesture and his eyes lit up in pleasure. She flushed and looked away, focusing on the other shops they passed.

They arrived at the restaurant, and Kayla couldn't help but gasp. Large fish tanks lined the walls and glowed with an eerie light. Shadows and colors danced upon the ceiling, simulating an ocean reef. Soft music played in the background and gave the entire restaurant an otherworldly feel. Kayla's eyes darted around the room as she tried to take in everything at once.

A trim, elegant-looking man approached and bowed low when he recognized them. "Good evening, it's an honor to have you with us. Please allow me to show you to our priority table."

Alec inclined his head, and they followed the man to a circular table on a raised dais. More fish tanks surrounded the table in a semi-circle, giving the illusion of privacy. Each of the tanks had hundreds of fish, brightly-colored corals, and strange tall grasses that seemed to dance beneath the water.

The man pulled out a chair for Kayla, placing her between Alec and Carl. Seara took the seat on the other side of Alec.

Their host handed each of them a thin tablet which appeared to be some sort of menu, but Kayla was too busy absorbing the surrounding details to look at it. Alec touched the screen and quickly scanned through it.

Carl looked around, seemingly impressed. "I've heard of this place but can't say I've ever been here."

"I think you'll enjoy it," Seara said, placing her napkin on her lap. "The food is marvelous."

Kayla noticed Brant standing nearby talking quietly to another man wearing the same OmniLab jacket with the Ouroboros symbol. His voice was too low to make out his words, but he pointed toward the door. The other man nodded and headed to the entrance. As though he felt Kayla watching him, he turned and met her gaze. He bowed ever so slightly in her direction before moving further from their table. Eyes narrowing, Kayla tracked the security officer's movements, not relaxing until he disappeared from sight. That guy was going to be a nagging headache until she figured him out.

Alec glanced up at their host. "Bring us a bottle of your best white wine to start while we look over the menu."

"Of course," the man replied and quickly hurried away to fulfill Alec's request.

Kayla shifted in her seat to get a better look at the fish tank next to them. She felt Alec's gaze on her but ignored him, fascinated by the colorful fish darting back and forth. She lightly tapped on the glass with her finger. The fish swarmed toward her, and she couldn't resist laughing in delight as they chased her finger.

"Why are they doing that?"

"They probably think you're going to feed them." Carl chuckled.

Her mouth formed a small 'o' shape. The thought both thrilled and intrigued her. "Really? Can I?"

Alec laughed and draped his arm across the back of her chair. "If that's what you want, we'll have it arranged. You seemed to enjoy watching the fish last time you were in my office. I thought you'd enjoy this restaurant. I'm glad to see I was correct."

She beamed a brilliant smile at him, touched by the fact he remembered her interest and brought her here because of it. Alec's breath caught, and he stared at her for a long moment. The intensity and longing in his eyes made her smile falter. *Shit.*

Kayla quickly looked away and snatched up the tablet menu to distract herself. It was impossible trying to focus on the selection while she could still feel Alec's gaze on her. He cleared his throat and put his hand over hers. "Would you like me to order for you?"

"Yeah, that might be a good idea," she agreed without looking at him. Pushing the tablet away, she dropped her hands in her lap and studied the ambience again. She couldn't handle his touch right now. "I still can't believe you guys eat like this. I've always just popped a packaged meal into a food preparation machine and been done with it."

When their host returned, he poured a small amount of wine into Alec's glass. After Alec had taken a sip and nodded at the man to indicate his satisfaction, the server poured the wine for the rest of the party. He then took their order and collected their tablets before disappearing again.

Kayla sipped her wine, surprised at the smoothness and flavor. "Wow, this is really good."

Alec smiled at her and swirled the wine in his glass. "Kayla, I was wondering if you'd be interested in beginning some training tomorrow morning. I have a bit of time that I've blocked off in my schedule, and I think it would be a good idea to begin as soon as possible."

Kayla fingered her necklace absently and nodded. She might as well learn what she could as long as she was here. At the very least, she could arrange to access OmniLab's records to get more information and then study energy manipulation on her own time. As soon as those water samples were finished, she was hightailing it back to the surface. She didn't quite trust her reactions around Alec, and the distance would probably help.

Carl glanced over at her, his expression filled with concern. "What's involved in this training? Is it dangerous?"

Alec gave him a cold look. "We don't discuss these sorts of things with outsiders."

"It's a fair question," Seara intervened and rested her hand on Alec's arm. "Carl knows more than most other people. He's already proven his loyalty, and his devotion to Kayla is obvious. I'm sure she's curious about the training too. We haven't had a chance to explain much to her."

Kayla nodded. She understood why the Inner Circle was secretive about their abilities, but there was no reason to keep it from Carl. "Is it just more energy being tossed around?"

Alec looked at her for a long moment and then glanced at

Carl. With a sigh, he said, "No. Since most abilities don't fully manifest until after puberty, we spend the majority of our childhood learning background and general information. I'm hoping to give you some of this foundation tomorrow. As far as actual energy manipulation goes, we need to discover the full range of your talents."

Kayla wrinkled her nose and took another sip of wine. *Well, shit. This sounds like it's going to be boring.*

"I'll make sure you aren't bored," Alec promised.

"Oh, fucking hell. I keep forgetting you can hear me."

Alec grinned at her. She scowled and finished her glass of wine. She needed some space and to clear her head. Kayla pushed away from the table. "Is there a lavatory around here?"

"Of course." Seara gestured toward a hallway. "It's right around the corner. Would you like me to show you?"

She shook her head. "No, that's okay. I'll find it."

Kayla stood and headed in the direction Seara indicated. The directions were spot-on and she located the restroom with ease. After finishing up and cleaning her hands in the sanitation machine, she stepped out of the room. On the opposite side of the hallway was a windowed door. Curious, Kayla stood on her toes to peek inside.

The doorway marked the entrance to a bustling, noisy kitchen. Workers rushed back and forth within the kitchen while others hovered over large steaming pots. Her breath fanned against the window as she leaned closer, fascinated by the activity. Suddenly, the hairs on the back of her neck prickled. She spun around to find Brant watching her.

"You've got to be kidding me. You followed me?"

He inclined his head. "Yes, ma'am. I've been asked to stay with you while you explore the towers."

She crossed her arms and glared at him. Too bad she didn't have the electrolaser gun or she might consider zapping him. Who needed an armed escort to pee? Unfortunately, Seara had confiscated the weapon, claiming Kayla couldn't carry it and wear that particular dress at the same time. Kayla had only relented after Seara promised to have a thigh holster delivered to their quarters that would fit under most dresses. At the time, it seemed like a fair deal. Now she was having second thoughts.

"I hardly think I'm going to get lost looking for a place to piss."

If her colorful language shocked him, he didn't show it. *Damn, I'll have to try harder.*

"Perhaps," Brant replied noncommittally and gestured toward the main seating area of the restaurant. "Shall we return to your table?"

Kayla hesitated and glanced at the kitchen door, not quite ready to go back and face Alec.

"Nope," she said with a grin, pushing open the door to the kitchen. If Brant was assigned to explore the towers with her, she'd take the opportunity to explore.

Large pots and pans covered the stoves, bubbling and simmering their mysterious brews. Rich smells wafted in the air, and she inhaled deeply, savoring the unfamiliar scents. Several people worked intently chopping food and stirring the pots. They all seemed to synchronize their movements as though they were engaged in an elaborate dance. A large-bellied man with a speckled white apron was the first to spot her. His mouth dropped open in astonishment, and he waved a large spoon to get her attention.

"Mistress Rath'Varein!" He bowed low. "Are you lost?"

She glanced at Brant, who was obviously displeased by her detour. Turning back to the man greeting her, she smiled. "Call me Kayla. And no, I peeked through the window and couldn't resist getting a better look. This is amazing. You cook all the food in here?"

He nodded, puffing out his chest at the compliment. "Yes. My name is Nicolas Martin. I'm the head chef for Bliss."

"Would I be in your way if I watched for a minute? I've never seen anyone prepare food like this before."

"You honor me," the chef said on an exhale and eagerly gestured for her to follow him. "You are always welcome in my kitchen. We are preparing your order right now. I would be delighted to show you."

Brant leaned close and said in a low voice, "Kayla, it would be best if you returned to the table."

No chance in hell.

She'd probably never get an opportunity like this again. Kayla shook her head and shooed Brant away before following the chef over to one of the pots. He tossed in some herbs and seasonings, chattering about the techniques used to bring out the flavors. She didn't understand most of it, but her stomach rumbled in appreciation.

He stirred the cream-colored sauce, and then gestured to it. "Would you like to sample it?"

Kayla perked up. "Really? I can?"

Nicolas pulled out a spoon and scooped up some sauce. He leaned forward, gesturing for her to open her mouth. Flavors exploded on her tongue as she closed her eyes to savor the sensation. When she finally opened them again, the cook was beaming at her with pride.

"Hot damn! This is freaking amazing! How did you learn to do this?"

"I trained for years in the culinary arts. Based on my specialties, I was awarded a position in this restaurant."

"I've never tasted anything like that," Kayla admitted.

Pleased with her enthusiasm, he offered, "We're making some of our garlic bread for your table. Would you like to see how it's done?"

Kayla nodded and followed him further into the kitchen.

As she passed, the workers looked up from where they were kneading dough and chopping ingredients to gape at her. Brant's scowl deepened, but he continued to follow her, his hand resting on his weapon as though daring anyone to approach.

They stopped next to another man who was in the process of pulling several large loaves of bread out of the oven. With practiced ease, he cut them open with a knife and used a brush to coat the inside of the loaf with a yellow substance. Cheese and herbs were sprinkled on it before it was sliced into smaller pieces.

Kayla gestured to the bread. "Could I try doing that?"

"Of course." He moved another loaf over to the counter in front of her. Kayla listened as he instructed her on the best way to position the loaf before slicing it and then explained how to spread the yellow mixture, cheese, and herbs on it. After she finished cutting the bread in small slices like the other cook, she put down the knife and grinned.

"Considering a profession in the culinary arts, my dear?"

Kayla whirled around and saw both Alec and Brant standing side by side. Alec was regarding her with mild amusement while Brant looked unhappy. Still excited over learning how to make garlic bread, she ignored Brant and flashed Alec a huge smile. "Nicolas just taught me how to make garlic bread."

Alec chuckled at her enthusiasm, then put his arm around her and drew her against his side. "You're truly a delight, Kayla. Chef Nicolas is one of the best chefs within the towers."

Nicolas flushed at the compliment. "Welcome to our kitchen, Master Tal'Vayr. I hope offering your fiancée a tour of our kitchen was acceptable."

Kayla froze at his words and her smile faded. *Fiancée?* She looked up at Alec. "Is there something you want to tell me?"

CHAPTER SIX

KAYLA HAD to hand it to him, Alec barely flinched. If it weren't for their shared emotional bond, she would never have believed he was anything other than the calm leader he projected. Even his eyes didn't betray his countenance. In her head, his silent voice promised, *"I'll explain outside. Please, play along."*

Her eyes narrowed at his words. She almost considered refusing until she felt his panic and concern. Her mouth parted in surprise at the uncharacteristic emotions. Alec was always so confident and focused. She'd seen him face off against the entire High Council without losing his cool demeanor. Whatever had him worried couldn't be good. She reached out across their bond to see if she could discern the cause, but he sensed her awareness and quickly suppressed his thoughts.

Damn, I need to learn how to do that.

"Yes, my love, we have much to discuss. Why don't we head back to the table? Our guests are waiting on us."

His tone didn't reflect any of the emotions she'd sensed.

Instead, he looked relaxed and even offered her an indulgent smile. *The bastard.*

Alec turned once more to the chef. "Thank you for giving my fiancée a tour, Chef Nicolas. I suspect she enjoyed it as much as she'll enjoy the meal."

"Oh, it was my pleasure," the chef replied, bowing deeply. "You're always welcome in my kitchen."

Alec dipped his head in acknowledgement and held out his hand to Kayla. She hesitated for a moment before accepting and letting him lead her out of the kitchen. The moment they were outside, she dropped his hand and whirled around to face both him and Brant.

"What was he talking about? Why the hell did he call me your *fiancée?*"

Alec winced at her furious expression and answered her silently. To any random observer, it would appear as though they were just staring at one another. It probably looked strange, but it was handy for keeping conversations private.

"We declared our formal intention to marry and for you to become my wife and partner at the High Council hearing. It's a matter of public record."

She shook her head in denial. That situation had been resolved with the destruction of the security bracelets. *"You know that was just a trick to get me out of wearing the High Council's leash. We're not getting married. I left the towers to go back to live on the surface with Carl."* The thought of Carl made her pause, a hint of worry creeping into her thoughts. *"Wait a minute. Does Carl know about this public record?"*

Alec didn't reply right away. After a long moment, he sighed and gave a brief nod.

"Call it off. Right now," she demanded.

He held up his hands in a passive gesture. *"If that's what you want, I will. But I'd appreciate it if you'd let me explain first. I hope that once you hear my reasons, you'll leave the engagement standing."*

Kayla blew out a breath, unwilling to make any promises. At the very least, she no longer felt guilty for hitting him earlier. She was sick and tired of people manipulating her for their own purposes. *"You can say whatever you want, but it won't change anything. I only agreed to play along to keep that damn bracelet off of me. You had no right to let people keep believing we're going to be married. I won't ever tie myself to anyone like that."*

Alec appeared genuinely remorseful, the weight of his guilt pulsing through their bond. *"I'm sorry, Kayla. I didn't want you to find out like this. I was hoping to have a chance to tell you about this privately. You have my word that I would never force you to do anything."*

Approaching footsteps interrupted them, and Kayla turned to find Seara and Carl entering the hall. Seara looked back and forth between them."You were gone for a long time. Is everything all right?"

Without looking away from Kayla, Alec replied, "The chef mentioned our engagement."

Carl crossed his arms. "I warned you she'd be upset."

Her suspicions confirmed, Kayla whirled around to look at Carl. She didn't bother to hide the hurt in her expression. How could Carl betray her like that? She'd been worried about his reaction, but he was just as guilty as Alec if he knew about the engagement and didn't say anything. "You knew about this and didn't tell me?"

"No," Carl protested and shook his head. "I just learned about it before dinner."

Seara interrupted, "Kayla, why don't we go take a walk? I think there are some things you should know."

Kayla was to argue, but the determined expression on her mother's face gave her pause. Instead, she scowled and grudgingly agreed. Seara turned to the two men. "Alec, why don't you and Carl go back to the table? We'll be along shortly."

Without waiting for a response, Seara led her out of the

restaurant. The last thing Kayla wanted to do was go for a leisurely stroll. It would be more therapeutic to kick something or leave the towers completely. She didn't sign up for any of this. What the hell was she doing here anyway?

Fuming silently, she continued to follow Seara down the unfamiliar thoroughfare. They approached a gurgling fountain and her mother took a seat on the edge. She motioned for Kayla to join her.

Kayla sat and leaned forward, tapping her fingers against the metallic edge of the fountain. Her entire body was coiled with energy just waiting to be unleashed. She wasn't used to sitting around when her emotions were riled up.

Her thoughts went back to Carl and she bit back a curse. A little warning would have been nice, but it definitely explained his attitude. Given that he'd heard about the engagement and then walked in on an intimate moment, Kayla was surprised he hadn't actually gone after Alec. She shook her head. *What a fucking mess.*

Seara's voice interrupted her thoughts. "You remind me a lot of your father."

Kayla raised an eyebrow, somewhat surprised by Seara's words. She'd been expecting to hear something about the little scene in the restaurant, not her father.

"Your father was a brilliant and charismatic man. When he was younger, though, he could be somewhat impulsive and reckless. Strangely enough, I think those qualities actually drew me to him. He was so ... alive. He believed his convictions so vehemently. It seemed like he could bring anyone around to his way of thinking by sheer will alone."

Seara smiled at the memory as her eyes took on a faraway look. "We had some rocky times in the beginning, but we managed to find a balance between us. I taught him the value of patience and temperance. In return, he shared with me his passion for life."

Kayla frowned and didn't reply. She wasn't sure what to say. Although part of her was curious, she had mixed feelings about being compared to a man she didn't remember. Another part worried that if she fully accepted her lost heritage, she'd also be forsaking the memory of her life as a ruin rat. Being a scavenger was a huge part of her identity and she wasn't sure she was willing to embrace this other world yet, not without losing something of herself in the process.

Kayla leaned back against the fountain wall and looked out at the surroundings in front of her. The scene contrasted sharply to the dirt and grit of life outside. She couldn't help but feel a twinge of contempt for the people milling around the commercial area. Some of them stared and whispered to each other as they passed. Others gave her and Seara more covert glances before looking away.

They were oblivious to the struggle for survival occurring right outside these walls. Kayla felt caught somewhere in the middle. She didn't belong to this new world, but she didn't quite fit into the world she'd grown up knowing either. Not anymore. One of the passersby halted in his tracks and a set of blue eyes met hers for a split second. Almost as quickly, the man turned and hurried down an adjacent corridor. Kayla sighed and rubbed her arms at the chill that went through her. She was tired of people gawking at her.

Her gaze fell on Brant, and she scowled at the sight of the security officer. As usual, he was standing nearby and casually leaning against a storefront wall. She'd been so angry when she'd learned about the engagement that she hadn't noticed he'd followed them from the restaurant. That wasn't like her. She was usually more aware and sensitive to her surroundings, but everything here seemed to be throwing her off.

She studied Brant and wondered about his true purpose. He stood close enough to keep an eye on them but far enough away to allow them a measure of privacy. His uniform and stern expression seemed to be enough to discourage people from coming too close to the fountain.

On the surface, he appeared relaxed, but his eyes were sharp. In some ways, he reminded her of some of the hardened ruin rats she'd known, ready to spring into action at the slightest provocation. There was something different about him though. She leaned forward to try to study him more intently and nearly gasped. All of the energy threads she'd come to sense around everyone and everything seemed to avoid him. They were completely absent.

Her eyes narrowed. There was no way he was a simple security escort. One way or another, she was going to find out more about him the first chance she got.

Seara clasped her hands in her lap, the movement drawing Kayla's attention.

"You know, I've lived in these towers my entire life. This is my home, and it's all I've ever known. I can't even begin to imagine how different this must be for you. I keep hoping you'll wake up one day and love our home the same way I do."

Kayla doubted it. In a strange way, she identified with the fish in the restaurant. They were both on display, outside their native habitats, and dependent on OmniLab for their survival. The cage might be pretty, but it was still a cage. "I don't belong here, Seara."

The older woman sighed and nodded. "I can understand why you'd feel that way. In the meantime, I'll just keep hoping to change your mind." She turned to face Kayla, her green eyes sparkling with moisture. "I'm glad you decided to come back and give it a chance, even if it's only temporary. I know I can't force you to feel something you don't feel. I wouldn't want that even if I could. But I'm so afraid of doing something or saying something that will push you away and the chance to know you will be lost."

She gave Kayla a sad smile. "When you were born, your

father and I were so excited. Watching you grow up and explore this world we helped to create was the greatest gift we could ever imagine."

Seara paused as her expression grew haunted. "When you were five, I found out I was pregnant again. I was supposed to have gone down into the ruins that day with you and your father. But your father insisted I stay behind because of the pregnancy. Catherine, Alec's mother, offered to take my place."

Kayla self-consciously reached up to touch the emerald necklace. She'd always wondered about the woman from her memory who'd saved her life. When she was young, she'd mistakenly believed it was her mother. "Alec's mother wasn't supposed to go?"

"No. It was a last-minute change. Then, when we learned everyone had been killed, I fell apart. In less than a split second, I lost everyone I cared about. I kept thinking it should have been me down there with you. Then, a few days later, I had a miscarriage."

Kayla closed her eyes, imagining the pain Seara must have gone through. She'd experienced enough loss to know words didn't mean much, but it was all she had to offer.

"I'm sorry."

Seara reached over and squeezed Kayla's hand. "Finding out you were alive and seeing you again has brought me more joy than you can imagine. It's also made me fearful I could lose you again. I don't want you to be unhappy here, Kayla. I don't want to lose you again. I'd do just about anything to make sure that doesn't happen."

"I'm not upset with you," Kayla admitted. She wanted to reassure her mother, but at the same time she didn't want to get swept away by circumstances either. "I enjoy spending time with you and would like to get to know you better. It's just everything is so different here. I don't want to be controlled or have someone else make decisions for me. I won't be pushed into anything."

Seara nodded and spoke in a voice too low for anyone to overhear. "I can understand that. Kayla, no one is asking you to marry Alec. The announcement was just that. A declaration. You don't have to do anything you don't want to do."

"Then why did the guy in the restaurant seem to think I am? Why not just tell everyone it's not true?"

Her mother sighed. "After Catherine died, Alec was angry, upset, and felt very alone. Edwin was always standoffish and hard on him. I saw a young boy who had lost his mother because she agreed to take my place. Alec turned to me because I was the closest thing he had to a mother. He became like a son to me. When he realized you were alive, part of the reason he was so determined to protect you was because of me."

Kayla picked at the hem of her dress. She knew Seara was right. Alec could have walked away and left her to her own fate, but he'd stood up and defended her. She might be grateful to him, but she wasn't going to just roll over and sign away her life either. In a way, it felt like she already had with their bond.

"So, what then? Are you suggesting I marry him as a thank you for keeping that damn bracelet off me?"

"No, of course not." Seara looked offended. Kayla wrinkled her nose and looked away. What was it about mothers that allowed them to instill guilt with one sharp look? Veridian's mother had possessed that ability too.

"Alec made up that lie to protect you. After you left the towers, things fell apart. A lot of people no longer trust his family name and that, coupled with Alec's age and lack of experience, has created quite a bit of unrest in the towers. Alec doesn't want to worry me, so he hasn't said much, but I see and hear more than he realizes." Seara's eyes lit with a strange light and Kayla wondered if her mother was as fragile as everyone believed. She recalled the way Seara stood up against Edwin at the council meeting and suspected that, under that delicate façade, the woman had a steel core.

"I believe one of the reasons the High Council hasn't gone after Alec is because I'm co-leader and fully supporting him. The fact you two are technically engaged is another reminder to everyone that our families are united and intent on doing whatever is necessary to protect the people in the towers."

Kayla's mouth dropped open. "You think the High Council wants to remove him?"

Seara gave a grim nod. "I'm sure some do. I believe there are dangerous politics at play and some of the councilors want power to shift to other families. If you remain engaged to Alec, their hands are somewhat tied. At least for the time being. Alec has already proven to be an excellent leader and has the best interests of the tower at heart. He just needs to be given more time so everyone else can see what I've known for years. If you end the engagement now, they could interpret it as friction between our families. I'm afraid some older members of the High Council will use that as an excuse to act against him."

"What do you think they would do to him?"

"I don't know," Seara admitted and looked away, but not before Kayla caught the raw pain in her expression. "But the last time someone moved against the High Council leader, I lost you and your father. I don't want to risk anything like that ever happening again."

Kayla felt the blood rush out of her head at the thought. She hadn't realized things were so serious. OmniLab was one fucked-up place. "You think they might try to kill him?"

"I would hope not, but I'd rather not take any chances. Alec is like a son to me." Her eyes pleaded with Kayla to consider the consequences.

Kayla frowned. She wasn't willing to risk it either. For all his arrogance, she still felt a strong connection with Alec. Her feelings for him went deeper than she wanted to admit. If pretending to be engaged would help prevent some sort of political maneuver against him, she'd agree to play along.

She sighed and watched the people passing by as they stared into the shop windows. Political intrigue, window shopping, and fancy clothing weren't part of her world and she felt ill-equipped to deal with it. Survival had been everyone's focus in the ruin rat camp where she'd grown up. But here, they willingly played political games and wandered aimlessly through the towers shopping for frivolous items. The whole thing disgusted her.

"If your High Council spent a fraction of their time looking at making things better for people rather than plotting against one another, they could make so many lives better both inside and outside the towers."

Seara sat up a little straighter and gave her a proud smile. "That's what your father used to say and why he expanded the trading districts."

"He did?"

"Yes. We used to just have outposts set up to look for new resources. Your grandfather started the outposts and began trading with some of the surface dwellers for information. Your father took it a step further, wanting to do more to help the people living on the surface. We don't have the resources to bring all of them into the towers with us. He figured by hiring them to locate artifacts and giving them a way to trade for supplies, we'd be giving them a better chance at survival."

The knowledge that her family had been the ones to create the trading posts floored her. She felt a wave of respect and admiration for these unknown individuals. "I didn't know that."

Seara nodded. "At first, there was a lot of resistance to the idea, but your father pushed through all of it. Many of the artifacts discovered by the surface dwellers are sent to our pre-war museum. Some of them end up in stores as curiosities for the people here to buy. Others are recycled and used to create new technology."

Kayla wondered where some of her camp's findings had ended up. She'd never given much thought to what happened after she turned the items over. No one did. They were just the means to purchase food, supplies, and keep the sun from burning them to a crisp.

As though sensing the direction of her thoughts, Seara leaned toward her. "I know how much the people on the surface mean to you. Protecting people is something that's in your blood. If you had the inclination, you could easily use your position to make things better for the people here and on the outside. Many people in the Inner Circle already respect you because of the way you stood up to Edwin and freed them. You could do so much more."

Kayla cocked her head. "What are you saying?"

"If you accept it, you have the power to make things better for everyone."

Kayla fell silent. Emotions and thoughts flooded through her as the enormity of Seara's words registered. She remembered all the senseless injuries and deaths she'd witnessed while living in Leo's camp. If they had access to the same type of medical care here in the towers, many of them could have been avoided. Veridian's mother would probably still be alive. *Maybe Seara's right. If I can help them, I need to do it.*

Seara had been watching Kayla's expression, and she reached over to gently squeeze her hand in understanding. Standing up, Seara said, "I know this is a lot to think about. Why don't we head back to the restaurant and get something to eat? I'm sure the men have had enough time to agree to some sort of temporary truce."

"I wouldn't count on it," Kayla muttered, but she stood anyway.

Seara laughed and linked arms with her. "Well, if they don't figure out a way to get along, they're going to have to deal with two very angry Rath'Varein women."

Kayla smiled at the image and began walking with her mother back toward the restaurant with Brant falling into step behind them. Once they were close to the restaurant, she paused and turned to Seara. "I'll meet you at the table. I want to talk to Brant for a minute."

Seara hesitated and then nodded before making her way back to the table. Kayla turned to Brant and pinned him with her gaze. He gave her another of his infuriatingly polite smiles as she stalked toward him.

"Come with me," she demanded without giving him a chance to argue. Gripping the sleeve of his jacket, she was surprised he didn't yelp at the contact. Kayla half-led and half-pulled him around the corner of the restaurant and into an alley. Dozens of empty storage boxes were piled high against the walls, making the alley somewhat cramped. At least they were out of the general traffic though.

She released him, and he quickly stepped away as though he didn't want to remain too close to her. Brant surveyed their new surroundings briefly before focusing once more on Kayla. She didn't miss how he positioned his body to continue to monitor the commercial thoroughfare and her at the same time.

"Did you change your mind about returning to the restaurant?"

Kayla tilted her head back to regard him. His hazel eyes skimmed over her, taking the opportunity to study her too. Although she didn't get the impression he intended her any harm at the moment, the lack of energy threads around him bothered her. It was time for some answers.

"Why is Alec having you follow me around?"

Brant squared his shoulders and clasped his hands behind his back. "You'll need to ask Master Tal'Vayr his reasons. I'm simply following orders."

Kayla put her hands on her hips. He could pretend to be nothing more than a drone if he wanted, but the shadows in his eyes told another story. She normally wouldn't push, but she had a suspicion that story involved her. "That's not good enough. You're armed, coordinating with other people in the restaurant, and have been following me so close all night that I wouldn't be surprised if you offered to flush for me on my next trip to the lavatory."

He didn't reply. Instead, he just continued to stand there and observe her.

She frowned, growing increasingly annoyed. "There's something about you that makes every single one of my senses go on alert. I'm beginning to wonder if it has something to do with the energy threads that disappear around you. I know there's no way you're a simple escort."

His eyebrows rose, but he still didn't reply. That flicker of interest made her hopeful she could extract some answers from him yet. Encouraged by the response, she took a small step toward him. He eyed her approach warily but didn't back away.

"On top of that, I've been asked to pretend I'm engaged to Alec to prevent some evil plot. Since Alec's ordered you to follow me around and you've seen me with Carl, you obviously know the truth about our relationship. So tell me, why the hell does he want you specifically to trail me? Does it have anything to do with the energy threads that avoid you?"

Something akin to irritation flickered across Brant's face. "Kayla, we should return to the restaurant. I'm sure Master Tal'Vayr will be happy to answer your questions in private."

That might be, but Alec wasn't here, and she had no

intention of being blindsided again. She cocked her head and decided to try a different approach.

"Master Tal'Vayr said *you* would answer my questions when he's not around. He's not here, so go ahead and fess up. What's your deal?"

Almost reluctantly, the corners of his mouth twitched. The slight smile made the hardness around his eyes less intense. "I was warned you can be quite ... headstrong. I suspect that was putting it mildly."

Her eyes narrowed at his description, but he didn't appear concerned. "Very well, I'll tell you what I can. I'm only permitted to discuss certain things, but I'll try to answer your questions as best I can without breaking my word."

She crossed her arms and waited for him to continue.

"Master Tal'Vayr is concerned about your safety, both inside and outside of these walls. I've been asked to keep an eye on you to make sure you remain unharmed and don't use your energy unintentionally."

Kayla's brow furrowed. "Using my energy unintentionally? Are you an Inner Circle member?"

Brant's shoulders stiffened at the question as his eyes flashed with some unspoken emotion. "No. I've been trained to detect energy channeling and to manipulate energy in such a way I'm able to neutralize an attack."

"Oh," she murmured, wondering if she'd touched a nerve. At the very least, it explained the absence of energy threads around him. "I thought anyone who can use energy was an Inner Circle member."

"Not exactly," he replied and his mouth tightened.

He definitely didn't like being compared to an Inner Circle member. *Interesting.*

"So if I channeled energy right now, you'd be able to tell?" She steered the conversation in what she hoped was a safer direction.

"Yes, ma'am." His shoulders relaxed slightly. "You're currently channeling a small amount right now. You have been since you arrived in the towers."

"No, I'm not."

He raised an eyebrow at her and she frowned. She concentrated, trying to figure out if she could somehow be channeling energy. She didn't sense it, but anything was possible. There was so much she didn't know. The earthquake in the ruins was proof enough. Apprehension filled her at the thought of triggering another event and she bit her lip in concern. "Do you know how I can stop it?"

Brant studied her for a long moment. "You may want to speak with Master Tal'Vayr about that. I'm sure he'll explain that sort of thing when he trains you. In an emergency, I can temporarily disconnect your energy flow."

"You can do that?" she whispered breathlessly. Hope filled her at the thought of being able to turn off the energy channeling at will. It could be the answer to her problems.

Brant seemed startled by her eagerness but nodded.

"Is it possible to do it permanently?"

He looked alarmed by the question and quickly glanced around to see if anyone was within earshot. "Mistress Rath'-Varein, we should return to the restaurant. I have already overstepped myself by discussing this much with you."

"Wait," Kayla protested. "Can you at least cut off my energy now so I can see how I'm channeling it?"

He hesitated and then shook his head. "It only lasts as long as I hold it in place. It's a tactic used to subdue someone from offensive energy attacks. I swore an oath to protect you. By using my abilities on you in that manner, I would effectively be breaking my word. I'm sorry, but I can't do that. You need to speak with Master Tal'Vayr."

Kayla sighed and inwardly cursed. Getting information out of Brant was like pulling teeth. She'd put up with it for now, especially if his presence also had something to do with the High Council targeting Alec. "Fine. Can you at least tell me what outside influences Alec thinks might be a threat? I get that he's worried I might blow someone up, but I'd like to know if he thinks someone might want to return the favor."

"I'm sorry, but I cannot say anything more about that. I was simply asked to protect you from anyone seeking to cause you harm," Brant stated with finality, ending any further discussion.

Something about the way he said it struck Kayla as funny. When she thought about it, the whole thing was ludicrous. Unable to resist, she burst into cathartic laughter. Brant seemed puzzled by her reaction. When her laughter finally subsided, she grinned at him.

He hesitated for a moment. "May I ask what you found so humorous?"

"I don't know what Alec is worried about happening," she admitted with a shrug. "To be honest, I'm more concerned about zapping someone by accident than anyone trying to hurt me. I've spent my whole life taking care of myself. I've seen things and done things that would probably give most of the people in these towers nightmares. Compared to what's on the surface, they live their lives surrounded by warm, fuzzy balls of fluff. I'm not like them. If I can't take care of myself, then whatever happens falls on me." She looked down at her hands with a frown. "It's just the energy stuff that I don't know about and apparently, I can't shut that off."

Brant gave her an incredulous stare. "No one deserves to be harmed if they can't defend themselves."

She shook her head and frowned. "Maybe they don't deserve it, but that's not how the world works. The only person you can always depend upon is yourself. If you get in the habit of relying on someone else and something happens to them, what then? If I fail for whatever reason, I'll either die or learn the lesson I'm handed. Life isn't always forgiving enough to give you second chances. And if you're fortunate enough to get a second chance, you better learn your lesson quick because you can be damn sure there won't be a third."

"You're unlike any Inner Circle member I've met," he murmured thoughtfully.

Kayla grinned, pleased by the comment, and bumped her shoulder against his arm. "That's because I'm a ruin rat. But you're all right, Fluffy. Even though you won't turn off my energy, I'm starting to kinda like you."

CHAPTER SEVEN

KAYLA SLID BACK into her seat. The tension at the table was palpable. Both Alec and Carl were watching her intently, and she had the impression they were both holding their breath waiting for her to issue her verdict.

Instead, Kayla ignored them and reached for her glass. She took a long sip and tried to gather her thoughts. She needed to make it clear she was going to do things her own way and in her own time.

When she finally lowered the glass, she announced in a low voice, "Okay. I know this isn't the place to have this conversation, but I'll say this much. Seara gave me some things to think about. I'm not angry anymore, but I'm also not happy that something like this was kept from me. I want you both to know that if either of you ever keep something like this from me again," she picked up the knife off the table and waved it at both of them, "I swear I'll cut off your balls, tie them to the back of my speeder, and drag them through all four districts."

Carl grimaced and took a long drink from his glass. Alec

looked equally pained but asked, "Do you still want me to renounce the announcement?"

Kayla squeezed her eyes shut. This was the hard part. It was like standing on top of a fulcrum and the slightest movement could send either end toppling. Through her shared connection with Alec, she could sense his apprehension and concern. Underneath, she could also sense deep feelings for her and his fear that he could possibly lose her. Although she couldn't sense Carl in the same way, she knew he was anxiously awaiting her decision too.

"No," she said in soft voice and lowered the knife, putting it back on the table. Alec didn't reply, but she felt his sudden rush of relief crash through their bond.

In a whisper so low only Alec and Carl could hear, she qualified, "But I'm not getting married."

Carl remained silent at her words, but his entire body tensed. She reached under the table and squeezed his hand gently, her eyes pleading with him to understand. He had to know she was only agreeing to this charade to protect Alec. He searched her gaze and whatever he saw there made him relax. He nodded and gave her a small smile before rubbing the back of her hand with his thumb.

She slumped in relief and withdrew her hand. He understood.

Seara's voice broke through her emotional rollercoaster. "Alec mentioned you received a tour of the kitchen. What did you think?"

Kayla straightened in her chair, thankful for the change of subject. "It was great. I've never seen anything like that. One of the chefs let me make garlic bread."

Her mother's laughter was a tinkling sound of merriment. It helped break up the rest of the tension. A moment later, several of the wait staff approached their table and placed steaming plates of food in front of them. A large basket of garlic bread was set in the center of the table.

Kayla looked down at the seafood pasta dish in front of her. It looked even better than it appeared in the pot. Unable to resist, she took a bite. Yep. No doubt about it. "This is even better than what I sampled earlier."

Seara smiled at her. "We have all sorts of different restaurants on this level that you might enjoy. Each has their own specialties. We'll have to try some different ones and see what else appeals to you."

Kayla wasn't sure she was willing to stick around long enough for that. Instead of agreeing, she stabbed her fork into the round-shaped pasta. "Man, Cruncher's going to be so jealous when I tell him about this. Think they'll let me take some home to him?"

Carl chuckled and shook his head. "I think he'd prefer the sandwiches."

She snorted. He was probably right. She wished it were possible to bring back some of these experiences to the other ruin rats. Taking another sip of the wine, Kayla once again considered Seara's words and wondered how she could make life better for the ruin rats.

"If you wanted to build another tower, not as big as these of course, how difficult would it be?"

Alec looked at her in surprise and then glanced at Seara questioningly. The older woman simply smiled and sipped her wine. Alec turned back to Kayla, his voice edged with caution. "It would depend on the scope of the project. What did you have in mind?"

"Let's say you wanted to create a smaller version of this tower. How would you go about doing it?"

Alec tilted his head, considering the question. "Well, I would decide the approximate number of people I wanted to house within the building and what amenities would need to be included, and then I would have our designers work up some ideas. From there, you'd need to determine what resources would be required to begin building. You'd need materials and labor, as well as a suitable building site."

"Kayla, where are you going with this?" Carl shifted in his chair to face her.

She glanced at him but didn't answer right away. Instead, she took another bite of her food. She didn't know if this was even possible. After she swallowed, Kayla gave a half-hearted shrug. "It might be nice if the ruin rats had a permanent home."

Alec glanced at Seara, who was still smiling over the rim of her glass. He chuckled and said, "Kayla, you are definitely your father's daughter. He proposed a similar idea many years ago." His face sobered as he added, "The cost and drain to our resources was too high though. The High Council argued against it."

"Oh." *Well, crap. There goes that idea.* Her shoulders slumped in dejection.

"That doesn't necessarily mean no," he said in a rush, placing his hand over hers. "If this is something you want, we can explore it. Seara can show you where your father kept his files. I'll be happy to go through them with you. If we provide suitable arguments to their objections, there's no reason why we couldn't propose your project to the High Council again."

Carl eyed Alec with suspicion. "Is something like this really a possibility?"

"We won't know until we get all the information. But if this is something Kayla wants and she's willing to make it happen, I don't see why not. I'll do whatever I can to help her."

Seara nodded in encouragement. "Sometimes all it takes is just one person to make an idea come to life."

Kayla pushed her finished plate away. If something like

this was within the realm of possibilities, she owed it to the ruin rats to try to make it a reality. Although some of them would balk at the idea of living under OmniLab's rule, there were others who would jump at the opportunity. At the very least, they'd have the choice. That was more than what they had right now. "Could I talk to one of the designers so we can figure out what would be needed?"

Alec nodded. "Of course. When you come to my office in the morning, I'll see about arranging someone to meet with you."

The conversation drifted off after that, each left to their own thoughts. Once they'd finished their meal, Alec escorted the group back to the Rath'Varein family quarters. Seara and Carl headed inside, but Alec stopped Kayla at the door.

"I just wanted to thank you again for allowing the engagement to continue."

Kayla glanced back into her family's quarters to Seara and Carl's retreating figures. "Seara's worried about you. She thinks the engagement will help protect you. I'm not going to pretend to understand the politics in this place, but I trust Seara."

Alec hesitated and sent another light wave of energy over her. His thumb glided along her jaw and traced across her lower lip. "It's not just about the politics, my love. My feelings for you are real."

Kayla frowned and took a step back. His touch, the energy ... it was confusing, overwhelming, and addicting all at the same time. Just like with any addiction, she needed to stop it. Now.

"Alec, don't."

He lowered his hand and his eyes shuttered, once more appearing the pragmatic High Council leader. "Very well. I'll come by in the morning around seven to pick you up. Does that work for you?"

She blew out a breath, hating the conflicting emotions inside her. "Yeah, that's fine."

Her eyes narrowed on Brant standing nearby. She gestured toward him. "Are you planning on telling me the real story about him tomorrow? He's pretty tight-lipped with the information sharing."

Alec glanced at Brant and nodded. "Yes. He'll be leaving in a few minutes, but he'll return in the morning. I'll have another security officer stationed outside your door tonight should you need anything. I'd appreciate it if you didn't leave these quarters without an escort until you're trained."

Kayla didn't like the idea of a babysitter, but until she learned more, she wouldn't object. In the meantime, she wanted another sort of answer. "Brant told me he was able to temporarily stop energy from being channeled. If so, can he permanently stop my ability to channel energy?"

Alec's eyes flashed with anger. Without answering Kayla, he spun around to confront the security officer. Brant's face visibly paled, but he managed to maintain his composure. He shook his head and said, "It's not the way it sounds, Master Tal'Vayr. I briefly explained some of my training. She asked for a demonstration. I refused. With regard to her question, I deferred to you."

Kayla's eyes darted back and forth between Alec and Brant. Alec looked as though he were ready to pummel the man. Not good. At least, not until she got some answers. She tugged on Alec's sleeve to divert his attention back to her. "Wait, does that mean it's possible? If I wanted to get rid of my ability to channel energy, could I do that?"

"No," he snapped. She flinched and dropped her hand, astonished by his uncharacteristic harsh tone. When she concentrated on their shared connection, she realized he was struggling to get his emotions under control. *Okay, this is definitely a touchy subject.*

After a long moment and several deep breaths, his shoulders relaxed a fraction and he turned away from Brant to look at her. "I apologize. I shouldn't have snapped at you. I know you're inexperienced and your curiosity is natural. It's just ... a rather sensitive and upsetting subject."

Kayla could sense his tension, anger, and an incredible sadness through their shared connection. She bit her lip and took a small step forward, resting her hand on his arm. Feeling someone else's emotions as acutely as her own still made her uncomfortable. Even so, she had an intense urge to try to ease his pain. She focused on gathering some of the energy around them and wove it in a comforting embrace.

Alec's eyes softened at her attempt to soothe him, and he murmured her name in a reverent whisper. Tightening his hand around hers, he pressed his lips against her forehead in a chaste kiss.

"Thank you, my love. It's all right though," he said quietly and gave her a small smile that didn't quite meet his eyes. "When the ability to channel energy is removed temporarily, it causes confusion and extreme discomfort. Other times, it can render someone unconscious. Brant uses it as part of his training to subdue an individual or stop them from harming themselves or someone else. Depending on the nature of someone's talents, ordinary methods to contain them may not work. He only uses this ability as a last resort."

Kayla nodded. That made sense, especially if Alec was concerned about her ability to generate another earthquake. She didn't want to risk another incident either.

Alec took both of her hands in his, and this time, she didn't pull away. Whatever was going on with him was serious, and he seemed to need the reassurance of her touch. He took another deep breath and said, "To answer the other part of your question, no. If you were separated permanently from your ability to channel energy, it would either drive you insane or kill you. It's part of who you are. You can't separate one from the other."

"Oh," Kayla said quietly as realization dawned on her. "It's the same thing as when people tried to remove the bracelets on their own."

"Yes. It's a similar concept." Silently, he added, *"It can be used as a weapon too. It's how my father killed Keith, and how I killed my father. The ability requires a great deal of energy, but it's a powerful weapon. My father was only able to do it with the assistance of the bracelets, and I was only able to do it with the help of several other Inner Circle members."*

Kayla blanched. Now Alec's tumultuous emotions made sense to her. Guilt flooded through her. She hadn't meant to make him relive such a painful memory.

"It's all right," Alec said more gently, sensing her thoughts. "I know this is difficult for you, but I want you to trust me. You have my word that I won't ever hurt you, and I'll do my best to answer all of your questions. It'll take time though. I hope you'll give that to me."

She looked away, unsettled by the events of the evening. The weight of their emotions still filled her mind. He was right though. She knew deep down that he'd never hurt her intentionally. Why was it so hard to trust him?

Kayla managed to nod. She wouldn't make any promises, but she'd give him what she could. "I'll try."

He gave her hands a gentle squeeze before releasing them. "Thank you. Why don't you head inside and get some rest? I'll see you in the morning."

She nodded again, and he leaned close to her. His mysterious scent enveloped her as he kissed her cheek lightly. "Goodnight, my love. Sleep well."

Alec turned away and approached Brant. Kayla watched him issue some last-minute instruction to the other man before heading back inside. When she entered the common room, Seara looked up. "Alec left?"

"Yeah. He's going to come by in the morning to start my training."

Seara stood and gave Kayla and Carl a smile. "All right. I'll let you two get some rest then. I'm so glad to have you back, Kayla."

They said their goodnights before the older woman headed down the hallway toward her room. Once she was alone with Carl, Kayla let out a long sigh and slumped against the wall. "Well, this has been a screwed-up day."

Carl nodded and slowly approached her. "I want to apologize for not telling you earlier about the engagement. Alec mentioned it while you were getting dressed."

She held up her hand to stop him. "I figured. You were fine until I left you alone with Alec. I had wondered why you were acting strange." She crossed the distance between them so they were standing inches apart. Lifting her hands, she cupped his face and let her fingers trail over the light stubble on his jaw. "Seara said there's been some trouble in the towers and asked me to keep the engagement ongoing for political reasons. I don't particularly like being part of this, but as long as you're okay with it and I don't have to marry anyone, I guess it doesn't matter."

Carl frowned and lowered his forehead against hers. "I wouldn't say I'm okay with it, but I understand the necessity of keeping stability in the towers."

Kayla pulled back to search his gaze and saw the storm brewing in his brown eyes. "It bothers you a lot," she stated, already knowing the answer.

He swore and took a step away from her, running his hands over his face. "Of course it bothers me. Even if you have no intention of marrying him, everyone in the towers believes it and I'm supposed to help purport this ruse. That's bad enough, but he's bound and determined to try to talk you into it too."

She shook her head, immediately rejecting his concerns. It wasn't even a matter of her feelings for him. Ruin rats simply didn't do marriage. Of course, they knew what it was, but such a convention was archaic and just led to inevitable heartache. It might be okay for the people living in the towers, but the surface was too dangerous to forge that sort of permanent ties. Leo, her former camp leader, had always advised against creating too many emotional bonds.

"No way. That's not going to happen. I'm not going to marry Alec."

Carl turned back to study her. "I'm glad to hear it, but that's not going to stop him from trying to convince you. I saw the effect the bond has on you. You're having trouble being around him, aren't you?"

Kayla groaned and kicked at the edge of the couch. He was right about the bond, but there wasn't much she could do about it while she was in the towers. She just had to keep reminding herself this was temporary. Once the water samples came back, they could leave and focus on mapping the cavern. It was easier to resist Alec's influence when she wasn't face to face with him. She'd just have to deal with the discomfort of being separated from him.

"I'll handle it. It's just for a few more days at most and then we'll go back."

Carl raised an eyebrow but didn't argue. He took a step closer and lifted her chin with his forefinger to look into her eyes. "You don't have to do any of this, sweetheart. If it becomes too much, say the word and we'll leave immediately. I don't give a damn about the audit or anything else. I'll be here for you no matter what you decide."

Raw emotion flooded through her at his words, and she melted against him. Once again, Carl knew exactly what she needed to hear. The fact he was willing to support her regardless of her decision filled her with unwavering gratitude and love. Curling her fingers around his collar, Kayla pulled him closer. She pressed her lips against his, letting him feel everything she wasn't able to put into words.

His instant reaction scorched her. As his mouth took possession of hers, his hands dropped down to cup her backside. He lifted her upward, letting her body slide against his. The hard evidence of his passion brushing against her ignited her further. Without breaking their kiss, she wrapped her legs around his waist.

Desperate, raw need filled her. She needed the connection and intimacy he offered, wanting to reassure both herself and him that they wouldn't lose this precious gift they had found in one another. Her fingers impatiently worked at his buttons, needing to feel the press of his skin against hers.

Kayla was dimly aware of him moving them in the direction of the bedroom. When he stumbled through the door and pressed her up against the wall, she whimpered into his mouth. "Now, Carl. I need you," she urged on a gasp, unable to wait any longer. Desire became a blinding need, and she clutched him tighter, knowing his needs were as great as her own. When he finally lifted her dress and took possession of all she offered, Kayla no longer knew who was reassuring whom and simply surrendered to the passion of the moment.

CHAPTER EIGHT

KAYLA WOKE up the next morning with Carl's arm wrapped around her. She didn't move right away, content to enjoy his warmth and comfort. After their initial explosive union the previous night, they'd finally managed to fall into bed where their continued discovery of one another became a tender and gentle exploration of sensations.

She lightly ran her fingers along the edge of his jaw, memorizing his features. His arm tightened around her, pulling her closer, and he mumbled something incoherent against her hair. She couldn't help but smile. She'd never imagined feeling this way about anyone. Every day with Carl was a gift, and she fell a little more in love with him. She brushed a soft kiss against his lips and slipped out of bed.

Picking up the discarded clothing off the floor, she headed to the bathroom and dropped them in the sanitation machine. The glint of the emerald necklace tangled in the clothing caught her eye. She carefully extracted it and held it in her palm, once again recalling the shared kiss with Alec. Her eyes squeezed shut. There had to be a way to keep their bond from overwhelming her.

Kayla opened her eyes again and stared down at the pendant. Without warning, fragmented memories rushed into her mind. Darkness and fear. Screams and a sense of urgency. A woman's face and then a pair of hands pushing her through a narrow crevice.

She shook her head, trying to clear it of these images. It had been years since she last dreamt of the ruin collapse. The dreams had plagued her often as a child, but they came less and less as she grew older. Lifting the necklace, she turned to face the mirror and slipped it over her head. It might not ever be possible to know the identity of the person who saved her, but she'd honor the memory of Alec's mother at the very least.

As she gazed into the mirror, her reflection seemed to shift and blur. A slender blonde with blue eyes returned her gaze and fingered the emerald necklace. Kayla stared in shock at the image. Then, just as quickly as it appeared, the image vanished and she was staring at herself again.

Her heart pounded, and she took a step back from the mirror. *Okay, Kayla, keep it together. You've seen these sorts of things before. It's just your imagination.*

But she wasn't in the ruins this time, and the face in the mirror was the same one that haunted her memories. She rubbed her temples and tried to make sense of what happened. Brant's words from the night before echoed in her mind as she lifted her hands to study them. Was it possible she'd channeled energy again without realizing it and caused this hallucination?

Kayla forced herself to look back up into the mirror again. Other than looking a little pale, it was only her reflection looking back. She let out a sigh of relief. At least she hadn't caused another earthquake.

She turned away from the mirror, determined not to use any energy until she got a better handle on it. In an effort to calm her nerves, Kayla took several deep breaths and focused on her morning routine, feeling marginally better by the time she finished.

Carl was still sleeping when she emerged from the bathroom. Keeping her footsteps quiet, she opened the closet door and nearly swore aloud at the sight. The small room was overflowing with clothing and a various assortment of shoes. Seara had obviously been busy.

Intimidated by the large selection, she frowned while looking through the clothing. She pressed a button on the far wall and drawers slid open, revealing a wide array of undergarments. Looking back at the clothes hanging in the closet, she scowled. Even if she wore something different every day, it would take months to run out of clothes.

Totally out of her element, Kayla closed her eyes and reached out, determined to wear the first thing she touched. When she opened her eyes and realized a formal evening dress was in her hands, she nearly growled.

She grabbed the outfit next to it instead. It was some sort of short, black dress with a swirling white pattern at the bottom. It looked similar in style to the dress she had on last night, although she was hardly an expert. At this point, it didn't really matter. If it covered her girly bits enough to placate the pretentious Omnis, that was good enough for her.

Kayla grabbed a set of silky undergarments, which she secretly admitted preferring over her old, more functional ones. Admiring their soft texture, she smiled. Carl's reaction to them last night had been even better. She'd have to bring some of them back to camp when they returned.

She finished dressing and then cursed as her gaze fell on the shoes. There was no getting around it. As much as she'd prefer to wear her boots or go barefoot, Seara would probably hunt her down if she tried it. For such a mild-mannered woman, her mother could be something of a tyrant when it came to clothing.

Kayla dug through the selection and found a pair of relatively harmless-looking white sandals. She slipped them on and wiggled her naked toes. It wasn't quite barefoot, but it would work.

Satisfied she had managed to actually dress herself, Kayla left the closet and shut the door behind her. She grabbed her commlink off the dresser before slipping out of the bedroom and heading down the hall.

She scrolled through her messages as she walked. There was a note from Veridian apologizing for not telling her about Jinx, and she smiled. From all appearances, her scavenging partner was head over heels for the spunky redhead. She was glad. Veridian hadn't been this happy in a long time.

"Good morning," Seara greeted. Kayla paused and looked up from her commlink in surprise to find both her mother and Alec sitting on the couch together.

"Hi," Kayla replied, then looked at Alec who was leaning against the back of the couch with his arm draped over the top. Golden hair fell neatly to his shoulders while his blue eyes blazed with an unspoken emotion as they scanned her up and down. She swallowed, feeling the heat of his gaze at his slow perusal. The pull along their bond flared to life, and she battled against the urge to channel energy toward him.

Kayla struggled to beat down the temptation and not give in. It seemed to be even worse when her guard was down. It didn't help that she was attracted to him either. "I didn't think you were going to be here so early. I thought you said seven."

He gave her a warm smile and stood. "I did, but I wanted to stop by this morning to speak with your mother."

"I didn't mean to interrupt. Do you want me to come back?"

Seara laughed and motioned for her to join them. "Of course not. Come sit down with us. I see you discovered your closet. I hope it wasn't too overwhelming. I know I got a little carried away, but you look lovely. That dress is a perfect choice."

Kayla muttered her thanks as she sat across from them. *Telling her I closed my eyes and grabbed the first thing I touched probably isn't the best idea.*

Alec choked on a laugh, and Kayla shot him a warning look. *"So help me. If you tell her, I'll hurt you."*

His eyes lit with amusement. *"Your secret is safe with me, my dear."*

Ignoring his teasing, she leaned forward. "What's going on?"

Alec gestured to the side of the room where a small table was set up containing several covered dishes. "We weren't expecting you to be awake so early. Would you like some breakfast? Afterward, we can head to my office to get started on your training."

She grimaced and shook her head, still a little rattled by the vision in the bathroom. The thought of eating made her stomach lurch in protest. Besides, it was better to get this whole training thing done than to delay the inevitable. "No, thanks. Let's go to your office." Kayla turned to her mother. "Seara, would you mind letting Carl know when he wakes up? I'll catch up with him later."

"Of course."

Alec stood and led Kayla outside toward the priority elevator. Brant had returned, and she gave him a small finger wave as he fell into step behind them. The security officer returned her greeting with another polite nod.

"You're still wearing the necklace," Alec observed, clearly pleased.

She touched it thoughtfully and debated whether to share

what happened with the mirror. Sensing her thoughts, he stopped and turned to face her. Concern etched his brow as Alec studied her. "What's wrong, Kayla?"

She hesitated and then glanced at Brant. Biting her lip, she told Alec silently about what she had seen. *"I know it sounds crazy,"* Kayla added when she'd finished. *"I probably just have an overactive imagination or something. I was still half asleep."*

"This type of thing has happened before, hasn't it?"

She nodded, thinking about all the times she'd seen faces or images in the ruins. Alec inhaled sharply. "We should discuss this in my office. It may change some of the training I had planned for you."

Kayla followed Alec to the elevator and Brant stepped in behind them. The security officer pressed the button to take them to the executive offices, and the doors closed. Alec was quiet, and she could sense several conflicting emotions coming from him. There was no doubt her words had troubled him. Apprehension filled her, and Kayla wondered if something was wrong with her.

"There's not," Alec said quietly.

"If you're going to be sifting through my thoughts, the least you can do is tell me what the hell you're thinking in return."

He nodded. *"Fair enough. I just need a few minutes to sort all of this out. I'll explain as soon as we get to my office. There's something you need to see."*

Kayla frowned. The doors to the elevator opened, and they stepped out into what she recognized as the executive offices. Alec had brought her here the last time she visited, but he turned down an unfamiliar hallway this time. "You moved your office?"

"Yes. I've taken over the High Council leader's office."

That made sense, even if it was a little weird. The last time she was here, it was Alec's father, Edwin, who had been the leader of the High Council. The difference between father and son was astounding. Although Alec seemed to possess a regal composure and nearly unflappable control, he wasn't cruel and power hungry. There was compassion and temperance within him, qualities Kayla couldn't help but admire. She wondered if part of that was Seara's influence.

A middle-aged woman with brown hair sat behind a large desk and rose at the sight of Alec. She offered him a brief bow. "Good morning, Master Tal'Vayr. Your messages have been transferred to your desk unit. As you requested, I made arrangements for our lead designer to meet with you this afternoon. The appointment is on your calendar."

He nodded and turned back to Kayla. "I'd like to introduce you to my assistant, Sheila Tousel. If you ever need anything, please let her know."

Kayla smiled at the older woman. "Nice to meet you."

Sheila beamed back at her.

"Brant, wait here," Alec instructed and led Kayla inside. Her eyes widened in astonishment. In addition to a regular office area, there appeared to be an expansive bar area, conference table, and living room. Large screens lined one of the walls in the office area. On the adjacent wall, a shelving unit displayed a vast selection of exquisite artifacts. The desk in the center of the office area was massive and looked as though it had been hand-carved centuries earlier. The entire office was almost as big as her entire ruin rat camp.

"Wow," she murmured, strolling through the office. After finishing her perusal of his new digs, Kayla sat down on the edge of his desk. "It's a lot bigger than I was expecting."

"The size has come in handy. I've spent more than a few nights here since I took this position. It's going to be a while before things are running smoothly again."

"That bad?" Kayla's voice was filled with concern. "Seara mentioned it's been difficult since you took over."

Alec waved off her concerns. "Any time there's a major shift in power, some people try to test the limits and push boundaries. It'll settle down soon enough, but we've had to remain vigilant."

Kayla frowned. Although he made light of it, she could sense his worry. "If this isn't a good time to do this, I can come back some other time."

Alec shook his head and walked over to her. "Not a chance. Having you here right now is the one bright spot in this entire mess."

Uncomfortable with the direction of his words, she looked away. "You were going to tell me what that was about in the elevator."

He hesitated and then nodded. "Yes. Your talents are unusual. Most Inner Circle members have only a few abilities, but you seem to have more than most people."

"What do you mean?"

"I'd like to show you something to see if my suspicions are accurate," Alec began and moved to stand behind his desk. He activated his computer terminal and typed in a few commands. An image appeared on screen, and Kayla gasped.

The woman on the display was the same one she'd seen in the mirror. "That's her. That's the woman I saw. How did you know?"

"That's my mother," Alec said quietly as he looked at the picture. "I believe you may have inadvertently channeled energy and seen an echo of the past."

"How is that possible?"

He shut down the image, and then his gaze briefly traveled back to the necklace around her neck. "Our energy is divided up into distinct groups, just like the elements. We have the ability to channel earth, air, fire, or water energy. Lesser known and extremely rare are those who can channel life or spirit energy. Spirit is the energy which draws all four elements together. In all our recorded history, there have been less than a handful of people able to tap into all of the elements at will. I believe you may have this ability."

Kayla frowned, watching him as he walked around the desk and back toward her. "I'm not sure I understand. Why is it called spirit energy?"

"This is a little more difficult to explain, but there are a seemingly infinite number of worlds or dimensions parallel to ours. When we channel energy, we tap into small rifts that exist in-between these worlds. Essentially, we're tapping into elemental energy from another world and pulling it through the spirit veil and into ours. We can also send it back. The energy threads you sense are ripples already existing between these worlds. There haven't been many studies since the talent is so rare, but people who channel spirit energy can control the veil. They have the ability to tap into these other worlds freely to use the energy we send back there. Most of us are limited to one element. However, spirit channelers don't have those same limitations. The other worlds call to them and they can open up new rifts, pulling energy from multiple elements. They can also sometimes hear and see echoes of the past."

"Echoes of the past?" Kayla asked hesitantly. "You mentioned that a few minutes ago. That doesn't sound good."

"All life is made up of energy," Alec explained. "When someone dies, their energy doesn't disappear. It transcends the spiritual veil. As a spirit channeler, you can recall this energy. You may see and hear things that occurred years before. Unfortunately, details on spirit channelers are sketchy, so we don't know the full scope of their abilities. A lot of the information was lost over the years."

Unease filled Kayla as she remembered all the times she'd seen images of people who used to live within the ruins. "So you're saying I can see people who have died?"

"Something like that. It's more that you're seeing the *echoes* of their energy. But even more importantly, you may be able to tap into more than one of the elements."

Great, she thought with a groan. *Not only am I one of the zap-happy circle freaks, but I also see ghosts.*

"It's not a bad thing," Alec explained. "It's an extremely coveted ability. You aren't just limited to one type of energy."

She threw her hands in the air. "How is this a good thing? I don't know how to use any of it, and I'm not sure I even want it. Other than giving me some tingles now and then, I don't see much use for it. If I was responsible for that earth-quake, that's not really beneficial."

He chuckled. "Maybe not, but there are several other talents which could be largely useful. You could help to revitalize the soil and make plants grow, redirect water and locate resources. There's really no limit to your potential. It's just a matter of learning how to tap into it."

Her eyes widened at the implications. "Okay, so how do I do that?"

Alec moved to stand directly in front of her, taking her hand in his. "The first thing you need to do is be able to recognize the different types of energy. Your mother is an extremely strong earth-based talent. We'll ask her to work with us later. I can also tap into earth elements to a lesser degree, but my talents are primarily air-based. I can show you that now, if you'd like."

"Air-based? But you read thoughts and influence people. How is that air-based?"

"That's not all I can do, Kayla," Alec admitted with a smile. Suddenly, the air around the room began to move. Kayla's eyes widened in amazement as a slight wind circulated through the office. It lightly caressed her skin and moved through her hair.

In addition to the physical awareness of his energy manipulation, she could feel the pulse of his controlled efforts along their bond. Through their shared connection, Kayla was able to explore the way he moved the energy throughout the room. Curious, she sent him a steady stream of energy and watched in fascination as it blended together to strengthen the wind in the room.

Her energy flowed through and around Alec, and he took a step closer, gazing at her as though seeking an answer to a question. Kayla shivered as he lifted his hand, stroking the back of his fingers across her cheek. The effect of his touch was immediate and indescribably powerful. Unfiltered sensation and emotion rushed through her, whispering vows that some long dormant part of her longed to hear. Alec released the wind and sent a teasing pulse of energy over her, caressing and setting her alight with desire. Kayla closed her eyes, unable to formulate a coherent thought as the exquisite awareness of his powerful energy merged with hers. Some unknown instinct rose from inside her and answered in kind with her own wordless response.

As more of her energy met with and surrounded Alec, he bent down and brushed his lips against hers in the barest of kisses. It was soft as a whisper but more potent than a drug. The sensations coursing through her were intoxicating. Tiny warning bells rang in the back of her mind, but she ignored them, too fixated on the energy to give them much importance. Kayla sent more energy toward Alec, and he returned it in the form of teasing, intricate waves tasting like a promise. Kayla trembled, marveling at the feeling and unable to remember the last time she'd felt so alive.

As Alec's energy continued to move across her skin, his touch was almost reverent as his fingers traced the edge of her collarbone. It felt as though his energy flowed through every inch of her, awakening and caressing along the way. Not wanting him to stop, Kayla opened herself up to the energy completely.

At the rush of power, Alec pulled her into his arms. His kiss became more demanding as he expertly teased her lips with his own. She was too far gone to think beyond the sensations rushing through her. Whimpering slightly, she leaned into him and begged him to finish claiming her.

Alec froze in shock at her silent plea. He pulled back slightly and looked down into her eyes, searching her expression.

"By the gods," he murmured in awe and traced his finger along the side of her face. "You are more exquisite than I ever thought possible. Completely uninhibited and ruled by your passions."

Her blood was still singing from the flow of energy. She wove a seductive web of energy around him as her hands explored his firm chest. He trembled slightly, and his fingers reflexively tightened around her. Kayla curled her fingers into his shirt as she pulled him down to her again. Whispers of ancient secrets and memories flowed through her as she kissed him.

"Claim me," she thought toward him, both demanding and pleading simultaneously.

"Kayla," he groaned. "You don't even realize what you're asking ..."

Alec wrapped his arms around her, but his face was filled with a combination of regret and longing. As though unwilling to let her go, he held her close and whispered, "You speak with the voice of your blood, my love. I belong to you completely, just as you belong to me. As much as I want to claim you here and now, I won't share you with *him*. As it is, I don't know how I can just let you go back to him again. Not now, not after seeing and experiencing everything you are."

Alec's voice trailed off, and he breathed in her scent as though trying to memorize it.

"Let the trader go, my love, and I will claim you," Alec promised softly. He released her and took a deep breath as he slowly withdrew his energy. There was no pain, just an aching sense of loss where she'd once felt complete.

When the energy was gone, Kayla shuddered from the withdrawal. A moment later, the realization of what had nearly happened struck her. She blinked back the confusion and slid off the desk, taking an unsteady step backward. Her hand flew to her swollen lips, still feeling the effects of his kiss.

Alec was watching her with a mixture of longing and tenderness. Both their residual passion and her confusion intermingled in a melting pot of raw emotion. Even without sharing energy, their shared bond had never been stronger. She ran a hand through her dark hair in agitation. What was she thinking coming here alone with him? She could kick herself. "Dammit! Not again! What did I almost do? I'm such an idiot."

"No, Kayla," Alec said with a sigh, "you're not an idiot. You're one of the most brilliant and alluring creatures I've ever met. You just haven't learned enough to go on anything other than instinct. Your abilities are ancient in origin. Watching you and feeling you channel energy is breathtakingly beautiful. It's passionate, fiery, and everything our kind used to represent. We've forced ourselves to stifle our abilities and instincts over the centuries so we blend in with outsiders. But you ... I don't even know how it's possible. Your instincts have remained untouched and pure."

Kayla frowned, still shaken by what had happened between them. "What kind of ass-backward compliment is that?"

Alec smiled at her. "It wasn't meant to be, my love. It was

a true compliment. You are everything I've ever dreamed our kind could be." He took a step closer and said softly, "I want you completely and in every way imaginable. I know you want me in the same way, but you need to resolve your feelings for Carl first."

She glared at him. "There's nothing to resolve. I love Carl." This ..." she gestured back and forth between them, "whatever just happened can never happen again. I'm serious. It can't happen."

He nodded patiently and took another step toward her, caging her against the desk. "I know you care for him, but has your blood ever sung the way it did just now for me? Have your instincts ever taken over when he touches you? Have you ever begged him to claim you? He can't give you what you need."

Kayla's eyes clouded as her temper kicked in. "Stop pushing, Alec. No, it's not the same, but I wouldn't want it to be. Do you think I *like* not having control over myself when the energy thing kicks in? Call it instinct if you want, but it's not me. At least with Carl, I *have* control over my choices. I choose to be with him. He may not be able to do the energy thing, but *I love him.*"

Alec closed his eyes and took a deep breath as though trying to steady himself. When he opened them again, Kayla knew he was trying to regain control of his emotions. "I know you do. You've openly said as much both to him and to me. But what you haven't admitted to yourself is how you feel about me. I can sense it in your thoughts and feelings. When you were in my arms, begging me to claim you, I felt the depth of your emotion. If our bond were merely superficial, it would be different. but it's not. We're connected on a deeper level than you could ever have with your trader. Why do you keep running away?"

Her stomach clenched and churned like a terrifying storm

brewing. How could she admit something she didn't even understand? Was Alec right? Were her emotions for him real, or was it just a by-product of the energy? She shook her head, denying him once again. "I can't. I'm sorry, Alec. I just can't do that."

"Then I'll continue to wait until you're ready," Alec said quietly and adjusted the strap on her dress. His hand lingered for a moment on her shoulder before he removed it. His frustration was obvious, even without their shared bond, but she couldn't give him what he wanted.

Even though I practically threw myself at him just now.

Kayla turned away and tried to rub the chill from her arms. She missed the warmth of his energy and that sense of connection. These strange thoughts and feelings were overwhelming, leaving her unable to find her balance.

"My sweet, beautiful Kayla," Alec murmured and lifted her head with the tip of his fingers. When she met his eyes, he gave her a small reassuring smile. "Just take a deep breath, my love. It's going to be all right. You don't have to do anything. Sometimes I have to keep reminding myself you're new to all of this. You have so much natural ability that it's easy to forget you haven't grown up here with us. I don't want to frighten you."

"I'm not afraid," she lied.

Although she was sure he knew the truth, Alec didn't dispute her words. Instead, he took a step back to give her space and clasped his hands behind his back. "I'll arrange to have someone who can manipulate water energy and fire energy provide you with a demonstration later. You'll need to create small connections with them just to observe them. I would suggest you not send your energy to mix with theirs. Even though you're already bonded, it will probably prove to be irresistible to them too."

She winced at the implication of his words. "I led you on

just now by sending you energy when you were doing the wind thing, didn't I?"

Alec gave her a wry smile. "Yes. I realized a few minutes too late that you weren't fully aware of what you were offering. The rush from sharing energy can be difficult to resist, especially when it feels the way yours does."

Kayla groaned and squeezed her eyes shut. "Okay, so don't share energy with someone unless you're ready to hop into bed with them."

He chuckled. "It's usually only with your bonded partner, my love. With a permanent bond, there's no filter and no limit. That's the nature of a permanent bond. You can create smaller connections with other people and send energy back and forth without it being an issue. It's necessary for teaching, sharing memories, or pooling energy to accomplish something one person can't do alone. The larger and more powerful the connection, the more intimate sharing energy becomes. Strong feelings for one another or sharing energy simultaneously only enhances the effects."

Kayla flushed, remembering how it felt to open herself completely to him. It was as though he knew every thought and feeling she'd ever experienced. "So it's like this with everyone? It just depends on how much energy you share with them?"

"Not quite. Each person's energy has a different ... flavor," he tried to explain. "The stronger and more potent your bloodline, the more desirable the energy. Different types of energy will usually be drawn to their opposing counterpart. So someone who channels air energy may be more drawn to an earth channeler. A fire channeler will be drawn to a water channeler and vice versa. Your emotions also are tied into it."

"So ... wait. If Seara's an earth channeler, does that mean my father channeled air energy too?"

"You would think so, yes," Alec admitted and rubbed his

chin as though he were considering her words. "It's possible to have a relationship with someone who isn't your counterpoint, but it's not as satisfying. Your father was rather remarkable in the sense he was able to channel both air and fire equally. Not many people have the ability to specialize in more than one element. Once he bonded to your mother, his ability to channel air became even stronger. He never lost his fire ability though. I can't help but wonder whether his strong dual talent is part of the reason you ended up a spirit channeler."

"If I'm a spirit channeler, I'm not your counterpoint," she pointed out. "How does that fit in?"

He gave her a slow smile. "You're unique and incredibly desirable. It's not just your level of power, which alone is impressive. You can connect with *any* of the elements. Your energy seems to shift to become your partner's perfect balance."

At her confused look, he added, "That means you're most likely irresistible to everyone, but you won't necessarily feel the same way. You'll only want to connect with someone who can return a significant amount of energy to you. Anything less will leave you ... unsatisfied."

Kayla couldn't help but laugh at his description. "Is that your polite Omni way of saying I won't have an orgasm?"

"Something like that." Alec chuckled, and his eyes glinted meaningfully. "If you're interested in a demonstration, I could show you how easily I could take you there with my thoughts alone."

She held up her hand to stop him. No way was she going down that road again. "I think you already proved yourself. I was about halfway to climaxing a few minutes ago."

He gave a half-hearted shrug as though to say it was her loss. He was probably right, but she'd already caused enough complications for one day. Kayla leaned against the desk while considering his words. Other than with her mother, she'd only ever made a connection with Alec. She wondered how small the connection would need to be to prevent something like this from happening with anyone else.

Hearing her thoughts, Alec offered, "I'll supervise your instruction. I won't risk anyone trying to claim you when you're already bonded to me. It's possible, of course, but the claim would be fleeting and wouldn't have the effect you need or desire."

Kayla wrinkled her nose. The details of this energy business seemed endless. "I don't understand. I thought a claim was a bond."

"It is, of sorts," he agreed. "A sexual claim is fleeting. It lasts as long as the energy does. It may last longer if you have feelings for the person you're with, but just like a bad relationship, it can be ended. A permanent bond is something much deeper and can't be destroyed. You tie your aura or soul to the other person in a permanent way. A sexual claim combined with a permanent bond reinforces and strengthens both."

Just like that, the metaphorical floor collapsed beneath her. She swallowed as the full impact of his words registered. "We have a permanent bond. You're saying my soul is tied to yours?"

Alec hesitated and then nodded. At her horrified expression, he sighed. "It's not as bad as it sounds. I won't ever hurt you, Kayla. It goes both ways too. You have a piece of me with you, just as I carry a piece of you. It's another type of balancing point."

Kayla shook her head, feeling overwhelmed. She slumped down in one of the chairs in front of the desk and put her head in her hands. "I don't want any of this. Can't we just turn it off?"

He moved behind her and rested his hands on her shoulders. As he gently kneaded her muscles, a soothing wave of energy washed over her. "I'm not trying to frighten you. It's truly a beautiful and amazing thing. If you give it time, you'll understand much more. You're trying to learn a lifetime of knowledge right now. Give yourself time to absorb all of it."

"Maybe," she said quietly and closed her eyes. The combination of his hands and the energy sweeping over her was wonderful. She considered telling him to stop, but it seemed to be his way of trying to calm and reassure her. She was coming to realize energy manipulation was second nature to him. *Damn, this is nice, but I don't like wanting it so much.*

Alec's commlink beeped, and he pulled away. He was quiet for a moment, reading. When finished, he raised his head and his eyes shone with an inner fire. Kayla stared at him, transfixed by the allure of his blue eyes. "What's going on?"

"The test results on your water samples are complete."

Her eyes widened, and she straightened in the chair. He had her full attention. The turnaround time was faster than she'd thought. "What do they say?"

"The water is potable." He scrolled through the message. "They found some minor contaminants, but it's safe. They suggest some minor filtering for drinking purposes but there were no unusual readings. This is excellent news. Another drinking source will take an enormous amount of pressure off our current water resource management. We may be able to lift some of our current restrictions and even utilize the water energy from the river."

She jumped up from the chair. "Oh, wow! Carl is going to freak out."

Alec nodded and mused, "I'll arrange to have some additional personnel and equipment sent over to map the cavern. Carl mentioned he didn't believe the river could be fully explored on foot. I'll speak with our researchers about acquiring some underwater cameras to navigate through these areas."

"What about floatation devices? We could just ride down the river and see where it goes."

Alec shook his head. "No. Not right away. Once the passage is mapped, that might be a possibility depending on where it leads. But some of these underground rivers are treacherous. We don't know how far they go, whether they continue to go underground, or if there's enough oxygen in deeper areas of the cave."

His concerns were valid, but they wouldn't deter Kayla from exploring as much as she could. She was anxious to get started. "Fine. I'll wait a bit, but I want to start mapping it immediately."

"Of course," Alec agreed, walking over to press a button next to the computer terminal. Less than a minute later, his assistant entered the room.

"Sheila, I need you to contact Director Borshin and tell him to put together an excavation and analysis team for an underground river. Mistress Kayla Rath'Varein will be the point of contact. Find out what equipment the teams will need and send the requisition requests directly to me for approval. If there's any other equipment Mistress Rath'Varein requires, put a priority on it."

Sheila nodded. "Of course, Master Tal'Vayr. I'll take care of it right away."

The assistant left the room, and Kayla shook her head. "You don't need to do all that, Alec. I feel like you keep giving me special treatment and it makes me feel weird."

"I am," Alec admitted and sat down at the desk. He folded his arms and leaned back in his chair. "You're going to have to get used to it. If you insist on overseeing the river analysis, I intend to make sure you have everything you need.

I'll do everything in my power to keep you as safe as possible."

Kayla pursed her lips. It was tempting to argue, but the thought of telling Carl the news about the water samples was far more enticing. "Okay, I'm going to go find Carl. I want to see his face when he hears the news. Are we done here?"

His eyes darkening at the mention of Carl's name, he hesitated for a long moment and finally nodded. "I have a few things I need to handle this morning. Brant can escort you back to your quarters so you can speak with your trader. I'll stop by in a couple hours and have the designer meet us at your family's quarters. If it makes you more comfortable, we can continue your training there."

"All right," Kayla agreed and opened her commlink to make sure Carl was still there. When he didn't answer, she frowned. It wasn't like him to not answer. With a shrug, she tried calling Seara. Her mother answered immediately but wasn't much help. Carl had left not too long ago, claiming he had some errands to run and would be back later.

Kayla sighed in disappointment and closed the commlink. It was too early for his appointment with Director Borshin. He must be on some other trader business or possibly visiting his family. She drummed her fingertips on the desk. Patience was never her strong suit, and she was itching to tell him the news.

Alec looked up from his monitor. "If you're that anxious to tell him, I can locate him for you."

She bit her lip. It was still unnerving how he knew exactly what she was thinking. "How?"

"Any time you use the main elevators, access certain areas, or make a purchase in the towers, it's tracked. In some areas, we use facial recognition and biometric scanners. He may be conducting some of his trader business on one of the lower levels. I can run a quick check to determine his last recorded location."

Intrigued, she walked over to Alec's computer terminal. He pulled up a display and entered in Carl's name. A list of purchases and locations appeared on the screen, and Kayla frowned. "That's kind of creepy. You can locate anyone in the towers?"

"Yes," he said and isolated Carl's recent activity on the monitor. "We use it primarily to eliminate criminal activity, to record shopping habits for product recommendations, and occasionally to help locate lost children. We don't usually make it a habit of spying on our residents though."

Kayla took a step back and shook her head. The idea that someone could track her every movement had her ruin rat instincts kicking in. This must have been how they discovered her location when she was last in the towers. "Thanks, but I should probably just wait until he gets back."

Alec looked at the screen thoughtfully for a moment. He typed in a few commands and pulled up another screen. Some unknown emotion flickered in his eyes briefly. "It appears as though he's at the Flamingo Café on Level Thirty-Two. I'll go with you to show you where it's located. Carl was just as anxious as you to get these results."

His offer and reaction surprised her. She glanced at the screen but didn't see anything unusual. Something felt off though. "You sure? I thought you had things you needed to do."

"I do, but my appointments can wait a bit. It would be best if I accompanied you if you're going to one of the public levels."

Alec stood and offered Kayla his arm. When she touched him, she got the distinct impression he was suppressing his feelings.

He led her out of the office, and Brant immediately stood

at the sight of them. Alec turned to Sheila and gave her some last-minute instructions about rescheduling his appointments. Once he finished, they headed toward the elevator with Brant falling into step behind them.

As they approached the elevator, Alec told Brant, "Carl is dining at the Flamingo Café on Level Thirty-Two. Kayla has some news she wants to share with him."

Brant nodded, and as soon as the elevator moved, he pressed a button on his wrist unit. When the doors opened, they stepped out into a busy commercial district. This area was markedly different than the area from the previous evening. It was busier, more congested, and lacked the rich decorations and elaborate fountains. The people were dressed more casually, and many seemed hurried as they walked in and out of the stores. Numerous armed security personnel patrolled through the large corridor.

One of the armed security officers approached them and bowed low. "Welcome to Level Thirty-Two, Master Tal'Vayr and Mistress Rath'Varein. We have four security details assigned to you on this level. Do you require an additional escort?"

Alec shook his head. "That won't be necessary. We'll be at the Flamingo Café."

The man gave a small salute before stepping away and conferring briefly with Brant. Kayla noted several of the armed personnel had circled around them and began following at a discreet distance.

She leaned in closer to Alec. "Why are they following us?"

Alec wrapped his arm around her waist and spoke silently in her mind. *"This area isn't part of the Inner Sanctum. It's open to the general population. Until things settle down in the towers, security has been heightened. It's nothing to worry about, just a precaution more than anything."*

It seemed like a pretty hefty precaution. She wondered

how dangerous the towers had become over the past month. As they walked through the crowd of people, Kayla was acutely aware of the surprised and curious looks when they were recognized. A small crowd began to gather as more people noticed them, and Kayla pressed closer to Alec's side. She'd never seen so many people in one place. Thankfully, the security officers encouraged these onlookers to keep moving and go about their business.

Alec took the attention in stride as they quickly approached the café. The restaurant was bustling with activity. Once again, the contrast between this place and the restaurant from the night before was obvious. The din of plates and loud voices echoed throughout the room. A ragged-looking man wearing a white shirt and a bright-red tie stood behind a desk studying his computer terminal.

Without bothering to look up, the man said, "It's going to be at least an hour wait unless you have a reservation. If you want to wait, register your commlink and we'll notify you when a table's available. Otherwise, you can try the café on Level Forty-One."

"No, thanks. I'm actually looking for Carl Grayson," Kayla said. "Do you know if he's here?"

"Lady, I don't care who you're looking for," the man began and looked up. When he recognized them, his face paled, and he stammered, "I-I—You—You're—You're Master Tal'Vayr and Mistress Rath'Varein!"

"Very good," Alec said, his voice dripping with irritation. "Now, perhaps you'll answer Mistress Rath'Varein's question."

"My apologies," he said and quickly began checking his computer terminal. Kayla started to pity the guy as he squirmed under Alec's gaze.

"Ca-Carl Grayson, you said? The trader?"

When Kayla nodded, he jabbed his thumb in the general

direction behind him. "He's over at one of the back tables. I'll take you to him right away."

The man scampered from behind his desk, practically pushing people out of the way as he led them through the crowded room of tables. As they approached the back of the restaurant, Kayla saw Carl sitting at a table with an extremely attractive dark-haired woman next to him. Her hand rested affectionately on his arm and she was laughing at something he said.

Carl looked up as they approached. His expression quickly became one of surprise and he stood. "Kayla? What are you doing here? I thought you were going to be busy this morning."

Kayla glanced at the woman sitting next to him. She was slender and petite with long, dark hair arranged in an elaborate style and large, wide-set brown eyes. Her face was heart-shaped with high cheekbones and full, pouty lips. She was absolutely stunning.

"We just got the lab results back, and I wanted to tell you what they found. Are we interrupting?"

Carl glanced down at his companion before shaking his head. "No, we were just having breakfast." He hesitated for a moment as though trying to come to a decision. Finally, he gestured to the woman. "This is an old friend of mine, Leah Monroe. Leah, I'd like you to meet Mistress Kayla Rath'-Varein and Master Alec Tal'Vayr."

The woman's eyes lit up at the introduction. "How wonderful. Carl, I knew you were acquainted with both Master Tal'Vayr and Mistress Rath'Varein, but I didn't realize you were on a first-name basis with them." She stood and extended her hand, giving both Kayla and Alec another long look. Her gaze lingered on Alec the longest and she batted her eyes at him. "It's a pleasure to meet both of you. We've already ordered, but please join us." She winked at Carl and patted him on the arm. "We can always finish catching up privately later on, darling."

Darling? Kayla's eyes narrowed on the woman before turning back to Carl. He looked pained at this development. Alec cleared his throat. "Kayla, if there are no objections, I think joining them is an excellent idea. You didn't have a chance to eat breakfast this morning."

At these words, the host quickly offered to get some additional chairs and disappeared. Kayla studied Carl, wondering what was going on. He caught her eye and shook his head, his eyes promising he'd explain later.

She frowned, wishing he could communicate wordlessly the way Alec could. She hesitated for a moment and then asked, "Would it be better if we talked later?"

"No, it's fine," Carl insisted and shot a warning look at Alec before gesturing to his companion. "Leah was just telling me she's now a journalist for *The Omni Observer*."

The host brought over two additional chairs and menus. "Is that so?" Alec inquired, holding out one of the chairs for Kayla to take a seat. "I believe I've heard of you. You report primarily on gossip and events concerning the Inner Circle, correct?"

After Kayla had taken her seat, Alec sat beside her and draped his arm across the back of her chair. His thumb idly ran across the top of her shoulder and over the strap of her dress in an intimate gesture. Carl stared hard at Alec's hand as he and Leah took their seats again. Kayla stiffened and started to shrug him off, but Alec's hand lightly squeezed her shoulder in warning.

"I need you to trust me and play along. This reporter could be a problem."

Kayla paused and cocked her head. Something was going on that she didn't understand. She turned to assess the unfamiliar woman again. Leah was sitting close enough to Carl that another inch or two would put her in his lap. The woman was practically rubbing up against him like an animal in heat. The whole scene was beginning to feel a little surreal and a whole lot wrong.

"Oh, yes. I'd absolutely love to do a feature about you two," Leah declared and gave them a brilliant smile. Her teeth seemed a little too white. Now that Kayla thought about it, her nose was a little crooked too. Maybe someone had broken it once. Although, that could just be wishful thinking. Her eyes were definitely asymmetrical though.

Unperturbed by Kayla's scrutiny, Leah chattered on. "I've been trying for weeks to get your assistant to set up an interview with you, Master Tal'Vayr. I know you must be busy, but the public is dying to know more about your relationship with Mistress Rath'Varein."

Leah put her hand back on Carl's arm and purred, "Honey, you should have· told me you knew Master Tal'Vayr and Mistress Rath'Varein personally. I never thought in a million years I'd be having breakfast with the leader of the High Council and his fiancée."

"Right," Carl muttered and took a sip from his drink.

Honey? Kayla's fists clenched under the table and her nails bit into her palms. Watching the intimate way Leah was touching and looking at Carl was excruciating. The urge to reach across the table and backhand the woman was becoming more and more attractive. She fumed silently, knowing she had no right to be jealous, especially considering what happened earlier between her and Alec.

A server came over to the table, and Alec ordered a cup of herbal tea for both himself and Kayla. She ignored the menu. Her appetite had fled the moment the woman started making bedroom eyes at Carl.

"I have to say, your story is one of the most romantic I've ever heard," Leah gushed. "Imagine living on the surface for all those years and then having Master Tal'Vayr find you and sweep you off your feet. I was practically in tears when I heard you two were engaged to be married. Was it really love at first sight?"

Carl choked on his drink. "Leah, I don't think they really want to discuss their personal lives with a reporter."

"That's all right, Carl," Alec said magnanimously, waving off Carl's objections. "I know many people are curious about our relationship." He made a show of looking around before leaning forward in a conspiratorial manner. "I knew there was something special about Kayla the moment we met. Her beauty, charm, and wit captivated me completely. I've been entranced by her ever since."

Alec lifted Kayla's hand and pressed a kiss on the back of her hand. Kayla gaped at him, dumbfounded by his solicitous behavior. Carl clenched his jaw in anger and struggled to appear impassive. The server took that moment to reappear and placed two steaming cups of tea in front of Alec and Kayla. She wondered at the wisdom of placing hot beverages on a table of occupants about to erupt into a knock-down, drag-out fight. Regardless of Alec's assurances, this was starting to look really bad.

"Would you like me to order for you, my love?"

Kayla blinked at Alec and barely managed a nod. He placed her order and took a sip of his tea. Once the server had disappeared, Leah leaned forward, eager to resume their conversation.

"Is it true you saved Mistress Rath'Varein's life at the council meeting?"

Alec's expression remained neutral, but Kayla sensed his emotional turmoil at the reminder of the council meeting. He was still coping with the death of his father. Concerned for him, Kayla opened her mouth to tell the woman exactly where to stick her nosy questions.

Alec quickly cleared his throat and put his hand on top of hers to stop her. "It was a difficult time for both of us. I'd rather not discuss it."

"Oh. Of course." Leah nodded in sympathy, but her eyes gleamed with the juicy tidbit of information.

Kayla's eyes narrowed. The amount of polite niceties being exchanged to cover the steaming piles of shit at the table was absurd. And if that woman didn't stop stroking Carl's arm, she was going to end up reaching across the table and bitch-slapping her.

Alec squeezed her hand. Whether it was an attempt at reassurance or to keep her hand pinned so she didn't make good on her intentions, she wasn't sure.

"Most of the information about the council meeting is public record. You can retrieve the details from the archives. As far as my personal feelings are concerned, let's just say there isn't anything I wouldn't do for her. Having Kayla in my life has been the greatest gift I could ever imagine, and I look forward to our future together."

Carl's expression was thunderous at the declaration.

"That's enough," Kayla told Alec silently, observing Carl's reaction. *"I know she's a reporter and you're trying to maintain an illusion, but you're being cruel."*

"How romantic," Leah sighed dreamily and fanned herself.

Alec took another sip of his tea. *"He should have considered the consequences before agreeing to meet with a reporter."*

Realization dawned. Alec had obviously known Carl was meeting with a reporter. That was the reason he had abandoned his other appointments to escort her to the café. He'd wanted to make sure he could direct the conversation.

Unaware of their silent communication, Leah leaned against Carl and looked up at him. "It was love at first sight for us, wasn't it, honey?"

"Is that so?" Alec raised an eyebrow and lowered his cup. "How fascinating. I had no idea Carl had a love interest here in the towers."

Kayla jerked her head up and looked at Carl in confusion. With those few words, her entire world shifted and all the blood rushed out of her face.

"What?" Her voice came out as a squeak.

"Oh, definitely," the woman chattered on, oblivious to the growing tension at the table. "Of course, we were teenagers when we first met, so it was probably more like lust. But either way, I haven't been able to keep my hands off him since the moment we first met."

Carl gave Leah a sharp look. "We were kids and ended things when I left."

The server took that moment to place a plate of pastries in front of Kayla. She eyed the plate distastefully, more tempted to throw it at the dark-haired vixen than eat anything.

"So you've known each other for a while?" Alec asked casually.

"Oh, we go way back." Leah ran her hand up Carl's chest playfully. "We were a pretty hot item before he left for the surface. Weren't we, honey?"

Carl gently removed her hand. He focused solely on Kayla as he explained, "Leah and I met during our classes at the Institute. We dated a couple years ago before I was commissioned as a trader. I ran into her this morning, and we decided to have breakfast to catch up."

"Uh huh," Kayla murmured, pretending to be interested in examining the contents of her plate. Her gaze fell on the utensils, and she wondered how well they'd work as a weaponized projectile. That bitch was going down.

Alec reached over and casually moved the utensils out of

reach. Kayla scowled at him and inwardly pouted at his attempts to curtail her bloodthirsty ambitions.

Leah leaned up against Carl, kissed his cheek, and teased, "I'm just biding my time until his contract is up and he comes back home to me. I'm not planning on letting him get away again."

Carl stiffened. "We can talk about it later."

Irritated with the whole situation and no longer willing to play this game, Kayla pushed away her untouched plate and stood. "Alec, I don't think I'm hungry after all. We should be getting back. You had all those things to handle this morning anyway."

"Of course, my dear," Alec stood and offered a polite smile to Carl and Leah. He put his arm around Kayla to lead her away, but before he could take a step, Carl jumped to his feet.

"Kayla, wait," Carl urged. He glanced down at Leah and added, "I'd like to speak with you about the samples from the lab."

Alec raised an eyebrow. "My fiancée wishes to return to the Inner Sanctum, Trader Carl. I'll have my assistant forward a copy of the results to you."

Carl ignored Alec, his worried gaze urging Kayla to listen to him. She hesitated and then nodded. "It's all right, Alec. After all, it's why we came here in the first place."

"Excuse me for a moment," Carl said absently to Leah. Stepping around the reporter, he followed Alec and Kayla into a back hallway near the restrooms.

Brant motioned toward an empty office. "I'll hold this room secure until you're finished."

Once the door shut behind them, Carl began, "This isn't what it looks like."

"What isn't?" Alec asked coolly and stepped around some

stacked boxes. "That you're conversing with a reporter who could potentially put Kayla in danger? If you make one comment or slip, Kayla could become a target. We discussed this exact type of thing. I was under the impression you had Kayla's best interest at heart. Obviously, that assumption was incorrect."

Carl's gaze hardened. "I'd never put her in danger." He turned to Kayla, and his eyes softened. "I ran into Leah on my way to my parents' place. I haven't seen her in over a year and she wanted to catch up. I didn't want to take her back to my parents' quarters because that would be asking for trouble. She can be persistent. I offered to take her to breakfast, chat for a bit, and then I was planning on leaving. I had no idea she'd become a journalist until after we sat down."

Confused, Kayla looked up at Alec. "What do you mean? Why would meeting with her put me in danger? I thought you were the one in trouble."

"Not exactly," Alec admitted with a sigh. "Seara told me she'd shared some of the growing troubles in the tower. Your mother is more perceptive than I realized. Unfortunately, it's true. There have been some recent threats against me. More recently, we've learned some specifics and tower security believes you're a potential target. Our engagement was originally meant to offer you some protection and show the towers our families were united. That's even more imperative now with these threats. It's well known in the Inner Circle that a bonded mate is sacrosanct. Any attack on you would also be construed as an attack against me and the towers. If this reporter suspects our relationship is anything other than what it seems, you could be in considerable danger."

Kayla frowned. Alec's explanation gave even more weight to Seara's words from the night before. She wasn't as concerned about herself, but the thought of Alec being in danger worried her. She may not fully understand the depth of her feelings for Alec, but she didn't want to risk anything happening to him either. "Okay, so what's your plan to stop this?"

"Ideally, Carl should leave and return to the trader camp," Alec suggested. "If you remain here with me, it'll give more credibility to our announcement. You'll have the opportunity to train and learn how to use your talents to protect yourself. You can still oversee the river evaluation, but you'll also be able to work with designers to discuss your idea to build another tower."

Carl scoffed and pushed away from the wall. "You'd like that, wouldn't you? You'd do just about anything to get me out of the picture. I wouldn't be surprised if you were responsible for this whole setup today with Leah."

Alec raised an eyebrow at the accusation but didn't respond. Carl's eyes narrowed. "That's it, isn't it? The whole scene out there was another ploy to manipulate Kayla into what? Making her jealous? Making her think I'd put her in danger by meeting with a reporter?" Carl took another step toward Alec. "Did you get off on putting your hands all over her in front of me? That whole charade came dangerously close to backfiring on you just now. Or is that your new goal? Push us so far to force the truth out so you can jump in and play hero again?"

"That's enough," Kayla announced, pushing against Carl's chest to stop him from advancing on Alec. She had her doubts about Alec knowing, especially given that he'd suddenly changed his mind about bringing her down here, but she didn't think he'd go so far to actually orchestrate the whole thing. "It was my idea to come find you this morning. Alec put aside his work to bring me down here to find you. He's been trying to help and protect me through all of this. You're not being fair."

"Nothing about this situation is fair, Kayla," Carl said in a low voice, his eyes flashing dangerously. "Leah asked me if I was seeing anyone, and I couldn't tell her the truth. Then I'm supposed to sit back and not say anything while everyone in the towers believes you and Alec are engaged to be married? To top it off, Alec is giving you these elaborate presents and going out of his way to try to win you over. And with that energy connection thing, it's probably just a matter of time before he actually does it. So no, Kayla, it's not fair. But there isn't a damn thing I can do about it."

Kayla froze in shock at Carl's words. She hadn't realized the depth of his feelings about the situation. Turning to look at Alec, she asked in a shaky voice, "Can you give us a minute?" Alec hesitated, clearly unhappy with the request but finally nodded in agreement.

Once he'd left the room, Kayla looked up at Carl and whispered, "What are you saying?"

"I don't know how long I can do this, Kayla," he said in frustration and rubbed his hands over his face. "You've seen the way people look at you and treat you here. You're part of the Inner Circle and that's a world I'll never belong in. Every damn person I've talked to in these towers has been carrying on about the fairy tale of Kayla Rath'Varein. The princess from the towers has returned, and Alec's a damn savior for bringing you back. And maybe they're right. I know better than most what it was like for you growing up as a ruin rat. You deserve the type of life he can give you and I can't."

Her heart thudded at his words, and she felt a sick, sinking feeling in the pit of her stomach. "How can you say that? You know that's not what I want."

Carl's face was pained. "If I took you outside right now, put my hands on you, and declared my feelings for you, I'd be arrested on site. Those security officers would assume I was trying to accost the High Council leader's fiancée. You can't ask me to sit by and pretend everything is fine when Alec has you on his arm like some sort of trophy. I love you, but I can't do that. I was a fool for thinking I could."

Kayla felt something within her break at his words. As much as she loved him, she could never put Alec's life or anyone else's life in danger just to appease Carl's jealousy. After everything they'd been through, how could he not realize the depth of her feelings for him? She swallowed, her throat suddenly dry as she wondered whether she was asking too much from him. If this situation were reversed, she'd be furious and wouldn't have put up with it at all. Anguish threatened to consume her at the thought that she needed to make a choice between him and someone else's life.

Unwilling to succumb to the jagged edge of despair and hopelessness his words evoked, Kayla struggled to bury her more vulnerable feelings and harness her fury and outrage instead. She couldn't afford to allow his words to break her or feel any doubt about her decision to protect Alec. The desperation and hurt might threaten to tear her apart, but focusing on her anger would offer enough strength to carry on in the face of her pain.

"No, Carl. You're only a fool for thinking I'm something I'm not. I'm not and never will be a trophy. No matter how they dress me up or what they call me, I'll always be a ruin rat. I'll never stop looking at a piece of jewelry and seeing my camp's next meal. I'll never stop looking at a security system and trying to figure out how to circumvent it. I'll never stop trying to figure out how to stay one step ahead of everyone else just so I can keep everyone I care about alive. Because, at the end of the day, that's what this whole charade with Alec is about."

"Then put an end to the charade, Kayla," Carl argued and took a step toward her. "Alec's a big boy. He can take care of himself. Stop living with one foot in both worlds. If you want to live on the surface, do it. If you want to stay here with

Alec, own up to it. Don't use the damned bond as an excuse. You're stronger than that."

Kayla reared back as though he'd slapped her.

"You self-righteous bastard," she hissed and shoved him away from her. Hard. "You don't know anything about it. You have no idea what it's like to lose yourself to this power. It's an addiction. It's consuming. Your will disappears and you become this other ... *thing*. A monster. You lose all control, but it's not you ... It's not ..."

Her voiced cracked as her eyes welled with tears. Carl's eyes widened, and he took another step toward her. "Shit. Kayla, I didn't mean—"

"No." She took a step backward, not bothering to hide the angry bitterness in her words. "I believed in you, Carl. I thought you understood how I felt about you. I was wrong, and that's on me, but you're wrong about something too. I don't belong here. I never have. When I look around at the people in these towers, I see nothing but shallow people who are obsessed with clothing, gossip, and politics. They have no concept of what life is really like."

Her eyes burned from the tears threatening to spill over onto her cheeks. "You've seen the ruin rat camps, but you haven't seen the outlying family camps. They're a thousand times worse. The only reason Veridian and I weren't shipped to one of those camps when we were kids was because I agreed to take risks other people weren't willing to take. You think I'm a good scavenger? It's because I didn't have a fucking *choice*. I went nose-to-nose with the traders because no one else would. My life, Veridian's life, everyone in that damn camp ... they were counting on me to do what needed to be done. No one else had the balls to stand up to any of you. And what did that get me?"

She let out an ugly, forced laugh. "I watched the mother who raised me die from an infection OmniLab medicine could have easily treated. Pretz was murdered simply because he protected me from a low-life Omni wannabe rapist. Then, I get attacked and nearly killed because another trader decided to use me to clean up the corruption. To make matters worse, I fell in love with that same trader. Even when my world went to hell and everything I knew was ripped away, I held on to the hope that I'd managed to find the one person I could believe in and trust."

Kayla closed her eyes at the onslaught of raw emotion coursing through her. Disappointment, hurt, betrayal, and an overwhelming sense of loss filled her. They were all useless emotions. She pushed them aside and dug deep to find the last of her dwindling strength. Her eyes hardened as she raised her head to look at him once more.

"That's what life *really* is, Carl. That's the ugly, dirty, gritty truth. It hands you hard lessons and forces you to adapt. When you get complacent and start to hope, it gives you an even harder lesson by taking it all away."

Whatever he saw in her expression made him pale. A look of panic crossed his face and he reached out, taking another step toward her. "Kayla, I never meant—"

She sidestepped him and pinned him with a glare. "No. Don't touch me. I don't belong with you either. One of the first things you learn as a ruin rat is to keep your distance from a trader. I broke that rule, just like I broke all the others. I'm the one who's really the fool, I suppose."

He froze and dropped his outstretched hand. "Don't do this. Please, God, don't do this, sweetheart."

She didn't answer. There was nothing else to say. Everything seemed to be falling apart around her, and she didn't know how to make it stop. She blinked back the tears as she turned away from Carl. She couldn't do this. Not now. She was destroying all of them.

Kayla fled from the room and ignored her name being

called from behind her. Her heart felt as though it were breaking into a thousand pieces. She ran back down the corridor toward the priority elevator, pushing her way through the masses of people in the crowded corridor. *Don't fall apart,* she told herself repeatedly. It became her mantra as her footsteps pounded on the ground in time with those words.

When she reached the elevator, Brant slipped in behind her. She hadn't realized he'd been following her, but she should have known. Kayla turned away, not willing to let him witness her misery. She must have been unsuccessful because his voice was almost gentle as he asked, "Do you want to go to your family's quarters?"

Not trusting herself to speak yet, she nodded and wrapped her arms around herself as though that gesture would prevent her from falling apart. Brant shot her a worried look before stepping forward and programming the control panel. Refusing to give into the tears that continued to threaten, she took several deep breaths as the elevator shot upward. When the doors finally opened, Kayla forced herself to slowly walk down the empty hallway toward her family's quarters.

Brant hesitated at the entrance. "Do you want me to go in with you?"

She shrugged, not caring one way or the other, and walked inside. Brant frowned and followed her just inside the common room. Thankfully, Seara was nowhere to be found. Kayla's movements felt almost robotic as she went to her bedroom, closed the door, and sat on the edge of the bed, dropping her head in her hands.

His words had hurt, but it went deeper than that. Their argument only helped to clarify her feelings for him, and the reality was terrifying. It didn't matter that she hadn't moved into his room at camp or not. She'd already tied herself to him in every way imaginable, and the thought of possibly losing him scared the hell out of her.

She would never have agreed to this engagement ruse if Alec weren't in danger. If her being here was a liability, maybe it would be better if she returned to the surface. Alec could keep pretending they were engaged until things settled down, and it would prevent any repeated incidents like the one earlier. At least now she knew to avoid using her energy, and they could put the training on hold until things settled down. The hardest part was the situation with Carl.

The bond between her and Alec was just complicating the matter, and she didn't trust herself enough to remain here until she got it under control. She needed some distance from both of them and time to think.

Kayla stood and walked over to the closet to pull out her bag. Without bothering to further analyze her actions, she quickly pulled off the dress and put on her old clothes and UV-protective gear. Grabbing her bag off the bed, she threw it over her shoulder and left the room.

Brant straightened as she entered, looking at her change of clothes and bag in surprise. "You're leaving?"

"That's the plan," she replied and headed toward the door. Brant stepped in front of her, blocking her passage and held up his hand. "I won't stop you, but you need to give me about thirty minutes to make some arrangements. Master Tal'Vayr won't want you to leave the towers without me accompanying you. It's not safe."

Kayla glared at him and dropped her bag on the floor. "Okay, this has gone far enough. I've allowed you to follow me around because, quite frankly, I had too much other stuff going on to give a damn. But I don't need or want a babysitter, and I'll be damned if I'm going to let you follow me out of the towers. I won't be responsible for what happens to you out there. So back off and sit your ass down."

Brant raised an eyebrow. "My apologies, Kayla. I know you're upset, but I swore an oath to protect you. I cannot allow you to leave without me."

Kayla's eyes narrowed at his choice of words. *Allow? Seriously? Fuck that.* She wasn't going to *allow* anyone to stop her from leaving. "This is your last warning. I don't feel like dealing with this shit right now, but I could definitely handle kicking someone's ass. Either get out of my way or it'll be yours."

"I can't do that."

"Fine," she snarled. The rush of adrenaline helped to clear the emotional haze from her mind. With her fist clenched, she took a step forward and swung at him. Brant caught her wrist, and there was a brief moment of surprise when she realized he might not be as fluffy as she first thought. *Nice reflexes,* she observed silently even though she'd telegraphed the move fairly well. Balancing on the balls of her feet, she widened her stance to take a more defensive position. Turning her body slightly, she used her elbow to jab him in the gut. He inhaled sharply at the contact and tried to make a grab for her, but she quickly moved out of the way. Kayla didn't have much physical bulk, but she was fast and knew how to fight dirty.

Brant lunged forward to grab her again, and she hooked a foot around one of his ankles. Twisting her body, she jerked her foot forward, trying to unbalance him. The movement caught him by surprise, and she thought there was a quick flash of approval in his eyes before he took them both down to the floor.

Kayla tried to push herself off of him, but he seized one of her wrists. With her free hand, she swung her fist to the side and connected soundly with his nose. Brant swore loudly as his eyes began to water. With a grunt, he rolled over on top of her, effectively pinning her against the floor.

Considering he was twice her size, Kayla was at a disadvantage in this position. She wriggled against him to no avail. He blinked to clear his vision and stared down at her, shifting his position slightly so she could breathe. With a huff, she blew the loose hair out of her face and glared at him. There was a trickle of blood coming from his nose, but Kayla felt little sympathy. After all, she'd warned him. Brant leaned over her and a few strands of short, dark hair fell across his forehead. *Not bad fighting skills for a pretty boy.*

He eyed her warily. "Are you done yet?"

"Not even close."

Kayla shifted and tried to jerk her knee up. Brant loosened his grip to stop her before she could connect. It was enough. With a twist, she escaped his grasp and scrambled to her feet. He swore again and lunged for her. She jumped out of the way and he bumped into one of Seara's tables. It toppled over and fell to the floor with a crash.

Knowing he was already off balance, Kayla threw her body weight into his. He slipped backward as she fell into him, and he moved to cushion her fall as they hit the floor. She kicked out her leg, feeling it connect with some part of him. He grunted, trying to grab her leg but she rolled over. Reaching down, she snatched the weapon from his holster and hopped to her feet. Aiming the weapon at him, she warned, "Stay down, Fluffy, or I'll zap you."

He scowled. "Fluffy?"

"Mmhmm," Kayla agreed, watching as the security officer propped himself up on his elbow.

Brant rubbed his ribs but didn't move any further. "I admit you handle yourself better than I expected, but I still can't let you leave without an escort."

She arched an eyebrow and reached down to grab her bag from the floor. "It doesn't look like you're in much of a position to stop me."

"Wait, Kayla," Brant said quickly. "It's the blasted Inner Circle who's plotting to move against Master Tal'Vayr. These aren't just threats. We've uncovered a definitive plot. If you walk out those doors without me, how will you defend yourself against them? Do you think it's a secret you can't control your energy? Master Tal'Vayr sent me to you for a reason. Your lack of training leaves you vulnerable. Any Inner Circle member could coerce you into using your energy bond against Master Tal'Vayr. Do you want to be responsible for his death?"

She paused and looked down at him, trying to decide if he was telling the truth. "What do you mean? Do you know who's behind these threats?"

"No," he admitted. "All we know is that someone wants Master Tal'Vayr and some other key individuals removed from the High Council. OmniLab's databases were hacked to obtain information about you. They were moderately successful and managed to retrieve some of your files. We haven't been able to trace the origin of these hacks yet. We believe their intention is to try targeting you in an effort to force Master Tal'Vayr into stepping down. I'm supposed to stay with you to prevent any other Inner Circle members from getting close enough to harm you."

"There aren't any Inner Circle members on the surface," she pointed out, more convinced than ever that leaving was the right decision. "Why would Alec want you to follow me there?"

Brant started to pull himself into a sitting position, and Kayla shifted the weapon in her hand. Acknowledging her threat, he stopped moving and remained still. "There are some Inner Circle members who aren't accounted for. It's also not as difficult as you might imagine, bribing people on the surface for favors. We monitor everyone who comes and goes, but deliveries and messengers are sent out to the trading camps every day. All of these individuals are outside our immediate reach once they're on the surface. We're auditing the camp records to look for any ties to people in the towers."

Kayla frowned and shifted the bag on her shoulder. The pieces were beginning to fall into place. The audit of Carl's records, Seara's fears, and Alec's concern all made more sense.

"No. Thanks for the info, but I can't stay here."

Brant started to object, but she held up her hand. "You'll be chewed up and spit out if you try following me, Fluffy. I can handle myself. But thanks for trying, and I'm sorry about this."

Kayla glanced at the weapon to make sure it was set to stun before firing at him. A low-pitched noise sounded, and the security officer grunted before his body went lax. She knelt over him to make sure he was unconscious before leaving the weapon next to him. His other weapon was still in her bag.

With another mental apology, Kayla turned and ran from her family's quarters. If she remembered correctly, she had only minutes before he regained consciousness.

The elevator moved quickly downward, and she took a deep breath when it arrived at the large entrance area. Melvin was sitting behind the desk and jumped up at her entrance. "Mis—Kayla, you're leaving?"

"Yeah, it's been fun," she said with a wave, not halting long enough for him to object. Grabbing her helmet from the rack on the wall, she put it on and headed into the adjacent parking area. The overhead doors slid open, allowing the bright sunlight to spill inside. Being an Inner Circle member apparently had its perks, and her speeder was parked in a priority area close to the exit.

Kayla climbed on the back of her speeder and fired up the engine. As she pulled out of the garage, she gave one last glance up at the towers. This was why it was always better to travel light. It had taken less than ten minutes for her to leave the towers and escape to freedom.

As she traveled across the desolate landscape, Carl's words came back to her. The tears she'd been suppressing began pouring down her cheeks. Leo had warned her against having a soft heart. When you let people in and allowed yourself to care about them, your emotions chained you more tightly than any possible prison.

Regardless of escaping the towers, Kayla wasn't truly free. She wasn't sure if it was even a possibility anymore. Her entire life was a huge mess and, for the first time, she didn't have a clue how to go about fixing it. Feeling lost, she programmed in the last known coordinates for her former ruin rat camp with the hope they hadn't moved on yet. Maybe going home would finally give her the answers she desperately needed.

CHAPTER NINE

IT TOOK Kayla only two hours to make an almost four-hour drive. When she recognized Leo's camp, relief flooded through her. The ruin rats rarely stayed in the same location for long, and the familiar shape of the camp was a welcome sight. By the time she pulled up outside the front entrance and climbed off her bike, Kayla was emotionally exhausted and numb. To make matters worse, she wasn't sure what sort of reception she'd receive from her former family.

Although Veridian had claimed her former camp leader didn't harbor a grudge for leaving, Kayla had her doubts. Leo was unpredictable, and most ruin rats were derisive when it came to traders and their crews. She had been one of their strongest objectors up until a few short weeks ago.

Just take it a moment at a time. With a deep breath, she grabbed her bag off the back of her bike and squared her shoulders. Putting a confident swing into her step that she didn't quite feel, Kayla headed inside. As expected, they'd monitored her approach and three people stood waiting for her at the entrance.

"Well, I'll be damned," Leo chuckled and shook his head

as she pulled off her helmet. "Looks like Mack won the bet after all. I thought it would take another couple of weeks before you got sick of playing with the trader. Guess you decided to come to your senses."

Leo was a tall, thin, balding man in his early forties who'd been leading the camp for the past ten years. Mack and Tharin were two of his scavengers who usually worked as a team in the ruins. They were both in their twenties and Mack, in particular, had been something of a scavenging mentor over the years.

"Not even close," Kayla replied with a trace of a smile. It was difficult to maintain her air of nonchalance when she felt nothing but relief at their greeting. She hadn't realized how much she'd missed the camp. Even the stale aroma of the air circulating through the vents and the flickering lighting was a welcome reminder she was home. "OmniLab asked me to conduct some scientific studies of alarming personal hygiene and weapon-grade body odor. I couldn't think of a more perfect specimen than you."

Tharin snorted. "She's got a point, Leo."

Mack broke into a grin and walked over to Kayla, enveloping her in a big bear hug. He was a heavily muscled man with short, dark hair and brown eyes. The rough, unshaven stubble on his face grated against her cheek, but she'd missed it all the same. "It's great to have you back, babe."

Leo glanced outside at her solo bike before turning back to her. "Where's Veridian?"

She gave a half-hearted shrug. "He's busy getting it on with a redhead back in Carl's camp."

Tharin's eyebrows rose. "Might want to tell him to be careful. Someone's putting something in the hydrating packs around here."

Kayla paused, cocking her head to study him. He'd joined

their camp about four years ago and had immediately fit right in with his playful banter and sharp wit. Only now, there were dark circles under his eyes and he appeared to have lost weight. "Oh? Something going on?"

Mack rubbed the back of his neck and frowned. "Kristin's implant failed."

Kayla's eyes widened at the news. "Shit. She's pregnant again?"

When Tharin nodded, Kayla squeezed her eyes shut. Kristin wasn't much older than she was and already had one child. Most ruin rats avoided serious relationships and especially pregnancy. Their lives were too dangerous and not conducive to family life. They tried to filter supplies back to the outlying family camps when they could, but it wasn't enough. Now that Kristin was expecting a second kid, there was a good chance she might be forced to leave. Kayla swallowed, recalling the deplorable conditions she'd witnessed during her infrequent visits to drop off supplies.

Most scavenger camps had a closed-door policy when it came to children. Leo was a rare exception. He'd allowed Veridian and Kayla to grow up in the camp. Kayla wasn't sure, but she suspected he'd been involved with Veridian's mother. They'd been scavenging partners for years before she died.

He'd also given an exception to Kristin's daughter because he didn't want to lose both Tharin and Kristin. Next to her and Veridian, Mack and Tharin were the best scavenging team he had. The news about another child was a concern though. Too many mouths and not enough income would be a problem. It didn't help that she and Veridian had left to sign up with a trading camp. Everyone in Leo's camp had to be struggling, even with the funds she filtered back to them.

"As if we don't have enough problems around here," Leo announced with a scowl. Yep. The camp leader definitely wasn't pleased with the news. He turned to regard Kayla with his sharp eyes. "Are you here for a visit or to work? I'm not running a damn halfway house."

She inclined her head. "I'll pull my weight while I'm here."

"You're on tomorrow then. You can run with these two since Veridian's not here. They've been off today and wasting my time. Mack, take her bag and throw it on a bunk. Tharin, go check on your woman and see if you can manage to keep your dick in your pants. I need a word with Kayla."

Mack picked up her bag from the floor with a wink. "Come find me when you're done, girl."

She nodded at him and the two men headed out of the narrow hallway. When they were gone, Leo crossed his arms and eyed her up and down. "I'm not going to ask why you came back. It's none of my business unless you want to tell me. But I need to know if your presence is going to jeopardize our trading relationships."

Kayla paused, momentarily surprised at the realization Leo didn't know about Carl, Alec, or anything else having to do with OmniLab. Had she really been that disconnected from her former camp? It was a relief in a weird way. For the first time in a long time, she could forget about energy channeling and just be herself again.

She shook her head. "It won't be an issue, Leo. If it becomes a problem, you have my word I'll leave."

"Fair enough."

He hesitated for a moment and then clapped her shoulder. For Leo, the small display of affection was the equivalent of Mack's welcoming hug. "Go get settled in."

She nodded, not trusting herself to speak, and turned away to hang up her jacket. Once the sound of his retreating footsteps had faded, she turned back around. The movement jostled Alec's necklace. Her hand flew up to touch the pendant. Thankfully, it had been hidden by her jacket when she arrived. She glanced around to make sure no was looking and then slipped off the necklace, stuffing it in her pocket.

Kayla headed toward the common room to find Mack, who was lounging on the decrepit couch. He gave her a chin lift when she entered. A few other people stopped what they were doing and called out greetings before turning back to their conversations. Mack chuckled and patted the spot next to him before draping his arm across the back of the couch.

"I heard you took out Ramiro's boy, Vex?"

"Yeah," she said with a sigh and settled in next to him. It still irked her that Ramiro was running around somewhere though. OmniLab blacklisted him, but he disappeared before they could take him into custody.

Mack nodded in approval. "Good girl. You know anything about this new trader they've got?"

"His name's Rand. He's solid. A lot like Carl."

"He any good at tracking?"

Kayla shrugged. "Your guess is as good as mine. He's smart, but he's still green. Carl's been showing him the ropes though."

"Too bad." Mack drummed his fingers on the edge of the couch. "We were thinking about heading back to his district when we relocate. Maybe we'll stick to the perimeter instead or head to Henkel's district."

"Not a bad idea." It was strange to think of them moving without her and Veridian. "Where have you guys been scavenging? I haven't heard about you in Carl's district lately. It's been pretty quiet."

Mack chuckled. "We've managed to snag a new temporary gig. Leo's been brokering with these new guys. They've been kicking some sweet equipment our way. Some of this shit is better than anything I've seen from OmniLab."

Kayla's entire body tensed, and she shifted to face him.

"What the hell are you talking about? Who's he dealing with?"

Mack stretched and propped his feet up on a nearby crate. "Some guys named Sergei and Lars. They've been coming here for the past couple of weeks. They paid Leo with food and some equipment to have us map the districts. They don't seem to be interested in the stuff in the ruins, just the topography and camp locations."

Kayla frowned. "You sure they aren't from OmniLab?"

"Hell no. The one guy, Sergei, has some sort of weird accent. I don't know where they're from, but they're definitely not Omnis. Last time they were here, they wanted us to finish mapping out Ramir— er, Rand's district for them. I'm guessing they'll want us to hit one of the other districts next. We'll probably do that tomorrow."

"Wait," Kayla interrupted. "So you guys aren't going into the ruins tomorrow? You're running mapping lines for these guys?"

"It keeps us in business, girl," Mack said with a chuckle and flicked her hair off her shoulder. "You know how this shit works. If they don't show up today, though, we'll hit the ruins."

Kayla wondered if there was a connection between these individuals and the surveillance aircrafts they'd seen on the radar. If that were the case, why were they using ruin rats to map the districts when they had such sophisticated equipment? She bit her lip and considered the possibilities. Unfortunately, she wasn't sure if voicing her concerns to Leo would do any good.

Kayla sighed and studied Mack. He was a few years older than her and had joined their camp when she'd been a teenager. He'd given her a hard time about scavenging when she was younger, but after he realized she wasn't a pushover, he'd taken her under his wing and shown her the ropes. Mack was a big guy who had a reputation for intimidating most people when he had the inclination. Although the majority of people in the camp gave him a wide berth, he had a soft spot for her. It was probably the reason Leo had paired her with his team tomorrow.

"What time are we going?"

"They should be stopping by later today to pick up the images. Depending on where they want us, we may need to head out early."

She nodded, and they lapsed into silence, each lost in their own thoughts. After several minutes, Mack leaned back and laced his fingers behind his head.

"So you gonna tell me why you're back?"

No. Not a chance. Instead, she opted for misdirection and batted her eyes at him. "Well, after pining for you for the past month, I gave into my urges and came running back. I just couldn't bear the thought of being separated from you for a moment longer."

"Damn, babe," Mack snorted. "You're getting to be scary-good at that. You could have just told me to mind my own damn business instead of breaking my heart."

Kayla smirked. "Fine. Mind your own damn business."

Mack eyed her up and down. She stiffened at the scrutiny and then forced herself to relax. His sharp eyes always saw too much. "If I had to guess, I'd say the trader put the moves on you. I'm just not sure if you moved back or broke his nose."

She stood. This was not a conversation she was going to have with Mack. Not now. Probably not ever. "Nice try, play-boy. You gonna show me this new equipment of yours or just brag about it? I understand if you don't have the goods to back up your story."

He raised an eyebrow and drawled, "Oh, I've definitely got the goods, darlin'. You just haven't had the privilege of enjoying them. But if you're talking about the new gear we picked up, sure. I can show that to you instead."

Kayla scowled and flicked him off. He laughed as he stood. "Glad you've still got your edge."

He gestured for her to follow him back into the tech room. The camp was relatively clean, but most of the equipment was run-down or falling apart. More than a few pieces were only operating by utilizing a combination of creative engineering and sheer luck. She found herself wondering once again if building another tower was a real possibility. Even if it was, she wasn't sure if the ruin rats would give up their nomadic lives for a chance to live somewhere permanent. Their distrust of OmniLab was so deeply ingrained they might reject it outright and claim it was an attempt to control them. It would have been her initial reaction too.

As they entered the tech room, Kayla noticed one of the computer terminals was offline. It had been having problems before she left. "It crashed again?"

"Yeah," Mack replied as he headed over to one of the boxes in the corner. "Kristin has been trying to get it back up and running without any luck. She got pulled off that to work on the photovoltaic system though. Seems like the whole place is going to shit."

"I'll take a look later," she offered and went over to the box. Mack pulled out an elongated instrument that looked similar to the image mappers she used at Carl's camp and handed it to her.

"It attaches directly to our bikes and records the topography on the surface. It also scans about a hundred yards underground. It's got some sort of echo system in place to pick up readings."

"Echo system?" She turned it over to assess the design. It would be interesting to take it apart to see how it worked.

Mack nodded. "So they said. They've given us some other

upgrades for scavenging too. We've gotten a couple of stability monitors and communication devices. We had to make some adjustments on the comm devices since they were designed for another language, but they're slick."

Kayla jerked her head up. "What language?"

Before he could answer, Leo strolled into the tech room, swearing and cursing up a storm. "Dammit, Kayla! You've been here for less than an hour and I'm already getting calls from Carl. Check your damn commlink. I'm not a fucking messenger."

Kayla blanched. "You told him I was here?"

"Who the hell do you think I am?" Leo demanded, clearly affronted by her question. "Of course I didn't tell that trader bastard anything. I told him what goes on in my camp is my business. He said if you turned up here to let you know he's looking for you. Some urgent bullshit or some such thing. Like I give a rat's ass what's got his panties in a knot."

"Thanks, Leo," she muttered and turned back to the equipment.

There was a heavy pause. Kayla lifted her head to find Leo and Mack exchanging looks. Leo turned back, pinning her with his gaze. "What? No smartass comment? No ranting and raving about a trader being up in your business? And you thank me? What the hell happened over there, girl?"

Mack raised an eyebrow and leaned against the wall, waiting for her response. Kayla frowned and turned back to the box to replace the image mapper. She needed to be more careful. Mack was wrong. She *was* losing her edge. Living in-between Carl's camp and the towers had changed her. It just hadn't been obvious how much until now.

She turned around to face Leo and crossed her arms over her chest. "Back off, Leo. My reasons are none of your damn business. If you have a problem with me being here and want to lose out on the credits I can bring in, fine. Say the word and I'll take off. I don't need your shit."

Leo was quiet for a moment, studying and considering her. Then, he nodded. "You're staying. I'll handle the trader."

Kayla bit back a sigh of relief. *One hurdle overcome.* She put her hands on her hips. "If you're done interrogating me, I want to know about these guys you're dealing with now."

Leo glanced at Mack, and the scavenger shrugged. "Yeah, I told her. If she's running with us tomorrow, she needs to know."

The older man harrumphed. "Fine. They showed up a couple of weeks ago and hired us to do some surveillance of the districts. The pay is fair and the work isn't dangerous, so we came to an agreement. I was planning on picking up and taking off last week for a new camp location, but I decided to wait until our business with them is done."

Now she was getting somewhere. "Do you know where these guys are from?"

Leo scowled. "I don't give a rat's ass if these guys are from the moon. They aren't paying us to ask questions. Just run the districts and turn over the results."

Of course he'd be narrow-minded enough not to ask questions. Idiot. She needed to warn him though. "Leo, before I left, Carl and Rand's districts were picking up air surveillance that wasn't from OmniLab. Are these guys connected?"

Leo waved off her words. "Not my problem. That's Omni shit to deal with. As long as we keep getting paid, I don't care."

Kayla clenched her fists in frustration, trying to resist the urge to smack some sense into him. She should have known he'd turn a blind eye to everything. "Fine. Stick your head in the sand and let your ass get a sunburn."

Leo's mouth twitched in a smile. "That's my girl. Now, check your damn commlink so I don't have to listen to more trader crap. Mack, go set Kayla's bike up for our tracking frequencies. Those damn Omnis have probably screwed up all her settings."

Mack nodded and picked up a toolkit sitting in the corner. They left the room, and Kayla grudgingly pulled out her commlink. She had several new messages from Carl, Alec, and Veridian. With a sigh, she opened Veridian's message. She wasn't ready to deal with either of the other two men in her life.

Carl had apparently contacted Veridian looking for her. They were all worried and wanted to make sure she was safe. Kayla frowned and typed in a short message letting Veridian know she was fine. She made it clear she had no intention of coming back anytime soon and wished him the best with Jinx. Figuring Veridian would let Carl know her reply, she closed the commlink without reading any of the other messages.

Needing to keep busy, Kayla walked over to the broken computer terminal and started taking it apart. The familiar sounds of the camp drifted into the room and had a calming effect on her. She missed Veridian's comforting presence, but either way, it was nice to be back in Leo's camp.

An hour later, Kayla had finished working on the computer and managed to get it back up and running. It was going to need to have a few components replaced soon, but there wasn't much she could do about it at the moment. She adjusted the terminal back into position before heading out to the common room.

Mack was sitting on the couch while Tharin and Kristin sat nearby. Kristin's two-year-old daughter, Marie, was playing on the floor. Her daughter was almost a tiny replica of her mother with curly chestnut hair and light-brown eyes. She chattered to herself while she played with some blocks someone had carved for her.

Kristin's face lit up at the sight of Kayla. "Welcome back.

I would have found you earlier, but Leo had me working on the solar system out back."

"No problem, Kris. It's good to see you again."

Kayla knelt on the floor and offered a little finger wave to Marie. The little girl's eyes lit up with recognition and she waddled over to Kayla. Tiny arms wrapped around her neck and Kayla gave Marie a hug. "Hey, sweetie. Did you get a new toy?"

Marie nodded and stuck her fingers in her mouth. Kayla kissed the top of her head and put her back on the ground. The little girl immediately went back to playing.

"I've missed her," Kayla admitted with a sigh and gestured to Kristin's slightly rounded belly. "Tharin mentioned you've got another one cooking?"

Kristin rolled her eyes and half-heartedly punched Tharin's arm. "Yeah. One wasn't enough apparently."

Kayla smiled, but she could tell Kristin was worried. Not only was her continued status in the camp a concern, it was no secret her pregnancy with Marie had been difficult. Hopefully, this one would be easier. Kayla sat on the couch next to Mack, and Kristin said, "We have about an hour before today's crew comes rolling in. We were going to watch one of those old pre-war vids Veridian sent over from OmniLab. You wanna join us?"

Kayla nodded and leaned back against the couch while Tharin programmed the computer terminal to run the program. As the movie started, she noticed Kristin snuggling up against Tharin. She felt a pang of sadness at Carl's absence but forced herself to put it out of her mind and focus on the screen.

The events of the day finally caught up with her, and she succumbed to her exhaustion. It was some time later before a hand gently brushed her hair away from her face. A husky voice murmured something in her ear, but she ignored it and snuggled deeper into the warmth wrapped around her.

The voice chuckled. "The crew just got back, darlin'. You gonna sleep all day?"

She murmured Carl's name and hooked her leg over his. One of her hands slipped under his shirt to touch warm skin. He always talked too much.

"Well, that answers that question. Guess you didn't break his nose."

Kayla opened her eyes and looked up into Mack's amused face. She was sprawled on top of him in a rather compromising position. At least Tharin and Kristin had disappeared so they weren't witnessing her blunder. She cursed and quickly sat up, pulling her hand away. Mack watched as she disentangled herself and then leaned back against the couch, putting his hands behind his head.

"I think you need to tell me what happened with that trader."

Kayla grumbled. "Have you always been this nosy?"

"No doubt," he replied, clearly enjoying himself. "You just had Veridian as a buffer before, so spill it. Why are you saying the trader's name in your sleep and climbing all over me? Not that I particularly minded that last part."

Kayla sighed and rubbed her face. There was no point in lying, not after what just happened. "We got into an argument and I left. There's no big mystery."

"What did you argue about?"

She hesitated. Although she'd been close to Mack, Veridian was the one she usually confided in. "He told me we didn't belong together," she said quietly and looked away. "And there was this other girl from the towers ... It just got complicated ..." Her voice trailed off. She couldn't bring herself to tell him about the whole situation with Alec and the reporter.

Mack nodded as though that cleared up his suspicions. "Uh huh. Those traders are all alike. I'm not sure why you'd get involved with one of them in the first place. You're smarter than that, babe. A real man wouldn't play those kinds of games with you."

Kayla shook her head. "It wasn't like that, Mack."

He was quiet for a long moment and then said, "Pretz was from a trader camp." She flinched at his words, but he ignored it and continued, "Now you've gone and gotten tangled up with a trader."

The direction of his words was clear, and she scowled, but he wasn't finished yet.

"Seems to me you need to start rethinking your choices. Getting involved with traders and their camps never ends well. If you don't want to shit where you eat, fine. There are plenty of other ruin rat camps around. But you should think about sticking with your own kind."

She let out a harsh laugh. If he only knew the truth. She didn't know who her own kind were anymore. Did she belong here? In Carl's camp? Or back in the towers with Alec? Dropping her head into her hands, Kayla rubbed her temples, trying to ward off the impending headache.

"Aw, shit. Come on. Get up and come with me."

She looked up to see Mack frowning at her. He held out a hand and pulled Kayla to her feet.

"You look like you're about to turn on the waterworks any minute. Personally, I'd like to kick the bastard's ass for you. But since he's not here at the moment, you've got two options. You can either come try your hand at wrestling me to get out your frustrations, or I'm taking you down into the ruins to let you screw over the trader by stealing under his nose. Take your pick. Although, if you try to take me on, you'll end up crying anyway. You don't have a chance in hell at beating me."

Kayla snorted, but his words had their desired effect. "I took you down once, I can do it again."

"You're welcome to try," he challenged and smacked her butt. "Go get changed and I'll meet you in the workroom."

Kayla jumped at the contact and cursed him under her breath. He just chuckled and jerked his head toward the door. She made a face at his back before heading toward the crew quarters. As she walked into the room with the bunks, Kayla noticed Mack had tossed her bag on the bed next to his.

She pulled on a tank top and a pair of shorts and headed back down the hall toward the workroom. Mack had cleared the area and looked up as she entered, raising an eyebrow at her attire. "You're almost too damn sexy to toss around."

She put her hands on her hips. "You're not too big to hit the floor."

Mack grinned and pulled off his shirt. He tossed it aside, and Kayla noticed a new tattoo on his chest. She leaned in closer to get a better look. It was in the shape of some sort of bird in flight. "Kris gave you some new ink?"

He rubbed his hand over the tattoo as though he'd forgotten it was there. A muscle in his neck worked, and he nodded. "Yeah. A couple weeks ago. Speaking of which, I'm still waiting for you to let me give you a tattoo."

Kayla crossed her arms. "You're not tattooing your hand-print on my ass."

"I can be flexible. We can put it somewhere else." His eyes roamed over her body as though he were considering his options

"Why don't you come a little closer and try saying that to me?"

With a grin, he lunged for her, but she quickly side-stepped him. Bouncing on her toes as the adrenaline rush kicked in, she nodded and gestured at him. "Okay, this is gonna be fun. Bring it on, big boy."

CHAPTER TEN

KAYLA GRABBED one of the hydrating packs from Tharin and took a long drink. She was hot and sweaty, but true to his word, the workout with Mack had left her feeling much better. She wiped her brow and smiled up at him. Mack drank his own pack down and wiped his mouth with the back of his hand.

"For a little thing, you've got some damn nice moves."

She grinned and bumped him with her shoulder. "You're not so bad yourself, big man."

Tharin shook his head and leaned against the wall. "I'm tired and all I did was just watch you two."

Leo interrupted their teasing by poking his head through the door. The camp leader quickly took in their appearance and scowled. "Lars and Sergei are about five minutes out. Quit jerking around and get to the entrance if you want in on this."

Mack nodded and grabbed his shirt. After he pulled it over his head, Kayla asked, "Are those the guys you were telling me about?"

"Yep," he replied. "You coming?"

"Hell yeah. I wanna meet them."

Leo frowned and warned, "No pissing them off, Kayla. These guys are our current meal ticket."

She fluttered her eyes innocently. "Me?"

"You see any other mouthy shrew around?" Leo retorted and headed out of the room. Mack grabbed another hydrating pack from the rationed supply and drank it as he headed to the entrance with Tharin. Kayla followed them.

A few minutes later, two men appeared in the entrance area. Kayla stood back and took the opportunity to study them as they pulled off their helmets. The first man was tall and solidly built with fair skin and nearly white-blond hair pulled back and tied at the nape of his neck. The other man was slightly less fair and had short, dark-blond hair and blue eyes. He was almost the same height as the first man but not as heavily muscled. The moment the second man glimpsed Kayla, he paused and did a double take. Then, his expression shuttered, and he turned back toward Leo. Kayla cocked her head, curious about the strange behavior. He seemed familiar, but she couldn't place him.

"Sergei and Lars," Leo greeted each of them respectively. "Welcome back."

Tharin took their helmets and hung them up. Sergei spoke with a strange accent as he said, "We are pleased to return."

"Let's talk in my office." Leo led them down the hall toward his office. Lars took the offered seat while Sergei remained standing. Kayla wandered over to Leo's desk and sat on the edge of it. Mack took a somewhat protective stance next to her while Tharin leaned against the wall.

"You remember Mack and Tharin from your last visit. This is Kayla, another one of our scavengers," Leo introduced them.

Lars didn't say a word and instead offered Kayla a brief

nod in greeting. A strange tingling sensation filled the surrounding air, and she absently rubbed her arms at the sudden chill. Kayla looked into the newcomer's eyes and had a strange sense of déjà vu. Something about this stranger reminded her vaguely of Alec. His eyes were almost the same brilliant blue, and they shone with intelligence. But unlike Alec, his had a dangerous glint.

Sergei stepped forward, eyes wandering over her figure, and gave her a charming smile. "Where have you been hiding this beauty, Leo?"

"She's been working at a different camp for the past few weeks and just got back this morning."

Kayla studied the fair man. "You have an interesting accent. Where are you from?"

"Our home is far away," Sergei replied with a vague wave. He leaned close to her. "But I could be persuaded to tell you more about it. Perhaps after our business is concluded?"

Kayla looked up into his steely-gray eyes. She wasn't particularly interested in flirting with him, but it would be foolish to pass up the opportunity to find out more about these guys. She offered him a smile. "Sure, I don't see why not."

Sergei gave her another appraising look before turning back to Leo and focusing on business. "You have information for us?"

Leo reached into a drawer to pull out a small data cube. "Got it right here. We finished mapping the district yesterday."

Lars stood up to accept it and then connected it to a tablet computer. A few moments later, he nodded. "Very good. The information appears complete. Sergei, the crew can start bringing in the supplies."

Kayla's eyes widened in surprise. Unlike Sergei, Lars spoke clearly without any trace of an accent. Sergei pulled out an unusual-looking commlink device and in a strange language began issuing instructions. He snapped the unit shut before turning back to Lars. "They go to unload equipment now."

Leo motioned for Tharin to go assist them. "Put everything in the workroom for now. We'll sort it later."

When Tharin left, Lars said, "We've been impressed with your work so far. If you're interested, we'd like to have another district mapped. Unfortunately, time is something of the essence. This needs to be completed within the next couple days."

Leo's eyes lit up. "Which district would that be?"

"The one directly to the east of this camp."

Kayla frowned uneasily. They were talking about mapping Carl's district. Before she could comment, Leo said, "We can probably get it done in about four days."

Lars shook his head. "It needs to be completed before then."

"That's going to be difficult. Not only is it one of the larger districts, but that trader's got some pretty hefty security around his camp. The outlying areas could be done sooner, but it's going to be damn near impossible to get close to his camp in that timeframe."

Mack piped up and suggested, "If Kayla makes the run with us, we can get it done in closer to two days. She knows the layout, routines, and can work through any security. We can pull Johnny in, too, if necessary."

Kayla glared at Mack, not appreciating being volunteered for duty when she didn't know the game or the players. She especially didn't like the idea of doing anything that put Carl's camp in jeopardy.

Lars studied Kayla. "How well do you know the camp?"

She shrugged, not willing to divulge too much information. "I'm familiar with it."

"We're prepared to compensate you generously for timely results."

"I might be interested," Kayla replied and leaned back on the desk. *Time to dangle the metaphorical carrot and see if they want to take a bite.* "But I'd like to know why you guys are interested in mapping these districts."

Lars's expression hardened. "Our reasons are our own. We're willing to compensate you for your efforts. That should be enough."

"Kayla," Leo warned.

Sergei asked Lars a question in the strange language, and Lars nodded in response. Sergei flashed a smile and took a step toward Kayla. His voice was warm as he said, "We are new here. You cannot blame us for wanting to learn more about this fascinating place and people."

Kayla glanced back and forth between the strangers with suspicion, wondering what Sergei had asked him. She was still uncomfortable under Lars's gaze, but Sergei seemed manageable. He was obviously interested in her, and it might be possible to use that to her advantage.

"Mapping areas seems a little forward when you're getting to know someone, don't you think?" she asked with a teasing smile. "Saying hello is usually where people first start."

Sergei chuckled, and his eyes danced with amusement. He lifted her hand, bowing over it, and gently kissed the top of it. "Hello, Kayla." Without taking his eyes off her, he added, "I will take this charming woman to see equipment while you finish here."

"Very well," Lars replied, but Kayla could feel the weight of his gaze on them as Sergei led her out into the hall. They headed back toward the workroom where Tharin and another unfamiliar man were putting boxes on the floor. Sergei spoke to the other man in his language. The man offered him a strange salute before heading out of the room.

"What language is that?" Kayla asked curiously, determined to find out as much about him as possible.

Sergei gave her a slow smile. "Russian. My people speak many languages though."

"Interesting. Most people around here only speak English."

"Perhaps I could teach you," he mused. "I would enjoy hearing my language from your lips."

Wow, this guy is pretty cocky. Figuring she'd get more information if she played along, she gave him an encouraging smile. "I wouldn't mind."

Tharin raised an eyebrow at Kayla. "Playing with the foreigners, eh?"

Kayla grinned and gave a half-hearted shrug. "We're just getting to know each other, Tharin."

Sergei leaned close to her. "I would enjoy getting to know you much better, *Milaya*. Perhaps I will bring over a bottle of vodka to share with you?"

"Sure. I've never tried that before."

He nodded, pleased by her answer. "I will see that it happens."

Kayla went over to one of the boxes on the floor. Keeping her voice casual, she asked, "So you're planning on staying around here for a while?"

"Mmhmm," he murmured. "For now, yes."

"Good to know," Kayla said and bent over to open the box, unable to hide her excitement at the sight of the equipment. It was definitely not manufactured by OmniLab. There were several communication devices, computer terminals, spare parts, and other miscellaneous pieces of equipment which seemed to be extremely well designed. "Holy shit! Did you check this out, Tharin?"

He snorted. "I've been too busy bringing all the shit in here."

She started digging through the box, eager to investigate each of the new devices. A strange-looking square piece of equipment caught her eye. Pulling it out, she tried to decide if it could be some sort of imaging device. "Okay, I'm impressed. You've got some neat little gizmos in here."

Kayla flipped over the unit and ran her hand along the back side of it. Sergei bent down next to her and made a point to brush his fingers down her arm before opening the access panel to reveal the display. "If there is some equipment you would like to get your hands on, we could come to our own arrangement."

She forced herself to keep her expression neutral. Kayla wasn't a fan of being touched by someone she didn't know, but it would be foolish to distance herself prematurely. There was too much she didn't know about these strangers. "Is that so?"

"Everything is negotiable."

"I'll keep that in mind." Kayla glanced down at the piece of equipment in her hands. "So is this an imaging device? It looks similar to others I've seen, except it's a little big."

"Yes, but not your typical imaging device. I will show you."

Sergei connected the unit to his commlink. "It detects specific compounds through walls, floors, solids, or liquids."

Kayla leaned over to study his commlink, intrigued to learn anything she could about new technology. The user interface was fairly simplistic but well designed. "Can it scan for multiple compounds or just one at a time?"

"One for now. We are working on improving design."

Fascinated by the implications of such a device, she looked up at Sergei. "Mind if I take a look?"

"Not at all." He handed over the unit and watched with open curiosity as she pulled up the source code for the device. She began scanning through it to familiarize herself with the programming.

Leo, Lars, and Mack finished with their business and came into the room. Leo started swearing at the sight of Kayla looking through the code. "Mack, Tharin, check the inventory before she starts taking shit apart and rebuilding it."

Mack and Tharin nodded and went over to the open box. Leo looked at the piece of equipment Kayla was using and scowled. "What are you doing with that?"

Without looking up from the screen, Kayla replied, "It's a compound scanner, but it's currently configured to search and identify only one compound at a time."

Sergei turned to Leo. "We will have improved design within weeks. Our experts work on modifying code to scan for multiple compounds."

Mack glanced up from inventorying the items and chuckled. "Twenty credits says she'll have it doing that within the hour."

"No bet," Tharin replied with a grin.

Kayla ignored them as she continued to study the screen on Sergei's communication unit. After several minutes, she glanced up. "I need another screen to compare the code. Tharin, would you mind setting up another terminal for me in here?"

He shook his head. "Sorry, Kayla. The other one's been broken for two weeks and we haven't configured these yet."

"I fixed it before the movie," she replied absently and went back to studying the screen.

Tharin snickered. "I should have known. I'll be right back."

He returned a few minutes later and hooked up the terminal for her. Kayla connected it to the commlink and scanned through the code in more detail. When she finally found what she was looking for, she grinned. With a few quick commands, she modified the code so additional requests could be added and then linked them to the existing databases.

"Okay, Sergei," Kayla said to the man next to her, "grab the unit and try running a scan for multiple compounds."

Sergei looked skeptical but picked up the unit. He aimed it toward the wall and used his commlink to enter several different common compounds. The lights on the device flashed, and a moment later, the results displayed on the screen of his communication device.

"Remarkable," Sergei murmured, clearly impressed. "Our engineers spend many weeks to work out problem you solve in thirty minutes."

"It just needed a woman's touch," she said sweetly.

Lars walked over to Sergei's commlink and glanced down at the display. He raised an eyebrow and said to Kayla, "You're quite talented. Where did you learn to do this?"

Mack chuckled. "She's been doing that shit since she was a kid."

"Beautiful, intelligent, and skilled," Sergei observed admiringly and closed the commlink. "I cannot help but wonder what other talents you possess."

"I've got a few others. But if you'll excuse me, boys, I think it's time for me to head to the showers. I'll see you around."

Kayla smiled to herself as she headed out of the room, confident they'd be giving her an opportunity to find out more about them. She glanced back to find Leo shaking his head in exasperation while Sergei and Lars both stared after her with fascinated curiosity. Yep. She'd dangled the carrot beautifully.

CHAPTER ELEVEN

KAYLA CLIMBED out of the shower and sighed, already missing the showers at the towers and even Carl's camp. She dried herself off and pulled on another pair of shorts and tank top before brushing out her dark hair. On her way out of the bathroom, she grabbed her dirty clothes and dumped them into the sanitation machine.

Mack was waiting for her in the hallway, leaning against the wall. He looked her up and down. "Not bad, but there's something to be said for the hot and sweaty look too."

She laughed. "The shower's all yours, if that's what you were waiting for. I know you prefer that one over the others. It's the only one with semi-decent water pressure."

He winked at her. "It also happens to be the only one that two people can fit into. Let me know if you'd like to try it sometime."

Kayla raised an eyebrow. "With that suck-ass water pressure? There's no way in hell I'd share the dribble that comes out of there. Wait your turn, bucko."

"A man can dream," he said with a drawn-out sigh. Then, his expression turned serious. "By the way, Lars and Sergei just left. I got the impression they'll be back soon though. It seems like our two new friends are pretty intrigued after your little display back there. Leo's a little concerned about their interest."

"You know me, Mack. I can handle myself."

He nodded, not disputing her claim. "No doubt, but the last time you pulled something like that, we ended up having to leave Ramiro's district. Just a warning, darlin'. Watch yourself with these two. Something about them rubs me the wrong way and not because they look like they want to take a bite out of you."

Kayla looked up at Mack and saw real concern on his face. It surprised and touched her at the same time. She gave him a reassuring smile and stood on her toes to kiss his cheek. "Thanks for looking after me, Mack. I've missed you."

"Same goes, babe. I'm going to hit the showers. If you feel like riding with us tomorrow, let me know. I'll rig your bike with one of the scanners."

"Maybe," she replied neutrally. The thought of mapping Carl's district still didn't sit right with her, but it might be the only way to find out what these guys were looking for. "I'm going to take a look at the scanners first. I want to see what types of readings they're capable of generating."

"They're still in the workroom. I'm going to hook them up a bit later. Do what you want with them until then."

Kayla nodded and headed to the workroom. Walking over to the desk, she picked up the first elongated device and studied it. On the surface, it appeared to be a well-designed unit, but it was easy to cover up a hunk of junk with a polished exterior. Besides, it was always possible to make improvements.

Hooking it up to the computer monitor, she worked through the code to determine the scope of the device. It didn't appear to be anything special or hazardous. It analyzed the ground surface, creating a map of the area and noting abnormalities in the collected topographical data.

With a sigh, Kayla turned her attention to modifying the device. She might as well try to cut down on their time out in the field. It only took a few minor tweaks to expand the mapping radius to almost double the distance without compromising the integrity of the results. Satisfied the new configuration would work, she disengaged the first unit and moved on to the next.

It took her over an hour to reconfigure all four of the devices. She left them on the desk for Mack to install in the morning. For now, she'd play along with these foreigners until she could find out more about them. If necessary, she could always corrupt the data before turning it over to them.

Drumming her fingers thoughtfully on the desk, she pulled out her commlink. Based on what Sergei had told her, Kayla guessed their facility was located somewhere near pre-war Russia. She wasn't ready to talk to Alec or Carl, so she called the only other person who could possibly help her.

When his image appeared on the screen, she smiled. "Hey, Rand! How's it going?"

The newest trader and Carl's longtime friend looked surprised to hear from her. She couldn't really blame him. They'd only talked a handful of times since they first met in the towers. Carl was the one who usually interacted with him since they both frequently had to discuss trader business.

"Kayla! It's been a while. You're looking well."

"Thanks," she replied. "Hey, listen, I've got a favor to ask. I'm a little out of touch with OmniLab at the moment, but I was wondering if you might have some information or could run a quick check through OmniLab records for me."

Rand's brow furrowed. "Out of touch with OmniLab? Is everything all right? Is Carl with you?"

"Everything's fine," she promised, not willing to elaborate

on the details. "I just need some information, and I really don't want to ask Alec or Carl about it right now. It's complicated."

Rand frowned. "I see. What sort of information?"

"I know you're more knowledgeable about pre-war living environments and cultures, but I need some information about another facility. Do you know if a group calling themselves the 'Coalition' originated in an area near pre-war Russia?"

"Just a moment," he said and turned away from the screen. A moment later, he nodded. "Yes. It appears their original facility was located in Russia, somewhere in the vicinity of a city called Egvekinot. I'll send the information to your commlink."

"Fantastic. Thanks."

Before she could disconnect, Rand said, "Kayla, wait. What's going on? I heard there was more air surveillance recorded in Warig's district earlier today. Director Borshin said this group still hasn't responded to our repeated attempts at contacting them. OmniLab has begun initiating procedures to disable or shoot down any of their aircrafts sighted within the districts. Have you discovered something about them?"

Kayla paused for a moment and shook her head. Although he had a right to know, she wanted to make sure her suspicions were accurate first. "I don't know yet. I might have found a connection. I'm trying to figure it out right now. I'll let you know if I find out anything else. Thanks again."

"No problem. Take care of yourself."

She ended the connection. All indications pointed to these guys being from the Coalition. What didn't make sense was why they were mapping the district and ignoring communication attempts from the towers. Her commlink beeped a moment later, and she scanned through the data Rand sent over.

The information on the facility was limited and mostly detailed their origins. It looked to be a militant group with different pre-war governments acting as their founders and leaders. There were a few references to their advanced technology, but the details about their culture and agenda was limited. There were a few other notes listing other facilities they had absorbed, but there was no other information about these groups once the Coalition had taken control.

Kayla frowned, surprised at the lack of information OmniLab had obtained about the group. With a sigh, she started to close her commlink. A new message from Veridian caught her eye, and she read through it.

Kayla,

I'm glad you're safe, but we're all worried about you. Carl told me what happened. I think you need to give him a chance to talk to you. Alec's been calling nonstop to find out if you've returned, and I think he's about ready to send out some teams from OmniLab to hunt you down.

Either way, I want to see you face to face. Say the word and I'll come to you. We've been through too much together for you to disappear on me.

V.

Feeling guilty, Kayla closed the commlink without replying. She wasn't sure how to handle the situation and needed more time to think. She'd hoped coming back here would give her time to figure things out. Instead, there were just more mysteries. Stretching her tired muscles, she headed down the hallway toward the crew's quarters.

It was comforting to be back at Leo's camp with all its familiarity. It was nice to just be herself again, without having to worry about people treating her differently because she was part of the Inner Circle. She'd always felt different on some level, but at least no one was trying to get into her head or dump energy on her while she was back in the ruin rat camp.

Several people were already sleeping when she entered the crew's quarters. Keeping her footsteps quiet, she tiptoed over to the bed next to Mack. Crawling onto the hard surface, she laid down and stared up at the ceiling. With nothing left to distract her, Kayla found herself once again replaying the scene from the restaurant. She desperately missed Carl, but his words and the look on his face had hurt deeply. Her guilt at what had happened with Alec in his office made the situation even worse. She'd made a mess of the entire thing. Kayla rolled over, buried her head in the small pillow, and tried to blink back the threatening tears.

"What's the matter, darlin'?" Mack whispered.

Kayla lifted her head to find Mack propped up on his elbow watching her. She shook her head and looked away. He sighed. "Aw, shit. That trader screwed you up pretty good, didn't he?"

She didn't reply. Mack pulled Kayla's bed closer and gestured for her to scoot over. With a sniff, she crawled over into Mack's bunk. He laid back down and put his arm around her. Keeping his voice low so as not to wake anyone up, he said, "Go ahead and cry, if that's what you need to do, darlin'. I'd like to kick the bastard's ass, personally. But since he's not handy, I'll just offer you a shoulder instead."

Kayla buried her head against his chest, and the tears she'd been holding back began to fall. Mack held her close, stroking her hair and whispering soothing words. It was a long time before she was finally able to drift off into a restless sleep.

———

ALEC RUBBED his temples and tried to keep his temper in check. Carl stood across from him, his stance rigid and appearing equally perturbed. Ever since Kayla had run off on them earlier, things had deteriorated and they'd both lost their tempers. Alec should have known pushing her into that situation in the café would backfire; her emotions and reactions were too volatile.

It would be convenient to blame Carl for the entire thing, but Alec knew he was just as much at fault. That was the point that grated on him the most. He leaned back in his chair to better study Kayla's lover. "You're sure she's back at her former camp?"

"Yes. She ditched the standard tracking device on her speeder, but I never told her about the secondary one I installed. She's there now, but Leo won't confirm or deny it. Veridian hasn't been able to get a straight answer, either, except to say she's safe."

Alec pushed away from his desk. Guessing wasn't sufficient. Anything could happen to her out there. With these unknown threats hovering over them, he couldn't afford to take any chances. The bond between them was still fragile. He'd hoped that once Kayla arrived at the towers, she would have been curious enough to embrace their bond ... and him.

He'd seen signs, and it had given him hope. The small looks, emotions he'd picked up through their bond, and even the way she tried to comfort him with her energy had indicated she was coming around. Alec just needed more time with her. Kayla was like a budding flower that just needed to be drawn out into the sunlight.

Alec moved to stand near the window and looked out into the darkness. If he closed his eyes, he could still feel the softness of her skin under his fingers and the taste of her energy on his lips. Without a doubt, she was exquisite. It was a constant battle to resist his urges to keep her close. It was tempting to just take her away from everything else, including her beloved trader. But he recognized if he pushed too far and too fast like he had today, he could possibly lose her forever. He'd already come close. Patience had never been his strong suit, but now it was a thousand times worse with these threats looming over them.

He turned back to look at Carl. "She's not safe out there. We need to convince her to come back."

Carl's jaw clenched, and his eyes flashed with anger. "I'll be damned if I'm going to force her to come back here. Go ahead and threaten me or my family again, but it's not going to happen."

Brant stepped forward and held up his hand in an attempt to keep the peace. "I think we're all trying to do what's in Kayla's best interests. Carl, you've said yourself that some of the conditions in these surface camps are hazardous. We can't protect her there. If we can convince her to either come here or return to your camp, she'll be safer. But right now, there's no one looking out for her. She could be in danger if anyone from the Inner Circle finds out her location before we do."

Carl sighed. "I know. The conditions aren't ideal, but Kayla grew up in that camp. They'll do what they can to look after her. There's no way in hell Leo would allow any Omni to walk into his camp. I've only been there twice, and they made it clear I wasn't welcome. If you try to push her into something she's not willing to do, she'll do the opposite just to spite you. Veridian seems to think she just needs more time."

Alec was quiet for a long moment. He tried to reach out across their shared bond, but he was too far away to get a good sense of her. If they had fully cemented their bond and claimed each other on all levels, he'd be able to sense her from any distance. Instead, he just felt the familiar ache of her absence. Frustrated, he idly rubbed his chest as though trying to ward off the pain.

"You have twenty-four hours to convince her," Alec declared and turned back to the window again. Although he wanted her back in the towers, it was far more important to assure her safety than his own desires. "If she's not back here or in your camp within that time, I'll send a retrieval party to the surface camp to extract her."

"That would be a mistake," Carl warned. "She'll turn away from both of us."

Alec turned back to the dark-haired trader. He couldn't help but feel envious of the man's relationship with Kayla, but he forced himself to put it aside. It was obvious the trader cared for her and believed he was acting in her best interest. Those same traits were the reason Alec trusted Carl with Kayla's protection.

"You're right," Alec agreed. "She would never forgive us for such a move. I've spent the last several weeks learning how much she values her independence." He turned back to the window again, wishing there was another option. "However, I would rather have Kayla hate me for the rest of her life than risk living mine without her in it."

———

KAYLA WOKE up early the next morning to her commlink vibrating in her pocket. She rubbed her eyes, slipped out the communication device, and turned off its alarm. Most of the camp was still asleep, but Mack and Tharin's beds were empty. Johnny was awake and starting to get dressed, so she knew they hadn't left yet.

She reached down, grabbed her bag from under the bed, and pulled out a change of clothes. After getting dressed and using the lavatory, she headed into the workroom to find Mack and Tharin packing up equipment. They glanced up when she entered, and Mack waved her over. "Morning, babe.

We're just about ready to head out. Johnny get his sorry ass out of bed yet?"

"Yeah, he's up. You guys need any help?"

"Nah," Tharin replied and snapped his bag shut. "Mack mentioned you modified the devices last night. You joining us?"

Kayla nodded and shoved her hands in her back pockets. "Yeah. The modifications should cut down on the time. I plotted a course that should take the four of us only about five hours to complete the outlying areas. We'll be done before you know it."

"Sounds good." Mack hefted up his bag. "I'm going to take this out to the bikes. Tharin, tell Johnny to get his ass moving. I want to get this done."

Kayla followed Mack to the front entrance where they pulled on their UV-protective gear before stepping outside into the cool, morning air. The sun wasn't up yet and the stars still shone overhead. She loved this time of day when the promise of the morning loomed just below the horizon.

She walked over to the bikes and programmed each of them to follow different courses. They would need to split up to cover more ground, but she was confident each of them could outrun Carl's crew if necessary. She hoped it didn't come to that though.

Kayla frowned and wondered about Lars and Sergei again. Neither of them were particularly forthcoming with information, but she suspected Sergei would be more receptive to her inquiries. If she could hurry up and finish the mapping by this afternoon, she could try contacting Sergei and learn more about them.

Mack spoke over her headset, "You zoning out over there?"

"Nah, I was just programming the courses. I'm done now."

Johnny and Tharin approached the bikes as Kayla climbed on the back of hers. They fired up their engines and took off across the barren landscape, riding hard for the hour needed to reach the perimeter of Carl's district. Mack ordered a stop, and Kayla stretched after dismounting, taking the opportunity to walk around for a minute while Mack activated all of the mapping devices.

"Done," Mack announced once he finished activating them. "Let's roll."

Kayla nodded and climbed back on her bike. With a wave to her companions, she took off along the route she had plotted the night before. She drove down abandoned streets of the district and passed various sectors along the way. Abandoned buildings which had once stood proud were run down and withering. In some cases, they'd collapsed completely. She couldn't help but wonder what it had been like when the streets were thriving with life and activity.

Her view shifted without even realizing it and a child with long, golden hair ran into the middle of the street. The ghostly image startled her, and she instinctively swerved to avoid hitting it. The speeder jerked to the side, spinning out of control, and as it hit the ground, she flew off and rolled across the hard earth.

Pain shot through her shoulder at the impact. From her location on the ground, she stared up at the now brightly lit sky and cursed her luck. *Fucking hell.* She definitely jarred her shoulder during the fall. Kayla winced trying to sit up. She carefully tried to move her injured arm and a cry of pain escaped her. Mack's voice came over her headset. "You okay, Kayla?"

She grimaced, wondering how she'd ever live this down. "I took a tumble, and I think I dislocated my shoulder."

"Where are you?" he demanded.

Kayla reached into her pocket with her good hand and

pulled out her commlink. Even the slight movement was excruciating. She gritted her teeth to keep from crying out again and managed to send the coordinates to Mack. "I just sent you my location. I'm close to Sector Four."

"I'll be there in a few minutes."

Kayla carefully stood, trying not to jostle her injured arm, and made her way toward her speeder. Other than a few scrapes and some bruises, nothing else appeared to be broken. Unfortunately, her speeder was on its side. There was no way to pull it back upright without the use of both hands. With a sigh, she slumped down on the ground next to it and prepared to wait.

True to his word, Mack pulled up a short time later. He climbed off his bike and set up the UV guard attachment to shield them from the sun.

"Shit, Kayla," Mack muttered as he pulled off his helmet and helped to remove hers. "What the hell happened?"

She blew out a breath. How was she supposed to explain laying down the speeder to avoid hitting a ghost? He'd think she was touched in the head for sure. "I thought there was something in the road. I swerved, and the rest is history."

Mack raised an eyebrow questioningly, but she didn't elaborate. He carefully helped remove her jacket and took a look at her arm and shoulder. He ran his hand up her arm and pressed his fingers into her shoulder to determine the extent of the damage.

"For fuck's sake, Mack," she cursed, and her eyes began to water from the pain. A wave of nausea washed over her.

He sat back on his heels and frowned. "Looks like you're right about the shoulder. I can pop it back in, but you're done for the day."

Kayla squeezed her eyes shut. "Just do it."

"It's gonna hurt, babe," he warned and tightly gripped her arm. She gritted her teeth and tried to brace herself for the inevitable. He flexed her elbow and rotated her shoulder. A screaming cry ripped out of her throat. The joint popped back into place and she felt an almost immediate sense of relief. It was still painful, but it was much more manageable.

"You're not going to be able to use that arm for a few days."

Kayla nodded, and he helped her stand. Mack went over and lifted her bike up off the ground. She watched as he crouched down to check for damage.

"It looks okay except for a few scratches. I'm not sure how well you can ride with only one arm though. I'll take it over to the side of the building. We can leave it here, and I'll bring one of the guys back with me to pick it up. Is there anything you need off it?"

"Just my equipment," she replied. "Sorry about this, Mack. I wasn't paying attention."

"Don't worry about it, darlin'. It happens. I'm just glad you're not in worse shape. You've had a rough couple of days."

Mack put his helmet back on and pushed her bike toward the building. He grabbed her bag and attached it to his bike before walking back over to her. Leaning down, he helped her back into her jacket and helmet.

After deactivating the UV guard, Mack sat on his bike. Kayla awkwardly climbed on behind him, careful to keep her injured arm as still as possible. He reached over, grabbed her good arm and put it around his waist, encouraging her to hold on as he fired up the engine.

Mack drove at a slower pace, but the ride was still miserable. Every bump and turn cause pain to shoot down her arm. It was a rough and nauseating two hours later before they arrived back at Leo's camp.

Kristin met them at the entrance and rushed forward to help Kayla remove her gear. "I heard you took a spill. You okay?"

"Yeah, thanks to Mack." Kayla tossed him another grateful look.

Mack gave the bottom of her chin an affectionate tap with his fist and winked. "Anytime, darlin'. Kris, can you take her to get changed and cleaned up? She needs to keep that shoulder still. The jacket helped, but it looked like there was some road rash on her arm too."

Kristin nodded and helped Kayla into the lavatory.

"I'm going to grab some of your clothes. Don't move that arm."

Kayla muttered an agreement and looked down at her arm. It wasn't pretty, but she needed to see how bad the rest of her looked. Using her good hand, Kayla unhooked her belt and wiggled off her pants. She kicked them aside and assessed her leg. The outside of her thigh had turned several unflattering shades of red and purple.

Kristin came back with clothes in her arms and scrunched up her nose at the sight of Kayla's injuries. "Definitely not your best look," she commented before helping Kayla remove her shirt. Once it was off, they both stared at her arm. It wasn't much prettier than her thigh. In fact, it looked far worse. The skin on her arm and shoulder was angry, raw, and swollen.

"Wow, you really did a number on yourself."

"No kidding," Kayla muttered, observing the damage. If she wasn't more careful, she wouldn't have to worry about seeing ghosts—she'd become one.

Kayla climbed into the shower, whimpering and cursing as she washed the grit out of the raw areas of her skin. It was a painful process, but the possibility of infection made it necessary. When the areas were as clean as possible, she stepped out of the shower. Kristin looked up, her eyes wide as she held Kayla's emerald necklace in her hand.

"This is gorgeous! Where'd you find it?"

Kayla hesitated, mentally kicking herself for forgetting about the necklace she'd left in her pocket. It must have fallen out when she undressed. "It was a gift. I had to promise not to sell it. It's some sort of family heirloom. I felt weird about wearing it though."

"A gift? To *wear*?" Kristin was seemingly shocked at the possibility. "Who gave it to you?"

"Someone from the towers," Kayla admitted. "It's a long story."

Kristin's eyes widened even further and she shook her head, dangling the necklace from her fingers. "Uh uh. No way. You're walking around carrying something worth who-knows-how-much and you're not going to tell me? Spill it."

Kayla sighed and grabbed her shorts from the counter. Using her good arm, she pulled them on. "Okay, but you better not breathe a word of this to anyone."

Kristin nodded, and Kayla briefly told her about meeting Alec and her ties to the towers. She left out the part about the energy, knowing Kristin either wouldn't believe her or it would freak her out. Kristin's eyes had practically bugged out of her head by the time Kayla finished. "That's crazy. So you left the towers because this guy wants to marry you?"

"In part," Kayla said as she struggled to pull on her shirt. Kristin stepped forward to help. "I just want to be with Carl, but I think he's having second thoughts. I needed to get away from all of it for a while, so I came back here."

Kristin nodded in understanding. "I can't believe you were born in the towers. What's it like there?"

Kayla frowned. How could she explain? There wasn't anything she could compare it to. "It's really different. The people there seem pretty self-absorbed, but some of them are nice."

The pretty brunette listened intently while Kayla tried to

describe the busy stores and restaurants. When she finished, Kristin sighed wistfully. "I wish I could see it."

"It's a possibility," Kayla admitted. "I don't want to get your hopes up, but I was talking to someone about building a smaller tower for the ruin rats. We'd need to figure out how to get the building materials and stuff, but he said it was a possibility. At the least, the idea could be presented to the Council."

Kristin's entire face lit up at the possibility. "Oh, wow. Could you imagine? I used to dream about living in those towers when I was younger. To think it could maybe one day happen. Maybe Marie could actually grow up there!"

"Don't say anything yet," Kayla reminded her. Although, Kristin's reaction gave her all the more reason to fight for the ruin rats and make the tower idea a reality. "I don't want to get everyone excited about it when it's still just being discussed. Someone proposed something like this years ago, and the Council rejected the idea."

"I won't," Kristin promised as she handed the necklace to Kayla. "You should wear that though. It's too pretty to sit in your pocket. Hide it under your shirt or something. I won't say a word."

Kayla hesitated and then nodded, slipping the necklace over her head. Kayla tucked the pendant under her shirt to keep it out of sight.

The girl smiled at Kayla approvingly. "Let's go put something on those cuts before they get infected. Mack's probably going to want your arm in a sling for a while too. He's being pretty protective of you since Veridian's not around."

Kayla grimaced at the thought of wearing the brace, but she followed Kristin out of the bathroom and toward the small medical room. Kristin opened a cabinet and handed her an immobilizing device. With a scowl, Kayla slipped it on.

Kayla shook her head when Kristin pulled out the small

tube of healing cream. She could deal with the discomfort for a few days. The camp's medical supply levels were too low to use it without dire need. If an infection started to set in, she'd deal with it then. Kristin nodded in understanding and put the medication away.

After they finished, Kayla headed back down the hall. Leo barked out her name as she passed his office. She sighed and stepped inside the room, prepared to argue with the grumpy camp leader. Mack was already in the room and had obviously told Leo about her accident.

"What do you want, Leo?" Kayla didn't bother to hide the irritation in her voice. Her shoulder was throbbing, and she just wanted to go sit down.

Leo scowled at her. "What the hell did you do? Forget how to ride with your eyes open? What am I supposed to do with you while you're healing up?"

"*Me*? You're about as useful as a mint-flavored suppository," she retorted. "Even one-handed, I'm still more useful than you. At least I can reconfigure some of those gadgets in the workroom. You're nothing but a bag of hot air."

"Then get on it, girl," Leo snapped, but his eyes twinkled with humor. His expression turned more serious as he added, "I'm glad you're okay."

She grinned at him and Mack stood. "How's the pain? You need something?"

"No, I can handle it."

Mack nodded. "I'm going to head out with Marshall to pick up your bike. I'll be back in a few hours. Think you can stay out of trouble until then?"

She gave a one-armed shrug. "I'll see what I can do."

As Kayla turned to leave the room, Leo said, "I hope you do. Sergei is stopping by in a bit, and we don't need trouble with him. He called to check on the status of the mapping. I told him it was progressing but there would be a slight delay since you were hurt. The rest of the boys will finish it up tomorrow."

She couldn't help but look at the bright side. At least being injured and stuck in camp would give her the opportunity to get more information out of Sergei. She just couldn't promise Leo she'd stay out of trouble while she did it.

CHAPTER TWELVE

KAYLA WAS SITTING on the floor an hour later modifying the settings on one of the new terminals they'd received from Lars and Sergei. Her arm was aching more than she cared to admit, and she put down the tool in frustration.

Sergei tapped on the wall before strolling into the workroom. His hair was pulled back like it had been the day before. He was wearing his UV-protective gear, but his jacket was open, revealing a dark shirt. Some sort of strange device that looked like a weapon was holstered at his side, and he carried a bottle in his hand. Kayla eyed the weapon with distaste. The one she'd borrowed from Brant was still in her bag. Ruin rats didn't carry such high-tech weapons because of their extravagant cost and upkeep, but maybe it was time to reconsider.

He gave her an appraising look. "I heard you were injured. How do you feel?"

Like hell warmed over. "Just a bump and a couple of bruises. I'll be fine."

Sergei extended his hand to help her off the floor and

gestured to the sling once she was standing. "That looks to be a bit more than a bruise. Is it broken?"

"Dislocated," she replied and peeked behind him toward the hall. "Is your friend here too?"

"Yes. Lars is with Leo. They are reviewing images you and your friends gathered today. You accomplished much, even hurt." He took a step closer to her and examined the brace. "May I inspect your arm? I have some experience with injuries."

"Not much to look at, but go ahead. Mack already reset it." Sergei put down the bottle before removing her arm from the brace. He ran his hand up her arm toward her shoulder and felt the joint. She winced in pain, and he raised an eyebrow at her.

"You have not taken anything for pain?"

"No, I can handle it," she replied stubbornly.

Sergei chuckled and put the brace back on her. "I am surprised you remained conscious when the arm was reset."

She frowned. So was she. "It hurt like a bitch, but I've been through worse."

He laughed outright. "You have spirit. I am impressed." There was a hint of admiration in his voice. He picked up the bottle from the floor. "I promised we would share a bottle of vodka. It may help dull your pain. Or I could show you my camp. We could correct your shoulder immediately."

Kayla was curious about his camp, but she wouldn't risk going anywhere with these guys until she learned more about them. There were limits, even for her. She shook her head. "I'll give the vodka a try."

Sergei nodded. She grabbed two glasses from the dining area before leading him to the common room. Sergei took the seat next to her on the couch and removed the protective barrier around the bottle. As he poured the clear liquid into the glasses, he explained that the sheath was designed to keep the liquid ice-cold. He handed one of the glasses to her.

"*Tvoye zdorov'ye!*"

He tapped his glass against hers before downing his drink. Kayla cocked her head at the unusual words but followed his lead. The cold liquid felt somewhat harsh against her throat, followed by a slight warming sensation as she swallowed—an interesting contrast. The taste was quite a bit different from the scotch Carl had given her, but it wasn't bad.

"What does that mean?"

"A toast to your health," he explained and leaned back, draping his arm across the back of the couch. "It seemed fitting, considering your shoulder. How did you manage to injure yourself?"

She wrinkled her nose. "I zigged when I should have zagged."

The corner of his lips twitched as though suppressing a smile, but he didn't question her further. Taking another drink, she took the opportunity to study him. Sergei was attractive, but with an unnerving intensity. He exuded confidence and even seemed to border on cocky. Kayla normally liked that in a man, but she had the impression every action and movement on his part was planned and deliberate, which made her somewhat guarded. Her only other option for information was Lars, however, and there was something about the other man that bothered her.

Sergei refilled his drink and considered her in return. "Leo said you worked another camp. Will you remain here now?"

"For a little while," she said noncommittally. "I'm not really sure what I'm doing yet. I just wanted to take a few days to figure things out. What about you? What are your plans when you finish mapping the current district?"

His eyes twinkled as he reached over to refill her glass.

"We have several plans in motion. We wait for now to see results."

Kayla resisted the urge to roll her eyes. She'd played these word games with traders more times than she could count. Unfortunately, her shoulder was aching and she wasn't in the mood to draw this out. It was time to step things up a notch.

She leaned against the back of the couch and gave him a playful smile. "If you're trying to go for the whole mysterious and sexy thing, I'd say you've got it nailed."

Sergei raised an eyebrow. Interest flickered in his gray eyes, and he gave her a slow smile. He reached over, lifted a tendril of her hair, and rubbed it between his fingers, watching her reaction. "I could say same about you, *Milaya*."

Kayla held herself still. It was all part of the game. She took another sip of her drink and peered up at him over the rim of her glass. "I've never been outside OmniLab territory. What's it like where you're from?"

"Ahh. You have interest in my home?"

When she nodded, Sergei smiled and lowered his hand to the back of the couch. His fingers brushed against her unin-jured shoulder. She had the impression he was testing her and trying to gauge her reaction to his touch. What was it with people putting their hands on her? Kayla didn't like it, but she'd play along for now.

When she didn't pull away, he lightly ran his thumb along the line of her shoulder. "I have been absent from my home for some time. For much of the year, it is cold with biting winds. There are large mountains, but our home is also near the ocean. When you look out, there is nothing but water as far as you see."

Kayla got caught up in his description. She'd never seen anything like what he described, except in pre-war images. "It sounds beautiful. I'd love to see that."

"Hmm," he murmured and continued to trail the back of

his fingers along her shoulder. "A woman like you would be well-received in our Coalition."

His words caught her by surprise. She attempted to cover by taking another sip of her drink. "The Coalition?"

He chuckled and leaned back. "I have been interrogating people for many years, *Milaya*. Your words say you are not familiar with us, but your eyes and body language deceive you. You have heard of us, yes?"

"Interrogating? What do you mean?" she asked hesitantly, lowering her glass.

"I ... apologize for any confusion," he said, brushing off her concerns. "Many words are difficult to translate. I am considered quite skilled at reading people. You obviously do not want me to know you have heard of us. Why?"

Kayla frowned, trying to decide how much to reveal. There was something strange about this conversation. It was almost as if he were engaging her in some sort of dance, but she didn't know the steps. Until she knew Sergei's motivation, he had the advantage. She didn't like that. At all.

"I've heard a little bit about the Coalition," she admitted. "But I don't know much."

He rested his elbow on the back of the couch. "What have you heard?"

She finished off her drink. "Just that your facility was formed by several pre-war governments. You guys have some pretty advanced technology, which I've seen for myself. You've absorbed some other smaller facilities, but no one has heard much about you for several years now."

"Interesting. You are better informed than most. Your information is fairly accurate." Sergei refilled her glass and tapped his against hers before taking another drink. "It was created around same time as your towers. Several governments worked together to build our facility. Only our best and brightest were accepted. We do not tolerate failure or weakness in any form."

"Survival of the fittest?" That was definitely a concept she understood. It was the basic premise of life as a ruin rat.

He nodded in approval. "Yes. Intelligence, strength, and perseverance are critical to survival. To accept anything less is foolish."

She might agree to some extent, but it still didn't explain their presence. "Are you here to try to absorb OmniLab?"

"Hmm," he murmured and ran his thumb against her arm again. "Not exactly. Our Coalition is dedicated to unifying various facilities around world. Only way to rebuild our world to its former glory is to work under single banner."

Kayla leaned back, sipped her drink, and considered his words. While it might be an interesting theory, it wasn't practical. Alec had made it clear that OmniLab would remain independent.

Based on what she'd seen, the Inner Circle and High Council seemed to have a sense of entitlement regarding their position within the towers. Unless the Coalition intended to work under OmniLab's banner, she didn't see it happening.

It was more than that though. The energy manipulation utilized by the Inner Circle set them apart from other facilities. Even though the residents of OmniLab were aware there were some differences between them and the Inner Circle, it wasn't openly discussed and their abilities were cloaked in mystery. Kayla had grown up without realizing energy manipulation was even a possibility. She wondered if Sergei or the Coalition were aware of OmniLab's hidden talents. If so, that added a whole other layer of concerns.

Kayla bit her lip at the thought. There were too many factors at play, and she didn't have enough information. Although she was confident Alec and OmniLab would never bow to anyone, they might be open to a possible alliance between the facilities.

He searched her gaze. "Where are your thoughts, *Milaya*?"

"What about an alliance with OmniLab?"

Sergei chuckled. "Do you think they would consider such a thing? From what we have seen, they do not even trade directly with your friends."

Kayla frowned and put her glass on the table. She was starting to feel the effects from the alcohol, and while it helped numb the pain in her shoulder, she needed to keep a clear head. She looked up at Sergei again. It was time for some straight answers. "So you map their districts in secret. Why not try talking to OmniLab directly?"

He studied her and asked casually, "What makes you think we have not?"

Her eyes narrowed. Was he serious? "We're just ruins rats as far as they're concerned. They would respond to another facility, unless you're avoiding them for some reason."

"I would like to propose another toast in your language this time," Sergei said and refilled her glass before handing it back to her. He gently tapped it with his. "To beautiful woman who knows far more than she pretends."

Kayla's eyes widened. "Oh, fucking hell. Are you just toying with me here?"

He simply smiled and finished off his glass. She scowled at him before tossing back her drink. The empty glass hit the table with a *clank*.

Sergei shrugged. "Perhaps somewhat, *Milaya*. We have both been trying to get information out of one another since we met. We have both been mildly successful. I am curious whether you will admit why you are interested in our motivations."

She frowned at him. "Because I think you guys are up to no good. Why are you hiring ruin rats to map the districts when you've been running aircraft surveillance through the districts for the past several days?"

He looked surprised by her admission. *Good. It's about time.*

"I see. How did you come by this information?"

"It was a little hard to miss. You flew over my damn head the other day."

He leaned forward. "Yet you believe it was us and not OmniLab. Why?"

She rolled her eyes. "Well, your little circle symbol was a pretty good indicator. I pieced together a couple of images."

Kayla stood to pull out her commlink and show him, but a sudden wave of dizziness washed over her. Sergei shot up from the couch and caught her before she could fall. He wrapped his arm around her waist to steady her. She blinked and looked up at him. The man had fast reflexes.

"You do not need to show me, *Milaya*. Perhaps you should sit back down. I suspect you are not able to handle your liquor as well as others."

Crap. She didn't think she'd had that much to drink. It had a bite, but the smoothness of the liquor had made it seem less potent. "I'm fine. At least, I think I'm fine. That stuff kinda sneaks up on you."

"Yes, it can," he agreed and shifted her slightly. With his free hand, he reached into his pocket and pulled out a small metallic object. She recognized the strange emblem from the aircraft.

His fingers hooked under the strap of her tank top and he affixed the small pin to the material. "This is symbol you saw, correct?"

Kayla looked down at the circular design and nodded. Sergei gave her a knowing smile and ran his thumb over the design. "Consider this gift. Circle symbolizes unity. Line marks our path. By wearing this, you will be viewed as friend to our people."

Her brow furrowed. Did she want to be viewed as a friend? She didn't trust him or their little group. Still, it couldn't hurt. It was better than being their enemy. Kayla looked up at him and paused at the intensity in his gray eyes. He slowly ran his fingers along her shoulder and traced her collarbone to the hollow of her throat. His gaze dropped to her mouth, and he murmured, "*Ty takaya krasivaya.*"

She swallowed. She just wanted information, not to be his next meal, and he looked like he wanted to devour her. "What does that mean?"

Kayla thought she saw a look of regret in his eyes, but it was gone quickly. He nodded toward her injured arm. "An observation. How is your arm feeling?"

"My arm?" She rubbed her shoulder in surprise. It still hurt, but it wasn't nearly as noticeable. "Oh, wow. A lot better. That vodka works pretty well."

"Would you like more?"

Before she could reply, Mack and Marshall entered the room. Mack's eyes narrowed on Sergei's arm around her, and then he scowled. "What's going on in here?"

"Hello, Mack," Sergei said in his accented voice. He lowered his hand but didn't move away. "Kayla and I are getting to know each other. I do not believe I have met your friend."

Mack's gaze shot to Kayla. She shook her head, letting him know everything was fine. He frowned but introduced his companion. Marshall was a thin, wiry individual who frequently paired up with Johnny. He'd come from another scavenging camp less than a year ago, and his eagerness to fit in had a tendency to annoy Kayla. Obviously pleased to be included in the conversation, Marshall rushed to sit down on the couch. "Nice to meet you, Sergei. It's good to see you back, Kayla. It's been a lot quieter around here since you took off."

She snorted and swayed slightly. Without Sergei's arm around her, the floor wasn't quite as steady. "Yeah, I think Leo's blood pressure shot up the minute I walked back in the door."

Mack's eyes narrowed on her. "You okay, babe?"

Kayla nodded and sat back down on the couch. "My arm doesn't hurt anymore."

He shot a suspicious glance at Sergei. "You get into the pain meds or something?"

She shook her head and pointed to the half-empty bottle on the table. Mack glanced at it and then asked Sergei, "What is that?"

"I brought vodka with me," he explained and waved his hand toward the bottle. "Please, help yourself. It helped with her pain."

Mack picked up Kayla's empty glass and poured a small amount of vodka into it. He sniffed it and then took a drink. "How much of this did she have?"

"Maybe three glasses," Sergei answered for her with a shrug.

Kayla leaned back and curled her feet up underneath her. She was feeling pretty warm and comfortable now. "It's good stuff. It might even be better than the pain meds."

"Uh huh," Mack replied and put the glass on the table. "Glad to hear it. We've got some bad news though."

"Oh?" Kayla reached for the glass Mack abandoned. Sergei sat back down next to her and topped it off.

Mack sighed. "Your bike is missing."

Kayla blinked at him in confusion. "Huh? What are you talking about? We left it by that building."

"We drove out there and it was gone. I don't know who picked it up. I suspect it was probably Carl. There were some tracks that led back in the direction of his camp."

"That dirty, rotten, thieving bastard!" She sat up straight.

"I bet he had a secondary tracking device on my bike. Crap. I got rid of one before I left, but he must have had a backup on there. He's too damn sneaky."

Sergei glanced back and forth between them. "You speak of OmniLab trader?"

Mack nodded. "Yeah. If Carl's got her bike, we can get it back. It's just going to be a pain in the ass."

"I can't believe he jacked my bike," Kayla muttered.

"I can," Mack said and ran his hand through his short hair. He leaned back on the couch. "We'll figure it out. You're not going to be driving anywhere for a few days anyway with that arm."

Sergei turned to look at her. "You know this trader well?"

"She worked in his camp for the past month," Marshall volunteered. "Before that, he was chasing her ass like you wouldn't believe. He tracked her for months."

"Shut up, Marshall," Kayla said in irritation.

Mack shot Marshall a warning look. The newer scavenger shrugged. "What's the big deal? Everyone knows Carl's been after her since we moved here."

"I see," Sergei said thoughtfully. "Is it common to work in trader camps?"

"Hell no," Marshall replied. "Kayla pissed off another trader named Ramiro. She stole this crazy-rare artifact from him, and he put a price on her head. Carl let her hide out in his camp since it was his fault Ramiro found her again. But she killed the bastard Ramiro sent after her. I heard she cut his throat—"

"Marshall!" Mack growled angrily.

Kayla slammed her glass down and shot to her feet. The room swayed, but she ignored it. "That's it, Marshall. If you were any brighter, you'd be in the damned visible spectrum. I warned you last time that if you started talking about my personal life again, I was going to kick your ass. Get your ass up out of that chair so I can knock it back down."

Marshall realized he had gone too far and swallowed nervously. Mack stood and held up his hands. "Whoa there, kitten. Calm down. He won't say another word or he'll have to deal with me too. Isn't that right, Marshall?"

"S-sorry, Kayla," Marshall stammered.

"Don't you dare tell me to calm down," she shouted and clenched her fist. She gestured to Sergei. "We hardly know anything about this guy and Marshall's telling him shit left and right. No one in this camp will breathe a word around a trader, but if a foreigner or anyone else walks into the room, he doesn't know how to shut the fuck up. If Marshall wants to say something, he can talk about his own damn life. Leave mine out of it."

"He's done, darlin'," Mack said gently. "As warranted as it may be, you're not in any condition to kick his ass right now." He turned to look at Marshall and jerked his head. "Marshall, go take a walk. Now."

Marshall nodded and quickly left the room. Mack turned back at Kayla. "He was out of line. I'll lay it out for him later. We good now?"

"I can take care of him myself," she muttered and sat back down with a huff.

Sergei watched the exchange with interest. He was quiet for a moment before he spoke. "You handle yourself well."

"You have no idea," Mack agreed without taking his eyes off Kayla. "Sorry about that, Sergei. That boy needs to learn to keep his mouth shut though. We don't take too kindly to people talking when they shouldn't."

He nodded. "I understand. Our culture is similar."

Kayla picked up her glass and took a sip. "No kidding. I've been trying to get you to talk since we sat down."

Sergei chuckled. "I've enjoyed every minute of it. It has been most enlightening."

Mack leaned against the wall. "Sergei, if you're going to be here for a while, Tharin and Johnny are going to have most of the district map finished today. Thanks to Kayla's modifications on your equipment, it's going much faster than we expected."

"Excellent," Sergei said and pulled out his commlink. He studied it for a moment and then stood. "Something has come up. We will return later. Contact me when information is complete and I will have equipment delivered, as agreed."

Kayla's eyes widened. "You're leaving?"

"Yes," he said abruptly. "I enjoyed speaking with you, Kayla. I look forward to seeing you again very soon."

He bent down and kissed her cheek before quickly walking out of the room. Mack watched him go with a frown. "Surprised he ran out of here like that. You were working the guy pretty hard, huh?"

"I tried," she said with a sigh and refilled her glass.

He raised an eyebrow. "Babe, I think you might have reached your limit with that stuff."

"Nah, I'm good."

"Uh huh," he replied and walked over to her. Mack plucked the drink out of her hand and her eyes widened as he finished it off. He picked up the bottle off the table and carried it, along with the empty glass, to the other side of the room.

"If you can manage to pick up the glass without falling on your ass, you can have it. Otherwise, you're switching to hydrating packs."

Viewing it as a challenge, Kayla carefully stood and started walking toward him. She only managed a few feet before she bumped into the table and stumbled. Mack grabbed her before she could fall. With a laugh, she teased, "You saved me again, Mack."

"You're pretty blitzed, babe," Mack said with a chuckle. He scooped her up and planted her back on the couch. "I'll grab you a hydrating pack."

She grinned at him. "I guess that works."

Mack headed out into the hallway, and she took the opportunity to stretch out on the couch. She enjoyed the warm, fuzzy feeling from the liquor. Her coordination might be a little faulty, but the liquor had definitely smoothed away the rough edges of pain. It was just too bad Sergei hadn't stuck around a bit longer. Closing her eyes, Kayla relaxed and let her thoughts drift until she heard shouting and a *crash* a few minutes later.

Alarmed, her eyes flew open, and she pushed herself off the couch, half-walking and half-stumbling toward the front of the camp where the noises came from.

Her eyes widened in surprise once she got to the entrance and saw Carl and Mack fighting one another in the front hall while Veridian and Brant were trying to separate them. *Fluffy managed to break free of the towers. Go figure.*

Mack grabbed Carl and shoved him into the wall. Carl hit the wall with a *thud* and pushed Mack back away from him. Carl took a swing at him, and Kayla winced as she heard his fist connect with Mack's jaw.

She stared at them for a minute, her earlier euphoria fading away. As the intensity of their fight focused her thoughts, Kayla tried to figure out how to stop them before they killed each other.

"*Leo!*" she yelled at the top of her lungs. A few moments later, Leo came running down the hall followed by Marshall. The camp leader quickly assessed the situation and let out an ear-piercing whistle.

The men paused briefly. "Enough! Knock it off!"

Carl's jacket was ripped, and he was bleeding from the side of his mouth. Marshall and Veridian each grabbed one of Mack's arms and held him back from attacking Carl again. Mack's shirt was torn, and it appeared as though Carl had done an equal amount of damage.

Mack glared at Carl. "You fucking trader bastard! Where the hell do you get off screwing with her?"

Veridian shook his head and continued to wrench his arm back, holding him in place. "Mack, you don't know the whole story. Carl came here to talk to her."

"He'll have to go through me if he wants to get anywhere near her," Mack threatened and finally managed to jerk away from Marshall and Veridian. "And what the hell are you doing bringing a fucking trader into our camp anyway?"

Veridian flinched at the accusation but didn't reply. Carl was about to answer until he spotted Kayla standing behind Leo. She bit her lip as he took a step toward her.

"Kayla, you can't run away like this. Give me a chance to explain."

She took a shaky step backward and stumbled. Forgetting her injury, she tried to use her arms to brace herself. She landed on her backside and cried out as pain shot through her arm and shoulder again.

Mack swore and leapt to her side. Carl started to move toward her, but Mack snapped, "Back off, Trader. You're not getting near her." When Carl froze, Mack turned back to Kayla and softened his gaze. "I told you to stay on the couch. What the hell were you doing?"

"Sorry," she managed, blinking back tears and clutching her arm. The numbing effects of the vodka had disappeared, and the throbbing pain was back with a vengeance.

"Shit," he muttered and scooped her into his arms. "Don't apologize. It freaks me out. Marshall, go grab the pain meds."

"No!" Kayla shook her head. "No meds, Mack. I can handle it."

"You're hurting pretty badly again. If you won't take the meds, you can have more to drink. Let's go check that arm and see if you pulled it back out," Mack said as he carried her back into the common room. Carl ignored Mack's threat and followed them into the room with everyone else trailing behind him.

Mack put her on the couch and grabbed the bottle of vodka from the other side of the room. He poured another glass and sat beside her.

"Drink it," he ordered.

She lifted the glass and swallowed it down quickly. The warmth filled her, and Kayla handed him the empty glass. Mack put it down and carefully removed the splint from her arm. His hands were gentle as he ran his hands up her arm toward her shoulder, feeling and prodding along the way. Kayla winced and bit her lip while he checked to make sure her shoulder hadn't popped back out.

Carl's eyes narrowed. "What the hell happened to her?"

"She dislocated her shoulder," Leo said in irritation and turned to Kayla. "Dammit, girl, you told me being here wouldn't interfere with our trading relationships."

Without taking his eyes off Kayla, Carl said, "Your trading relationships aren't an issue, Leo, but I'm not leaving without her. When I go, she's coming with me. That arm needs to be properly treated."

"You already had your chance." Mack snarled and stood, taking a protective stance in front of her. "You're going to stay the hell away from her. You traders are all the same. You think you can just jerk her around because she's a ruin rat?"

"You don't know what the hell you're talking about," Carl snapped.

"I know you screwed with her head pretty damn good."

"Stop it!" Kayla tried to push Mack out of the way. He took a small step to the side but didn't budge. The pain in her arm was excruciating, and she didn't want to have to deal this on top of her shoulder. Her brain was fuzzy enough as it was. "Carl, I don't want to talk to you right now. Just go away and leave me alone."

Carl shook his head. "I'm not leaving until we work this out. If you want to take a swing at me, too, you're welcome to it, but I'll be damned if I'm going to let you disappear again."

Veridian frowned. "Kayla, give him five minutes. You owe him that much."

Kayla glared at Veridian. His betrayal at bringing Carl here cut deep. "Like hell I do. I don't owe him a damn thing. Whose side are you on anyway?"

"Yours, Kayla," Veridian answered, an apology in his eyes. "Always yours."

She looked away, still unhappy by Carl's presence, but she couldn't bring herself to be angry with Veridian. He didn't know everything that had happened, and that was her fault. She hadn't told him.

Mack crossed the room and got right up into Carl's face. In a low, rumbling voice, he said, "You heard her, Trader. Get lost."

Carl's fists clenched, but he stood his ground and warned, "I suggest *you* back off. This has nothing to do with you."

"Mack," Leo said sharply and pointed to the door. "Get out of here. I don't need you making this any worse."

"Fuck that, Leo," Mack said, crossing his arms. "I'm not going anywhere until this asshole is gone."

Leo stepped forward. "You really want to go up against me, boy?"

Mack scowled and moved away from Carl but didn't leave the room. Leo's eyes narrowed on Carl. "Trader, you have no business being in my camp and interrupting my operation. I think it's time you left."

"As long as Kayla's here, it's my business. Even though Mack took a swing at me, I don't have any issues with you and your camp right now. I'd like to keep it that way."

Carl turned to Kayla, his eyes softening as he looked at her. "I never meant to hurt you or push you away. If you really want me to leave, I will, but I hope you'll give me a chance to fix this."

Kayla opened her mouth to speak, but she couldn't find words. The love that shone in his eyes enveloped her in its warmth, weakening her resolve. None of this was Carl's fault. She wasn't being fair to him. The whole thing with Alec, the engagement, the energy ... it was all just too much. She'd hurt him too. Taking a deep breath, Kayla nodded in agreement.

Leo sighed and shook his head. "Damn women and their fickle minds. Go ahead and talk. We'll be in the other room."

"I'm not leaving her alone with him."

"It's okay, Mack. I'll be fine," Kayla assured him, although she had her doubts. Carl had a way of turning her to mush when she was clearheaded. She wasn't sure she stood a chance against him now. She didn't know if she wanted to.

Mack apparently still had his doubts too. He frowned and hesitated. "You sure, darlin'? I'll stay if you want."

Kayla nodded. Mack gave Carl a hard look and then followed Leo, Veridian, and Marshall out of the room. Brant remained behind and leaned against the wall on the far side of the room. Carl jerked his head toward the door, but Brant stood his ground.

"I have my orders, Trader. I'm not leaving."

"Hiya, Fluffy," Kayla said with a small smile. She still felt a smidgen of guilt about fighting dirty and smacking him down with his own weapon, but he shouldn't have gotten in her way.

Brant didn't reply, but his mouth folded into a hard, firm line. It was obvious he wasn't happy with her either.

A puzzled expression crossed Carl's face. "Fluffy?"

"Yeah. I shot him with his own weapon. Sorry about that. I tried not to hurt you too bad."

"You didn't hurt me," Brant replied. He hesitated for a moment and then added, "It's a little difficult to adequately defend yourself against someone you've been ordered to protect. It was an interesting lesson to learn." A small smile traced his lips. "You fight like a crazed tigress."

Kayla grinned and slumped against the back of the couch. Carl sat next to her, his eyes roaming over her and lingering on the bruises and abrasions before stopping at her shoulder. The concern in his eyes touched her, and she drank in the sight of him. It had only been a day, but she'd missed him. A small cut at the edge of his mouth where Mack had hit him caught her attention. She lifted her uninjured hand and touched it gently.

"Does it hurt?"

At her words, Carl reached up to touch his lip. "Your friend obviously doesn't think much of me. He's got an impressive right hook. Let's leave it at that."

"He doesn't like traders," Kayla said with a soft smile. "No one here does. You guys are *baaaad* news."

Carl studied her with a frown and glanced at her empty glass. "How much have you had to drink?"

"Mmm, a bit." She stretched out her legs, trying to remember how much she drank. Maybe three? Four? They were small glasses. She could probably use another. "My arm hurt so Sergei gave me some vodka. Can you hand me another glass? It still hurts."

Carl hesitated a moment but poured a small amount of the clear liquid into her glass. She drank it quickly. It didn't burn as much anymore. Strange how that happened.

"What happened to your arm?"

"I crashed my bike so I wouldn't hit a ghost," she said matter-of-factly. The thought of trying to avoid the ghostly figure struck her as funny and she laughed.

"A ghost?" Carl frowned, clearly confused. "Maybe you've had too much to drink, sweetheart."

Kayla shook her head. "Yep. Alec said it was an echo of the past. I don't think I like ghosts much though. They run into the road and almost get you killed. Or they jump out at you in the mirror."

Brant's sharp intake of breath caught her attention. She turned to find him staring at her in disbelief.

Carl flicked his gaze toward Brant. "What? What does that mean?"

"She's an untrained spirit energy channeler," Brant said in a near whisper. There was no mistaking the awe in his voice.

Carl's expression was bewildered. "I know she's untrained, but what's a spirit energy channeler? Is what she's saying accurate? She actually saw a ghost?"

"Yes," Brant said without taking his eyes off of her. The security officer was studying her as though she were some sort of exotic creature capable of disappearing at any moment.

Even intoxicated, she didn't like the scrutiny. Kayla waved her empty glass in the air. "I could use another."

Carl took the glass and put it on the table. "Maybe you should wait a bit. We found your bike. It's back at my camp."

"That's nice," she mused and then frowned. "Hey, wait, you stole my bike!"

"No, it's safe," he corrected. "We found it for you and traced your coordinate history back to Leo's camp. Do you want to come back with me and get it? We can fix your arm too."

Kayla bit her lip, trying to think. There was a reason she

came here, but her thoughts were fuzzy and it was hard to concentrate. She was supposed to be figuring something out, wasn't she? "I don't think so. I think I want to be a ruin rat again." She lowered her gaze. "I don't want to hurt anyone. I don't want to hurt either."

Carl closed his eyes for a minute and took a deep breath. He lowered his forehead to rest against hers. "I know, sweetheart. I don't blame you for feeling that way. I was out of line with what I said to you back at the towers. I had no right to put you in that position and ask you to make that kind of choice. I know you probably wanted more time before seeing me again, but I couldn't stay away."

Carl's closeness and words captivated her. She inhaled deeply, trying to memorize his scent. There were a thousand times today that she'd thought about him, wishing he were there. Kayla needed this man like she needed her next breath. He was her biggest strength and greatest weakness all in one. The thought terrified and exhilarated her at the same time. She ran her fingers lightly along the contours of his face. "I didn't think you wanted me anymore."

"Not want you?" Carl gaped at her and wrapped his hand around her wrist, holding her to him. "Kayla, I've wanted you from the first moment I saw you. Why do you think the situation with Alec frustrates me? Every time he puts his hands on you, I want to drag him out of the Inner Sanctum and show him exactly what I think of him."

Brant cleared his throat, and Carl glared at him. "If you're going to sit here and listen, at least pretend you're invisible."

"Your treasonous comments aside, I'm not sure how well you can reason with her if she's intoxicated," Brant pointed out.

"What do you suggest?" Carl asked in a dry tone. "I think we're a little too far down the evolutionary track for me to club her over the head and drag her back to my cave."

"Pick her up and take her out of here," Brant replied casually. "Or I'll do it myself. She's not safe here, especially if she's what I suspect. She needs to be returned to the tower immediately. She's in no condition to argue the point. This location is not secure."

"No," Kayla sat up in a panic as his words registered. A wave of dizziness washed over her, and she put her hand on Carl's arm to steady herself. She couldn't handle the energy right now. Not like this. She had to keep her distance from Alec before she made things with Carl even worse. "I don't want to go back to the towers yet. I can't."

"It's all right, sweetheart," Carl said in a soothing voice and put his arm around her. "You don't have to go back there. No one is going to make you do anything you don't want to do."

Kayla relaxed at his words, confident he wouldn't let anything happen to her. Brant scowled. "It's not your place to make such promises, Trader. You have no idea what you're dealing with here. She needs to be in the towers."

"You're not touching her," Carl snapped. "She'll either come with us willingly or she'll remain here. I won't force her to do anything she doesn't want to do, sober or not. Frankly, she's probably safer here than just about anywhere. There's no way in hell these guys would let anything happen to her, and they have no love for the towers. You saw what happened when I walked in the camp. The only reason we're even talking to her right now is because she agreed to it."

"You underestimate the Inner Circle's reach," Brant warned. "You don't think these people can be bought for a handful of credits?"

Carl ignored him and turned back to Kayla. She was having a difficult time following the conversation, but she got the impression she was going to have to kick Brant's ass again. It would have to be later though. It seemed like too much trouble right now.

Kayla laid her head against Carl's chest and closed her eyes as she listened to his heartbeat. "You really do smell good," she murmured and snuggled against him.

Carl brushed his lips against her hair and tightened his arms around her. "Why don't we get your things and I can take you back to my camp? Would you like to go back there instead?"

She snuggled deeper into his arms and tilted her head up to kiss him. He returned her kiss gently, careful not to jostle her.

"Sweetheart, let's go get your arm fixed," he urged. "It looks like it hurts. Where's your bag?"

"Mmm ... crew's quarters."

"Can you tell me where that is?"

"I can show you," a voice came from the hallway. Kristin walked into the room and eyed the two men. She offered Carl a warm smile. "I'm Kristin, and you must be Carl."

"Yes, I don't believe we've met."

"No, we haven't. I've heard quite a bit about you though. It's nice to finally meet you. I'm guessing you're here to convince Kayla to go back with you?"

"That's what I'm hoping," he admitted.

Kayla traced her fingers along his jaw. "He's too pretty to be a trader. Don't you think so, Kris?"

Carl sighed and shook his head in exasperation. Kristin laughed at his reaction. "Sergei mentioned he brought over a bottle of vodka. Looks like she got into it."

The room was starting to spin, and Kayla closed her eyes. The spinning feeling continued even with her eyes shut. It was beginning to look like she needed to avoid men bearing gifts of alcohol.

"I don't think any of us thought she'd be staying here

long," Kristin said to Carl quietly. "I can take you to the crew's quarters to collect her things. I figured she'd be going back with you when I heard you were here. She cares about you a great deal."

"I'm going to grab your bag and then take you back to my camp, sweetheart. Is that okay?" Carl's voice was a warm breath in Kayla's ear.

She nodded and put her uninjured arm around his neck, too tired to argue anymore. She'd go anywhere as long as Carl was with her. When he lifted her, she snuggled against him and blissfully slipped into unconsciousness.

CHAPTER THIRTEEN

THE GUILT WAS EATING AWAY at Carl. He'd pushed Kayla too far too fast. What the hell had he been thinking by demanding she abandon Alec to his fate? Insisting she make a decision right then and there was just foolish. She had been letting him in little by little and he had to go and push her past the breaking point. The whole situation with Alec had pressed all his buttons, and he'd lost it.

It was too soon. He had to remember Kayla was still coming to terms with everything—her life as a ruin rat being over, her identity as an Inner Circle member, the energy, and their relationship.

Their argument had opened his eyes though. Kayla never talked about her past except the one time he'd pushed her to talk about Pretz. That had ended in a disaster too. Carl had an idea, but he'd never fully realized the depths of her pain or the responsibility she felt at keeping her camp companions safe.

He scrubbed his hands over his face and paced the length of the small medical room. He'd come so close to losing her. Again. When they were arguing and that light had gone out of her gorgeous green eyes, he'd thought it was over between them. Although he couldn't prove it, and the High Council leader hadn't admitted it outright, Carl was convinced Alec had orchestrated the entire event in the café.

He'd thought it odd when Leah approached him that morning. They hadn't seen each other for a long time, and she'd never come on as strong as she had that day. He'd wondered about her prodding questions about life on the surface but assumed she was just trying to catch up. At least, until she admitted to being a reporter.

The warning signs had all been there. It was more than her insistence that they catch up and the heavy flirting. Leah had always been a troublemaker with a penchant for gossip. Her tendency to be self-centered and shallow overshadowed any redeeming qualities she might have once possessed. Someone must have promised her something rather elaborate to pull off that stunt.

Carl had been sure Kayla was going to leap across the table and yank out the reporter's hair. Although it was probably wrong of him, he'd found Kayla's jealousy endearing. The corner of his lips lifted in a small smile as he shook his head at the thought. God, he was crazy about the woman. He turned back to look at her motionless form again, and the smile disappeared.

"Quit beating yourself up, Carl. She's fine," Jinx said and adjusted the vital sign monitor. The redhead reached into a drawer and pulled out some medicinal cream. She tossed it to him, forcing him to stop pacing long enough to catch it. "If you're going to be in here, you can at least help."

Carl looked down at the small container and tightened his fingers around it. Jinx was right. He needed to focus and not obsess like a lovesick idiot. He put a dollop of the cream on Kayla's arm and gently began to rub it in.

"The liquor's been flushed out of her system, and the ligaments in her shoulder are almost done regenerating. She'll be a little sore for a day or two, and she'll need to rest that arm."

Carl nodded at Jinx's words, distracted by the bruises on Kayla's skin, and he was reminded of the first time she'd come to his camp as he'd applied the cream to her. It had taken everything he had not to grab her then and kiss her senseless. He'd wanted to touch her so badly, and the cream had been a perfect excuse.

A chair scraped across the floor and drew Carl's attention. Veridian scooted over to sit closer to Kayla, shaking his head sadly.

"I should have been there. I should have gone to Leo immediately to see if she'd gone back. Why didn't she tell me where she went?"

Jinx's hand dropped to Veridian's shoulder. The growing affection between them was obvious. Jinx rubbed his shoulder. "She probably just needed some alone time."

Veridian hung his head. "She thinks I betrayed her. You didn't see her face, Jinx. She was furious with me when I went to Leo's camp."

Jinx opened her mouth, but Carl held up his hand to stop her. This was his fault, and he'd accept the blame and responsibility. "You're wrong, Veridian. Kayla loves you. She didn't want to tell you because she was avoiding me. It had nothing to do with you. Your messages were the only ones she responded to."

Veridian looked up at him and his eyes grew cold. The protectiveness Carl had witnessed before came flaring to the surface. "Then you need to fix whatever happened between you two. I'll encourage Kayla to leave your camp before I'll risk losing her if it comes down to it. She's the only family I have left. I won't lose her because of you *or* OmniLab."

Carl's mouth formed a hard, thin line, but he gave a curt nod, unable to blame Veridian for being upset.

Carl looked down at Kayla again and put his hand over hers in a solemn oath. "I intend to fix this. I won't lose her either."

———

KAYLA WOKE up to the beeping of a vital sign monitor and squinted against the harsh light in the medical room. Carl was sitting beside her, watching her anxiously.

"Hey there," he said softly as her eyes focused on him. "How are you feeling, sweetheart?"

She frowned and blinked at him, assessing her condition. Her throat was dry and her shoulder ached, but she was alive. She moved to sit up slowly, and Carl leaned over to help her. Glancing around the small room, she groaned. "Crap. I hate being in Medical. How did I get back here?"

"We brought you back to treat your shoulder. You passed out. Mack and Leo weren't going to let me take you, but Kristin and Veridian argued with them. Leo finally relented. Mack was still pretty pissed though. He's not one of my biggest fans."

"Yeah, I noticed," Kayla muttered and rubbed her eyes as she recalled the events that had occurred in Leo's camp. Was she really ready to be back here and face everything?

She looked up at Carl, who was watching carefully. His face was unreadable, but it didn't escape her notice that he'd gotten up to stand between her and the door. Was he worried she'd run again?

"You dislocated your shoulder and tore the ligaments. Mack said he reset it in the field but there was still some damage. Is it feeling better now? The regeneration finished about thirty minutes ago."

Kayla gingerly stretched her arm and tried to rotate her shoulder. It felt better, but it was still sore. Instead of the sharp pain from earlier, it now felt as though she'd just had an extensive workout. "Yeah, I'm just a little sore and really thirsty."

Carl reached over and grabbed a hydrating pack from the counter. He handed it to her, and she took a long drink. The cool liquid helped wake her up a bit more.

"We flushed the alcohol out of your system. You've also got some nasty bruises, and the skin on your arm and leg is raw. It's healing, but we were focusing on your shoulder first." Carl leaned over and carefully removed the vital sign monitor. "You want to tell me how you got hurt?"

Kayla scrunched up her nose and made a face. Not particularly. Every time she recounted the story, it made her feel like more of an idiot. What kind of ruin rat couldn't even stay upright on their own bike? "It was stupid. I was driving and not really paying attention. I thought I saw something in the middle of the road. I swerved, lost control of the bike, and had to lay it down."

Carl remained silent. She frowned, not able to remember whether she'd said something about the ghost when she'd been drinking. Either way, no way was she going to admit to it while she was sober.

Carl sighed and dropped the monitor into the drawer. "I'm just glad you're all right."

So was she. Carl turned back and searched her face. Her throat suddenly felt dry again. Their stupid fight haunted her. Kayla didn't like this distance between them, but she wasn't sure how to fix it.

Whatever he saw in her expression made him take a step toward her. He brushed her hair away from her face, tucking it behind her ear. Kayla leaned into his hand, relishing the tenderness in his touch. He trailed his fingers down the line of her jaw and dropped his gaze to her mouth as he grazed her lower lip with his thumb. Her breath hitched at the longing on his face. She was a complete and total dumbass for trying to push him away.

"I'm sorry, Kayla. I thought ... God, I was so stupid. I shouldn't have said those things to you or asked you to make a choice like that. I never meant to hurt you. I was just so damn frustrated."

The pain in his eyes felt like a lance through her heart. "Carl, I ..." Kayla looked away, needing to get her emotions under control.

"Sweetheart, talk to me." He sat next to her. "Give me a chance to fix this."

Kayla squeezed her eyes shut. Why was it so hard to tell him how she felt? She'd never been good at talking about things. It was as if saying the words made everything more real and put into perspective everything she could lose. The thought of losing Carl terrified her.

She bit her lip and forced herself to open her eyes and meet his concerned gaze. "I—I don't know what to do, Carl. I know everything with Alec and the stupid energy stuff is tearing you apart. It's hurting me too. This is why I didn't want to go back to the towers in the first place."

Carl took her hand and kissed it lightly. Goose bumps broke out along her arm at his touch. She wanted to throw herself into his arms and just pretend the entire thing never happened.

"I know, sweetheart. I won't ask you to go back there again. If you want to stay on the surface indefinitely, we can do that. I don't want to lose you."

She withdrew her hand. After everything that had happened, Kayla wasn't sure she deserved him. She folded her hands in her lap and lowered her gaze. "I need to tell you something. You may not still feel that way after you hear it."

Carl's expression was guarded as he waited for her to continue. Kayla took a deep breath and tried to gather the courage to say what she needed to tell him. Her stomach began doing nauseating flip flops, but she tried to ignore it. "Before I went to see you at the café, I was working with Alec in his office. We ... Well, I kissed him again and things got a little intense between us."

Carl froze, and his entire body stiffened. Anger and hurt flashed in his eyes. "Does this mean you want to be with him?"

Kayla shook her head, wanting to make him understand. "No, I don't. I want to be with you. That's what I've always wanted. I care about Alec, but it's not the same. Whenever he starts doing that stupid energy channeling thing, I feel like a different person. All I can think about is the way the energy feels. I can't control it, and what's worse is I can't promise it won't happen again. I wish I could, but it feels like this overwhelming force pulling me toward him. He keeps telling me I'll eventually be able to control it, and maybe that's true, but I can't spend years trying to master this damn thing when he's in my head and pouring energy over me."

"Wait a minute," Carl interrupted and put his hand over hers again. The small gesture helped to reassure her that maybe they could work through this. "Kayla, I know this wasn't the first time you kissed him. But I want you to think very carefully for a minute. Have you ever kissed him when he wasn't channeling energy in your direction?"

Kayla was thoughtful for a moment and then shook her head. "No. It's only when our energy mixes. As soon as it stops, my brain starts working again."

"Does he know this?"

"Yeah," she said slowly, recalling Alec's words. "He wanted me to learn to recognize the different types of energy. When I sent energy back toward him to increase it, that's when he kissed me. I didn't realize sending energy back through our connection was an invitation to have sex."

Carl's hand reflexively tightened over hers. "Did you?"

"No! It didn't get that far. Alec stopped and told me he wouldn't share me with you. When I realized what almost happened, I kind of freaked out."

Carl ran his hand over his face. "I know you care about Alec. I'm trying not to say anything bad about him in front of you, but he's had years to master this energy crap. He must know damn well what he's doing to you. You're inexperienced, and I suspect he's using that to get what he wants."

She started to argue, but Carl put his finger against her lips. "Hang on. I don't think that scene in the café was a coincidence. I can't prove it yet, but after you left, we started arguing. I know you said it was your idea to come to the café, but Alec knew way too much about my relationship with Leah. I don't think it was a coincidence she bumped into me that morning. I think he somehow engineered the whole situation in the hopes you would get jealous and go running to him. Unfortunately, it backfired and you ran away from both of us."

Kayla frowned, wondering if it were possible. She recalled how Alec had suddenly changed his mind about going with her to tell Carl about the water sample results. She'd known he was hiding something from her. Could that be it?

"Why would he do something like that?"

"Because he wants you," Carl said in frustration. "If I'm out of the picture, he thinks you'll willingly go to him. The only reason Alec hasn't gone after me outright is because he knows it'll push you away. He admitted that much to me. So he's trying to manipulate things in any way possible, either through energy or jealousy, to get what he wants."

"That doesn't make sense," she argued. "When I feel his emotions and feelings, they seem sincere. Alec wouldn't do anything to hurt me."

Carl nodded and squeezed her hand. "I'm sure he cares

about you, sweetheart, but he's also a man used to getting his way. I suspect, for the first time in his life, he sees something he wants and believes he's entitled to have, and it infuriates him that he can't have you."

Kayla sighed and leaned back. It was too much. "I don't know how to feel about all of this. I don't want to go back to the towers until I can figure it out. I'm worried about the threats against him though."

Carl brushed a kiss against her forehead. "Don't worry about the threats. Alec has a host of people working security for him. We're both more concerned about you and making sure you're safe. I think the biggest question is whether you're going to stay here or go back to Leo's camp."

Kayla winced, not sure how to answer that. She didn't know who she even was anymore. "I don't want to leave you, but I don't want to keep hurting you either. I thought just getting away from everything for a while would help. At least when I'm in Leo's camp, I'm just another ruin rat."

Carl paused and considered her for a long moment. She could almost see his mind working. "I see. You wanted to just go back to your old life and forget everything?"

Kayla shrugged. *Not everything. Just some of it.* "It sounded like a good plan at the time. The execution didn't go quite as well as I'd hoped."

Carl sighed and rubbed his hands over his face. "Kayla, you know that won't happen. It doesn't matter where you go. You're still a Rath'Varein. You can't change that."

"I know," she said in exasperation and pulled away from him. "I'm reminded every single damn day. If I'm not in the towers with people staring at me, I'm getting all sorts of equipment and gifts from Alec. I'm tired of the special treatment and bullshit. I'm not a fucking princess."

Carl winced at her words. "I shouldn't have said that to you."

Kayla slid off the examination table. She really wanted to break something. "It doesn't matter whether you said it or not. That's what people think, and it's not me. I grew up just like Kristin, Marie, and Mack. I'm not any better than them or anyone else. It doesn't matter who my parents were or whether I can channel energy." She whirled around. "If any one of them had hurt themselves, would you have brought them here to fix them up? Or am I just some Omni obligation?"

Carl didn't blink. "I would have done what I did *regardless* of your status in the towers. I love you, Kayla."

His words made her pause, and her anger dissolved. She nodded and exhaled slowly. "Yeah, you would have. I shouldn't be yelling at you about this. You tried protecting me even when you thought I was just a ruin rat."

Carl put his arms around her, drawing her close. She leaned against him and curled her fingers into his shirt. The sound of his heartbeat was a soothing balm.

"You're absolutely right about what you said, sweetheart. Your unique perspective gives you the ability to see things on a larger scale. I think a lot of people in the towers have forgotten about the world outside of those walls."

"They're mostly just a bunch of self-absorbed idiots," she muttered in irritation. "Kristin's pregnant again, and even though she didn't say anything, she's scared. If there's a way I can keep all of them safe, I'm going to do it. They've worked their asses off every single day just trying to survive. Those idiots up in those towers wander around and window shop. They play their little political games and are obsessed with their power. There's a whole world outside that doesn't ever touch them."

"Kayla, what you're saying is true, and I agree that changes need to be made," Carl began. "But you're also talking about an institution which has been in existence for over two centuries. A lot of people are going to be resistant to change. I think your tower idea for the ruin rats was a great start though."

"You do?"

He nodded. "I've seen what it's like here on the surface. Most of the people in the towers don't have any idea. It's definitely something we should explore. Even if the tower idea doesn't pan out, there are other ways we could help them."

He brushed another kiss against her forehead. "But right now, you need to hold off on saving the world and take care of yourself first. If you keep injuring yourself, you won't be able to help anyone. You need to get some rest and let your shoulder finish healing."

Too tired to argue, Kayla merely nodded in agreement. He took her hand and led her out into the common room. Cruncher, Brant, Veridian, and Jinx were sitting at the table together. The conversation halted when they entered, and Veridian stood.

Kayla lowered her head, hating the look of apprehension on her scavenging partner's face. "V, I'm sorry. I didn't mean what I said back at Leo's camp."

Veridian let out a breath and walked over to her, enveloping her in a hug. "I was worried about you," he admitted. His expression was stern as he added, "Don't you dare do that again. Promise me you'll tell me where you are next time. We're family, Kayla."

Shame flooded through her. Kayla bit her lip and nodded. Of all people, she shouldn't have ignored Veridian and put him through that. She would have killed him if he'd done the same to her. His shoulders relaxed at her agreement.

"Are you feeling better now?"

"Yeah." She looked over at the table where Brant was sitting and stiffened at the sight of the Omni security officer. "What the hell is he doing here?"

Brant rose from his chair. "I was hoping to speak with you if you're feeling better."

Kayla scowled. There wasn't any reason she could think of that would make his presence acceptable. If he was trying to convince her to return to the towers, he was in for a disappointment. She still had a lot of contacts in the ruin rat world. She could easily hop camps for the next several months and stay off OmniLab's radar indefinitely.

Carl put his arm around her waist and drew her close. Whether it was to keep her from running again or pummeling the Omni, she wasn't sure. Was she really becoming that predictable?

"Let's go into my office and at least hear what he has to say," Carl suggested and led the way down the hall. In a voice too low for Brant to hear, he added, "You can always get rid of him later."

Kayla frowned but nodded. They entered the office, and she took a seat on the edge of the desk while Carl positioned himself next to her.

Brant's gaze darted around the office before centering on Kayla. She tapped her fingers impatiently against the desk, eager to be done with the conversation so she could tell him where to stick it. The thought that he was going to try meddling in her affairs pissed her off.

"Thank you for speaking with me. As I mentioned to you before you left the towers, Master Tal'Vayr is concerned about your safety," Brant began and clasped his hands behind his back. "I was asked to assist Trader Carl in locating you and to make sure you're safe. Master Tal'Vayr is aware you've returned to the trading camp. If you've decided not to return to the towers at this time, he's requested that you allow me to remain here for the time being."

Kayla paused, surprised at his words. "I have a choice?"

"You do," Brant admitted with a frown. "Master Tal'Vayr

is willing to discuss it with you, but the decision rests solely in your hands. If you do not want me to remain, I'll return to the towers. If you allow me to stay, he's instructed me to not interfere with any of your decisions. I will simply act as a security consultant until the threat against both of you is eliminated."

Carl sighed and crossed his arms over his chest. "Alec's good. I'll give him that much."

Brant looked irritated at Carl's remark but remained silent. Kayla looked up at Carl in confusion. "What do you mean?"

Carl shook his head and didn't elaborate. Kayla frowned at him and then shrugged. "I don't care. Do what you want. It's not my place to make your decisions for you."

Brant looked at her in surprise. His gaze darted back and forth between her and Carl. "You don't have a preference?"

"Not particularly," she admitted, already bored with the conversation. "It's not my camp. As long as you leave me alone, I don't care what you do. It's your life. I'm not responsible for your choices. If you get into my business, though, we're going to have problems."

Brant's brow furrowed. The security officer was silent for a long moment before he said, "If there are no objections, I'll stay. I have to say, your reaction is rather unexpected. When Master Tal'Vayr told me to make the offer, I was convinced you'd tell me to leave."

"You gave her a choice," Carl said dryly. "Kayla's only obstinate when someone tells her what to do. Apparently, Alec learns quickly."

"Hey!" Kayla huffed, mildly affronted.

Carl put his arm around her and brushed a kiss against her temple. "I happen to like that about you."

She smirked at him. Carl looked at Brant and then

gestured toward the door. "If you're going to be staying, you can take an empty room in the crew's quarters."

"Thank you," Brant replied. "I'd like to review the security system you currently have in place. Master Tal'Vayr has authorized the installation of additional cameras and sensors around the perimeter. The equipment will be delivered tomorrow afternoon."

Carl gave a curt nod. "Xantham and Cruncher can walk you through the security system in the morning."

"Wait, more equipment?" Kayla frowned.

"Yes, ma'am. Master Tal'Vayr doesn't want to take any chances with your safety."

"Oh, good grief," she muttered. "Nothing is going to happen to me here."

"That's what we're going to make sure of," Brant said grimly. "If you'll excuse me, I need to make some calls. Goodnight." He turned and strode out of the room.

Once he was gone, Kayla looked up at Carl. "What didn't you want to tell me when he was in the room?"

Carl sighed. "Alec gave you that choice knowing it was the only way you'd agree. He knew you'd get pissed if he tried to force it on you. But given a choice, you lose your resistance."

Kayla frowned and protested, "I do not."

Carl merely raised an eyebrow at her. *Crap. He has a point.* She groaned and lifted her hands in surrender. "Okay, maybe you're right. I just don't like people pushing me about things."

"I know, sweetheart," he said, easing her off the desk. "I don't blame you. Brant will follow Alec's instructions to the letter though. If he says he won't interfere, he won't. We'll just let this play out and see what happens."

She nodded. Carl took her hand and led her into his private quarters, closing the door behind them. He walked over to the edge of the bed and sat beside her. Tucking a strand of hair behind her ear, he took her hand in his. They both stared down at their entwined hands as he traced small circles on her palm.

"I was worried I'd lost you," he admitted with a frown. Kayla lifted her head and looked into his dark-brown eyes. The raw pain, concern, and overwhelming love in them staggered her. She reached up to touch the worried crease on his forehead and wished she could erase the hurt she'd caused. Even though they'd only been apart for a short time, she'd missed him more than she'd ever thought possible. It was unnerving how much she'd come to depend on him. It was more than depending on him though. It was the sharing of small moments and looks that let them know exactly how they felt and how much they cared about one another.

Not for the first time, Kayla wondered what it would be like to share a bond with him. As her fingers caressed his face and moved downward across his chest, she realized it didn't truly matter. In some ways, they already had a bond. It might not be the same as the one she shared with Alec, but it didn't make it any less. When she left Carl behind in the towers, she left a piece of herself too. Whether he knew it or not, this trader owned part of her soul. Carl was her balancing point in every way that truly mattered.

He leaned forward and pressed a kiss against the corner of her mouth. Moved by his tenderness, her lips curved upward at his gentle touch. Almost reverently, he brushed another feather-light kiss against the other side of her mouth.

Kayla parted her lips slightly as he built the anticipation with his whispered caresses. As though he had all the time in the world, he began trailing small kisses along her jaw, teasing and nibbling along the way. Each place he touched was like a direct line to her heart, coaxing forth her feelings for him and binding them even tighter. His touch was tender and soft, but she could sense the controlled passion that brimmed just under the surface. His hot breath fanned her face and tempted her mercilessly with his closeness, but he remained just out of reach.

Impatient to taste him, Kayla leaned forward and pressed her lips against his. In a wordless response, she showed him with her kiss what her heart had long since known. The depth of her feelings for him were consuming and undeniable. She fisted her hands in his shirt, demanding everything from him and promising everything in return if only he accepted her offer. He didn't refuse her silent request. Instead, Carl captured her lower lip between his teeth and lightly nibbled on it before sweeping in and taking possession of her mouth.

She let out a soft moan. Without breaking the kiss, Carl reached over and pulled her onto his lap so she was straddling him. Even through their clothes, the new position connected them intimately. He pressed against her core and she whimpered, wanting everything he offered.

Kayla pulled back and looked down at the man who'd captured her heart. He reached up to cup her face, and his eyes darkened with unfettered desire. In his gaze, both the memory of the past and the promise of the future reflected back at her. She realized this was what she'd been searching for when she went back to Leo's camp. All the answers she'd needed were right here.

She'd been wrong in the café when she thought all her hope had been stripped away and lost. As she looked into eyes filled with a mixture of reverence and need, Kayla realized the promise of the future wasn't ugly, dirty, or gritty.

It was beautiful.

She was home.

There was so much she wanted to say to him. She wished he could look inside herself and understand the depths of her feeling for him. She didn't want to ever see doubt in his eyes again.

"I love you, Carl. You're the man I want to be with."

His hands tightened on her hips as he held her in place. "Kayla, I don't think I can ever let you go."

"Then don't," she replied and reached up to loosen his ponytail. Her lips curved into a smile at the sight of his dark hair falling past his shoulders. It was such a small thing, but the sight of his unbound hair was a shared intimacy she treasured. With her fingertips, she combed through his hair and then lightly traced the contours of his strong jaw.

For the first time in her life, she wanted someone to keep holding on to her and not let go. The thought of being bound to someone didn't frighten her, as long as that someone was Carl. Time and time again, he had shown her he would always be there for her. Even when she'd tried to push him away, he'd respected her feelings but had never abandoned her.

Most importantly, he never pushed her to be something she wasn't. He challenged her intellect and her ideals but accepted who she was and supported her unconditionally. Sometimes it seemed he knew her better than she knew herself.

Kayla brushed her fingers over the softness of his lips, amazed at how this once hated trader had become such an important part of her world.

"Sweetheart," Carl murmured and captured her hand in his, kissing her fingertips. "Where are your thoughts?"

She shook her head, not sure how to put everything she was feeling into words. "I was wrong back at the towers. You are my hope, Carl. You're my home."

His eyes softened at her words.

"Kayla," he whispered reverently as he brushed his thumb over her cheek, "you humble me."

Her face flushed, and she looked away. Carl's hands were firm but gentle as he tilted her chin upward. "No, please, sweetheart. Don't look away."

She bit her lip, uncomfortable with the vulnerability she'd

exposed in her confession. Carl searched her face. "I always believed the towers were my home, until I met you. Now, I've come to realize none of that matters. It's just a place. You're my hope, too, Kayla. You're my hope, my home, my everything. Whether we're here on the surface or in the towers, my heart belongs to you."

His words floored her, and she blinked back tears, overcome by emotion. She needed him. Now. Desperately needing to feel the press of his skin against hers, she reached down and pulled her shirt over her head. She tossed it aside and looked down at him in open invitation, reminded of the first time they'd been together. His hungry gaze lowered to her breasts, and she shivered at the desire in his eyes.

"Show me," she urged, demanding action rather than words. He didn't refuse.

With one swift motion, he flipped her over and pressed her back against the mattress. Yanking his shirt over his head, he threw it aside and lowered his body over hers. He bent down, taking one of her nipples into his mouth. It hardened instantly. Kayla gasped and threaded her fingers through his hair, pulling him closer.

She arched her back, wanting to feel more and wanting him to take more. Every part of her belonged to him in that moment, and she offered it freely. His rigid hardness rubbed against her core as she whimpered at the sensual assault. Nearly mindless with desire, she reached down, desperate to release him from the confines of his restrictive pants.

He released her nipple and grabbed her hands, preventing them from reaching their goal. She let out a frustrated groan, and he chuckled but didn't relent. His mouth moved to lavish attention to her neglected breast and she tossed her head back, digging her fingers into his arms as he drove her to new heights of pleasure.

He unhooked her belt with nimble fingers, and cool air hit

her legs as he slid off her pants. Lowering himself down her body, Carl teased every inch of her with his clever fingers and tongue. When he stopped and pressed a kiss against the most intimate part of her, she gasped.

The feel of his tongue exploring her hidden depths sent her soaring in a wave of exquisite sensation. When he moved to focus on the overly sensitive nodule that was the center of her pleasure, she cried out and writhed in ecstasy. It was too much, but he was relentless. His hands tightened on her hips, forcing her to keep still as his tongue and lips demanded a response from her body. With a loud cry, she couldn't do anything but obey as waves of euphoria crashed over her.

She struggled to catch her breath and dimly heard the sound of a zipper. A moment later, he was right there and hovering over her. She looked up into his passion-filled gaze and put her arms around him, surrendering to him completely.

When he finally slid inside her, she was more than ready. She wrapped her legs around his waist, drawing him closer. He moved slowly within her as she clung to him tightly, begging for more. He increased his pace and she met him, stroke for stroke, until their frenzied mating reached a crescendo. When she finally cried out again in a second release, Carl exploded inside her, ejecting his pent-up heat.

He collapsed on top of her, burying his face in her hair. As they both struggled to catch their breaths, Carl wrapped his arms around her and pulled her close. She couldn't protest, even if she wanted to.

When she finally managed to get her breathing under control, Kayla reached up and pressed a hand against the side of his face. "That was ... Wow. You make a pretty convincing argument for staying."

He chuckled at her words and shifted his weight off of her

but didn't release her. Instead, he turned them both on their sides and nuzzled her neck.

"Is that so?"

Kayla lightly ran her fingers across his chest, unable to resist teasing him. "Mmhmm. You're impossible to resist. You're too damn pretty. It's no wonder Leah was all over you."

He paused and lifted his head to look at her with sincerity in his eyes. "You're the only woman I want, Kayla."

Her stomach fluttered at his words. Leaning her head against his chest, she pressed a small kiss against him. His arms tightened around her as she cuddled against him, enjoying the warmth and security he offered. Content with the knowledge that she was finally home and in his arms again, they laid together for a long time before sleep finally claimed them both.

CHAPTER FOURTEEN

KAYLA WOKE up early the next morning and lazily stretched out under the blankets. Her shoulder felt almost completely back to normal with only the slightest hint of soreness. She turned to look at Carl and smiled to herself. His eyes were still closed and he was breathing the deep, regular breaths of sound asleep.

She scooted over closer to him and propped herself up on her elbow. Leaning down, she kissed his bare chest. He made a noise that sounded like a muffled grunt. Kayla smiled to herself and shifted over top of him. She slid down his body, peppering small kisses along the way.

He groaned and threaded his hands through her hair. She paused her sensual assault to peek up at him and found him watching her with heavy-lidded eyes.

"Good morning, sweetheart."

His voice was raspy from being unused during the night. With a small smile, she lowered her head, intending to resume her tactile exploration. Before she could begin, Carl's commlink began beeping loudly. He swore and reached over to grab it.

Kayla started to scoot away, but he wrapped his arm around her to prevent her from going too far. Carl flipped open the commlink and pressed the audio button. His voice was curt as he snapped, "What is it?"

Xantham's voice came through the speaker. "Boss, we need you in the comm room. We've got movement on the radar. It looks like our flying friend is back."

"Damn! Try to use the outlying cameras to get a visual on it," he ordered and released her to climb out of bed. "I'll be there in just a second."

Kayla reached down and grabbed their clothes off the floor. She tossed his pants to him and quickly began pulling on her clothes. As they ran out of the room, Brant met up with them, falling into step behind them.

"OmniLab has been notified about the breach."

Carl nodded but didn't stop until they reached the communications room. Xantham looked up as they entered and pointed to the radar screen. Carl moved to the control station to try to pinpoint the aircraft's trajectory. Kayla reached over to check the cameras Xantham was manning when a loud explosion rocked the entire camp.

"Shit!" Xantham hit the alarm and began pressing buttons furiously. "We've got a fire in the maintenance room. Something hit our shield and one of the UV shield generators is out. The other is losing power. I'm engaging the emergency backup in critical areas."

"Xantham, get everyone up and into their gear *now*! Tell Cruncher to get down to the maintenance room," Carl ordered as he grabbed a fire extinguisher. "We need to get that shield back up now. Brant, stay with Xantham and see if you can redirect more power to the backup shield."

Kayla ran after Carl as he headed toward the maintenance room. Smoke was already creeping out from the crevices around the door. She stood back as Carl kicked it down. It burst open and thick white smoke poured out. Kayla covered her face and turned away.

Carl started spraying the fire retardant on the flames as Kayla moved behind him and grabbed the emergency toolkit off the wall. One of the UV shield generators had been completely destroyed. The other didn't appear to have much surface damage, but the two devices were linked together. It was possible the explosion had short-circuited the other generator.

Kayla knelt and yanked open the cover of the UV shield generator. She peered inside and coughed as smoke continued to fill the room. Her eyes burned, making it difficult to focus on her task.

The internal circuit board looked as though it had sustained some damage. Some of the wiring also appeared burnt. If they didn't get it running soon, the entire camp could be in a lot of trouble. The emergency backup would only give them a few minutes.

"Kayla, get out of here!" Carl shouted as he continued fighting the flames.

She didn't respond, too busy focusing on pulling out the burnt wiring. Using the wire cutters, she quickly cut off the ends. All the wiring needed to be replaced, but there wasn't time. A quick fix was all they could afford. Luckily, ruin rats specialized in quick fixes.

Kayla got up and ran back toward the tech room. The air was clearer here, and she took a moment to catch her breath as she dug through a box. She grabbed a new circuit board and a handful of wiring and raced back toward the maintenance room.

Carl was coughing but had managed to get the flames under control. The ventilator fan had been damaged, though, and the room was still full of smoke. It would have to wait. The entire camp would be at risk if they didn't get the generator up and running. She crawled back toward the UV shield generator and cut out the damaged circuit board.

Cruncher appeared and Carl shouted, "Cruncher, see if you can get the fans working in here. We need to clear out the room!"

Cruncher nodded and covered his face with his shirt as he investigated the fans. Kayla quickly spliced the wiring and connected it to the new circuit board. She flipped the switch to power on the unit and it booted up with a loud beep.

Relieved, she turned to the system monitor next to the shield generator and programmed it to recognize the new circuit board. A moment later, the fans started up and smoke started clearing from the room.

Carl put down the extinguisher and wiped his brow. It didn't help much. His entire face was darkened with soot. He coughed and took her arm, pulling her to a standing position.

"We need to get out of here until it clears. Come on. Cruncher, you too."

Her mission accomplished, Kayla let Carl lead her out of the room. Several strange men in dark, UV-protective suits and helmets were waiting for them in the hallway. They pointed some sort of strange weapon-looking devices at them. Carl stepped in front of Kayla and held up his hands. "We're not armed."

A familiar man approached them with his helmet in hand. Kayla peeked around Carl and her eyes widened when she recognized him. "Sergei? What are you doing here?"

The foreigner gave her a small half-smile and said in his accented voice, "Hello again, Kayla."

Carl's brow furrowed as his gaze darted back and forth between them. "You know him?"

Kayla nodded and mentally kicked herself for not mentioning Lars and Sergei earlier. With everything that had happened, she'd allowed her personal crisis to take the front seat to much more important issues.

Crap. This was exactly why Leo had warned me against getting soft. Emotions screw everything up.

Sergei chuckled. "We are acquainted. Come, join your friends in other room."

He spoke some sharp words in his language to his companions. Roughly, the group was searched and the strange men ushered Kayla, Carl, and Cruncher toward the common room. The rest of the crew was already sitting at the center table in the room, with half-dozen armed men training weapons on them. Brant, however, was nowhere to be seen. Sergei motioned for them to have a seat.

Once they were seated, Xantham leaned over to Carl and said in a hushed voice, "I'm sorry, Boss. They came out of nowhere. The fire must have been a distraction. There are a couple more in the tech room going through our system files. They grabbed Brant and took him somewhere else. I think he killed one of them."

"Silence!" Sergei demanded. "I want access codes to your system."

Carl lifted his chin and glared at Sergei. "I'm not telling you anything until you explain why you're here."

Sergei motioned to one of the armed men who stepped forward and delivered a swift blow to the side of Carl's head with the base of his weapon. Carl jerked back with blood trickling down the side of his face.

"Sergei, stop!" Kayla cried in shock, trying to reconcile this violence with the same man who had been flirting with her the day before. "Why are you doing this?"

Sergei ignored her and continued to focus on Carl. "That was only warning. What are your codes?"

Carl wiped his face. "The main terminal code is CRYET-

Z64, but you won't be able to get into OmniLab from here. Access is restricted."

Lars walked in from the hallway and spoke sharply to Sergei in Russian. Kayla watched both men closely, trying to pick up clues to determine their intent in attacking the camp. Carl was right. The main access code would only give them access to the camp's records. If their goal was to target Omni-Lab, they were in for a disappointment. OmniLab might be able to access the camp's records, but the flow of information didn't go both ways.

Lars took that moment to look over at her. His piercing blue eyes held her gaze for a long moment, and she was once again struck by the familiarity. She knew him from some-where. He pulled out a small tablet-sized computer and handed it to Sergei.

Sergei glanced down at it and then looked up at Carl. "We will discuss rest of codes later. When did your guest arrive?"

Carl glanced at Kayla and frowned. She shook her head, not having any idea why they were asking about Brant.

"He arrived yesterday," Carl admitted.

"I see," Sergei said, checking something off on the tablet. "What is his position at OmniLab?"

"Security," Carl bit out.

Kayla glanced at Carl again. He was still bleeding. It wasn't too bad, but she wasn't going to just sit there and do nothing. Making her movements deliberately slow so they couldn't be confused, she stood up. She'd be damned if she let them think they intimidated her.

One of the armed men pointed his weapon at her and motioned for her to return to her seat. Kayla shook her head and pointed to the food preparation area. "Call off your goon, Sergei. I'm getting a cold compress to stop the bleeding. You can either shoot me or tell him to get the hell out of my way.

If you want the rest of the codes from Carl, it's in your best interest to make sure he's healthy."

"Kayla, don't," Carl warned, reaching up to pull her back.

"They could have killed me already if they wanted me dead," she said in irritation as she shot Sergei a meaningful look.

Sergei's expression was mildly amused, and he held up his hand to the guard. The guard lowered his weapon slightly but continued to watch her. Kayla ignored them and walked over to the food preparation area. She grabbed a wet cloth and then took out a cold compress from the bottom bin. She brought them back over to Carl and gently dabbed at the cut on his head. He eyed the intruders and asked in a low voice, "How do you know these guys?"

"I met them at Leo's camp," she admitted and handed him the compress. "But they weren't such assholes over there."

Sergei overheard her comment and chuckled. He walked over to her and removed the forgotten pin from the strap of her tank top. Kayla's eyes narrowed as he pocketed the miniature device. Was it a tracker?

"You forced us to change our plans, *Milaya*. Meeting you at Leo's camp was unexpected surprise. If you stayed, we would not have needed to raid this camp just yet. Your ICS agent was ordered to bring you back to towers. We were not willing to risk you slipping out of our hands."

Kayla blinked. How did he know Brant was an ICS agent? "You're here because of *me*? I haven't known you long enough to piss you off yet. What did you do with Brant?"

"He is being ... questioned. But no, you have not angered us. We are far more interested in what you can do for us."

Carl looked at Kayla in alarm and whispered, "Do you know what he's talking about?"

She shook her head, but a troubling notion entered her

mind. They wouldn't have gone to all this trouble just because she'd programmed their little doohickey. Something else was going on.

Sergei put his boot on the seat of one of the chairs and leaned forward to study both of them. "You are Carl, correct? Employed by OmniLab as trader?"

Carl nodded and continued to eye Sergei with suspicion. "Yes. My name is Trader Carl Grayson, and this is my camp."

"You hire ruin rats to work in your camp? That is how you met Kayla?"

Carl's jaw tightened, but he gave Sergei a curt nod.

Kayla sighed and crossed her arms over her chest. This was stupid. Once again, they were playing twenty questions. Only this time, Sergei didn't bring her anything to drink and had men pointing weapons at them instead. She much preferred the first round of questioning.

"Why are you here, Sergei? I thought you wanted to unify the facilities. Raiding an OmniLab trader camp is just going to piss them off. I know *I'm* pissed, and it's not even my camp."

A slow smile spread across Sergei's face. "We have our own ways of doing things."

She leaned back and pouted. The foreigner was just as infuriating today as he was yesterday.

A moment later, several men came into the room carrying boxes of supplies from the tech and storage rooms. Sergei glanced at the boxes before motioning for the men to take them outside. Kayla scowled as the men stripped the camp. Some of those toys were hers!

Zane leaned over to Cruncher and whispered something to him. Cruncher nodded and shifted positions slightly to move in front of him. Kayla stiffened when Zane slid out his commlink and opened it. *Crap. Not good.* Even with Cruncher trying to block his activity, Zane was right in Sergei's field of vision.

Kayla stood to try to distract the armed men. Holding out her hands, she said, "Sergei, if you tell me what you want, we can work it out."

"In due time, *Milaya*."

She huffed and put her hands on her hips, slightly shifting her position to draw his eyes away from the activity behind her. "You could save us all a lot of time and trouble if you just tell us what you want. Once we come to an agreement, we can be done with this. These weapons and threats aren't necessary."

Sergei's eyes made a slow perusal of her body, lingering on her curves before returning to her face. The corner of his mouth lifted in a small half-smile. "We have what we want. We are now tying up loose ends."

Carl's jaw clenched as he stood and grabbed Kayla's hand, pulling her behind him. Sergei chuckled at the protective gesture and shifted his gaze to something behind Carl. Sergei narrowed his eyes and pulled out his side weapon. Without saying a word, he fired. Jinx cried out as Zane collapsed on the floor.

Kayla spun around, her eyes widening in horror as Zane clawed at his chest, choking and gasping for air. Jinx tried to prop him upright, but it didn't help. Kayla dropped down next to Zane and yanked up his shirt. There was nothing. No wound, no injury ... nothing to indicate what was preventing him from breathing. A moment later, Zane's eyes unfocused and his body went still.

Kayla felt for a pulse, knowing it was futile. Jinx looked at her hopefully. It was no use. Jinx choked on a sob. Veridian bent down and pulled the weeping woman into his arms.

Kayla continued to kneel next to his body. Her heart

wrenched as she realized he was truly gone. It had happened so fast. He'd been alive one moment and now ...

She shook her head in disbelief. There would be no more playful banter, no more stealing his fruit sticks, no more competing against him for the best times at working locks. Kayla pulled her hand away. The strange weapon had managed to kill Zane without leaving any sort of mark.

Sergei walked over to Zane's body and picked up the dropped commlink. He threw it to one of the other armed men and spoke harshly in his language.

Kayla rose to her feet. "You slack-jawed, repugnant bastard!"

Without waiting for a response, Kayla leapt at Sergei. Carl wrapped his arm around her waist and held her back. She struggled in his hold and glared daggers at Sergei. She'd kill him. She'd drag his rotting carcass on the back of her speeder through all four districts. She'd attach electrodes to his balls and flip the switch. She'd douse him with his own vodka and light him on fire. She'd—

"Kayla, don't," Veridian warned.

Carl leaned down and spoke in her ear. "He's right. Don't antagonize them. I don't like the way they're looking at you."

To hell with that. She glared at Sergei. "Screw them. If they want to kill us, they will. The bastards are just playing with us."

Sergei raised an eyebrow. "You are quite spirited, *Milaya.*"

Asshole. I'll show him spirited. Just wait.

Carl's arms tightened around her, but his next words were directed at Sergei. "She's right. Look, if there's something you want, start talking. We'll cooperate. There's no need to hurt anyone else."

Kayla stopped struggling, but Carl continued to cage her with his arms. Lars stepped over to Sergei and spoke to him quietly for a moment. Sergei nodded, and Lars headed down the hall toward the tech and communication rooms.

In that moment, something had changed—she just wasn't sure what. Carl sensed it as well because his body tensed behind her.

Sergei motioned to the table. "Sit. We finish soon."

Carl pulled Kayla back and nudged her toward the chair. She scowled but sat next to him. Sergei turned back to the tablet computer in his hand while the guards continued to watch over them.

Kayla fumed silently until an idea occurred to her. She fidgeted in her seat for a moment, trying to decide the best way to implement it. At Carl's curious look, she casually tapped her fingers on her belt where a small knife was embedded. It had come in handy last time she was attacked in the ruins by Ramiro's henchman.

His eyes widened in alarm. He leaned toward her and said in a voice too low to overhear, "Let's just see where this goes, Kayla."

She didn't respond and instead kept her focus on Sergei. He was still studying the computer screen in his hand. "Hey, Sergei, are you going to keep us long? I need to pee."

Sergei glanced up from the computer and studied her for a long moment. She blinked at him and tried to keep her expression innocent. The bastard had no idea what he was about to unleash.

Finally, he inclined his head and said a few words to one of the guards. The guard motioned for Kayla to go ahead. She walked down the hall toward Carl's office and private quarters with the guard following close behind her.

There were more men searching through Carl's office. They glanced up as she entered and almost immediately turned back to what they were doing. Angered by their trespassing, Kayla clenched her hands but forced herself not to react as she continued into Carl's private quarters. There was another man in there going through his belongings.

In total, there had to be at least twenty men in the camp. This was a well-orchestrated attack. The options for getting out of this situation were growing increasingly limited. She had the knife in her belt and Brant's secondary weapon in her bag. If she could get that weapon or steal one of the guard's weapons, it might buy them some time. At the very least, it would give her a chance to contact Alec and let him know the proverbial excrement had hit the ventilator.

Kayla ignored the man rustling through Carl's belongings and headed toward the bathroom. Her commlink was on the nightstand next to the bed but there was no way to grab it while the guard escorting her watched so closely. He followed her inside the bathroom and slid the door shut behind them. He motioned toward the toilet and waited, clearly indicating he wasn't going to give her any privacy.

She squared her shoulders and took a deep breath. Carl was going to strangle her for what she was about to do, but there weren't any other options.

Throwing herself into the role, Kayla turned around and gave the guard a coy smile. "I don't know if you understand what I'm saying, but I'm pretty sure there are some things that are universal."

The guard looked at her questioningly and motioned again toward the toilet. Kayla shook her head and sauntered toward him, putting an exaggerated swing into her step. She reached down and gripped the hem of her shirt. With another small smile, she slowly pulled her shirt over her head. The guard's eyes widened and immediately lowered to her breasts.

Kayla tossed the shirt onto the counter and crossed the distance between them, lightly resting her hands against the guard's chest. He swallowed, took a half-step back and barked out some words in his language. He gestured toward the toilet, but it didn't have the same emphasis it had a moment ago.

She shook her head to say she didn't understand. Lowering her head a fraction, Kayla peered up at the guard through her lashes. Suspicion was etched across his face, but he continued to watch her intently as though waiting for her to make a move.

She complied.

With single-minded determination, Kayla reached up and slowly began unzipping his jacket. He grabbed one of her wrists with his free hand and said a few more words to her. She didn't bother to respond. Instead, she ran her free hand up his chest and brushed her fingertips over his mouth. When she licked her lips, the guard's gaze dropped to her mouth. Kayla bit back a smile at the turmoil in his eyes. *Show a man some boobs and they short-circuit.*

She ignored the weapon he held in his other hand. If she gave it any attention, the ruse would be up. Instead, she stepped closer to him, allowing her breasts to brush against his chest.

The guard's eyes widened slightly at the contact and he released her wrist. His gaze lowered again and there was no mistaking his interest.

Yeah, you're getting the idea now, she thought in annoyance but hid her emotions. He still held the weapon in his hand, but judging by the growing bulge in his pants, she had his complete and total attention.

The guard put the weapon on the counter and pulled her against him. It was the move she'd been waiting for. Kayla worked her hand down to her belt as though she were going to unfasten her pants. The knife embedded within her buckle slid out. She palmed the knife and reached up as if she were going to kiss him. In one fluid movement, she neatly sliced the knife across his throat. Almost as soon as he staggered, she brought the knife back down in the other direction.

He gripped his throat with a strangled cry and emitted a high-pitched keening noise. Blood gushed from the wound as Kayla shoved her hand against his mouth to keep him quiet. He gurgled and thrashed as he collapsed on the floor but became still in a matter of seconds. When she was sure he was dead, she removed her hand. A wave of nausea hit her at the sight of the blood on the floor and the realization of what she'd done.

Kayla ran to the toilet and emptied the contents of her stomach. It was too much. She retched again and sank to the floor shaking uncontrollably. Wrapping her arms around herself, she leaned back and took a deep breath, reminding herself why she was doing this. They'd killed Zane. They could kill the others. She did what had to be done. *An eye for an eye and all that crap.*

Kayla crawled to the sink and splashed water on her face. She wanted to scrub her skin to remove the memory of the man's touch and erase the image of his death. She peered into the mirror and at her reflection, barely recognizing the ghastly image of the woman staring back. A watery mixture of blood and soot from the fire smudged her cheeks and dripped down her face.

Her gaze caught on the emerald necklace still hanging around her neck, sparkling in the light. It was a sharp contrast to the macabre image in the mirror. She reached up and gripped the necklace, renewed determination filling her. Alec. She needed Alec.

Grabbing a nearby cleaning cloth, she wiped herself off before picking up her shirt and pulling it on. She shoved the knife back into her belt before bending down to search the guard. Other than his weapon, the only other thing of note was a strange commlink unit. She flipped it on and frowned at the strange, foreign letters that appeared on the screen. It might come in handy. She stuffed the commlink into her back pocket and grabbed the weapon from the counter.

It looked somewhat similar to the device she'd used in the towers. Unfortunately, all the settings were written in that unfamiliar lettering. She'd have to just hope for the best. Gripping the lightweight weapon in her hand, she cracked open the bathroom door.

A guard was rummaging through cabinets in Carl's private quarters. If it weren't for the soundproofing in the bathroom, she would have already been caught. She bit her lip, wondering what they were looking for, and then her gaze fell on her commlink. She'd have to sneak past the guard in order to get it from the nightstand.

It's risky, but I've already gone this far.

The guard's back was turned, and Kayla quietly slipped out of the bathroom. Keeping her footsteps light, she moved cautiously behind him. The stolen weapon seemed to grow heavier with each step and her grip around it tightened. As she approached, his commlink beeped.

Kayla's instincts kicked in. She quickly dove behind the bed. Her heart pounded as the guard answered the device. She risked peeking over the bed and saw his back was still turned toward her. He was silent for a long moment as he listened to whoever was speaking on the other end. When the voice fell silent, the guard snapped the commlink shut and headed for the door to Carl's office.

Kayla breathed a sigh of relief at her lucky break. Snatching her commlink off the nightstand, she quickly slipped out the back door and into the main hallway. Another guard stood at the end of the hall with his back facing her. She swallowed and ducked into a storage closet. Time was running out. Someone would come to check on her any minute, if they weren't already on their way. Flipping open her communication device, she hunched down amongst the boxes to call Alec.

Alec's face appeared on the screen almost immediately. "Kayla? Seara and I have been worried about you. I wanted to apologize about what happened in the café with Carl. Are you all right?"

She blinked. How did he not know about the attack? Brant said OmniLab had been notified about the aircraft sighting. She shook her head. Something wasn't adding up. "Shut up, Alec. That's not important. We've got a problem over at Carl's camp." She quickly relayed the details about the attack and originally meeting their captives at Leo's camp.

Alec's expression was grave. "Is there any way you can get out of there? Where's Brant?"

"I haven't seen him since he told us you'd been notified about the aircraft. They're not keeping him with the rest of us." She paused to listen for any sounds outside the door. So far, it was still silent. She turned back to the video screen. "Look, Alec, they already killed Zane. If there's a way you can help get everyone out of here, we need to do it fast."

"Kayla, listen to me very closely," Alec said urgently. "Brant never notified me, and this is the first I've heard about this. I'll do what I can to rescue your friends, but we've been digging into the archives to get more information about this group. They've been active in our territory longer than we realized. The Coalition was originally a multi-government-funded organization, but they've shifted into something worse over the years. OmniLab is one of the largest facilities on the planet, and up until now, they've avoided any conflicts with us. Something must have changed for them to launch an attack on one of our camps. If there's any way you can get out of there safely, I need you to do it. You have my word we'll make every effort to rescue your friends. But if they have access to Carl's system, there's a good chance they'll learn about your parents and your connection to OmniLab. They're going to focus on you."

Kayla frowned, considering the possibilities. "If they're focused on me, they'll leave everyone else alone."

Alec's expression became thunderous. "Dammit, Kayla, don't make yourself a target. This is not a game. Don't you understand? I would do just about anything to get you back safely."

A shout echoed from outside, and Kayla winced. The dead guard had apparently been discovered. She didn't have time to argue. "Look, I stole a guard's commlink, but I can't read it. It's in some strange language. I'm going to upload the information to you so you can sort through it."

Alec paused, and his brow creased with concern. "How did you manage to steal a commlink?"

Kayla connected the guard's commlink to hers and uploaded the information. "Stop asking stupid questions. I killed him while he was trying to grope me."

Alec stared at her with a combination of shock and horror. She sighed and rubbed her temples. They really did come from two different worlds.

"You've got the information. Go through it and see what you can learn. I'm going to see if I can figure out what these guys are doing."

"Kayla, don't," Alec urged. "Stay hidden. I'm sending out a team to your location right now."

She shook her head. She didn't have time to keep bickering. "I'll do what I have to do. They're already searching for me. Just hurry up and get here as quickly as you can. Preferably before I get my ass killed."

Kayla disconnected from the call and cleared the transmission history from her commlink. If they learned about her connection to Alec or anything about the underground river, it wouldn't be from her end. Unfortunately, it would only be a matter of time before they discovered the information on Carl's system.

There were thousands of files stored on their servers. There might be a chance they hadn't accessed them yet. If she could get to one of the main terminals, she could tap into the system and destroy them. The trick was getting access to a console.

Determined to give it a shot, Kayla shoved both comm-links into her back pockets. Gripping the guard's weapon tightly, she cracked open the door. The need for speed outweighed the need for subterfuge, especially since her escape had already been discovered. Carl's office was the closest terminal with server access, but it was swarming with men. She'd have to make it to the maintenance room and hope the fire hadn't damaged the console.

The guard in the hallway spotted her. With a shout, he rushed toward her. Reminding herself this was necessary, she squared her shoulders, pointed the weapon, and fired.

Just like Zane, he staggered and clutched his chest, struggling to breathe. She watched in horror as the world seemed to move in slow motion as the guard fell to the ground. Her body count was just racking up. More guards were approaching fast.

"Shit!" She darted down the opposite hallway and ran straight into another guard.

The guard shouted something in his language and lunged for her. Kayla pointed the weapon at him and pulled the trigger. Nothing happened. *Crap. It's a one-hit wonder.*

He tackled her, knocking the wind out of her. The weapon went sprawling down the hall. She struggled for breath and rolled over, trying to get out of his reach. He grabbed her ankle and hauled her back toward him. She had a brief moment where she wondered what they fed these guys. He was huge. She tried to claw at him, but he grabbed her wrists. Panic set in and she delivered a swift kick to the groin. The guard howled in pain and released her hands, cupping himself protectively. Kayla scrambled to her feet and ran.

She flew down the hall and into the crew's quarters. As far as she could tell, the room was empty, but voices and running footsteps were rapidly approaching. Kayla dove under Veridian's bed. His dirty clothes were shoved underneath it, and she silently gave thanks for poor housekeeping habits. Kayla curled into a ball and moved the clothing in front of her to better hide her from view. It was a temporary solution though. She had to get out of there as soon as possible.

Kayla held her breath when she heard someone run into Veridian's private quarters. She stared at their boots for several seconds as they supposedly looked over the room and disappeared. Kayla assumed they'd gone to check the next private area.

There was a small grate in each of the private areas that tied into the main ventilation system for the entire camp. If she could crawl inside, it might be possible to get to the maintenance room without being spotted. It was times like this that her small stature came in handy.

Kayla pushed the clothing aside and climbed out from under the bed. She crept over to Veridian's desk and shuffled through the disorganized mess. There were a handful of spare parts he'd been rehabbing to send to Leo's camp. She grabbed a small tool that could work as a makeshift screwdriver but was really designed for more detailed work.

Kayla knelt next to the grate and quickly unscrewed it. She pulled off the cover and cringed at the metallic scraping noise. *Crap.* It was no use. She just hoped the guards were far enough away they hadn't heard it.

It was going to be a tight fit, but she didn't have much of a choice. She bent down and climbed into the ventilation system. The tunnel was too narrow for her to turn around, and Kayla swore silently at the realization she couldn't replace the cover. If the guards went back to check Veridian's room, they'd figure out where she'd gone. She needed to move quickly.

Crawling on her stomach, she used her elbows to pull herself along. The ventilation duct was narrow and circular in shape, limiting her range of motion. At least she didn't have to worry about one of those giants coming in after her.

Kayla climbed through the feeder pipe until she reached the main system. Here, it was slightly larger, and she was able to get up on her hands and knees. Unfortunately, she was now above the main portion of the camp. Too much noise would alert them to her location. She gave a silent thought to Carl and hoped he was okay. If they both made it out of this, he would probably end up strangling her himself. Putting aside these thoughts, she moved slowly and tried to stay as silent as possible. When she reached the next set of feeder tubes, Kayla paused.

Closing her eyes, she tried to imagine the camp's floor-plan. The maintenance room was her best bet to get to a console without running into more of Sergei's men. She headed down one of the smaller tubes, hoping she'd chosen the right direction. As she approached the grate, Kayla peered down and realized she was overlooking the communications room.

Damn twisting tubes. This was definitely not where she wanted to be. There were three men in the communications room standing over a figure strapped to a chair. Kayla looked closer and barely recognized Brant. His head slumped down against his chest and his shirt was soaked in blood. He wasn't moving.

Panic gripped her. This didn't make sense. Alec had said Brant never notified him about the attack. Was Brant a traitor? But if so, why was he being tortured? Was he even still alive? Kayla bit her lip, hoping Alec's promise of help would arrive soon. She was no longer sure any of them would make it out alive.

She scooted backward away from the grate. A metallic clang sounded, and she froze as her foot hit one of the supporting metal bands and knocked it loose. Kayla winced as her foot throbbed in pain, but she didn't dare move. If she crawled backward, the ventilation system might collapse under her weight. She was stuck.

The men below looked up in her direction and started talking excitedly in their language. Brant stirred in the chair, and she felt a moment of relief he was still alive.

Kayla silently cursed her predicament. Alec's ability to manipulate people's thoughts would come in handy right about now. She'd love to be able to wave her hand in front of them and say, *"These are not the ruin rats you're looking for."*

One of them called out, and a moment later, Kayla heard another voice. Through the tiny slats in the grate, she recognized Lars. She hung her head. *Great. This day just keeps getting worse and worse.*

Lars looked directly at the grate and held up a small device. "Kayla, we know you're in the ventilation system. My finger is on a button right now which will instruct my men to execute one of your companions. If you come out in the next minute, I won't press the button. If I have to wait one second more, someone *will* die. Every minute thereafter you stay hidden, another will be executed until they are all dead. In the meantime, I've ordered them to begin tearing apart the ventilation system to find you."

Brant lifted his head. His nose was bloody and one of his eyes was swollen shut. It wasn't a good look for him. He struggled against his bonds, and shouted, "Don't do it, Kayla. Get out of here!"

Lars spoke sharply to one of the guards and they struck

Brant again, knocking his chair over from the force. Brant hit the floor with a grunt. Kayla squeezed her eyes shut. She couldn't let anyone else get hurt.

"Fine, you puke-inducing piece of crap. Just leave him alone," Kayla relented and climbed toward the grate. Lars spoke to the guards and one of them unscrewed the cover. The guard reached forward and helped pull her out of the vent. Once she was standing, Kayla jerked away from him and glared at Lars.

Lars motioned for the guard to search her. "A wise, if sentimental decision, even if your choice of words was not."

The guard confiscated the two commlinks and handed them to Lars. He flipped them open and quickly scrolled through them, irritation crossing his features. "Who did you contact?"

Kayla shrugged. "I don't know what you're talking about."

Lars stepped closer and narrowed his eyes. He grabbed her arm, jerking her upright, and sent a powerful rush of energy through her. She gasped in shock, and the energy suddenly cut off.

Crap. He's an Omni.

CHAPTER FIFTEEN

KAYLA GAPED AT LARS. "You're another one of those freaky, zap-happy, woo-woo guys?"

He quickly released her. She stumbled backward, pressing against the wall. It wasn't as far away from him as she'd like, but it was a start.

He was pissed. He clenched his fists, and his piercing blue eyes reminded her of the sky before a storm erupted. She swallowed. This situation just went from bad to apocalyptic.

Without taking his eyes off Kayla, Lars held out both commlink units to one of the men in the room and issued some curt instructions. The man nodded and flipped open Kayla's commlink before turning back to the system computer.

The other two guards lifted Brant and his chair, setting him upright. Kayla glanced back at Lars and slowly pulled away from the wall, angling as far away from him as possible. Lars made no further movement toward her and simply watched as she knelt in front of Brant to inspect the damage.

Brant's expression was fierce, and he glanced at her briefly as though assessing her well-being before focusing on their captor. Lars's tempestuous eyes were nothing compared to the fury and promise of retribution reflected in Brant's gaze. In a low voice, Brant said to her, "You should have run."

Kayla frowned. They'd beaten him severely. It wasn't just his face either. Brant's arms were covered with bruises, and judging by the ripped and stained shirt, it extended to other parts of his body. Why would they have targeted him like this? They'd ignored everyone else in the camp except Zane. Kayla stood and turned to Lars, prepared to demand some answers. "Why are you doing this? Brant didn't do anything to you. None of us did. Most of the people here are ruin rats just trying to survive. If you have an issue with OmniLab, take it up with the towers directly."

Lars looked surprised by her words but made no move to respond. Instead, he cocked his head and frowned as he continued to study her.

She blew out a frustrated breath and turned back to Brant. Guilt flooded through her. It was impossible to escape the feeling she was responsible for not only his injuries but also for Zane's death. There were too many coincidences, and they all seemed to circle back around to her. Life as a ruin rat wasn't great, but it was much simpler than all of this.

Kayla put her hands on her hips and glared at Lars. "He needs a first aid kit."

"I'm fine," Brant snapped.

She wrinkled her nose. "Seriously? You're dripping blood all over the floor. If you think this is fine, I'd hate to see what you look like when you're not."

Lars crossed his arms over his chest. "He's not your concern."

Oh, really? Kayla resisted the urge to kick him. Instead, she stormed by him to get one herself. Lars grabbed her and shoved her against the wall.

"Get your hands off of her!" Brant shouted as he jerked against his restraints.

Lars didn't even glance in his direction and kept Kayla pushed up against the wall. He grabbed her wrists and pinned them above her head. There wasn't even enough room to try to lodge a cheap shot to his groin. He looked down at her expectantly, and she had the feeling he was waiting for something. Kayla stared back at him, refusing to let him intimidate her. She'd already killed one of their men, maybe two. So far, they'd gone out of their way not to hurt her, but they hadn't blinked at killing Zane. They wanted something from her or they would have killed her by now.

Brant bit out a harsh laugh. "You're a fool. She's untrained."

"I can see that," Lars said quietly without taking his eyes off Kayla. "She knows enough to be extremely useful though. If you try to interfere again, I'll kill you myself."

Kayla's eyes widened, and she suddenly felt uncertain. They had to be talking about the energy stuff. Brant obviously knew Lars could channel energy. Had he tried to stop him? Was that why they'd beaten him? She was definitely out of her element here.

A vibration filled the air—that was the only way to describe it. She glanced at Brant, but he wasn't looking at either one of them. His eyes were clenched shut, and it appeared as though he was in an excruciating amount of pain. Lars pulled away from her and spun around, backhanding Brant.

"I warned you. Do. Not. Interfere." he bit out before reaching down and grabbing the restrained man by the throat.

"Stop!" Kayla jumped at Lars, effectively distracting him from Brant. One of the other men in the room grabbed her and pulled her away. Using the heel of her hand, Kayla pushed upward with all her strength and heard the *crunch* of the guard's nose breaking. She twisted out of his grasp, raking her nails across his arms in the process. The man cried out in pain, clutching his nose, and released her.

Lars whirled and tackled her. She fought against him, kicking and punching. He shouted something in a foreign language and then two more men grabbed her. Her arms were yanked in front of her and quickly bound. One of the men bent down and tied her feet together.

Kayla's eyes glittered angrily as Lars picked her up off the floor, tossing her over his shoulder. She tried to wriggle away, calling him every colorful name that came to mind. His grip never lessened, and he gave her a swift smack on her rump. The shock was enough to make her freeze for a split second. Then, with renewed vigor, she continued to shout at him and pounded her bound fists against his back. Lars ignored her and continued to carry her toward the common room.

"You putrescent mass of walking vomit. I bet you couldn't pour piss out of a boot with instructions on the heel. You're nothing but a sore that won't go away. You're the one-celled organism that lives on the slime produced by pond scum. You—"

Lars swatted her butt again, causing her to yelp. "Be silent or I'll gag you."

Kayla clamped her mouth shut and fumed. They entered the common room, and she heard Sergei chuckle. She tried to twist around to see him, but Lars held her fast.

Carl jumped up and started to rush toward her, but two guards grabbed him and held him back. Lars unceremoniously dropped Kayla in one of the empty chairs.

"If you hurt her, you're a dead man," Carl threatened. The guards shoved him back toward his chair. Carl knelt next to her, searching for injuries. "Are you all right?"

She nodded, not trusting herself to speak yet. Oh, she had

lots to say, but most of it would result in a stinky bit of cloth shoved in her mouth.

Lars gestured to her and spoke to Sergei. Even though she didn't understand the words, Kayla could hear the anger in his voice. Sergei listened quietly for a long time, a slight smile playing on his lips as he gazed at Kayla. Finally, he burst into laughter. Lars chuckled and shook his head. It was the first sign of human life she'd seen from the man. It was quickly gone though. He turned away and spoke rapidly into his commlink.

Sergei approached Kayla, looking down at her with an equal measure of appreciation and grudging respect. "I knew you were spirited, but you exceed expectations. You killed one of our guards, stole his weapon, and neutralized three more. I'm impressed, *Milaya*."

Carl's eyes widened. Veridian dropped his head in his hands and sighed. Kayla simply shrugged and eyed her wrist restraints. Guess there wasn't much of a chance in getting Sergei to release her.

"If I wouldn't have taken a wrong turn in the vents, it probably would have been more." She bit her lip and glanced at Carl. "Uh, sorry about the ventilation system. I think I broke one of the supports."

Carl let out a long exhale. "I hardly think it matters. They could have killed you, Kayla."

Kayla turned back to Sergei. "I can handle myself just fine."

Sergei tapped briefly on her restraints, a reminder of her capture. "Perhaps not as well as you think."

She leaned back and offered him a brilliant smile. Restraints would only hold her until she had the opportunity to use her knife on them. Cocky bastard was in for a rude awakening. Sergei looked at her curiously for a long moment as though trying to figure her out. One of the men from the tech room interrupted and called him and Lars over.

With one last glance at Kayla, Sergei turned to the newcomer who handed Kayla's commlink to Lars. The guard's voice was animated as he pointed at something on the display screen. Lars studied Kayla's communication device for several minutes and then his eyes narrowed on her. *Uh oh. Not good. They must have been able to reconstruct the data.*

"We're leaving. OmniLab is on their way here," Lars snapped. "She sent the contents of Mikov's communication device directly to Alec Tal'Vayr."

Sergei nodded and barked some instructions into his commlink. Kayla shrugged as a flurry of activity erupted around them. "Well, it's not as though I could read it for myself. Sergei didn't have a chance to teach me his language yet."

Sergei raised an eyebrow and gave her a slow smile. "You may still get the chance, *Milaya*."

She laughed. Sergei might be an asshole, but in another time and place, she might have actually liked him. Too bad he played for the wrong team.

Lars scowled and took a step toward her. Now *this* guy was a different story. Lars freaked her out, but she'd be damned if she let him see it.

"You speak with Alec Tal'Vayr regularly. There are more than a dozen transmissions from him in the past few weeks. How well do you know him?"

Kayla cocked her head. Could Lars be the threat Alec was worried about? She leaned back, lifted her bound hands, and flashed him the universal one-fingered symbol of contempt.

"I'm not telling you a damn thing. If you were on fire and I had a glass of water, I'd drink it."

Lars motioned to one of the guards and he stepped

forward threateningly. Before the guard could put his hands on her, Carl jumped up and grabbed the man's wrist. "Wait."

Carl turned to Lars and spoke quickly. "Kayla met Alec a month ago when she visited the towers with me. They haven't known each other very long."

Lars held up his hand to stop the guard. "Interesting." He motioned to Sergei. "We're out of time. Bring Kayla and Carl with us. Kill everyone else."

Lisia had remained silent up until then, but at these words, she leapt out of her seat with tears streaming down her face. "No! You promised no one would get hurt!"

Everyone spun around to stare at her. Carl's jaw hardened. Elyot stared at his sister as though he'd never seen her before, and his voice came out as a pained whisper. "What did you do, Lisia? *Please* tell me you're not responsible for this."

Her hand flew to her mouth, and she trembled. Her gaze darted back and forth between them. "They ... I didn't want anyone to get hurt." She grabbed Elyot's arm and pleaded with him. "I did it for us. Carl was going to throw us out at the end of the month. I couldn't go back to that life. The Coalition promised to give us a place with them if I helped them. They just wanted Kayla."

Elyot shrugged out of her grasp. "He only threatened to terminate our contract because you've been acting like a jealous bitch. How could you do something like this? You betrayed Carl? Kayla? *All* of us?"

Lisia's eyes widened as she shook her head, denying his words. "No! That's not true. It's all because of Kayla. Everything was fine until *she* showed up." She turned to glare daggers at Kayla. "Ramiro promised to get rid of you if I let him into our system. You've ruined everything! You were supposed to die. Just you. Not Zane."

Lisia crumpled into the chair and sobbed. Everyone stared, dumbstruck by her words.

Xantham slapped his hand on the table. "Fuck me. I *knew* I had all those backdoors sealed shut. Goddamnedmotherfuckingbullshit. That's how Ramiro got in. I *knew* I wasn't losing my touch." He pointed to Cruncher. "Didn't I tell you something screwy was going on?"

"Enough," Lars declared and motioned to the guards. Kayla's eyes flew open. Jinx burst into tears again and Veridian put his arm back around her. To hell with that. There's no way she'd let them touch anyone else. Kayla jumped to her feet and pulled the knife from her belt. She raised her bound wrists and held the knife against her throat.

"If you kill them, I'll cut my own throat," she threatened. "My name is Kayla Rath'Varein. I'm the daughter of the former leader of OmniLab's High Council. My mother is currently one of the co-leaders of the High Council. Alec Tal'Vayr, the other co-leader, is a close friend of mine."

Carl gaped at her. "Kayla, what the hell are you doing?"

"So it's true," Lars mused but didn't appear surprised. "You're the daughter of Andrei Rath'Varein?"

Kayla straightened her shoulders and inclined her head slightly but didn't remove the blade. If it got Veridian and everyone else out of this mess, she'd admit to being a thirteen-foot, green-skinned, radioactive man. "I am."

Lars clasped his hands behind his back and scanned her up and down like a specimen under a microscope. He gestured to the camp's crew. "Yet you would sacrifice yourself to save these people? Especially after one of them betrayed you?"

Sergei watched the exchange curiously. Carl and Veridian looked horrified at her admission. Kayla tried to ignore them and kept her eyes focused on Lars. If she kept looking at Carl and Veridian, she'd lose her nerve. "I don't particularly want to die, but if you lay a hand on anyone, I'm prepared to end my life. If that happens, I promise you that you won't see a damn thing from OmniLab. Instead, Alec and my mother will use every single last resource in the towers to wipe out the existence of your entire 'Coalition'."

Lars crossed his arms and studied her. "And if I agree to leave these people unharmed, you'll turn over your weapon and come with us willingly?"

"Yes."

She heard a sharp intake of breath from behind her, but she didn't turn around.

"What's to stop me from killing them after you turn over your weapon?" he challenged.

This was where it got tricky. She had a suspicion, but it was time to see if she was right. Kayla took a deep breath and reached for him with one of her energy threads. He latched on to the connection as though he'd been waiting for it. It felt distinctly different than the connections she'd created with Alec and Seara. She swallowed back her unease. Even just having a small link with him made her uncomfortable. She didn't trust Lars or understand energy channeling enough to know the risks of what she was attempting.

It made her realize that, beyond her protests, she did trust Alec. He had been right this whole time. Their connection wasn't superficial. The bond she shared with Alec scared her because she didn't understand the power, not because she had reservations about him.

Kayla pushed aside these thoughts and forced herself to face her fears. Taking a deep breath, she sent a strong wave of energy over Lars. His eyes widened in astonishment and something else she couldn't discern. Maybe greed? She felt his elation and his hunger for more power, but beyond that, she wasn't sure. With a shudder, Kayla broke the connection abruptly before he could channel anything back toward her. She wasn't ready to experience that.

Lars started to take a step toward her but stopped

himself. He hesitated and then gave her a curt nod. "You have my word. Your friends will not be harmed."

She wasn't sure what he'd garnered from that little energy show, but if it got them out of this situation, she'd take it. "I also want you to leave Carl behind. I'm far more valuable to you than him."

Carl shook his head and moved to stand beside her. "Forget it. Absolutely not. I'm not letting you go alone with them."

"Shut up, Carl," she snapped without looking away from Lars. If Lars agreed, she'd go skipping and whistling with these assholes and damn the consequences. She needed to keep Carl safe. She couldn't lose him.

Either way, they needed to finish up this little negotiation. It was getting harder to keep her hand from trembling while it held the blade. It would be really pathetic if she nicked her own throat because of nerves.

Lars shook his head. "The trader comes with us. That's not negotiable."

Kayla sighed. "Well, it was worth a try." She lowered the knife but twisted it around to slice through her bonds. Reaching down, she did the same to her ankles before offering the knife to Lars. He frowned but took it from her and then spoke to Sergei in his language. Sergei nodded in agreement and issued some commands into his commlink. A few minutes later, the rest of the armed guards came into the room bringing the last few remaining boxes. Kayla rubbed her wrists and watched as they headed toward the exit.

Sergei motioned for Carl and Kayla to follow them. Kayla stopped for a moment and glanced over at Veridian. She wanted to say goodbye but didn't want to make their relationship obvious. Veridian met her gaze and seemed to understand what she was thinking because he gave her an almost indiscernible nod and put his arm around Jinx, pulling her close.

Kayla gave Veridian a small reassuring smile as she turned away. She'd rather see the worry currently in his eyes than risk losing him. He'd be okay. Alec knew what Veridian meant to her and wouldn't let anything happen to him.

The thought startled her. She'd never relied on anyone to take care of what was hers. There was no doubt in her mind she could count on Alec though. Both Carl and Alec had somehow managed to slip past her defenses and become an integral part of her life. She didn't really understand how it happened, but it was too late to do much about it now.

Lars waited at the entrance and instructed them to equip their UV-protective gear. Kayla reached over and grabbed her equipment off the rack and began pulling it on. Once she finished, Lars motioned for a guard to bind her again. Obviously, he didn't trust her. The guard pulled her arms behind her back, and she heard a small beep as the new restraints locked in place. She scowled. It would be more difficult to wiggle her way out of these. The guard turned and did the same to Carl.

Before she could get a good look at the restraints on Carl, they ushered them outside into the bright sunlight. Numerous bikes surrounded the front of the camp. Lars took Kayla toward his bike and motioned for her to climb into the companion car. It was awkward trying to climb into the strange speeder without the use of her hands, and Lars quickly grew impatient. He picked her up with surprising ease and put her inside before climbing into the driver's seat.

Kayla counted a total of eighteen individuals who'd participated in the attack. Their bikes flew across the desolate landscape in a tight formation. She had to admit their assault and even their current movements were well-organized and efficient. The fire had been a clever distraction. They'd managed to infiltrate the camp and secure everyone within a matter of minutes. She'd used a similar diversion tactic more than a year ago when she'd stolen the Aurelia Data Cube.

They drove south for what seemed like an eternity, past all the normally recognizable landmarks. Kayla wasn't sure how far they traveled, but she was fairly certain they were either outside OmniLab territory or just on the border. Either way, the area was unfamiliar and she had only a vague notion of their approximate location. The bikes slowed as they approached an unusual rocky formation. Upon closer inspection, Kayla realized it wasn't a natural rock formation. They had used some sort of masking device to disguise their camp. She'd love to get her hands on the technology to see how it worked.

A small glance at Lars quickly erased any hope of getting him to show it to her. He turned off the engine to the bike and lifted Kayla out of the companion compartment. Her butt was numb from sitting in one place for so long, but he didn't give her a chance to stretch before gripping her arm and leading her toward the camp entrance. She nervously tried to look around as they headed inside and relaxed when she spotted Carl. Sergei was escorting him behind her.

Lars pulled off her helmet when they stepped inside the renegade camp. She couldn't help but try to take note of the layout and any possible exits. The camp was larger than it appeared from the outside. Unlike the trader camp, the supports were all temporary, and it looked as though it had been hastily constructed. Even so, the material appeared much more substantial than what they used in the ruin rat camp.

Well, I held up my end of the deal. Everyone's safe, and I came willingly. Doesn't mean I stay willingly though. But hell if I know how I'm going to get out of this mess.

Lars took her arm again and led her down a hallway

toward a large office. It was smaller than Carl's office and sparsely furnished. Other than a desk, a few chairs, and a small cabinet in the corner, the room was empty.

Lars motioned toward one of the chairs. Kayla sat and tested the limits of the restraints again, trying to determine how they worked. One of the guards came into the room, spoke briefly to Lars, and handed him a small tablet computer. Lars looked down at the tablet and dismissed the guard with a wave of his hand.

Sergei entered a moment later with Carl and motioned for him to sit. Carl took the chair next to Kayla, his expression worried. "Are you all right?"

"Never been better," she replied dryly and flexed her wrists. Ruin rats weren't meant to be in captivity. The bonds were starting to piss her off. She leaned back and tried to surreptitiously get a good look at Carl's wrists. When he realized what she was trying to do, he shifted his arms slightly to provide her with a better view.

The restraints were solid in design without any obvious weaknesses. A small key reader of some sort was embedded on the side. It offered some possibilities if she could get the cover off. Without having access to any tools, she'd either need to palm the key from Sergei or find a way to short-circuit the unit. Kayla glanced around, trying to figure out if there was anything in the room she could use.

Lars ignored them and continued to study his tablet. Sergei pulled up a chair and sat down backward on it. He faced Kayla and rested his arms across the back of the chair.

"Lars believes your towers will pay large amount for your return. It is shame. I believe you would do well with us. But who knows? If your towers do not agree to terms, we may come to our own agreement."

Kayla shifted in her seat, trying to feel along the edge of

the restraints for the key reader. "Release me and I'll show you what I think about that."

"A woman with such fire is rare," he observed with approval. "It is admirable. But do not forget your place. If you resist or try to escape, we will not kill you. You will wish for it though."

Kayla rolled her eyes at him. "Yeah, yeah. You're a real badass. If you really wanted to hurt me, you would have done so by now. But I think we both know OmniLab won't pay for damaged goods."

Sergei laughed and leaned back. "Not only spirited, but smart too." His eyes darkened dangerously as he added, "There are many ways to inflict pain without leaving marks."

The door slid open, and Kayla's eyes widened as she recognized the man standing in the doorway.

"Hello, Kayla," Ramiro said with a cruel grin.

CHAPTER SIXTEEN

ALEC PACED HIS OFFICE, listening to the conversation. Brant's battered image filled the screen as he reported to Thomas, the head of security in the towers, on the events that had transpired in the trading camp. All Alec's worst fears were coming to fruition. He didn't know how much longer he could remain in the towers when Kayla was out there somewhere with those people.

It had been sheer torture not going after her when she fled from the towers, but this was a thousand times worse. The only small comfort was he could sense her faintly through their bond. He knew she was still alive. Other than that, he had no way of knowing if she remained unharmed.

If he'd sent a team to Carl's camp to guard her instead of a single agent, this wouldn't have happened. She would have hated it and maybe him, but it no longer mattered. He'd suffer through her contempt for the rest of his life if she remained unharmed. Alec squeezed his eyes shut. He'd even be willing to let her live in peace with Carl if he had some assurance she would be protected.

It wasn't a matter of their bond anymore or that he loved

the willful and headstrong woman. Kayla was the first spirit channeler in generations. He'd listened to his heart and allowed her to walk out the doors in the hopes she just needed a little more time to accept their bond. Instead, he'd let her walk right into harm's way.

"She admitted to providing them with information about Kayla's location and the layout of the camp. She was also responsible for intercepting my transmission to the towers warning of the attack. The financial records support—"

Alec jerked his head up and interrupted Brant's report. "Who did you say was responsible for this?"

Brant paused and glanced at Thomas. "Lisia Carpan, a surface dweller. She was recruited by Trader Carl Grayson a year ago. She's being interrogated by one of our agents as we speak."

Alec walked over to his desk and pulled up the woman's file. He scrolled through her information and frowned. There was nothing remarkable about her skillset. The fact she was recruited in the first place was surprising. "What did they offer her?"

"From what I've gathered from the other camp occupants, she believed Carl was revoking her contract at the end of the month. The Coalition offered both her and her brother a place within their organization. Her brother is being interrogated as well, but at first glance, he appears innocent. Other members of the camp have also stated Lisia Carpan was instrumental in helping to coordinate the attack against Mistress Rath'Varein several weeks ago. Apparently, she provided intel to Ramiro Lucas. We believe she may be one of the links we've been looking for."

Alec's eyes narrowed at the mention of the former trader. Ramiro had disappeared right after Kayla's birthright had come to light, and they hadn't been able to locate him. "Are you insinuating Ramiro is working with the Coalition?"

"Yes," Brant replied. He hesitated and then added, "Lars Cerulis was also here. He appears to be a key player within their organization."

Alec's knuckles whitened as he gripped the edge of the desk. This was much worse than he could have imagined. He'd thought Lars and the rest of his family had perished. There could be only one reason they'd allied with the Coalition. Alec's throat tightened at the thought. "Does Lars know who she is?"

Brant grimaced and nodded, making it clear he understood the implications of this news a little too well. "Yes. He knows she's Andrei Rath'Varein's daughter. Kayla was the reason for their attack."

————

FOR THE FIRST time since they arrived, Kayla felt a taste of real fear. Ramiro was a massive figure and reminded her of a pre-war tank. His menacing eyes observed Kayla with a combination of hatred and contempt. She knew he blamed her for losing his trader status and his expulsion from OmniLab towers. In retaliation, Ramiro had sent one of his goons to kill her and nearly succeeded.

Carl straightened in his chair. Kayla could almost see the air ripple around Carl from barely restrained fury. "You traitorous bastard. You're the one who gave the Coalition information about us?"

Ramiro didn't even glance at him. Instead, he walked over to Kayla and raked his eyes over her. "I wasn't expecting you to be still digging around in Carl's camp. I heard a rumor that some little ruin rat bitch moved up in the world."

Her heart thudded, but she forced herself not to react. Men like Ramiro got off on fear. Feigning a look of boredom,

Kayla shrugged. "Is that all you've got? I've been called worse by better than you."

Ramiro laughed, and her blood went cold. She'd had nightmares about that laugh. He leaned in close enough she could smell the stench of his sweat. She had to struggle not to gag. In a low whisper that was loud enough for only her and Carl to hear, he said, "I told you before that I intended to collect. From the way it's looking, I'm going to get much more out of the deal I made with the Coalition. I'll have to arrange a private thank you later."

She scowled and brought her leg up swiftly into his crotch. Ramiro howled in pain. Two for two. It was a good cheap-shot day. He lifted her from the chair and slammed her against the wall. She cried out as her previously injured shoulder hit the wall, jarring it again.

"You little whore."

Even though he was still bound, Carl charged Ramiro and used his weight to knock Ramiro backward into the wall.

"Enough," Lars ordered. "Until we finish our business with OmniLab, they are both to remain unharmed."

Sergei grabbed Carl and forced him to sit. Ramiro yanked Kayla up and shoved her toward her chair.

Lars assessed Ramiro with cold disdain. "The information you provided us was outdated and useless. We've confirmed Edwin Tal'Vayr is dead. The new leader of the towers is Alec Tal'Vayr. What do you know about him?"

"Alec Tal'Vayr is Edwin Tal'Vayr's brat. He must have taken his father's place. He's just some snotty Inner Circle member who enjoys flaunting his title. That's all most of them are. Some have different weird abilities but most of them are just stuck up prigs."

Lars tossed the tablet onto the nearby table. "I see. Do you know what sort of abilities Alec Tal'Vayr has?"

Ramiro shrugged. "Hell if I know. We're not included in

their little circle. I'm thinking the whole thing is probably just to keep other people from challenging their authority. Some of them can talk to each other with their minds, if you want to believe the rumors. Some of them can control people and even kill with a thought. I think it's all just a bunch of bullshit though."

When Lars didn't reply, Ramiro added, "They're all just a bunch of pompous asses who enjoy looking down their noses at everyone else." He stuck his thumb out toward Kayla. "If this one here could do anything, she wouldn't be sitting here right now."

"I see." Lars focused on Kayla once more but didn't contradict Ramiro. For some reason, Kayla had the impression he didn't want to Ramiro to know much about their abilities. She tucked the information away to possibly use later.

Leaning back in her chair, she glared at Ramiro and hoped she had a chance to ask Alec to use his influence on this asshole. There were a lot of embarrassing and painful displays she'd enjoy watching. Maybe she'd have him strip naked and run through the ruined streets until his skin melted off. Yep. That would be a good start.

Before Lars could question Ramiro further, one of the guards entered the room and spoke rapidly to Lars and Sergei. Lars raised his eyebrows and looked down at his tablet computer. Sergei walked over and looked down at it too.

Lars laughed loudly. Kayla swallowed back her unease at the uncharacteristic sound. Lars lifted his head to look at her, his blue eyes ablaze with an inner fire. "This changes things quite a bit."

Carl shot her a concerned look. She shook her head to indicate she didn't know what they could have found.

Lars walked around the desk and held out the tablet to her. "You know Alec Tal'Vayr far better than you led us to believe. Their records indicate you're engaged to be married."

Kayla squeezed her eyes shut and slumped back in the chair. She didn't need to look at it. It was just her luck the stupid engagement thing would come back to bite her in the ass.

Ramiro snickered. "Well, well, sleeping your way to the top, huh?"

Kayla opened her eyes to glare at him. "If that's the case, is it any wonder why you were bypassed completely? I've been more aroused by shit on the heel of my boot."

Ramiro's eyes narrowed, and he took a threatening step toward her.

Carl straightened in his chair and nodded toward the former trader. "You might want to rein your boy in."

Lars frowned. "Enough. It's a fool who gets riled by a woman's words. Take them to a holding room until the others arrive."

With a cruel look, Ramiro yanked Kayla back to her feet. Sergei took Carl and led him down the hallway. Kayla watched them stop at a door and Carl gave her an alarmed look as Ramiro continued taking her further down the hall. Carl turned to Sergei. "Don't leave that bastard alone with her."

Sergei ignored Carl's plea and pushed him inside the room. The door slammed shut behind them, and Ramiro grinned down at Kayla. A chill went through her at the look in his eyes. She swallowed and said, "Looks like you're licking someone else's boots now."

"That's what you think." Ramiro squeezed her arm tighter, and Kayla winced in pain. She refused to cry out. It would only encourage him.

Ramiro pulled her toward a small room and shoved her inside. She stumbled and tried to catch her balance, hindered by the restraints still on her wrists. She looked around nervously. It was a tiny, windowless room with a small cot, a sink, and a toilet. Ramiro closed the door behind them and unhooked his belt.

Oh, shit. Kayla backed away, but the room was small and there wasn't anywhere to go. She tugged at her restraints, but they didn't budge. Ramiro stood between her and the door, closing in on her.

"Nowhere to run now, you little whore," he sneered and grabbed her. "You need to be taught a lesson, and I'm going to give it to you."

She went to kick him, but he was expecting it this time. Ramiro slammed her up against the wall, knocking the wind out of her. He grabbed her shirt, and she heard it tear as he shoved her face-down on the cot. His heavy weight pressed down on top of her. The smell of his sweat choked her, and the memory of Pretz fighting him flooded into her mind.

"Get off me, you disgusting sack of shit!" she yelled and tried to push him off.

Ramiro yanked her head back by her hair. She cried out in pain as her eyes welled with tears. "Oh, I'll definitely get off, you little bitch. Don't you worry. It's just too bad Pretz and Carl aren't here to watch. I wonder if Alec Tal'Vayr will still want you when he finds out his fiancée is nothing but a whore."

The sound of his zipper was like a bucket of ice water being thrown over her. Her breath hitched. Kayla felt energy well up inside her, and she opened herself completely to its power. Energy snapped and whirled around her in a kaleido-scope of sharp colors and the earth began to tremble and shake.

"What the hell?!" Ramiro scrambled back. Dimly, Kayla heard shouts from the hallway as the walls continued to shake. As she continued channeling the energy, she heard the echo of a thought urging, *"It's too much, love. You need to pull back."*

"Alec?" There was no response, but the energy was quickly becoming too much to control. With a pained gasp, she released the energy and the shaking stopped.

A moment later, the door to Kayla's cell flung open. Sergei, Carl, and another armed man rushed inside. When Carl saw Kayla's condition and Ramiro's unbuttoned pants, he charged him. He tackled the former trader and shoved him against the wall. Carl took a swing and his fist connected squarely with Ramiro's jaw. Ramiro used his bulk to shove him backward. Carl grappled with him as they wrestled each other to the floor.

Kayla rolled over and scooted herself back against the wall, pulling her legs up to get out of the way of the two men. Sergei yelled in his foreign tongue, and several armed men rushed into the tiny room and separated the fighters.

Sergei's eyes landed on her. He reached for her wrists, and she heard the telltale beep of the bindings being released. Sergei removed them and tucked the restraint into his pocket.

Kayla rubbed her wrists, trying to ignore the trembling in her hands. She looked up to meet Ramiro's stare. "It must suck to know that forcing yourself on someone is the only way you'll ever get laid. No woman is willing to get anywhere near your pathetic excuse for a dick."

Ramiro snarled at her. "Next time, bitch, I'm going to make you beg for it."

Kayla held her head up high, refusing to let this bastard intimidate her. "That'll never happen. I wouldn't fuck you if the world were flooded with piss and you lived in the only tree."

Sergei whirled on Ramiro and glanced down at his unfastened pants. "You were ordered to return her unharmed. We do not condone rape."

Ramiro didn't have time to react before Sergei pulled out

his weapon and fired. There was a slight hissing noise and then Ramiro clutched his chest, gasping for air, surprise etched on his face. Kayla watched with a strange sort of detachment as he collapsed on the floor. His body twitched and then remained still.

She blinked. It all happened so fast. Two of the guards bent down to remove his body from the room.

"Wait!" Kayla jumped off the cot. Sergei held up his hand to stop the guards and looked at Kayla questioningly. She walked over to Ramiro and stared down at the man who had caused her so much grief.

His death wasn't enough.

He should have been made to suffer in the same way Pretz suffered. He should have been forced to experience the same pain he'd subjected Veridian to when his arm was broken. He should have experienced the same degradation he tried to force upon her. He should have been made to feel every ounce of pain he'd ever inflicted.

She spat on his lifeless body. It wasn't nearly enough, but at least it was a small form of payback. Without saying another word, she turned and sat back down on the cot.

Sergei's mouth crept upward in a small smile. He gave her a nod of approval before motioning the guards to continue taking Ramiro from the room. Once he was gone, Sergei gave her and Carl a considering look. He then instructed the remaining guards to release Carl.

"You will temporarily share this cell. The other was damaged a few minutes ago during the earthquake."

Carl nodded. "Thank you."

Sergei inclined his head, and the armed men followed him from the small room. When the door closed behind them, Kayla leaned back against the wall. She wrapped her arms around her legs and pressed her forehead against her knees. She couldn't seem to stop the tremors going through her.

Carl leaned down toward her and she flinched, not able to handle being touched yet. "Just ... I need a minute."

He stopped, and she heard the cot creak as his weight settled on the edge. Now that it was over, emotions and memories flooded through her. She could still feel Ramiro's hands on her, and she wanted nothing more than a hot shower to wash away the memory. She took a deep breath and choked on a sob.

Don't lose it now, Kayla. You will get through this.

She took a few more deep breaths and looked up at Carl.

"Kayla? Did he ..."

"No," she said quietly. "Apparently, earthquakes aren't conducive to rape."

Carl fisted his hands and looked away. After a long moment, he sighed and leaned forward to rest his elbows on his knees. "I'm so sorry. It took me too long to convince Sergei to check on you. My cell was damaged when the earthquake hit, and he didn't have a choice but to bring me here." Carl paused and lifted his head. "Was that you? With the earthquake? The wall split open in my cell and I thought ... was it you?"

She nodded and rubbed her arms, thankful for the distraction. The room hadn't felt this cold when she first came in. She was freezing. "I think so. I don't know how I did it though."

"Can you do it again?"

Kayla shrugged. Right now she wasn't sure she could stand, much less cause another earthquake. "I just channeled a whole hell of a lot of energy. I'd probably end up bringing the entire place down on top of us if I tried. I don't know how it works."

He was quiet for a moment and then said, "If we can figure out what triggered it, maybe we can use this to our advantage. Can you tell me what happened?"

Kayla frowned. She saw the wisdom in his request but didn't want to relive the experience. She took a deep breath and forced out the words. "Ramiro brought me in here and told me he was going to teach me a lesson. I went to kick him again, but he pushed me onto the bed. He put his hands on me and ... oh shit, he ..." Her voice trailed off as she choked on a sob, unable to say the words. It was too much.

Carl wrapped his arms around her and pulled her onto his lap. She buried her head against his chest, desperate to soak up his warmth and chase away the chill. In a soothing voice, he said, "Shhh, it's okay. He can't ever hurt you again."

"I can't ... I can't think about it right now."

"It's all right, sweetheart. You don't have to say anything. I won't let anything happen to you," Carl assured her. He tightened his arms around her, and she felt his lips press against her hair. He rubbed her back, continuing to warm her with his touch. She curled her fingers in his shirt, enveloped in the safety of his embrace.

"Everything's going to be fine. Alec said he felt your energy pull the other day when you caused the other earthquake. Maybe he felt it again just now and can trace it. Either way, I'm sure he's tearing apart all four districts trying to find you."

"Maybe," Kayla whispered. She hoped it was true, but there was no way she'd wait around for someone to rescue her. She'd figure out a way to get them out of this situation, even if she had to bring down the entire building in the process.

CHAPTER SEVENTEEN

KAYLA WATCHED as Carl twisted the metal clamp on the cot back and forth. Just a little more and ... there. With a grunt, Carl managed to snap off the piece of metal. She took it from him and began trying to pry the cover off the door-locking mechanism.

"I've never seen a keypad like that one," Carl observed from over her shoulder.

She hadn't either. One of the corners lifted slightly, and she moved on to the next. Even though she wasn't familiar with the design, it had the same function as any other door lock. Just like with most other things in life, underneath the fancy exterior, it shared a common purpose. The trick was getting under its skin.

She glanced back at him. "See if there's anything else we can use to hold this edge up. I need something flat to slip underneath it."

Carl turned away and began searching the room while she continued working on the keypad. Kayla heard the distinctive sound of footsteps approaching, and she scrambled back from the door. Carl caught her around her waist and pulled her behind him. She slipped the piece of metal into the waist-band of her pants just as the door slid open.

Sergei entered with two armed guards and pointed at Kayla. "You will come with me."

"Excuse me?" Kayla let out a bitter laugh. "I don't give a damn what you want."

Carl glanced down at her. "No. If she goes anywhere, I'm going with her."

"She comes alone. We either take her willingly or by force. That is your choice."

Kayla made an obscene gesture. "Does that mean fuck off in your language too?"

Sergei spoke to the guards and one of them grabbed Carl. Kayla watched as Carl's pent-up frustration finally had a target and he attacked the guard trying to restrain him. Sergei shouted into the hallway and two more men came into the room.

One of them reached for her. She sidestepped him by using one of the moves Mack had shown her. With her elbow, she gave him a sharp jab to the gut. When he hunched over, she spun around to kick him. He shoved her up against the wall and pressed his forearm against her throat, cutting off her air.

Just before she passed out, the guard abruptly removed his arm. She bent over, resting her hands on her knees and tried to take several deep breaths. *Crap. That hurt.* She rubbed her throat, convinced her bruises were going to have bruises if things kept going at this rate.

Kayla glanced up to see that three of the guards had subdued Carl and forced restraints back on his wrists. Sergei *tsked* at her and shook his head before gripping her arm and leaving the room.

She was marched back to the office she'd been in earlier. Lars was in the room and looked up when they entered. At least she didn't have to deal with restraints this time. Sergei nudged her toward a chair, and Kayla took a seat, debating her limited options. Even if she managed to find an opportunity to escape, she wouldn't leave Carl behind.

She crossed her arms and glared at her captives. "Are we going to keep playing musical chairs here? Because being dragged back and forth is really starting to piss me off."

Sergei went over to a cabinet in the corner of the room and pulled out a hydrating pack. He tossed it to her before sitting back down across from her.

Kayla caught it but hesitated for a moment. Now they were playing nice? She didn't trust it, but she wouldn't say no either. It was vital to keep herself sharp to get out of this situation. She opened the hydrating pack and took a long drink.

Lars studied her with a frown. "Why is her shirt torn?"

Sergei spoke rapidly in his language. Lars's expression darkened. He said a few curt words and Sergei nodded in response.

Kayla finished the hydrating pack and crumpled the container. She threw it at Sergei. He caught it easily and winked at her. *Damn. I need to work on my aim.*

"If you two are finished talking about me, you might want to tell me why you dragged me back here."

Lars frowned. "I understand you had a rather unpleasant experience with Ramiro. Sergei has assured me Ramiro was properly dealt with and will no longer be a problem."

"You must be pretty desperate if you enlisted someone like Ramiro for help to begin with."

"It was no surprise he fell from honor in your towers," Sergei said with a shrug. "His usefulness to us was short-lived. Now he is no longer problem."

Lars walked around the desk to stand closer to her. He clasped his hands behind his back in a move that reminded her of Alec. She couldn't help but wonder about his connection to OmniLab.

"I admit I was curious about your talents after your little display back at the trader camp. The amount of energy you channeled was substantial, but it didn't even seem to faze you. Then, you produced an earthquake to get out of a bad situation. You have my compliments. Your talents are earth-based?"

Kayla leaned back in the chair and kicked her feet up so they rested on the edge of Sergei's chair. Nope. No way. She wasn't getting into a conversation with Lars about energy crap. She ignored him and studied the wall instead.

Lars frowned. "The skill and power required to create an earthquake is no small feat. I find it strange though. You don't seem to have the temperament of an earth-based talent."

She made a show of stretching and yawning. If an earth-based talent had the temperament of her mother, then nope. Kayla wasn't even close. She hadn't realized personalities aligned with the type of energy someone could manipulate. That information might come in handy.

"I see you've chosen to be difficult."

Kayla snorted. He had no idea. Lars picked up his tablet and entered a few commands. "There's someone who would like to meet you. He'll be here in a moment."

"Sure, why not?" she retorted. "It's a regular freaking party in here."

Sergei chuckled and tapped the toe of her boot. "I am curious. If you are one of these Inner Circle members, why do you choose to live outside your towers?"

At Sergei's question, Lars looked up from his computer and waited for Kayla's response.

She dropped her feet to the ground and leaned forward. "First of all, they're not *my* towers. Secondly, I don't like being locked up. It pisses me off. A pretty cage is still a cage."

Before Sergei could reply, the door slid open and an older man with gray hair entered. It was difficult to determine his age. The lines etched upon his face seemed more of a tribute to the trials he'd experienced rather than the decades he'd survived. The moment he stepped into the room, his gaze immediately focused on Kayla. Recognition filled his blue eyes, and he gave her a wide smile.

"So you were right, Lars. Andrei's daughter managed to survive all these years. I'd recognize you anywhere. You have the look of your mother."

Kayla straightened in her chair and wondered about their ties to the towers. Other than the traders, she'd never heard of any Omni living on the surface. It was strange enough to see Lars here, but the appearance of this man made her wonder how many of them were running loose in her playground.

Sergei stood and offered the older man the chair. He thanked Sergei graciously and sat across from Kayla. This man carried himself with the same air of authority she'd seen in other Inner Circle members. It made her twitchy.

"My name is Trenon Noltreck," he introduced himself. "I doubt you have any memory of me though. You were a small child when I last saw you."

Great. Another trip down memory lane. Kayla was beginning to wish Alec had never stepped foot in Carl's camp and found her. She crossed her arms over her chest, not willing to play nice. After all, they were keeping her here against her will.

"So you're from those freakish towers too, huh? That's just great. Another zap-happy circle freak to join our little party."

Trenon looked surprised by her response and glanced at Lars. "Yes, I was from the towers originally, as were you. Like you, we didn't leave by choice. After your father died, five families challenged Edwin Tal'Vayr's claim to rule the High Council, and all five families were exiled from the towers and imprisoned."

Kayla recalled the empty seats she had seen at the High Council meeting. "Edwin's dead. If you want to go running back to the towers, be my guest. Your empty seats didn't look all that comfortable, but as far as I'm concerned, you're welcome to them. None of this has anything to do with me."

Trenon gave her a sad smile. "I'm afraid it does, my dear."

She scowled at him. The old man was pissing her off with his attempts at familiarity. She wasn't his dear or anything else. "I fail to see how. I didn't even know I was born there until recently. Besides, if you're an Omni, why the hell did you attack Carl's camp?"

"We're not Omnis," Lars bit out, his eyes flashing with anger. "The day they exiled us from the towers was the day *any* loyalty we felt toward OmniLab died."

Trenon held up his hand to silence the younger man. "I understand you've lived on the surface most of your life. However, the actions taken against us weren't conducted by a single individual. There were several members of the High Council who were responsible for our imprisonment and the deaths of our family members and friends. We seek retribution against all of them."

Her jaw dropped, and she shot to her feet. "Seriously? This is all about *politics*? You attacked Carl's camp and killed one of my friends to get back at some idiots on the High Council?"

Trenon's eyes hardened. "Blood is on your hands as well, Kayla Rath'Varein. There are always casualties in war. It's an unfortunate necessity. However, your presence on the surface has given us the opportunity to demand justice from the High Council for their crimes."

Kayla clenched her fists so tightly that her nails bit into her palms. "You've definitely got a couple of screws loose if you think I'm going to help you in any way. You bastards abducted us."

"I have no intention of harming you, my dear." Trenon's tone became placating. "Just the fact you are in our custody will give us the footing we need to make our demands."

Lars stepped forward and handed the computer tablet to Trenon. "You might be interested to know that even though they only met a month ago, she's engaged to Edwin's son."

Trenon looked at Kayla in surprise. "Is this true?"

Kayla swore under her breath. She was going to kill Alec for letting that announcement stand. "I'm *not* getting married."

The older man studied the tablet quietly for several minutes. When he finished, he considered her thoughtfully. "You've only known about your heritage for a month?"

She didn't answer.

"Lars, I want you to determine the scope of her talents," Trenon told the younger man and handed the tablet back to him. "If Alec is intent on marrying her this quickly and without any formal training, I want to know why."

Sergei leaned against the wall and chuckled. "I suspect many reasons."

Lars spoke sharply to Sergei and the man merely shrugged. Trenon gave them both disapproving looks. "Lars, please proceed."

As Lars approached Kayla, the older man explained, "This will only take a few minutes and won't hurt. Lars will just need to form a strong connection to test you."

Kayla backed away from Lars. She pressed herself against the wall and shook her head. "Screw you. If I wasn't going to let Ramiro touch me, I'm sure as hell not going to let you get near me."

Lars narrowed his gaze on her. "I am only interested in learning the extent of your abilities and talent. If you want to be difficult, we can drug you and determine the same thing. It's your call."

Kayla hesitated and then nodded in resignation. Above all else, she did not want to risk being drugged. Lars took another step toward her and reached out to touch her cheek. The intimate gesture unnerved her, and she resisted the urge to jerk away from him. She shuddered as he established a connection with her. It felt *wrong*. She didn't know how else to describe it, but it made her miss the purity of the connection she shared with Alec.

His blue eyes held hers as he probed her energy threads and connections. Kayla felt as though she were being stripped bare and her soul exposed. It was more than she could handle. She gathered a large amount of energy around her and pushed it toward him. Lars abruptly broke the connection.

He moved his hand to her throat in a threatening gesture. "If you try that again, I promise I'll retaliate and you won't enjoy it."

"I didn't enjoy being probed much either," she retorted. "Whatever you have in mind can't be much worse."

"Lars," Trenon warned.

"I'll handle this," Lars snapped without looking away from her.

Kayla sensed energy begin to swirl around him, and her eyes widened in surprise as a sudden wind began to circulate throughout the room. The surrounding air was sucked away and disappeared into the strange vortex. Even though he didn't tighten his grip around her throat, Kayla struggled to take a breath. Lars used the distraction to force a new connection with her. Energy flooded through her. It was no longer a timid exploration. Light and color bombarded her as Lars pushed to see how much energy she could handle.

She was reminded of her experience at the hands of Alec's father. Furious, she found a calm oasis in her mind and opened herself to the energy storm raging around her. Channeling both her own energy and the storm, Kayla redirected the attack back onto Lars. His eyes widened in shock when he realized she was assaulting him using his own tactics. He abruptly ceased the energy flow, and Kayla took another gasping breath as he once again severed their connection.

He shook his head and stared at her as though seeing her for the first time. There was a hint of awe in his voice as he said, "I was wrong. Your talents aren't earth-based."

She slid away from him, keeping her back against the wall. Her eyes darted to the door. She definitely needed to get out of here.

Lars glanced back at Trenon. "She channeled earth energy earlier, but she just now channeled my own air energy against me. Each time, her energy has a different nuance as though it changes its resonance to reflect mine."

The older man gaped at him. "That's impossible. Are you suggesting she's a spirit channeler? There hasn't been one among us in centuries."

"It's more than just a dual talent. I've never seen anything like it. If so, this explains why Alec bonded to her so quickly," Lars said quietly and looked down at her with a trace of pity in his eyes. "I'm surprised he allowed you to leave the towers." He lifted his hand and brushed his thumb across her check. A light trickle of sympathetic energy flowed over her. "He must be desperate to get you back."

Kayla jerked away from him. His hand froze in midair, as though he hadn't realized what he'd done. He slowly lowered his hand but didn't move away.

She swallowed. "How did you know we were bonded?"

Trenon's expression became thunderous. "Are you saying

he *claimed* her? Even if she is a spirit channeler, I can't believe he bonded to an untrained Drac'Kin."

"I can," Lars murmured as he continued to study her. "You didn't experience her energy. I've never felt anything like it before. She doesn't just channel it. It's part of her." He frowned and searched her gaze. "Did you even know what you were doing when you formed this bond?"

Kayla narrowed her eyes. The pity in Lars's eyes had unsettled her, but these personal questions were just pissing her off. She would not have this conversation with this creep. She jabbed her finger against his chest. "You ask a lot of questions but don't give very many answers. I'm not telling you a damn thing. You attacked Carl's camp, set it on fire, killed my friend, and then kidnapped us. I'm thrown into walls, smacked around, nearly raped, mentally probed by zap-happy circle freaks, and now you're asking me all sorts of personal questions. I've had a really shitty past couple of days and I'll be *damned* if I'm going to tell you anything."

"You're absolutely right, my dear," Trenon said diplomatically and stood. Kayla looked at the older man in surprise, wondering what sort of game he was playing now. "Sergei, I want you to take her to Miranda and see that she's given a chance to clean up and get something to eat."

Kayla shook her head. "No. Take me back to Carl."

"The trader?" Trenon raised his eyebrows and exchanged a look with Lars. "I'm sure you would be more comfortable in Miranda's quarters. We'll make sure he receives the same courtesies though. In exchange, I hope you'll give me the opportunity to speak with you after you've had a chance to rest."

She frowned. Okay, so their plan was to keep them separated for now. Kayla didn't like it, but it wasn't as though she had a choice. At least she'd get the chance to learn more about the layout of the camp.

CHAPTER EIGHTEEN

SERGEI ESCORTED Kayla through the narrow hallways of the compound and stopped outside an unfamiliar door. He knocked briefly, and a woman's voice called out for them to enter. He slid the door open and motioned for Kayla to step inside.

It was about the same size as the office, but there were two beds set up in the room. A desk with a computer terminal sat in the corner. Like the rest of the camp, it was relatively sparse.

A slender woman in her late twenties was seated at the desk and stood when they entered. Her golden hair was braided away from her heart-shaped face. She wasn't particularly beautiful, but there was something about her features that captured your attention. She wasn't a woman you'd easily forget. Her gray eyes softened slightly as she studied Kayla and smiled.

Sergei looked between the two of them. "Your father, he said to have her cleaned up."

Miranda nodded in understanding but didn't look away from Kayla. After several long seconds, she seemed to realize she hadn't said anything and laughed. "Forgive me. It's just strange to see you again, especially all grown up."

Kayla frowned and glanced at Sergei. He was leaning against the wall watching them. He'd apparently been instructed to hang out and play guard. She sighed and rubbed her forehead. "I've been getting that a lot today. Trenon is your father?"

"Yes. I was a teenager when we were forced to leave the towers. But I suppose you've already heard the story."

"He didn't mention he had a daughter," Kayla admitted as she assessed the room. It was another windowless room with two doors. Sergei guarded the entrance, and the other door was an unknown. The presence of a computer was promising though. "I thought Trenon and Lars might be related."

Miranda shook her head and opened a bag that was lying on one of the beds. "No, we're not. But over the years, we've become a family of sorts. It was the only way to survive. I'm sure, given your own situation, you can understand that." She glanced at Kayla before pulling out a shirt and handing it to her.

"Unfortunately, I don't think my pants will fit you. If you'd like to shower and get cleaned up, there's a bathroom through that door." Miranda gestured to a closed door. Kayla took the shirt and glanced at the door. That solved one mystery.

"Are you hungry? I can arrange to have something brought to you."

She frowned. Was all of this an attempt to lower her defenses? She'd been through this before with traders offering various things in exchange to get what they wanted. "Will something be taken to Carl?"

"I'm assuming you're referring to the trader?" At Kayla's nod, Miranda smiled. "I'll make the arrangements, if it hasn't already been done."

"Thanks." Kayla headed to the bathroom. Shutting the

door, she looked around the room. It was basic in design and reminded her of the camp's bathroom. There was nothing much in here she could use to escape. At least she could try to wash off the memory of Ramiro though. With a sigh, Kayla pulled off her clothes and stepped into the shower. The water pressure was slightly better than expected, and she quickly scrubbed her skin.

When she finished, she pulled on the black shirt Miranda have given her. The material was soft and lightweight, but it was different from anything she'd seen created by OmniLab. It was more form-fitting and lower cut. She frowned at the realization Alec's necklace was noticeable under the material.

There wasn't much she could do about it. With the metal piece hidden in the waistband of her pants, the only other place to hide the necklace was her pockets. Those were usually the first places searched.

Sergei straightened from his post at the door when she walked back into the room. Miranda gestured to a plate over on the desk. "The food was just delivered. Help yourself."

Kayla sat down and glanced at the computer terminal, itching to get her fingers on the controls. She forced herself to take a bite of the prepackaged meal instead, chewing automatically and barely tasting the food.

Miranda sat on the edge of one of the beds and folded her hands in her lap. "They're taking a meal to the trader now. If you'd like, you can stay here with me tonight. It'll give us a chance to get to know one another better."

Kayla raised an eyebrow. Did they really think she'd suddenly become best friends with them simply because they offered her a shower and some food? She might be susceptible to bribes, but she wasn't that cheap. She swallowed another bite and waved her fork. "I'd rather stay with Carl."

Miranda cocked her head and seemed genuinely surprised

by her response. The woman glanced at Sergei and then said noncommittally, "I'll see if Lars will agree to that."

Of course he wouldn't, but they weren't ready to show that hand yet. They were still playing nice. Kayla shrugged. Whatever. Time for some information gathering. "How did you guys end up hooking up with the Coalition?"

The woman's face darkened. "OmniLab imprisoned us on the surface for several years. Thanks to Lars and his talents, we managed to escape, and the Coalition discovered us. They listened to our story and agreed to help us in exchange for our loyalty."

Kayla poked at the food on the plate. "How many of you are there?"

"Not as many as when we left the towers," Miranda said with a sigh. "We lost several people while we were imprisoned. If OmniLab had provided us with basic medical care, we would have been able to save them. As it was, they barely gave us enough food and water to survive."

It sounded like the situation in the ruin rat camps. She imagined it would be difficult for someone used to the opulent luxury in the towers to adjust to the harsh life outside. In some ways, Kayla decided she probably had an easier time of it. Unlike Miranda, she couldn't remember ever living in the towers.

Miranda looked down at her hands. "I lost my mother before we were forced out of the towers. She was one of the people in the ruins with you and your father when it collapsed. It was difficult when she died, but it was easier for me to understand. Accidents happen. What Lars and the others went through was so much worse. Lars not only lost his mother in the ruins, but after we were imprisoned, he watched his father and sister die from an illness that could have been easily treated."

Kayla's fork froze in midair. Dammit. She didn't want to

feel sympathy for these people. It was bad enough they'd all suffered huge losses. It would make things even worse if they knew the ruin collapse hadn't been an accident and that Alec's father had orchestrated the entire mass murder. Would they blame Alec for his father's decisions?

She pushed away her plate, unable to stomach eating anything else. "I get that you're pissed off about what happened. I don't blame you. But none of this has anything to do with me. If you have a problem with OmniLab, you should take it up with them."

Miranda leaned forward. "You're one of us, Kayla. We channel the same energy you do. If you trace our lineage, you'd find we share ties of blood too. We don't want you to be hurt by any of this. We just want your help to bring justice to those who deserve it."

"You have a twisted way of asking for help," Kayla muttered.

"I know. We didn't expect you to be on the surface, or things probably would have happened differently."

"Why don't you let us go then? I can ask Alec to help you."

Miranda shook her head. "I'm sorry, but it's not that simple. Alec may have not been responsible for what happened, but he's a Tal'Vayr. Lars wants ... never mind. I've said too much already. But it's not just Alec. We all want the High Council to be held responsible for their actions."

Alarm bells started to go off in her head. "What does Lars want with Alec?"

Miranda hesitated before she spoke. "Is it true you're bonded to him?"

Kayla frowned, unsure how much she should reveal. She sort of liked the woman, but that was probably their plan. It wasn't a coincidence that they put her in here with Miranda. Out of all of them, Miranda had a warm and appealing nature that was difficult to resist. Lars already knew about the bond, so there wasn't much harm in admitting it.

"Yeah, we're bonded. It was accidental though. I got in a little over my head and Alec bonded with me to save me."

Miranda's eyes widened, and she leaned forward. "Do you care for him?"

Whoa. Kayla gave Miranda a sharp look. "That's none of your business."

"You're right," she said, backpedalling quickly and holding up her hands. "I apologize. I'm just surprised. I've only heard of bonds between two dedicated partners."

Kayla shrugged. "Yeah, well. Accidents happen."

"I see," Miranda murmured and cocked her head. "Lars said you can channel spirit energy. I've never heard of anyone being able to do that before."

Kayla frowned and didn't answer. Word had gotten around quickly. Lars must have sent Miranda a message the moment Sergei brought her here. Kayla glanced over at Sergei who, at first glance, appeared engrossed in his commlink. When she didn't respond to Miranda, he looked up and met her gaze. Yep. He was hanging on every word.

Miranda scooted forward. "If there were a way to remove the bond you share with Alec, would you be interested?"

Kayla's eyes flew back to the woman sitting on the bed. "How? I was told it was permanent."

Miranda gave her a sad smile. "I've learned nothing in this life is permanent. Things can change, even so-called permanent bonds. If there were a way to sever your bond, would you want to remove it?"

Kayla hesitated. She had the feeling there was more to this question than the woman was leading her to believe. "I don't know. I thought it was permanent, so I've never considered an alternative. There's no point in speculating about what-ifs."

"I see." Miranda picked at the threads on the blanket. She seemed to be deciding whether or not to say something. A knock at the door interrupted them. Lars entered and spoke with Sergei for a moment. Sergei nodded and then disappeared down the hall.

Miranda stood and gave Lars a warm smile. "I was about to call you. Kayla has asked to be returned to the trader rather than staying here."

Lars raised an eyebrow. "What is the trader to you?"

Kayla put her hands on her hips and glared at him. "That's none of your business."

His eyes raked over her as though trying to ferret out her secrets. Suddenly, he stopping studying her and crossed the room toward her. Kayla bit back a groan, knowing he'd spotted the necklace. He lifted it and ran his thumb over the green stone. His eyes flew up to meet hers. "Did Alec give this to you?"

She pressed her lips together and didn't answer.

Miranda stepped forward and interrupted before he could say anything else. "Lars, could I speak with you for a moment?"

He continued to stare at Kayla for a long moment before releasing the necklace and moving away. He inclined his head, and Miranda motioned for him to join her outside. As soon as the door closed behind them, Kayla dove for Miranda's bag. She rifled through it and found some sort of small multipurpose tool. Kayla grinned and slipped it into her pocket before readjusting the bag so it didn't appear to have been touched.

She could still hear the low din of voices outside, so she moved over to the computer terminal and turned it on. The system was different than what she was used to working with, but there were some similarities. She entered in a few keystrokes and scowled as the computer rejected her commands. She continued to make several more attempts and then watched in satisfaction as the data retrieved from Carl's camp was erased. With a satisfied grin, she pulled up a diagram of the camp and began memorizing the layout.

If her calculations were correct, Carl was being held on the opposite side of the camp. As long as the earthquake damaged no other areas, she could get to him pretty easily. The biggest problem was she didn't know how many people were living within the camp.

Unfortunately, most of the other information on the system was indecipherable. Strange characters displayed on the screen that she could only assume were in some other unfamiliar language. Frustrated, she shut off the monitor and began drumming her fingers impatiently on the desk.

Miranda and Lars reappeared several minutes later. Miranda seemed pleased by something, as evidenced by her cheerful smile, while Lars rubbed the back of his neck. Kayla couldn't help but wonder what Miranda had said to him. He seemed frustrated. Kayla wasn't sure if that boded well for her or not.

Her skin suddenly prickled, and she rubbed her arms. Something wasn't right. Her eyes narrowed at Lars. "What the hell did you just do?"

Lars raised an eyebrow. A slight smile played across his lips, making him appear almost approachable. Almost.

"You're extremely sensitive to energy manipulation, aren't you?"

"Lars," Miranda warned and shook her head.

He sighed and gave a small shrug. "I simply channeled energy around you to see if you would notice. Most people wouldn't have even realized it."

Kayla scowled. "I'm not a damn test subject."

"This isn't the way," Miranda said softly.

Lars blew out a breath and held out his hand. "Very well.

Come along, Kayla. I'll have Sergei take you back to the trader."

She eyed his hand with suspicion. *Nope. Not gonna happen.* She shoved her hands in her back pockets and nodded toward the door. "Sounds good. Let's go."

He darted a glance at Miranda, but she shook her head at him. He grumbled under his breath and lowered his hand before opening the door. Lars took her to the room across the hall which seemed to be used as some sort of tech or communications room. Sergei was leaning over a man working on a console and they both looked up when they entered. He gave Kayla a slow smile and murmured something in his language.

Lars gave Kayla a long, lingering look. "Yes, she does." He then cleared his throat and focused again on Sergei. "Kayla has asked to be returned to her cell for the evening instead of remaining here."

Sergei straightened and nodded. "I will take her." He held out his hand to her. "Come, *Milaya*," he instructed, and she slipped her hand in his. Lars frowned, but Kayla shrugged. Sergei wasn't going to zap her.

She followed Sergei back through the maze of the camp and tried to recall the image of the floorplan on the computer. Kayla was fairly confident she could find her way around once they were on their own. Trying to avoid the numerous people in the camp would be the biggest challenge. To make matters worse, judging by the interested glances and number of men she counted, she and Miranda were likely two of the few women in camp. Blending in would be difficult.

She suspected the Coalition had a secondary location. Miranda seemed to just be visiting, and Trenon had recently arrived from somewhere else. They could be right under OmniLab's nose if they had the same type of masking ability in their other camp.

Sergei opened the door and gestured for her to enter. Carl was sitting on the cot but stood when she entered. He'd changed into different clothing and his hair was still slightly damp. She hurried over to him, and Carl pulled her into his arms.

Sergei chuckled. "Ah. So *that* is why she insisted on returning."

She felt Carl tense, but he didn't reply. They could think whatever they wanted. Kayla didn't want to admit it, but she'd been scared out of her mind since they attacked Carl's camp. She needed this. She needed Carl and his reassurance. The sound of the door closing and the lock engaging sounded from behind her.

"Are you all right, sweetheart?" Carl tilted her head back to look at him.

There was a small cut above his eye she hadn't noticed before. She frowned and looked over the rest of him. His knuckles were bruised and raw from the earlier fighting.

Reassured that his injuries were minor, she nodded and told him everything that had happened.

After she finished, he was quiet for a long moment and then said, "I think it's safe to assume they're not going to be ransoming us back to the towers for supplies."

"Yeah, I've gotten that impression," she muttered and reached into her pocket to pull out the stolen tool.

He chuckled. "I've never been more thankful for your ruin rat ways."

She grinned at him. "I'll remind you of that next time you start bitching at me for being reckless."

Carl bent down and took possession of her mouth. Kayla kissed him with all the desperation she'd been feeling since they arrived. He took control of the kiss, promising with actions rather than words that he would appreciate her even more once they were safe and alone.

He pressed one last kiss against her lips before pulling away. "Are you sure you want do this? We can wait a bit longer to see if Alec shows up."

Kayla shook her head. "He would have been here by now if he knew our location. I don't know what these guys are planning, but I don't think we should wait to find out. I don't know enough about the energy stuff to protect myself against Lars. He's powerful. I think he's probably as powerful as Alec, but I really don't want to find out for sure."

Carl took the tool from her and studied it. "How do you want to do this?"

She removed the metal clamp from her waistband. "We need to get to the entrance to get the rest of our UV gear. Unfortunately, there are a lot more people in the camp than I expected, and they all seem to be armed."

Carl frowned. "They took me to a shower area down the hall, so I got a brief look around. There's only one guard stationed at our door. As long as we're able to surprise him, I should be able to disarm him and get his weapon. Think you'll have any problems working the lock on the door?"

She smirked. "Have you forgotten who you're talking to?"

He chuckled. She took the tool from him and bent down in front of the door. If she had her frequency detector, she could probably bypass all the wiring. Unfortunately, she'd have to make do with what she had. Kayla handed the metal clamp to Carl and instructed him to use it as a lever to remove the cover panel. Once the cover was removed, she used the multipurpose tool to strip and re-splice the wiring.

After several minutes, she looked up at Carl and nodded. "It should work. You ready?"

Carl shook his head and placed his hand on her shoulder. "Not yet. As soon as I go after the guard, I want you to head directly to the entrance. Don't wait for me. I'll catch up. You need to get to the towers. That's the only place you're going to be safe from these guys."

Kayla straightened her shoulders and put her hands on her hips. "Forget it. We're staying together. I'm not going anywhere without you."

"Dammit, Kayla, you're the one they want. They aren't interested in me."

Kayla shook her head and took a step toward him. Panic welled inside her as she curled her fingers in his shirt. "Please, Carl, don't ask me to leave you behind while you try to rescue me. I can't—I can't ever do that again. I lost Pretz because I listened to him when he told me to run. Don't ask me to do that. I can't lose you. It'll destroy me."

Carl's eyes softened, and he pulled her against him. His breath was warm against her ear as he said, "God, Kayla, I didn't even think. I'm sorry. I just want you to be safe." He brushed a kiss against her neck. "We'll do this together. Okay?"

She clung to him and nodded against his chest.

He pulled back and kissed her forehead. "Go ahead and disengage the lock, sweetheart."

She took a deep breath and twisted the last set of wires together. The door beeped and slid open. Carl lunged forward and slipped his arm around the guard's neck, jerking him backward in a chokehold. The man thrashed and fumbled for his weapon as Carl cut off his supply of air.

The guard was unconscious in a matter of seconds. Carl dragged him back inside the room and quickly removed the guard's jacket and weapon. He tossed the jacket to Kayla. "Put it on."

Kayla slipped it on while Carl studied the weapon. She zipped up the jacket and looked over his arm at the device. "I couldn't read any of the settings on that thing when I took it from the guard in your camp. I just clicked and fired. It only worked once, so there may be some reset mechanism that you need to press after you use it. Don't count on it for more than one shot."

Carl nodded. "That'll have to work. Let's go."

He stood and looked out into the hallway. After a moment, he motioned for Kayla to follow him. They walked quickly down the hall and paused at an intersection. Two guards were talking and walking in the adjacent direction.

"Hang on," he whispered to Kayla. "They're leaving."

She nodded, pressing her back against the wall as Carl leaned forward to watch the guards. A shout rang out from behind them, and Kayla turned to see a guard running in their direction.

"Come on!" Carl shouted and grabbed her hand. They ran down the opposite hallway and into two more guards. Carl pushed Kayla behind him and fired the weapon toward them. One of them collapsed on the floor and the other turned and pulled out his weapon. The guard pointed it at Carl and fired.

"Carl!" Kayla cried out as he staggered and fell to the floor. She knelt next to him as the two guards rushed up to her. One of them grabbed her around her waist and started to pull her away. Without thinking, she filled herself with energy and felt it flow through her hands as she pushed against the guard restraining her.

He screamed and released her abruptly. The other guard ran toward her, and Kayla instinctively threw a large amount of energy toward him. He flew backward into the wall. Kayla dropped back to the floor next to Carl.

"No!" she yelled, tears filling her eyes. She planted her hands on his chest, shaking him and pleading with him to get up. More footsteps and shouts rapidly approached, but she ignored them. Carl had to be okay. She couldn't lose him. A moment later, Lars grabbed her by the waist and lifted her away.

"Let go!" she screamed and threw a large amount of energy toward him. He deflected it and tried to circle it back around toward her. She shrugged it off and opened herself completely to the surrounding power. The ground began to tremble as she channeled increasingly more energy. Caring and reason left her. None of it mattered. They'd killed Carl.

A biting wind whipped around them, and she realized Lars was trying to subdue her again by cutting off her air. Enraged, she tapped into his energy, yanking it from him and redirecting it back toward him, lashing at him with it like a whip. Lars struggled against her onslaught, trying to stop her attack and suppress her energy with his.

She was dimly aware of Trenon and Miranda running down the hall toward them. Fury ripped through her. They were all responsible for taking Carl away from her. She now fully understood how Alec was able to kill his father. The mantle of judge, jury, and executioner was one she'd willingly adorn.

"By the ancestors," Trenon whispered as he stared at Kayla and Lars.

She ignored Trenon and forced more energy toward Lars, who had dropped to one knee and pressed his hand against the wall in a desperate attempt to stay upright. The energy whipped through her, threatening to steal parts of her soul. She didn't care. If it took away everything, maybe it would also take away the pain. Tears streamed down her face.

She dimly heard Miranda calling out to Lars, but the roar in her head was too loud. Even if she and Miranda shared ties of blood like the woman claimed, they weren't family. How could family take away the one person she'd allowed herself to love completely?

The surrounding air shifted, collapsing a nearby wall. There was a scream in the distance, but Kayla no longer cared if the entire building fell down around them.

Miranda reached for Lars, and when they touched, a painful rush of energy shot out toward Kayla. They must have merged their energy against her. Kayla cried out and winced, raising a hand toward Miranda to stop the onslaught. Energy erupted from her hand, and Miranda stumbled backward. When the woman fell, Kayla turned her focus back to Lars.

He was still struggling to keep her from turning the energy storm back toward him. Kayla could feel him growing weaker and she pressed on further. Miranda stared at them in fear and grabbed the weapon Carl had dropped on the ground. With shaking hands, Miranda pointed it at Kayla and fired.

Pain flooded through her at the impact. With a gasp, Kayla staggered and released the energy she was channeling. Darkness edged at the corner of her vision, and she felt Lars catch her as she began to fall. Her eyes closed, and her last thought was of Carl as she faded into darkness.

CHAPTER NINETEEN

KAYLA WOKE UP FEELING DAZED. Her head was pounding, and she whimpered at the harsh light flooding the room. A sharp voice issued a command, and the lights dimmed. Kayla risked opening them once again and found herself looking up into Lars's startling blue eyes.

"Take a few deep breaths and move slowly. The dizziness will pass in a minute."

Lars slipped his arm around her and helped her sit up. As he predicted, a wave of dizziness washed over her. She tried to ignore it and gauge her surroundings. She was back in Miranda's room. Lars was sitting on the bed next to her, and Trenon was sitting on the opposite bed. Sergei leaned against the wall watching them while Miranda was nowhere to be found. It was just as well. The bitch had shot her, and Kayla wasn't feeling very forgiving.

A wave of nausea rolled through her. She pulled her legs up and wrapped her arms around them. Why wouldn't they just leave her alone? Kayla lowered her head to her knees and muttered, "Go away."

Trenon leaned forward and said in a no-nonsense tone, "I

understand you've been through a great deal, my dear. I've tried to be patient with you, but after that display, we need to talk. I'm afraid it won't wait."

Kayla turned her head to glare at him. Even the slight movement made her stomach roil. "All of you can go fuck yourselves. I'm done."

Lars glanced at Trenon and then said, "We'll take you to see Carl after you answer our questions."

Her eyes flew back to Lars, and she grabbed his arm. A slight tingle went through her at the contact, but she ignored it. If he was lying, her new life's mission would be to make him suffer. "He's alive?"

Lars glanced down at her hand on his arm. "Yes, like you, he was merely stunned."

"I want to see him," she demanded and tried to climb off the bed. Unfortunately, her legs didn't seem to want to support her weight yet. Lars pulled her back down to sit on the bed before she fell.

"You can see him after you answer our questions."

She pulled away. "No. I don't believe you. I want proof he's alive."

Lars nodded to Sergei who brought over a small tablet. She eagerly took the tablet and saw a video image of Carl. He was sitting up in a bed and rubbing his chest as though in pain. Miranda and a guard stood next to him.

It was real. Carl was alive. Tears welled in her eyes as she choked on a sob, burying her face in her hands. All of this was too much. She thought she'd lost him.

"He'll be fine," Lars assured her. "As soon as you finish answering our questions, we'll take you to him."

She nodded and wiped away her tears. As long as Carl continued breathing, she'd answer whatever questions they wanted. "All right. What do you want to know?"

Trenon's eyes lit up, and he inched forward. "Where did

you learn to manipulate multiple types of energy simultaneously?"

Her brow furrowed. "Huh?"

"In the hallway, you were channeling earth, air, and fire energy at the same time. Where did you learn this skill?"

"I did?" she asked in surprise and tried to remember exactly what had happened. All she remembered was being really pissed off. When Lars tried to cut off her air, she tried to turn it back on him. Other than that, she wasn't sure. At some point, she just gave herself up to the energy and let it consume her. She had no idea how to duplicate it.

Lars searched her face and frowned. "You don't have any idea what he's talking about, do you?"

Kayla hesitated and then shook her head. There was no point in lying. "No. Alec told me about the different types of energy the other day, but he only showed me how he could manipulate air energy. I left before he could have someone show me the others. I don't know how it happened."

Trenon gaped at her. "You're telling me that display was purely instinctual?"

"I don't give a shit what you call it," she snapped. "No, I haven't been trained. I've spent less than a week in those freakish towers and I have no intention of going back. Anytime I get involved with OmniLab, everything goes to shit. I thought you killed Carl. I don't know what the hell I did or how I did it, but it might be a good idea not to piss me off in the future." She crossed her arms. "If those are all your questions, I'd like to see Carl now."

The look of shock on Trenon's face was almost comical. Lars, on the other hand, was eyeing her with skepticism.

"Before you erased the data we gathered from Carl's camp —which we're in the process of reconstructing—I read your bio. You're smart, Kayla. A little *too* smart. You're not gullible, and you don't trust easily. Otherwise, you wouldn't have survived this long on your own. Miranda indicated the bond between you and Alec wasn't intentional. How did it happen?"

Kayla frowned, not wanting to tell them about the bracelets that linked energy together. She'd made sure the instructions on how to create the bracelets was destroyed, but information never truly disappeared. Instead, Kayla asked the question that had been plaguing her since Miranda put the idea into her head. She hoped they wouldn't fixate on the other. "It was an accident. I didn't know what I was doing, and Alec stepped in to help me. Miranda said there may be a way to remove the bond though. Is that true?"

Trenon and Lars exchanged looks and Lars nodded. "Yes, it's possible."

"How?" Kayla demanded. "Alec told me it was permanent. Now both you and Miranda are telling me it can be removed? If that's true, I'm going to cut off his balls when I get hold of him."

Lars raised an eyebrow. "So you didn't go into this claim willingly?"

"Dammit, no," she hissed and stood up. Although a little shaky, her legs seemed to be functioning again. Kayla ran a hand through her hair in agitation. None of this made sense. Could Alec have lied to her about something like that? She didn't think so, but anything was possible. She needed answers. All she'd been getting were half-truths and tidbits of information.

"This whole bond thing has been a pain in my ass since it happened. If it can be broken, why the hell did he let it go on this long?"

Trenon shot Lars a warning look. Lars cleared his throat. "Kayla, it's apparent that he took advantage of your inexperience. You mentioned that Alec showed you how he can channel air energy earlier?"

"Yeah," she muttered in irritation and began pacing the confines of the small room.

"We probably share similar abilities," Lars suggested.

She stopped pacing. Where was he going with this? "Well, yeah, you can both do the wind thing. Although Alec never tried to suffocate me with it."

"What else can Alec do?"

Kayla's eyes narrowed. Even if Lars had given her reason to question the bond between herself and Alec, it didn't mean she trusted him. "Yeah, like I'm going to tell you that. Even though he's a cocky prick and I'm going to enjoy making him sing several octaves higher when I get through with him, I'm not giving you assholes any advantages over him. You killed Zane, almost killed Carl, and you're holding us here against our will. Alec may piss me off, but I trust him a hell of a lot more than you."

Trenon rubbed his chin in thought. "You care for this trader, don't you?"

She whirled on him. "Don't you dare touch him. He has nothing to do with any of this."

Trenon held up his hand. "That depends solely on you. We may be able to come to an arrangement to make sure he remains in good health."

Kayla swallowed and took a step back. Her internal alarms were starting to go off as a sick feeling began to creep into her stomach. "What sort of arrangement?"

Lars shook his head. "No, Trenon, we won't harm the trader and risk a repeat of what happened earlier." He focused on Kayla once again. "But we can offer to release him, unharmed, and send him back to OmniLab towers. In addition, we'll also remove the bond you share with Alec."

Her eyes narrowed. "What's the catch?"

Trenon nodded to Lars. The younger man stood, clasping

his hands behind his back. "In return, you'll agree to allow me to claim you."

Kayla stared at him, completely dumbfounded. The silence in the room was practically deafening.

"Let me get this straight," she said in an eerily calm voice. "You want to remove my bond with Alec and replace it with your own?"

"Yes."

"Are you fucking kidding me?!" she shouted, gesturing wildly with her hands. "You think I'd ever *willingly* let another zap-happy circle freak throw energy at me and turn me into a brainless idiot whenever he wants? Fuck you and the speeder you rode in on. There's no way in hell I'm letting you claim me. I don't want anything to do with you people."

Her rant seemed to take Lars off guard. "Are you telling me Alec uses your bond to take advantage of you?"

She looked startled for a minute and then shook her head. Waving off his concerns, she said, "What? No, Alec's not like that. It's none of your damn business anyway."

Kayla sat back down on the bed and crossed her arms over her chest. Lars was quiet for a moment and then asked, "If I gave you my word I would never use our connection in that manner, would you consider it?"

She huffed and glared up at him. "Yeah, right. Like I'm going to take the word of someone who killed my friend and abducted me. Let me be very clear here. If you were the last man on earth and I was the last woman, humanity would be doomed."

"I see," Lars said calmly. "It's obvious you didn't know what you were doing when you formed the bond. I would imagine Alec's ability to channel energy was irresistible to you, especially without any formal training. Is that why you left the towers?"

Kayla stared down at her hands and shrugged. "I don't

belong in the towers. That life and those people don't make sense to me." She looked up at her captors and shook her head. "I don't even understand you guys. You have this vendetta against the High Council and you want to punish them, but for what? Do you want your place in the towers back? Are you looking for revenge?"

She made a wide, sweeping gesture. "There's a whole world out there. There are thousands of people struggling to stay alive right now. Some of them are dying from starvation or from not having proper medical supplies. I know you've seen this. You've experienced it. You've lived it. How can any of you justify wasting your time on this political bullshit if you've experienced the precariousness of life? Why are you wasting your time focusing on revenge instead of embracing each and every moment you're alive?"

Kayla looked over at Sergei, who was watching her with a sharp gleam in his eyes. She understood him far better than Lars and Trenon. Maybe she could reason with him. "I know you couldn't care less about their politics, Sergei. You're only in this for the end result. You want to use OmniLab's talents to help with rebuilding, but you want to do it under your organization's banner. I get it. It's a more noble cause than what they're trying to do, but it won't work."

Sergei cocked his head. "Why not?"

She gave him a sad smile. "People in power don't easily relinquish their power. OmniLab may agree to work with you, but they won't ever bow down to you. How much is a power struggle worth to you? Is it worth possibly losing all those lives and great minds just so you can say you're all part of the Coalition? Why not just let them keep their independence and work with you? You're both working toward the same goal. Who cares if you share the same name?"

Sergei raised an eyebrow and didn't reply. Trenon sighed and pinched the bridge of his nose. "You are truly your father's daughter, Kayla Rath'Varein. If he had lived, he would have been proud of the woman you've become."

"I don't know much about him," she admitted. "I've only heard bits and pieces. But if you truly called him and my mother friends, why are you doing this to me? You're taking away my free will just like OmniLab took away yours. Where's the justice in that?"

Trenon and Lars looked at each other. Lars sat on the bed next to her and sighed. There was a defeated look in his eyes as he said, "I never thought I'd be shamed by a girl who barely reaches my chin. You're right, Kayla. Our intention was to force out the corruption in the High Council and take our rightful places. I won't lie and say I don't still want that though. They need to be held accountable and punished for their crimes."

"Then let me talk to Alec," she urged. "I know he'll do what's right."

Lars let out a bitter laugh. "You're wrong. Alec knows what happened to us. He was there when his father and the other councilors made the agreement to exile us from the towers. He might not have been able to stop it, but he could have given us warning. He had plenty of opportunities. In fact, I was with him when they came for us. He never said a word. He just watched as they arrested us."

She shook her head, denying his words. "I know he's not perfect. He's made mistakes, but he's a good man. If you give him a chance, he'll make this right. There must have been some reason he didn't say anything before. Alec wouldn't have done that unless he didn't have a choice."

Lars studied her and shook his head in disbelief. "Unbelievable. You're in love with Carl *and* Alec, aren't you? How the hell did Alec manage to gain your loyalty within such a short amount of time?"

Kayla opened her mouth to argue but couldn't vocalize

the words. She looked away. Lars was right. How could a complete stranger have seen what she'd been denying? She loved both of them. She realized in that moment that although she didn't want to lose Carl, she didn't want to lose the bond she shared with Alec either. Alec was right when he called her on it in the towers. What was between them wasn't superficial. She didn't understand it, but she'd been so focused on denying their energy bond that she'd denied her feelings too.

Lars sighed and lifted her chin with his fingers so he could gaze into her eyes. "I know Alec far better than you could imagine, little one. He would never have been able to bond with you unless he cared for you. I suspect sharing a bond with you and watching you with your trader is its own form of torture."

She frowned. Lars and Alec were close to the same age. "Were you friends in the towers?"

"We were much closer than friends." Lars reached down and lifted the emerald necklace from her neck once again. He ran his thumb over the pendant. "I never thought I'd see this again. My mother was wearing the matching stone to this one when she died." He lifted his gaze to meet hers and gave her a bitter smile. "Your precious Alec is my cousin. Our mothers were sisters. My Uncle Edwin was the one who had us imprisoned."

CHAPTER TWENTY

KAYLA'S EYES WIDENED. Everything began to make sense. Lars had no idea what Alec had experienced at the hands of his father. Edwin Tal'Vayr had been a crazed tyrant who ruled with an iron fist. His son hadn't been immune to his wrath. Alec had walked a narrow line trying to appease the man and act as a buffer to protect the people he cared about.

"You need to talk to him," she urged Lars. "There are things about Edwin you don't know."

Lars raised an eyebrow. "I had a younger sister named Anna. She was your age, or she would have been if she'd survived that first year on the surface. Instead, she died from pneumonia. We couldn't do anything but watch as she struggled to breathe. One vial of medicine could have saved her. One!" His eyes hardened. "There isn't any excuse that can justify what happened to her."

Kayla squeezed her eyes shut. She could understand his pain. She'd experienced it enough watching her own camp-mates and even Veridian's mother die. It was senseless, and these deaths could have been easily prevented. No one knew that more than her. But even so, Lars was blaming the wrong person. Alec wasn't responsible for what happened to Lars's sister. Kayla opened her mouth to tell him everything, but a screeching alarm began blaring throughout the camp.

Sergei shouted in his foreign tongue and ran out the door. Lars shot to his feet and grabbed Kayla's arm.

"Trenon, get to the east exit. Sergei will meet you there with Miranda."

The older man didn't hesitate and rushed from the room. Lars's grip tightened on Kayla's arm as he pulled her out of the room. Across the hall was the communications room she'd seen earlier. Lars began barking orders to the two men stationed within the room. She didn't know what he was saying, but it was clear they were wiping their systems clean.

She looked up at Lars. "Alec's here, isn't he?"

He glanced down and gave her a curt nod. "I suspect as long as you two are bonded, he'll be able to sense you. That little display over your trader probably acted as a beacon and drew him right to us."

Kayla glanced at the men who were finishing up. "What are you going to do?"

Lars looked down at her and shook his head. "I can't exactly take you with me, can I? You'll just light up the room again and not in a good way."

Her brow furrowed. Kayla wasn't sure she liked the sound of that. The two technicians headed out, but Lars made no move to follow them. The look in his eyes made her nervous. She started to take a step backward, but he stopped her. He wrapped his arm around her waist and pulled her close. A warm pulse of energy floated over her skin and seemed to fill her from within. She shivered from the sensation. It wasn't a bad feeling. It was just different from the way Alec's energy felt. Lars drew her close and leaned down, his mouth hovering a breath away from her ear.

"You have options, little one. Don't believe everything Alec tells you." He pressed a kiss against the side of her neck.

"Let her go, Lars."

Lars drew back slightly to look at someone standing behind her, but he didn't release her. Kayla twisted her neck to find Alec and Brant standing in the hallway.

Alec was staring at Lars with a thunderous look on his face. The High Council leader's blue eyes lit with fury as his fists clenched. He reminded Kayla of a fallen hero intent on vengeance. The energy in the room became tight with tension. Unable to resist, she reached out to Alec with her energy threads.

As though he sensed it, Lars pulled her closer. His arm tightened around her, and a cool blanket of energy enveloped them, thwarting her efforts to reach Alec. She felt a sharp nick against her side and gasped. Lars had pressed a knife against her. "I was wondering when you'd show up, Alec. I'm surprised you let this little one out of your sight. She has some amazing talents and doesn't even realize the full scope of her potential. And her taste? Exquisite. It's a shame you let her get away."

Lars leaned down and nuzzled the side of her neck. Kayla's eyes widened, but she didn't move. It was obvious Lars was trying to bait Alec. Unfortunately, judging by the expression on Alec's face, it seemed to be working. Kayla was tempted to push him away, but Lars was too much of an unknown. The knife digging into her side was a heady deterrent. Since she was rather attached to her organs, she'd play hostage for now.

"What do you want?" Alec bit out.

Lars jerked his head toward Brant. "For starters, send your minion away so we can talk."

Alec's jaw clenched, and he jerked his head in agreement.

Brant's expression darkened, but the security officer moved back down the hallway and well out of range.

"What would you give me for her, cousin? How much does her life mean to you?"

"Anything," Alec replied in a whisper and glanced down at her. "Just name your price."

In that brief second, Kayla met Alec's gaze and recognized his overwhelming fear and love for her. She desperately wanted to reach out to him, but their bonded connection was strangely silent. She couldn't feel him through Lars's energy cloud.

"Is she worth a vial of antibiotics? That was the cost of my sister's life. Or a metabolic booster? That was the price of my father's life. Or a crate of food? Several of the others paid dearly for that one."

Alec flinched at his words, but Lars wasn't done.

"Good. Now you know what it's like to put a price tag on someone you love. There's nothing you can offer me, Alec. I've already lost what I held most dear. I'm going to enjoy watching as everything you care about is torn away. You'll learn what it's like to lose everything little by little until there's nothing left. Not even hope. The seeds have already been sown, cousin. It's just a matter of time before it comes to fruition."

"I don't blame you for hating me," Alec began and held out his hands in a passive gesture. "It's been years, Lars. My hands were tied. I couldn't do anything for you back then. I had no idea you were still alive until a few days ago. If I had known, I would have searched for you the moment I took control of the towers."

"You think that would have made up for everything?" Lars laughed, and Kayla felt a trickle of warmth on her side as the knife pricked her. "You traitorous bastard! You knew what the Council planned. You could have warned us. Instead, you sent us to our deaths."

Alec shook his head and glanced down at the knife. He swallowed, and then his eyes flew back up to Lars. "I'll accept whatever judgment you have for me, but don't hurt her. If you felt her energy, you know who and what she is. Kayla's innocent in all of this, more so than any of us. Don't take out your anger on her. Please. Release her and I'll take her place."

Lars was silent for a long moment. Kayla wondered if he was taking Alec's words to heart, but his next words left her cold.

"I never thought I'd ever hear Alec Tal'Vayr plead for anything. In a way, it's fitting. I never begged for anything until my sister became sick. OmniLab ignored my pleas." His arm around her tightened, and she inhaled sharply. "You're right though. I know exactly what Kayla is and just how precious. That's why this will hurt you more than anything. You were the one who let this happen."

Lars bent down and pressed another kiss against her neck. His voice was a low whisper in her ear. "I hope you can forgive me for this one day, little one."

Kayla frowned, trying to figure out what he was apologizing for when she felt the sharp, stabbing pain of the blade sinking deep into her side. She cried out in agony as the pain ripped through her. Lars yanked the knife back out and shoved her toward Alec. She stumbled, clutching at her side.

"Kayla!" Alec cried out and caught her as she began to fall. Lars turned and ran down the hall in the opposite direction. Brant began chasing him, but Alec shouted at him to stop.

"Forget him, Brant. Get a medic over here now!"

Kayla whimpered as the pain radiated through her. She dimly heard Brant's footsteps running away as Alec gathered her in his arms. He pulled off his jacket and pushed it against the wound. She glanced down and wished she hadn't. It was bad. Worse than she thought. It was apparent even to her that she was losing too much blood.

"Shh, you're going to be okay. It's going to be all right. I won't let you go again."

Kayla was aware she could once more sense their bond. She didn't know how Lars had suppressed it, but she was glad to have it back. Alec wrapped her up in a calming band of energy and cradled her. It helped a little, but the pain was overwhelming. She was beginning to feel lightheaded. The floor beneath her grew wet and sticky.

"Alec," she whispered, trying to reach up to touch him. The movement proved to be too much, and she dropped her hand.

He kissed her forehead. His blue eyes held hers and she was taken aback by the tenderness in his gaze. "It's okay, love. You don't need to talk. Just rest. They're going to be here in a minute. You're going to be fine. Just stay with me."

A minute might be too late. She was having too much trouble keeping her eyes open. She didn't want to pass out before he heard the truth. It was imperative she seize the moment while she still had it. Before it slipped away.

"I need to tell you ... You were right. I'm ... I'm sorry I didn't tell you before. I was scared."

"Shh," he urged. "It's all right. You don't need to say anything. Just hold on."

Kayla swallowed. Her fingers were starting to go numb. The pain was nearly unbearable, but she had to push past it. She needed to tell him in case she didn't have another chance. She'd hurt him so much by denying him and their bond. She loved Carl, but her feelings for Alec went just as deep. They were just different. She couldn't deny it anymore. She didn't want to.

Carl was a choice. He grounded her, challenged her, and understood her in a way no one else ever had. With Alec, though, he unlocked something inside her that had been dormant for too long. Alec pushed her to cross normal boundaries and explore her innate potential. She needed him to know how much he meant to her and how she felt about him.

Kayla opened herself up and fully embraced their bond, sharing everything she was feeling. She poured her love for both men into their bond and tried to show him what they meant to her. Even so, it wasn't enough. She needed to say the words.

"I love you, Alec."

She heard his breath hitch as his arms tightened around her. A drop of wetness fell on her cheek. Was she crying or was it him? She wasn't sure it mattered. It was impossible to keep her eyes open any longer. She was cold. Why was she so cold?

With a sigh, Kayla closed her eyes one last time and let herself slip away into the darkness.

CHAPTER TWENTY-ONE

ALEC WALKED past the two guards outside the door and entered the large medical room. The stark-white surroundings were broken up by the vast array of flowering plants Seara kept bringing into the room. None of the doctor's complaints made the slightest bit of difference. Seara was determined to make it look like a floral shop.

Carl glanced up briefly when Alec entered, but the trader immediately turned his attention back to the still form beside him. Alec paused by the edge of the bed and looked down.

Kayla's eyes were closed, her dark hair framing a face that was still too pale. Seeing her like this—in the large bed and surrounded by machines—made Kayla seem fragile and delicate all at once. A small smile touched his lips at the realization she'd probably hit him for thinking about her that way.

They'd removed the last of the bandages an hour ago. Most of the drugs had cleared her system, and the physicians were just waiting on the order to wake her up. Part of Alec wanted to keep her here where he knew she'd be safe and protected. At least while she was asleep and recovering, no one had made any attempts on her life and she hadn't tried to escape the guards.

It was a small comfort to know the knife injury hadn't done too much damage. He suspected the attack was more of a warning and a way for Lars to escape. If Lars had truly intended Kayla harm, she wouldn't be here right now.

"You can't keep her in a bubble."

Carl's words broke through Alec's thoughts. He sighed and pinched the bridge of his nose. "I know. That's why I'm here. The doctors will bring her around in a few minutes, but I needed to speak with you before they did."

Carl lifted his head to look at him but didn't speak. The trader's face was marked with exhaustion. His eyes were red, and he wore a several-days-old beard. Alec had been monitoring her visitors and knew Carl hadn't left her side except for a few minutes at a time. Even then, it was only when Seara or Brant was there to take his place.

Alec turned back to Kayla's sleeping figure. He could sense her just below the surface of consciousness. He sent a light thread of energy over her and enveloped her in a caress. She embraced it and wrapped herself in his warmth like a blanket, snuggling into a deeper sleep. His eyes softened as he watched her. She wasn't fighting him anymore. At least not subconsciously.

A surge of love flowed through him, but Alec swallowed it back. It was too dangerous for him to allow his emotions to dictate his decisions. They'd almost cost him what he treasured most. Given these new threats, he needed to be even more careful now. No matter what he had to do to protect her, Alec wouldn't allow anything or anyone to hurt her again.

"She can't go back to the surface with you. It's too dangerous."

"I know," Carl agreed and lifted Kayla's hand into his. The trader pressed his lips against the back of her palm.

Alec watched the intimate gesture but couldn't bring himself to get angry. With the words and emotions Kayla had shared with him in the hallway, something inside him had unleashed. She'd finally acknowledged her feelings for both of them. What that meant for the future, he wasn't sure, but he could no longer bring himself to feel envious of the trader's relationship with her. If anything, he felt a strange sort of kinship with the man.

Carl lowered her hand but didn't release it. He looked up at Alec once more, pinning him with his dark gaze. "I'd like to formally request to be released from my trading contract and return to OmniLab permanently. I'll submit the documentation to Director Borshin by the end of the day."

Alec took a deep breath and clasped his hands behind his back. He'd been expecting this. Carl's feelings for Kayla ran too deeply for him to be able to walk away.

He shook his head. "I can't allow you to do that."

Carl's eyes hardened as he stood. The trader's barely restrained fury only further cemented his decision. Alec held up his hand to halt his advance. "I understand the reasons for your request, but I have to deny it. Instead, I've temporarily suspended your contract. Orders have been issued recalling you to the towers immediately."

Carl froze, and his eyes narrowed with suspicion. Alec didn't blame him for not trusting this news. Carl glanced down at Kayla before turning back to him. "Why?"

Alec sighed. He suspected Carl wouldn't believe anything except the truth. "Kayla's too unpredictable. I don't believe she'll agree to stay in the towers without you. Even if you remain here, there's no guarantee we can convince her to stay. The Coalition is still out there, and I know Lars is planning something. I need your help to keep her safe and out of their hands."

Meeting Kayla had changed something inside him. There

had always been clear lines drawn between the different social groups, but she'd managed to blur all of them. Alec never dreamed he'd be standing here asking a trader for help or reaching out to her former ruin rat camp and asking for their aid. Kayla had no idea just how far-reaching an effect she had on all of them.

In the short time she'd been in the towers, she'd touched many lives. Many of the Inner Circle members had never met her, but that didn't stop their adoration and devotion for her efforts in freeing them from the oppression of the bracelets. Other tower residents heard rumors of her escapades in the kitchen at Bliss and loved the fact she'd embraced one of their own. They'd seen her walking down the common corridors and even visiting one of their public cafés. She refused her title and insisted everyone speak to her with the same familiarity they'd greet an old friend.

Kayla didn't understand or see how she'd influenced all of them. Her actions and reactions were trickling down and affecting everyone. She challenged each of them to question their beliefs and even their way of life. Alec shook his head in exasperation. She'd end up either destroying all of them or making them greater than they'd ever been.

He swallowed back the rush of emotions and lifted his head to look at the trader. "Help me convince Kayla to stay. Give her projects and help her build that damned tower for the surface dwellers. Keep her busy and show her the prototypes in the Research and Development Lab. Do whatever you need to do to keep her here as long as possible. I don't care what it costs. It won't last, but every day she remains is one more day we have to hunt down Lars and the Coalition."

Carl was quiet for a long moment. Then, he chuckled and shook his head. "You understand her far better than I gave you credit for. You only suspended my contract so I can go after her in case she takes off again."

"Yes," Alec agreed, although it pained him to do so. "She trusts you. If she decides to leave again ..." His voice trailed off, and he shook his head. "She agreed to return to your camp because she loves you. You were the only one able to get through to her. Brant told me what happened."

Carl sat back down and rested his elbows on his knees. "You really love her, don't you?"

Alec glanced down at the dark-haired woman who had stolen his heart. "From the time she was born, it was expected we would end up together. I resented having my future planned out, but I couldn't resist her even then. I loved her in the way only a child can love another child. When the ruin collapsed and we thought she'd died, I grew up loving her memory and the possibility of what could have been. But now, all those feelings pale in comparison to the reality of her. I love her as the woman she's become."

Alec reached out to touch her cheek and sent another light wave of energy over her. "I'll always love her, which is why I'm entrusting her to you for safe keeping. No one else can protect her as well as the person who loves her as much as I do." He turned to meet Carl's gaze. "You have my word that I'll no longer attempt to interfere in your relationship. There's too much at stake. I need an ally, not more enemies. Help me protect her. Please."

Carl studied him for a long time. When he didn't respond, Alec felt a moment of panic at the thought the trader would reject his offer. By capturing Kayla's heart, the dark-haired man in front of him held more power than the highest Inner Circle member. From the look on Carl's face, he knew it. The role reversal humbled and unnerved Alec.

Carl gave him a curt nod, acknowledging the unspoken words between them. He extended his hand. "For Kayla's sake, I'll agree to be your ally."

Alec accepted his hand and felt the balance of power shift

even more. It was a hold he'd gladly relinquish as long as Kayla remained safe. "Just don't let anything happen to her. She's my heart."

"I won't," Carl agreed and glanced down at Kayla again. He reached over to tuck her hair behind her ear. In a softer voice Alec barely heard, he added, "She's my hope and my home."

Alec squeezed his eyes shut as the memory of Kayla's emotions and her love for both of them flooded through him. Her capacity for love was staggering and made him determined to be worthy of it and of her. Unable to wait a moment longer, he went to find a doctor to awaken her, confident that Carl would keep her safe in his absence.

ABOUT THE AUTHOR

Jamie A. Waters is an award-winning science fiction and paranormal romance author. Her first novel, Beneath the Fallen City (previously titled as The Two Towers), was a winner of the Readers' Favorite Award in Science-Fiction Romance and the CIPA EVVY Award in Science-Fiction.

Jamie currently resides in Florida with her two neurotic dogs who enjoy stealing socks and chasing lizards. When she's not pursuing her passion of writing, she's usually trying to learn new and interesting random things (like how to pick locks or use the self-cleaning feature of the oven without setting off the fire alarm). In her downtime, she enjoys reading, playing computer games, painting, or acting as a referee between the dragons and fairies currently at war inside her closet.

You can learn more by visiting: www.jamieawaters.com